CAFFEINE NIGHTS PUBLISHING

Remission

ED CHATTERTON

Fiction aimed at the heart
and the head...

Published by Caffeine Nights Publishing 2016

Published in Great Britain by
Caffeine Nights Publishing
4 Eton Close
Walderslade
Chatham
Kent
ME5 9AT

www.caffeinenights.com

British Library Cataloguing in Publication Data.

A CIP catalogue record for this book is available from the British Library

ISBN: 978-1-910720-69-1

Cover design by

Mark (Wills) Williams

Everything else by
Default, Luck and Accident

Acknowledgements:

A number of people have been invaluable in getting this book to this point. In the very beginning, Amanda Bromfield was kind and brave enough to share her experiences of receiving a cancer diagnosis. On the medical side I have had good advice from my daughter, Dr Sophie Chatterton. I do need to point out that any errors on that side of things are entirely my fault, not hers. Many of the Berlin and Scotland sections were researched and discussed with Peter and Linda Moreleigh (the original Girl With The Dragon Tattoo) and the book would not have been the same without their help, support and friendship. For police matters I once more shamelessly used Christine and Stewart Parkinson for their experience in the field. Again, any procedural errors are mine, not theirs. Sebastian Ross-Hagenbaum checked my German and has (hopefully) saved me from any major clangers (usual caveats apply). Pete McDowell was kind enough to point out some errors I made regarding the reality of violence. My agents, Tara Wynne in Sydney and Rebecca Richie in London, were extremely useful and supportive in getting the final draft tighter. And, although not directly related to *Remission*, the enthusiasm and support from Nat Lawley at Escapade Media for getting *The Art of Killing* adaptation of *A Dark Place To Die* to TV has been a source of inspiration to keep writing this series. Kudos also to Phillip Bowman at Enjoy Entertainment for his championing of my books. Thanks too to Darren Laws at Caffeine Nights for his enthusiasm and for Susan Hunt's expert editing which saved me from embarrassment. Lastly, I know that it is mandatory for any writer to thank his or her partner for their support and I'm certainly not going to stray from that tried and tested formula: Annie Chatterton, thank you for everything.

To:

The heroic and stoic Dave Heggie and my wonderful sister, Ali Heggie, and to the McGinn family, who have lived, and are still living, with the reality of this bastard disease.

Also by Ed Chatterton

Remission

1

Liverpool, October 9th

He could never be called a poetic man, but the dark beauty of the naked girl arcing backwards through the rain in a cascade of broken glass will return to Halloran time and again in the small hours, jolting him awake in a guilty twist of knotted sheets. He's seen worse accidents before, but always after the fact; the dead already cooling, the vehicles at rest, all violence done and only the injured to deal with.

Now Halloran has a front row seat for the horror.

Idling at the stop light on his regulation Yamaha he watches as the driver of the white Mercedes van, squinting through the squalls gusting in off the river, blows straight through a red just as the ugly metal skeleton of an empty car transporter groans across his path. Halloran opens his mouth to shout something but before he can draw breath the accident is already happening. The transporter crosses the filter lane and the Merc driver's eyes open wide. He stamps on his brakes but, on the slick tarmac, it's too little too late. The laws of physics will not be denied.

Time crawls. Seconds are sliced, and then sliced again and again until, finally, the front wing of the Mercedes van slams hard into the side of the transporter.

The van windscreen explodes and the girl floats balletically across the space in front of Halloran. In those brief moments, with his adrenaline spiking, it seems to the bike cop that he is able to differentiate each glittering teardrop of water, every separate scratch and slice on the girl's flesh. More details will come back to him later: the sound of metal on metal, the girl's scarlet blood vivid against the rain-blackened tarmac, her white skin, the grumble of the bike underneath him.

She clips a stanchion at the very back of the transporter and her face is turned towards Halloran. Blood from a fresh wound traces a parabola through the air. She's young, he registers. Eighteen? Nineteen? Too young for this.

And then, sickeningly, she hits the unforgiving road and, as if slapped across the face, Halloran is jerked back into the here and now.

To his left the Mercedes grinds to a halt against the bollards while the transporter broadsides a Nissan coming from the other direction, the gaping mouths of the car's occupants briefly swimming into Halloran's view before they hit. There's another vehicle too, somewhere, but Halloran only registers that as a blur on the edge of his vision.

He's got his eyes on the girl.

If by some miracle she's still breathing he can, at least, prevent her being killed by a rubber-necking driver. The transporter and Nissan slide to an uncertain stop, clinging to one another like awkward dancers at the end of the song. Halloran flicks on his blues and guns the bike out into the centre of the intersection. From the initial impact of the Mercedes into the transporter to this moment has been less than ten seconds.

Halloran parks the Yamaha next to the woman in the road, dismounts and starts talking into his radio as he bends over her. It's going to take a lot longer than ten seconds to sort this out. This isn't a crash.

It's a killing.

2

Liverpool, October 9th

Malignant.

Was there a more frightening word in the English language? If there is, Frank Keane can't think of one and when he hears it coming out of the mouth of the man sitting across the desk, Frank makes a sudden involuntary nervous noise somewhere between a bark and a laugh: an automatic response to the bitter little joke. So funny you'll kill yourself laughing.

Medavoy's expression doesn't change. People react in different ways and he's seen most of them before. It's in the nature of every organism to decay, but most of the time everyone's too wrapped up in the humdrum to notice the song winding down. We keep doing things that mean nothing, imagining that the dance will last forever. Now, with a single word, the music stops for Frank and is replaced with the absolute bleak certainty that, for him, everything there has ever been or ever will be is fucked, completely and forever, amen.

Through the first-floor windows of the medical centre Frank's home city now appears as alien to him as the surface of Jupiter. At the intersection a line of cars halt, each touching their brakes as they pull into line, the red bulbs of the tail lights splintered into diamonds on the rain-spotted glass. Go. Stop. Go. Stop.

'Malignant?' Frank repeats. The word is awkward in his mouth. He feels like an actor. There are lines to be said in this scene and some of them are his. The trouble is he doesn't want to play the role.

Medavoy nods and Frank gets a sudden flash of a succession of people sitting in this same chair getting bad news just like his, their stricken faces riffling past at high speed like a deck of cards under the dealer's thumb. You win some you lose some.

'I'm afraid so, Mr Keane. I'm sorry.'

'Jesus Christ.'

A tidal wave of nausea washes through Frank and he slumps back in the chair.

Cancer. *Of course.* Frank feels the grim satisfaction of the hypochondriac having his nightmares realised. This day has been coming his whole life. He'd known it all along. Medavoy is just the messenger.

'It's bad news,' Medavoy says. 'No getting around that, unfortunately.'

Frank finds it difficult to look Medavoy in the eye, as though there's something shameful about being ill. Dirty. Probably a Catholic thing. He focuses instead on the fading yellow bruise high on the doctor's cheek. The bruise raises a flicker from Frank's cop instincts but it's probably just golden oldies rugby, something like that. Medavoy has that rugger bugger look about him. Early fifties, chunky, red-complexioned, sandy hair and a public school voice tinged with the softest of Liverpool accents. A bit like Charlie Searle. Jesus, Charlie Searle. A week already and Frank still hasn't told Charlie about the other thing. Now *this*. What a –

'Mr Keane?'

'Sorry.'

'We were discussing your prognosis? It's important you understand the way this all came about.'

'Right.'

'So . . . on your first visit you complained of headaches. Pronounced headaches.'

'I'd been shot,' says Frank. 'Wouldn't that have something to do with it?'

His hand strays to the meandering scar that runs across his scalp, a permanent reminder of his last investigation which, surreally, had come to a bloody end in California. Frank's nose had been smashed and he'd taken bullets. Frank knows he'd been fortunate: the head shot had been little more than a graze and the medics in the US had saved his shoulder. Koopman, Frank's old boss at Liverpool MIT, had lost an arm.

Medavoy speaks calmly. 'The trauma from your wounds go some way to explaining the pain but a number of other indicators got me worried. This is why I ordered more blood tests and why you had the EEG over at Broadgreen yesterday.' Medavoy raises his head and looks directly at Frank. 'Sadly, as I said, the result confirms my most pessimistic suspicions. You almost certainly have an intracranial solid neoplasm. A brain tumour. Cancer, in other words. Worse, the cancer is malignant. It's growing and you will require surgery – that's if the tumour is not too big already. I'm telling you this in advance of arranging a biopsy but I'm afraid that may only corroborate what we already know. The key, though, is that we do need to know for sure.'

Medavoy glances at Frank and then down at his file.

'You could argue that you've been lucky. If you hadn't been shot, if you hadn't been receiving post trauma treatment, then this might have been found too late.'

'Shouldn't they have picked this up in America?'

Medavoy shrugs. 'This is an extremely aggressive tumour. In all likelihood it has arrived post-operation. You've been recuperating for several months. There was time for this cancer to take hold without alerting anyone and whoever was looking after that would not necessarily be looking for cancer. Coming in here for ongoing treatment *was* lucky. I know it doesn't seem like that.'

Medavoy leans forward and speaks with increased conviction. 'This is potentially survivable, Frank. It's not an absolute death sentence. Not yet. If the operation is do-able, and if we're successful, there are a number of possibilities we can look at and a treatment plan we'll put in place starting in two weeks when we have the data back on the biopsy. You'll be spending a few days in hospital afterwards. The procedure is under general anaesthetic. I know it's difficult to think clearly right now but this type of cancer, while aggressive, does have an increasing survival rate. Not so long ago this diagnosis was invariably terminal.'

Frank realises he'd been mistaken about *malignant*. It turns out that there is a much worse word after all.

'And now?'

'I don't like to put a percentage on this kind of condition, Mr Keane. Not at this stage.'

'Give me a number.'

'If I had to guess I'd say slightly better than ten percent. The EEG shows a clear tumour. The biopsy will tell us the size and malignancy.'

Ten percent. OK. A long shot. Better than the lottery. It's the first thought he's had in the last five minutes that is even remotely positive and he clings to it like a lifebelt.

'If surgery is required, 'continues Medavoy, 'that will be a positive outcome.' He looks at Frank. 'But I have to tell you that the biopsy may very well show that there is little we can do if the cancer has metastasised beyond a certain point. If that's the case then it becomes about managing the disease.'

'Managing?'

'If we can't operate we will try and manage the pain and quality of life, as best we can, in the time you have left.'

Frank makes a rapid inventory of the seven days he's been back in Liverpool. A week of worrying. A week of trying to pick up the threads of his old life: a life that now seems to belong to someone entirely different. A week of watching TV and catching up on MIT case files and drinking tea. A week worrying about the fallout from what happened in America, about the envelope on the plane, about Charlie Searle, about doing the right thing, about the bullet in his shoulder, about his career, about women in general and Jules and Em in particular. A week of not noticing the weather, of forgetting that breathing was a luxury, of talking shit. A completely wasted week.

Frank will need a specialist, and Medavoy will recommend a good one. If Frank prefers there are others that Medavoy can call. There is a further problem due to Frank's extremely rare blood group – something that Medavoy seems downright excited about – but they'll cross that bridge when they come to it. Medavoy mentions dates and health regimes and drugs and consultants. There will be another hospital appointment next week to perform the biopsy.

Frank can almost hear the grinding of gears as the medical machine begins the process of pulling him into that world, appointment by appointment, sample by sample. There will be sickness and blood, panic and boredom jostling with the thousand indignities of a slow drift into nothingness.

Frank isn't really listening. He's thinking about the envelope.

3

Liverpool, October 9th

On her last day on earth Sarah Coughlan gets out of bed a couple of minutes before eight. She walks along the landing towards the bathroom to do her hair, put on her war paint and take her meds. Her father's been gone an hour but she can hear the reassuring clatter of her mother downstairs in the kitchen. Like always, she's got the radio on too loud and a steady stream of moral outrage echoes up the stairs of the semi, the nasal whining, tired pop and stale jokes of the local phone-in as familiar to Sarah as the wallpaper in the hall and just about as noticeable.

'Is that you, Sarah?'

Her mother's question that's not a question, the same every morning, cuts across the digital drivel.

'No,' says Sarah leaning over the banister. 'It's Judy Garland.'

She varies the answer each morning depending on her mood: Angelina Jolie, the Dalai Llama, the ghost of Michael Jackson, Kenny Dalglish's older sister, a frog.

'Oh good. I like Judy Garland.'

Her mother starts to say something else but Sarah's already in the bathroom.

Later, after their world has collapsed, when all is lost and the days stretch out in endless deserts of despair, a numbed Mary Coughlan will endlessly scavenge these tiny exchanges for any scrap of comfort or, more often, pick at them like a scab in order to rub vinegar into the always fresh wound.

Why didn't I say more?

Why didn't I hold her, stop her, save her?

Why Judy *fucking* Garland?

In the bathroom Sarah methodically takes her medication, the bottles lined up neatly on the glass shelf reserved for them, the levels checked by her mother daily. Sarah cleans her teeth, brushes her hair and starts putting her make-up on for the last time. She hears 'Somewhere Over the Rainbow' being systematically slaughtered downstairs, the tune belted out by her tone-deaf mother across the phone-in chatter: a kitchen karaoke car-crash.

'Ouch,' murmurs Sarah, wincing at herself in the mirror. 'Sorry, Judy.'

Sarah takes care with her make-up. In remission since last year's illness, she likes to do things deliberately now, the repeated patterns of behaviour a comfort after the chaos of leukemia that, until today, the Coughlan's had thought would be their worst nightmare.

Back in her bedroom, drugs in her blood, full slap in place and her hair piled high, Sarah dresses for college in art-school retro and is ready for the world. She checks her phone on the way downstairs, enters the kitchen and turns the radio down from cacophony to bearable.

'Oh Sarah.'

Mary Coughlan hands over a mug of tea and regards her daughter's appearance with an expression of such absolute disgust that it would not have been out of place had Sarah entered the kitchen sporting a dress made of dismembered puppies. 'Is that *really* what you're wearing?'

'Have you seen my phone charger?' Sarah takes the tea from her mother and starts poking around behind the kitchen appliances.

'You have some lovely dresses. Why don't you wear something *nice*? For me.'

'I'm sure I left it here last night. Have you been tidying up?'

Without taking her eyes off her daughter, Mary Coughlan slides open a kitchen drawer and hands Sarah the charger.

'Some brighter colours would be good. You used to wear such pretty things. I don't know why you wear all those old clothes.'

'Mum,' says Sarah, her attention on her phone. In the background something a radio caller says gets Mary's attention. Sarah plugs in her charger, eats her toast in relative peace.

The ebb and flow of family life. Paradise in hindsight.

At 9.32 a.m., Sarah Coughlan opens the front door and steps into the rain falling on Menlove Avenue, her head bent over her phone. Mary Coughlan watches her daughter walk in the direction of the bus stop.

'See you later, love,' she shouts but Sarah already has her headphones on.

The next time Mary Coughlan will see her daughter will be on a mortuary slab at the Royal.

4

Mid-Atlantic, October 2nd. Liverpool, October 9th

A week ago. A lifetime ago.

Doing his best to look like he belongs at the at the pointy end, Frank is on his way back home after four murky months floundering in some very deep waters in the US. He's wearing a set of generic department-store clothes given to him in Atlanta by a Loder Industries spook called Ashland. The bruising from the facial surgery on his broken nose is still angry enough around his hollowed eyes to suggest a story of extreme violence which only the more charitable passenger would assume was the product of an accident. The Frank Keane who'd left Liverpool is not the same Frank Keane on the Delta triple-seven heading into Manchester. He's got a lot of explaining to do, a lot of answers to come up with and his problems are about to get a lot worse.

About two hours into the flight, a snooty flight attendant slides through the darkened cabin and hands Frank an envelope containing a headache the size of Anfield.

The envelope contains the unpalatable information that DI Frank Keane, senior plod on Merseyside's Major Incident Team, is now in possession of twenty-five million shiny US dollars in a Belgian bank account he never opened but that has his name all over the paperwork just the same.

He's never even been to fucking Belgium.

Worse, although the note and message aren't signed, Frank has the cast-iron certainty that this mother of all bribes comes directly from the Dark Overlord of Hades and Destroyer of Worlds himself; namely Dennis Patrick Sheehan, the monumentally connected ex-US

Secretary of State, CEO of Loder Industries and not a man to be taken lightly under any circumstances. Frank – along with his former MIT boss, Menno Koopman – had pursued Sheehan's deranged actor son to Los Angeles after a series of killings in Liverpool. Frank's in no doubt that the twenty-five million is a forceful reminder about the wisdom of Frank not going public with the family link between the gunman and the all-powerful Sheehan. He assumes Koop had been given the same deal but since he hasn't heard a murmur from Koop since the shootings, that's just guesswork.

No comebacks, no strings, says the note. Declare it, don't declare it: the money is legit.

Right.

You can put lipstick on a pig but no-one's going to mistake it for Scarlett Johansson, even down the darkest of alleys. Large unexplained sums of money tucked into the back pockets of senior cops usually meant one thing, and Frank's boss, Charlie Searle, won't be slow in putting two and two together and coming up with twenty-five million reasons to suspend him, or worse. A bribe is a bribe however you dress it up.

Frank has to hand it to Sheehan – the money is a genius-level move that simultaneously puts Frank's balls in a vice if he took it and coats everything he might say against the American with the stink of corruption if he doesn't.

Sheehan could easily have used more permanent methods, Frank's under no illusions about that. A late night visit from a Loder Industries cleanup crew is all it would take for his link to the ex-Secretary of State to be closed forever. There'd be no paper trail leading back. No clues. Just a dead Liverpool cop with a stinking pile of iffy money in a Brussels bank. Easy.

Instead, by forcing the cash onto Frank, Sheehan keeps him on a leash: if Frank tells Charlie Searle about the money – if he does the right thing – then he would be tainted by association and suspended faster than you can say goodbye. No smoke without fire and all that.

If he keeps quiet then he is complicit. Either way, Sheehan wins.

Since getting back, Frank has kept quiet about the money. He'd been meaning to tell Charlie – he had – but the moment just hadn't arrived.

After *malignant* he's not sure it ever will.

Outside the medical centre, after Medavoy has given him the paperwork he needs, after the biopsy appointment has been made, after the death sentence has been passed, Frank finds himself on James Street in the cold October rain. Once again he is struck by the details. An ambulance screams past heading east, closely followed by a gleaming red fire truck. An accident in the wet. You get a lot of them. People become careless. He watches the emergency vehicles until they're out of sight, aware that he's been standing on the pavement longer than is normal. Whatever normal might be for someone who has just had the news he's had.

Soaked, and cold, Frank folds the sodden sheets of medical data in half and puts them inside his jacket pocket. He looks at his watch. Ten forty-five.

He turns his feet towards the car park and to work. He can't think of anything else to do.

5

Berlin, October 9th

The fine point of the blade hovers momentarily over the stretched white flesh before it bites in and neatly divides the skin to reveal the scarlet tissue below. The hand holding the scalpel presses deeper and slices confidently through the flesh in a line that starts just below the throat. Blood seeps out behind the shining steel like the wake from a speedboat.

'Drain,' says Ilsa Bruckner without taking her eyes from the incision. Chopek, the secondary, slips the tip of the suction tube behind Bruckner's scalpel and mops up. From the other side of the table, Eve Paulasson, the head theatre nurse fits the retractors that will hold the incision open. Behind Paulasson is her assistant, holding the tray of required equipment.

As soon as Bruckner has finished the cut she places the scalpel on a steel tray at her elbow and picks up another, smaller, instrument. Over her surgical mask she glances quizzically at Mahmood Hussain, the anaesthetist for today's list.

'Everything as it should be, Hussain?' she asks.

'Of course,' says Hussain. 'Everything normal.'

Bruckner says nothing and turns back to the operation feeling, as always, that satisfying controlled adrenaline that comes when she holds a life in her hands. Opera plays softly in the background. Bruckner busies herself over the patient and her team move quietly in the hard pool of light from the central overhead lamp, a coven gathered round the fire.

Strictly speaking, Bruckner doesn't need to do this part of the procedure, and it's been a bitch of a day, but she likes to keep her hand in. Elle Chopek will be pissed about not getting the lead but she knows better than to chirp up about the situation. Bruckner runs a tight ship and likes to keep her juniors on their toes.

Time passes in *Operationssaal 6* as the procedure ebbs and flows against a backdrop of gently clanking steel, music and murmured voices. From time to time there are electronic beeps and, from outside, the muted sound of a ringing phone. In some clinics the chief surgeons encourage jokes or banter, but not Bruckner. She's all business, all the time. At a point in proceedings she places her instruments down and turns away, her latex-covered fingers streaked with blood.

'All yours, Dr Chopek,' she says. With a nod to Hussain and Paulasson, Ilsa Bruckner pushes open the theatre door with her hip and heads for the clean-up station. She strips off her bloody gloves and mask and places them in the disposal bin along with her plasticised apron and bib. She steps out of her gown and places that in the steel-sealed laundry trolley next to the shower room. At her locker she takes off her surgical scrubs and adds them to the laundry. Her plastic shoes go in the recycling trash. She opens her locker and places her bra and pants in her holdall and takes a towel from the stack. Most of the surgical team prefer to shower at home but Bruckner always cleans the day off her as soon as possible. Bruckner takes her time, paying particular attention to her fingers and hands. She washes her hair three times.

After dressing in her street clothes Bruckner hoists her holdall onto her shoulder. She checks her phone as she heads to the car park. As she opens the back door she almost collides with one of the clinic maintenance crew.

'Sorry,' the man says stepping back and letting Bruckner pass.

'That's fine, good night.'

Bruckner puts her holdall in the boot of her Audi – one of the last left in the small lot –and pulls out through the automatic gates onto the linden-lined streets of Spandau, glad her work is over for the week.

Some distance away, on the opposite side of the street, the driver of a grey Volvo fires off a last rattle of images, puts down the Nikon and starts the engine. For this person, the evening is just beginning.

6

Liverpool, October 9th

Work turns out to be a bad idea.

More than four months out of the Merseyside Major Incident Team – along with the little matter of Sheehan's money – had left Frank Keane feeling like an outsider when he came back. His absence had been subsumed in the daily grind of gore and paperwork which make up the days at MIT. They'd grown used to him not being around and, when after his return, it's been hard to get the old rhythm back, especially as Frank is reluctant or unwilling to talk about California.

He hasn't told Searle about the twenty-five million.

He'd meant to, right away, but somehow days had passed and it hadn't happened. Every night the burden grows and Frank always resolves to do it in the morning.

Now, after Medavoy's bombshell, Frank's worries about the money seem almost childish.

Frank has been happy to let Harris shoulder most of the workload and she, along with everyone else at MIT can see that whatever happened in America's left its mark. But as distracted as he has been since getting back, today he looks like something the dog brought up.

'Jesus,' says Harris, looking up as he comes into the office. 'Chin up.'

Frank doesn't understand what Em Harris is saying at first. Chin? He raises a hand to his jaw.

'What?'

'Listen, I know you've not exactly been Charlie Chuckles since getting back but a gob that miserable should come with an advance warning.' She waves a sheaf of papers around the MIT office. 'It's not like we've got much to smile about in here but there is a limit.'

Considering what he'd just been told, Frank had thought he was coping pretty well. Obviously not.

'Well, yeah. Sorry.' He moves off towards his office consciously trying to move naturally and finding even that difficult. All his movements seem rigid, his responses dull.

Behind him Harris turns her head back to her work.

She's been using Frank's office more frequently in the last month or two and as she takes her seat she sees Theresa Cooper, the only other woman in the room flick a glance her way. Harris freezes her out. Cooper's expression is one of sympathy but Harris isn't in the mood for female solidarity right now. She stabs a finger at her keyboard and glares at the list of work that appears on screen.

Frank closes his office door and sits down. Familiar things surround him. The stack of files with his department name on each, the smell of old paper and air freshener, the 'view' from the window, are all as they should be and yet they seem to belong to someone else.

He pulls his chair in closer to the desk and opens the computer in an echo of Harris on the other side of the dividing wall. He sits blankly, staring at the long list of crimes and filth and graft onscreen and tears leak from his eyes without him being aware of a thing. His face is static and the salt water drips steadily onto the cheap surface of his desk. He's like that when DS Rose walks in after a brief tap on the door.

'Boss –' Rose stops mid-sentence and freezes. Frank doesn't look up.

Rose hesitates in the doorway and then steps back outside, his face stricken. Seeing Frank cry is like seeing your dad cry. It's just wrong.

As the door shuts, Frank turns his head.

For the first time he notices the tears and wipes them with the back of his hand. Had someone been in? He can't remember.

What do you *do* when you've been diagnosed with cancer?

Frank turns to the computer and writes a detailed email to Charlie Searle outlining the Belgian cash. He attaches the scans that have been sitting in a file on his desktop since he got back from the US. Frank looks at the email for a long while before pressing 'send'. He writes another email to the Merseyside Police Occupational Health Unit requesting a leave of absence and detailing Medavoy's diagnosis.

Then, because he knows he has to get out before he starts screaming, Frank pushes back his chair and walks out of MIT without speaking to anyone. He doesn't know if he'll ever come back again. Right now he doesn't know if he wants to.

From her desk, Harris watches Frank leave and gets an odd feeling that she's seeing him for the last time. She glances over towards Frank's empty office, ashamed that a tiny part of her is glad.

7

Liverpool, October 9th

If he half-closes his eyes and looks hard at the tiny upstairs window, Willy Schneider can almost see him pushing the horn-rims back up his beak of a nose, the black quiff flopping down as he hunches in concentration over the cheap strings of the prized Gallotone.

Schneider, smiling the dazed smile of a pilgrim at the altar, leans his forearms on the big steering wheel and gazes through the rain-streaked windscreen at the drab suburban semi like it's the Taj Mahal at dawn.

'He lived here until he was 22, man. There is an album called *Menlove Avenue.* Did you know this, Klaus?'

Menckel, slumped in the passenger seat, plucks one of his headphone buds out and shrugs.

'What?'

'An album. *Menlove Avenue.*'

'What's an album?'

Schneider peels his eyes from the house and looks at Klaus Menckel like he's an alien. He's young, maybe 21, Willy's not too sure, he only met him last week in a bar behind *Alexanderplatz* when the call came through from Gottlenz. Schneider is originally from Hamburg and even after years in Berlin, the thick *Berlinerisch* of Menckel is sometimes difficult to understand. When Schneider had asked if he was Klaus, the guy had said no, the name's K-Man; only his ma ever calls him Klaus and she's, like, dead.

Right there Schneider knew he'd be trouble. Klaus – there's not a chance of Willy ever using that 'K' shit so Klaus is the best Menckel will get, at least on this trip –is tall, dressed conservatively in black jeans and a charcoal zip-up. His choice of clothing has more to do with orders from above than personal choice. Discretion is the key on these runs. Menckel has his blond hair razored short and the air of someone accustomed to violence. He looks like a thousand other Marzahn *prolos* Schneider has seen come and go. The graffitied concrete East Berlin district where Menckel was spewed out has been producing them since before the wall fell.

'Music, you peasant. An album is music,' says Schneider, turning back to stare at the house.

Menckel looks bored. Schneider's been banging on about this old shit ever since they rolled up to the target. Menckel's tastes lie with the type of hate and death grind they play before the meetings, get the troops revved up and ready. Landser, Das Reich, Bloodshed, maybe some speedcore Gabber once in a while if he's getting up or if the boys are heading up to the estates at Neukoelln or Lichtenberg to mess up some sand niggers. Or real niggers, queers, kikes. Any ethnic homo Jew fucker they can find.

'OK,' says Menckel. 'I'm biting. Who lived here? Satisfied?'

'John Lennon.'

'Who?'

'Fuck off!' Willy Schneider more or less levitates. He twists 180 degrees to look the punk in the eye. 'You're kidding me, man! You don't know John Lennon? The Beatles? For fuck's sake, who doesn't know the goddam Beatles? *Scheisse!*'

'Calm down. You'll give yourself a heart attack, old man. People will notice. And no, I don't know Lennon. Is he dead? Was he a musician?'

Schneider throws up his hands dismissively and then settles back, sulking. There's a pause before he speaks. 'Yes, of course he's fucking dead, you dickhead! Got shot in 1980.'

Menckel sits up a little straighter, a light in his eyes. 'Really? Where? Here?'

'New York,' says Schneider. 'You're interested now there's some blood, hey?' He's turned away so he doesn't see Menckel smiling. Menckel knows exactly who John Lennon was but it's fun to get Schneider's blood pressure rising. Keeps things interesting on these outings. It can be boring. So much waiting and waiting.

They'd taken the Zeebrugge ferry overnight and picked up the plain white Mercedes Valente in Hull, the keys stashed inside the exhaust.

Just like Gottlenz had told them, the vehicle was in the car park. No need to take a risk crossing in the vehicle. Someone else had gone across with the Merc the day before. After collection, Schneider and Menckel were in Liverpool by nine.

Now it is almost time and, despite his hard talk, Menckel feels his guts tighten.

'She live here?'

Schneider doesn't turn away from Lennon's house. 'No, she lives down the street a little. But this is a good place to be. Always tourists coming so no-one looks twice at us. See?'

Schneider points to a tour bus which has pulled up across the street. Not bad. Menckel has to give Schneider that one. The old guys get old for a reason sometimes and Menckel's smart enough to know that he should pay more attention to the Schneider's of this world if he wants to keep rising. To a point.

'I know who Lennon was,' says Menckel after a while. 'I was just fucking with you.'

Schneider grunts.

'He was a peacefuck, hey? Married that Jap bitch. Fucking gook.'

Schneider sighs. 'Here we go.'

'What?'

'All that Nazi crap. Why do you care about the Japanese? You meet a lot of Japanese in Marzahn?'

Menckel's lip curls. 'Japanese, Taiwanese, Chinese. All these fucking foreigners are the same. Dirty Turks and niggers and Jews. We need to get rid of them again. All the filth coming over to Germany. You can't fucking move in Berlin without tripping over some Muslim fucker. Kill them all.'

'That worked out well last time, hey?'

Menckel starts speaking again and Schneider turns to look back at Lennon's house, trying his best to tune out the little prick, sorry he said anything. That was the problem with Gottlenz using his little Nazi acolytes for this work. All that pointless venom. Schneider has no particular feeling for Yoko Ono one way or the other, but the bile that jumps to Menckel's lips at any reference, no matter how oblique, to 'ethnics', wears Schneider out. How do they do it? It must be exhausting. He waits for Menckel to finish his tirade and then lets the silence develop.

For almost five minutes the only sound is the rain on the roof of the Mercedes. Then Schneider nudges Menckel. 'There.'

He points down Menlove Avenue towards a young woman walking along the pavement. Schneider nods. 'It's her.'

'Sure?'

'It's her. They sent pictures.'

'You haven't kept them, have you?'

'Do I look stupid? No, wait, don't answer that one.' Schneider leans across to get an angle on the woman. 'This is her alright, trust me.'

'Nice,' says Menckel. 'She'll look good in the back, hey?'

'It's not a fucking knocking shop, Menckel. You know what Gottlenz said.'

Menckel rummages around inside a backpack in the footwell and comes up holding a large steel kitchen knife he'd bought at a hardware store on the drive west. There was no sense bringing weapons with you when you could just pick them up off the shelf. It isn't like he plans to use the thing. Just showing her the knife will do the trick.

'Keep that out of sight,' says Schneider. 'We're not ready.'

'Just making sure everything's there,' says Menckel. The truth is that this is the part he likes best. The chase. The feeling of domination. The moment when a line is crossed. He caresses the handle of the knife and waits as Schneider pulls out from the side road opposite the Lennon house and swings the van round in a smooth U-turn at the crossroads.

They come up on the girl from behind. It's a quiet spot but Schneider makes no attempt to hide or to move quickly. Instead he stops the Mercedes up a few metres past the target, the wheels half on the road and half on the grass strip next to the pavement. Menckel, a map in hand, steps out and smiles at her. He pulls his jacket up over his head to shelter from the rain. There are no other people within a hundred metres and traffic is light.

'Hello, please,' he says giving a lift to the second word. Hello *please?* His German accent reassures her. She's used to the tourists at the Lennon house.

'Hi,' she says.

'We are lost,' says Menckel in halting English. He waves the map and she steps closer to the van. Now Menckel lifts the knife from under the map and shows her. He moves in close. 'Don't panic,' he says, pressing the blade against the fabric of her coat. She jerks back automatically but Menckel stuffs the map in his pocket and grabs her arm. 'Nein. No. Nothing stupid, Sarah. I do this before, yes? Understand?' She looks startled at the use of her name.

'What?' She is close to panic.

'Easy,' says Menckel. He applies a little more pressure to the point of the knife in her ribs and keeps smiling. The side door to the van slides open.

'Get in or I kill you.' His voice is level and she obeys as he knows she will. Menckel pushes her inside the van and the door slides shut. To anyone watching the Mercedes pull away they have just seen someone pick up a friend in the rain. A kindly act.

Schneider pulls out into the traffic and, in the back, Klaus Menckel starts to do what he has to do.

8

Berlin, October 9th

Most of the surgeons live outside the city, in sprawling leafy suburbs to the west but Ilsa Bruckner prefers her high-ceilinged apartment on *Lerhter Straße* where she can look out across Berlin from the rooftop garden. Her building, although an old one, is the tallest for several blocks and she has all of the top floor to herself. Bruckner parks the Audi in the underground carpark and takes the lift to the eighth.

Behind Bruckner on *Lerhter Straße* the driver of the Volvo pulls up and settles in to wait. If past experience is anything to go by Bruckner will be in there at least an hour. On Fridays she is in the habit of going out, often to some kind of ritzy art event. The driver of the Volvo makes a note of arrival time in the file and reclines the seat a fraction, stifling a yawn. There has already been a full day at work before this.

At six thirty, Bruckner, wearing a dark blue silk dress with a long black jacket and carrying a glittering black clutch bag, emerges from the building and gets into a waiting taxi. From what can be seen from the Volvo, there is already someone inside the cream-coloured cab. The Volvo slips into the traffic several cars back and tails them to the newly-renovated opera house on *Unter den Linden*. Familiar by now with Bruckner's habits, the Volvo peels off and parks in a disabled slot a hundred metres from the theatre. The driver steps out into a well-heeled audience streaming towards the performance.

Up ahead, Bruckner and her companion, a solidly-built, florid-faced man in his late forties, are already walking up the steps. Bruckner pauses on the first step and looks around for a few seconds before continuing into the theatre.

The driver of the Volvo sags. A long evening ahead beckons. An ad for tonight's performance printed on a long banner slung from a lamp post flutters in the evening breeze. Wagner. Again?

This part of the boulevard is a nightmare for observation. No warm bars or convenient cafes and no parking zones on the main drag. All the driver can see is a cold bench under the trees next to the Humboldt Gallery. It'll be two hours before an intermission and another two after that. These culture vultures like to get a big dose of boredom when they go out. The option of giving it a miss tonight looks better than ever.

'Screw it,' murmurs the driver. 'One more. One more.'

In a street behind the opera house the driver orders a coffee and takes a window seat. There's no need to be sitting out there longer than is absolutely necessary.

Wagner. *Fuck*.

9

Liverpool, October 9th

'A bad one,' says John Halloran into his radio mike. He's standing above the prone woman at the centre of the intersection.

'She dead?' says a voice behind him.

A fat man in a tracksuit is goggling down at the blood and broken body. Incredibly, Halloran detects a faint hint of a leer in the onlooker's face.

'Go back to your vehicle, sir,' Halloran says with an effort. In the distance he hears the first siren. 'Now,' he barks as the man lingers. Halloran notices a phone in the man's hand. 'And if you take one image, I'll stuff that fucking thing up your arse, got that, dickhead?'

'You can't speak to me like that.'

'Move,' growls Halloran and the man backs off.

Halloran shakes his head and turns back to his job. He's normally part of a two-person bike assignment but today there's flu going around and his regular partner, Logan, is sick. This is all going to be on him.

The rain, already heavy, is coming down now like it has a point to prove. Halloran has already asked for ambulance and fire before he steps off the bike. 'We'll need a couple more bods for traffic control, too,' he adds.

He takes off his helmet and puts it on the bike seat. A man wearing a suit stands half in and out of his car looking confused.

'You,' says Halloran pointing a finger. 'Stop anyone trying to drive through, OK?'

The man steps out of his car and stands uncertainly in front of the stationary traffic. It'll do. Halloran has no time to organise anyone on the other side but there's no shortage of public-spirited citizens willing to help. And have a good gawp at the excitement while they're at it, thinks Halloran, before repressing the thought as ungracious.

There's a long streak of blood on the wet road. The Nissan is on its side, there's another car with a damaged front end and the Mercedes van is wedged under the back of the transporter. The traffic is backed up on all four ways in and out, some drivers standing helplessly, others drumming fingers on the driving wheels. Halloran notices a couple of people filming the whole thing.

He bends over the young woman, sliding off his gloves as he does so. Before he touches his fingers to her neck he knows she's dead. Her wrists and hands are lacerated.

A middle-aged woman, her eyes wide, moves towards the body and places a coat over her. Halloran moves to stop her and then thinks again. The coat will protect the evidence – if there is any – from the rain.

There's also the chance that the coat will destroy some evidence but on balance Halloran thinks it's worth it. At least he's considered the matter should it come up later. Right now there are dozens of decisions to be made, each of them requiring rapid action so he doesn't waste too much time in contemplation.

'Stay here,' he says to the woman who'd brought the coat. 'Don't let anyone move her. I'm going to check on the others.'

The woman nods and Halloran heads to the Nissan.

There is noise coming from inside as Halloran approaches. He leans into the vehicle through the passenger window, steeling himself for what he'll find. There are two men in the car, one of whom, the driver, has a badly broken leg. He is screaming. Next to him the passenger is unconscious, his face a mass of blood. Rain hammers into the car through the broken window. Halloran pays no attention to the screamer; noise means life. Instead he puts a finger inside the unconscious man's mouth and hooks his tongue out of his throat. The man coughs but seems to be breathing. Without help Halloran can do nothing to get these two out. He checks there's no sign of fire and that the engine isn't still running.

Halloran leans back out and sees the driver of the transporter wandering aimlessly, staring into the distance, his hands moving oddly. 'You OK?' says Halloran. There's no response.

'Sit down over there,' says Halloran pointing to the kerb. The man nods and slumps heavily onto the wet concrete.

'I didn't do nothing,' he says and Halloran nods.

'OK. Don't move. An ambulance is coming.'

Halloran leaves the transporter driver and moves to the white van. He hears sirens and senses the traffic parting for an emergency vehicle. They were quick. He hopes it's the medics first.

The Mercedes van is in a bad way. Two men stand over to one side, looking twitchy. Civilians. Workmen of some sort. One young, one older. Halloran's not sure if they were in any of the vehicles involved in the crash.

'Hurry up!' says the younger of the two men as Halloran approaches. 'He's fucken dying in there, dickhead!' Halloran doesn't reply. The man looks shocked and Halloran has found that with witnesses to crashes like this one, anger often follows, especially with the young. He can deal with that later. The priority is the guy in the van although, from what he can see, it doesn't look hopeful.

'He's dead,' says the older man, his tone more conciliatory. 'I think. I had a look.'

'OK,' says Halloran. 'Could you just step back onto the pavement?'

The cab has been crushed in on itself, almost folded in two, the driver still in his seat, his head horribly mangled as it made contact with the steering wheel. Blood is still pouring from a gaping wound in his neck. There's no arterial power to the flow so even if Halloran didn't already know the guy is dead, that would have been enough.

He leans through a gap in the glass and sees that the blood is gathered in a pool against the edge of the door. If he opens it, it will splash across the road. Not the best of looks given the number of people watching but it can't be helped.

'Stand back,' he says to the two bystanders. He braces himself and grips the slippery handle of the cab door. It resists the first pull and then springs loose sending Halloran dancing back three quick paces. The pooled blood splashes onto the wet, black road as though someone has emptied a full bucket.

'Shit!' The older witness puts his hand to his mouth. The younger one looks like he's going to faint.

'Can you get him out of here?' Halloran gestures at the young man. The last thing he needs is another body at the scene. 'But don't go far. We'll need statements.'

The older man nods and says something Halloran doesn't catch but it doesn't matter because the two are moving away, glad to be clear of the carnage. Behind them an ambulance edges onto the intersection. Halloran points in the direction of the Nissan and holds up two fingers. There's no need to explain anything, the paramedics know better than him what the priorities are.

Free of immediate medical duties, Halloran steps across the rain-spotted blood and hoists himself up on the cab step and looks closely at the dead man. The driver is in his late thirties, well built with short black hair. Other than almost being decapitated by the steering column he is relatively untouched by the crash. He's wearing dark clothes and, Halloran notices, black leather gloves.

He checks the cab for paperwork. The man is someone's family and it'll be Halloran or some other poor plod who has to let the wife or parents know. Names will be useful.

Halloran takes a quick look inside the cab but there's nothing obvious on show. He tries to see if the driver has a wallet but if he has he's sitting on it and, while Halloran is keen to make progress, that can wait.

Halloran drops back down to road level. The blood from the man in the Merc, now mingled with the rain, snakes out across the intersection, red against the black, following some unseen contour of the road surface towards the gutter. Halloran moves to the back of the van as the second police vehicle arrives. At almost the same time a fire crew pulls through the traffic, another ambulance tucked in behind. Leaving the newly-arrived personnel to their tasks, Halloran pulls open the rear doors. He takes a few seconds to absorb the contents.

'Jesus,' he says and takes out his mobile.

10

Liverpool, October 9th

'Run that past me again, sir. Frank Keane came back from his little jaunt to the US with twenty million dollars tucked in his back pocket?'

'Twenty-five.'

'Jesus.'

'Well, yes, precisely, Peter.'

Charlie Searle sits back in his chair and blows his cheeks out. He glares at the email from Frank Keane as if he can make it disappear simply by wanting it so. He closes his eyes for a moment but when he opens them, there's the damn thing still sitting there.

'It doesn't look good,' says Moreleigh. 'Not going to play very well with Lupus if they get a sniff.'

Pete Moreleigh from the Merseyside Police Media Unit doesn't share his boss's concern. He's never really warmed to Keane and as far as he's concerned if the head of MIT gets scooped up into the current anti-corruption witch-hunt – ironically brought in on the back of a case that Frank Keane was closely involved with – that would be fine with Moreleigh.

'No,' says Searle. 'It isn't.' Just contemplating the outsider bastards from Operation Lupus sticking their filthy investigative hands into MIT's underwear drawer is enough to make Superintendent Searle feel queasy. What they'd do with information that one of his own officers has twenty-five million US dollars of dubious origin, doesn't bear thinking about.

And they will hear about it because Charlie Searle is going to have to tell them. He just wants to talk it through with Moreleigh first. Peter can make it seem better. That's what he's there for.

'What does he say happened? Where did the magic millions appear from?'

'He hasn't. Not completely, anyway. Says it's connected with all that cloak and dagger bollocks in Los Angeles.'

Moreleigh raised his eyebrows. 'What in God's name did he do out there?'

'Classified,' says Searle. 'Believe me, I've asked and got my knuckles rapped pretty hard and pretty damn quick too for my trouble. Left me with an aversion to pushing deeper in case the next time I lose a finger. Or worse.'

Searle's face clouds at the memory. Running headlong into a grade A bollocking from the Chief Constable had given Charlie Searle a few sleepless nights. Which is another reason he's called Moreleigh in for a chat. While this stuff is not strictly a Media Unit problem – not yet – Moreleigh's got a good nose for taking the right line with the upper echelons at Merseyside Police and has carved out a niche as Searle's de facto advisor. Well-dressed, smart, and, under all that middle management veneer, as dangerous as an open box of used hypodermics.

'Well I think Frank Keane is gone,' says Moreleigh. 'No-one is given twenty-five million dollars without having done something wrong. Or winning the lottery. And I don't see Frank standing in the corner of a Spar rubbing the coating off a scratchy, do you?'

'No, not really. But he says it's legit.'

Moreleigh pulls a disbelieving face.

'I know,' says Searle. 'But Keane's attached the paperwork. Company in his name, trading figures, stock options, the lot. Looks pretty convincing at least at first glance.'

'Except he himself says it was a gift.'

'True.'

'Did he say who from?'

Charlie Searle drums his fingers on the desk. 'Ah.'

'Ah?'

'Yes, Peter, very fucking 'ah'. Frank did mention a name but I don't think I'm going to share that information with you. I don't think I'm going to share that information with anyone. In fact, I really wish Keane hadn't shared the information with me.'

'You can't hide it forever.'

'Can't I?'

Moreleigh shrugs. 'It'll come out somewhere along the line, sir.'

'Not this one,' says Searle. 'I have a feeling that this name should never be spoken out loud without a lawyer present.'

'It's not Voldemort is it?'

'I wish. No, it's better you don't know, Peter. For all I know Frank may be a fantasist.'

'He's never struck me as the type. And, from what you tell me, he did get some incredible medical treatment over there. Someone was pulling the strings. I really think you should kick this one up to the CC.'

Charlie Searle holds Moreleigh's gaze and says nothing.

'You mean you already have?'

Searle nods. 'Doesn't want any part of it. Pushed it back down to me. Said I was best placed to handle it.'

'Oh.'

'That's right. This is our mess for now. And as far as Frank's new friend is concerned, the fewer people who know, the better.'

'OK,' says Moreleigh. 'Let's move on.' He leans forward. 'Have you told Milner about the money yet?' Mark Milner is the head of Operation Lupus. Operating from the first floor of the Merseyside Police HQ on Canning Place, the team of Londoners have been there for the past month and are about as welcome as a dose of cockney chlamydia.

'No,' says Searle. 'But I will.'

'You have to. Keane's toxic. At the very least it'll mean a suspension while he is investigated.' Moreleigh looks directly at Charlie Searle across the desk. 'You need to put distance between yourself and Frank Keane. He's dead wood, Charlie, even with his high flown connection.'

Searle frowns a little at the use of his own first name. 'We're not on the golf course, Peter,' he murmurs. 'And Frank Keane has been, until now at least, an exemplary officer. He was shot in America in the line of duty, let's not forget.'

'Sorry, sir. But we don't actually know the detailed circumstances of his injury, do we? Which wouldn't be a problem unless someone in the press decides to ask.' Moreleigh doesn't miss a beat. 'No, Keane has to go. I'm not buying this story of his. If this money isn't connected to Perch I'd be amazed.'

Perch. Even the name of the former disgraced MIT senior officer seems to leave a smell in the air. And Moreleigh's right. Despite Keane's assertions, twenty-five million is a lot to explain away. Searle's going to give Frank to Operation Lupus. Feed him to the wolves. Literally.

'There's something troubling me about Frank coming forward with this,' says Searle. 'If the money *is* dodgy, why did he tell me about it?'

'Because it'd come out anyway.' Moreleigh speaks with hard certainty but Charlie Searle's not so sure. Someone on the take doesn't email his superior officer about it unless there's a very good reason. And this is what's worrying Searle. All that US nonsense Frank found himself mixed up with . . . not knowing what happened continues to nag. The official version; that Frank Keane was pursuing a murder case against Ben Noone, an actor mixed up in a violent sex crime in Liverpool, had seemingly evaporated. Noone? Nothing to see here, move along please. Charlie Searle couldn't even discover what had happened to the American and so far Frank Keane hasn't told him. Since the intervention by the CC there has been a tacit understanding – at least by Charlie Searle – that the best thing that can happen to this particular sleeping dog is to lapse into a coma. Searle becomes aware that he's stopped listening to Moreleigh who is in full flow.

'. . . either way, he has to stand aside. Take a suspension while it's investigated.' Moreleigh looks at his boss. 'You agree?'

'Y-es,' says Searle. Once Frank had emailed about about the money the only thing that could be guaranteed is that Frank Keane would not be a serving officer for some time. And besides, there's something else. Something he hasn't told Peter Moreleigh.

Charlie Searle looks at the laptop. 'It may all be moot anyway.'

'Moot?' In this office, with a view out over the curving Hilton hotel and the Liverpool One development behind, the word seems medieval.

'Moot.'

Searle turns the screen towards Moreleigh.

'Frank had some other news.'

11

Liverpool, October 9th

Ambitious though she is, Em Harris never really allowed herself to contemplate the idea that Frank Keane might *not* come back from chasing Ben Noone around California. Certainly Superintendent Searle got very shifty whenever pressed about Frank's return date. *Deep waters*, is all he'd said – whatever the hell that meant. She got nothing from Frank either while he was in the US. Not a call, an email, zilch.

Then he showed up last week, changed in some fundamental way.

He hadn't, yet, explained what had happened and Harris had reluctantly readjusted to her old role. She had got used to her seat behind Frank's desk and, although she took care never to let it show, a small part of her had been disappointed when he came back to MIT.

And now he'd gone again.

Harris considers calling Searle to see if he knows anything but rejects it. She'll find out soon enough and calling him will make her look weak. Harris is self-aware enough to know her own ambitions mean that Frank being absent is good for her.

Still, she could do with knowing *something* about what's going on.

'Saif.' Harris calls DI Magsi from his desk. She indicates that he should close the door.

Magsi's a smart cop and one of the newest faces in MIT. Drafted in to make up the numbers on the Noone case he's become a permanent fixture. Too junior to worry Harris with his own ambitions he's becoming her go-to man when things need finesse. DC Rose and Caddick and even Theresa Cooper are all a little . . .

clumsy compared to the subtler, slyer, Saif Magsi. And like Harris, Magsi has had to rise in a force with far fewer 'ethnics' than should be the case. They both know the score and that helps.

'DCI Keane has left for the day.' Harris lets that hang so Magsi hears the subtext. He waits patiently for whatever is coming. 'You have some contacts at Canning Place, right?'

Magsi nods. 'I know a few blokes, yes. Ma'am.'

Harris glances up at the 'ma'am' but there's no trace of irony on Magsi's face. The king is dead, long live the queen.

'Good,' says Harris. She keeps her head down. 'So if you heard anything about DCI Keane you'd let me know?'

'Hear things?'

Now Harris looks up. 'Jesus, Magsi I was hoping you'd make this easy.'

'Sorry, ma'am.'

'I'll spell it out. There's something going on with DCI Keane. I'd like to know what that is without asking in an official capacity. There are reasons for me being so roundabout.'

Magsi doesn't need to ask what she means. Rumours that Roy – MIT's nickname for their boss – had some trouble are flying around the office. Harris isn't the only one who wants to know what's going on.

'With it involving DCI Keane obviously we need to be very careful.' Harris looks at Magsi. 'Just keep your ear to the ground.'

Magsi nods. 'Of course.'

Neither of them seriously think that Frank's dirty although there is always that possibility, especially after the Perch investigation. But there's something going on and Harris wants to know what it is without revealing her need to know. There will be smoke if not actual flames. Frank won't be sitting in this chair for a while yet and Harris can already feel the shifting in the office as the team slowly realise that whatever happens, this will be the reality for a while yet. Harris will be boss.

'Get me the general feeling about the situation. Don't try and do anything funny. Just get whatever hard information you can. OK?'

Magsi nods. 'I'll get cracking. Ma'am.'

'What else is there? Anything new come in?'

The MIT workload in a city like Liverpool is always heavy but there has been a small hiatus in recent months. There are the drug killings and domestic murders, an explosives case, extortion; the usual, in other words, but the main bulk of MIT's recent business is dealing with the aftershocks of the Ben Noone business. Seven dead and Searle putting heavy pressure to sew the whole thing up as a sordid story of inter-family paedophilia and murder. It's not how Frank had seen it and his trip to the US had been intended to prove it. Where that case stands now, Harris doesn't know. That was another weird thing: the deafening silence about the Noone enquiry. To judge from the reaction by Searle – and Frank, come to that – the whole case was done with in Liverpool, the US fishing trip a bust. Explanations? None.

'Not much,' says Magsi. 'I've got a bit of a funny one though. A traffic incident this morning. Two dead. Just down by the Pier Head.'

'I passed it coming in,' says Harris. 'Why are you looking at a traffic incident?'

'Well there are a few things off about it, ma'am. A mate of mine's a bike cop and he was right on the scene. In fact he's still there. He wants us to come and have a look. I was just about to go and do just that.'

Harris looks out of the window. The rain is coming down heavy. 'Stair rods' her mother called it. Harris isn't entirely sure what a stair rod is but she thinks of them every time there's weather like this. Her mother too.

'How good a mate?' she says.

'He's solid,' says Magsi, 'Won't move until we get someone down there. He's got the medics screaming blue murder to let them take the victims but he wants us to see it first. Says it smells.'

Harris stands up. She could do with getting stuck into something unrelated to bloody Frank Keane and his miserable gob for a while. 'Get your coat,' she says to Magsi. 'Let's go and see what your traffic cop wants.'

12

Liverpool, October 9th

He's not a believer. He's not.

Yet here he is all the same, each step taking him closer and closer to the god he doesn't believe in. Frank tries to tell himself that where he's going is just a reaction to the diagnosis and he needs somewhere to clear his head, but something in a recess of his mind is telling him different.

Other than funerals, too many to count, Frank Keane hasn't been to church for a very long time, the last occasion the day he got married. Maybe that's why he doesn't go to the Catholic cathedral now but instead chooses the Anglican. At least there'd be no temptation to talk to a priest there.

Whatever the rationale, after leaving the office and driving into the city, Frank finds himself heading in the direction of the red-brick pile at the wrong end of Hope Street as far as a Catholic is concerned. The rain's coming down heavier now, and as he turns a corner he sees the top of the cathedral poking above the fake Georgian terraces is almost shrouded from view. It won't be much of a vista today but that doesn't matter.

This is a massive building. Massive in the same way as a battleship. The Anglican has none of the soaring gothic grace of a Notre Dame or a Canterbury but in the flat grey light it could pass for something military or alien; its main door jutting forward like the prow of an abandoned spaceship.

Inside, the hushed halls echo with the whispered conversations of the few visitors. Frank feels odd being inside the 'other' church. His mother would not have approved and he had never been able to tell what his father thought about the whole business. Frank can't remember much about him. He'd left when Frank was in his late teens and had always been a remote figure. He's been thinking a lot about his father recently; specifically about the change that came over him when Frank was small. Frank hadn't thought about that much before the diagnosis but now he sees that his father had been two very different men. The early memories Frank has of him are sunny – a man with an easy smile and time in abundance. Later, after whatever happened to change him had happened, Keane senior withdrew and then, finally, left.

Inside the cathedral, one of the first things Frank sees is a handwritten neon artwork mounted on the wall below a soaring triple-vaulted stained glass window. *I Felt You And I Know You Loved Me.* Frank blinks, unsure of how he should feel about the neon inside such a space. Is this what churches do now? A label tells him it is a Tracey Emin piece and he tries not to be too Daily Mail about it because he likes the sentiment.

He walks the length of the nave and buys a ticket for the tower from an overly talkative volunteer. Frank takes the rickety lift to the second level and walks up the vertiginous ladder-way before emerging into the light on top of the cathedral. The square platform is deserted. Frank, never good with heights can't believe he's doing this but the cancer makes the vertigo fade, the fear less important now he has something concrete to worry about. He walks gingerly across to one of the slit-like gaps between the crenellations and looks out north towards the Pier Head. The rain masks his view of the Welsh mountains but he can still make out most of the rain-sodden city below. From here the place looks neat and orderly. Frank breathes in the cool damp air and thinks about his cancer, thinks about the microscopic platelets careering through his blood, thinks about the people going about their business. The good. The bad.

He needs to speak to someone but can't think who. His parents are long gone and he has no siblings. There isn't even a cousin. Em Harris would have been the obvious choice but since they'd slept together during the Nicky Peters case things have been tricky. In the end, the view of the Wirral prompts him to call Julie, his ex.

He doesn't know why but it feels strange using the mobile up here, like he's trying to get a direct line to God.

It takes a while before there's an answer.

'Jools,' he says. 'It's Frank.'

'Where are you? It sounds windy.'

'It's not important. Listen, can I ask a favour? Do your folks still have their place in Helsby?'

The barn is less than twenty miles from where he is now – if the weather was clearer he could more or less see it – but Cheshire might as well be another planet.

'Are you alright, Frank?' Something in Frank's voice betrays him. Julie always did have a finely tuned radar.

'No,' says Frank. 'I just need a bit of a break, really. Get away from the flat. I'm taking a bit of time off. I think I went back too soon.'

'A break in Helsby? In October? Wouldn't you rather go overseas?'

'I can't.' *Because I have a fucking brain tumour.* It would make so much sense to tell her but the words won't come out. He wouldn't have been able to explain why he doesn't want anyone to know, except he doesn't. Not yet anyway . . . maybe never.

'Is the place empty?'

'They'll be in Spain until November,' she says. 'No-one's renting it at the moment. The keys are in the usual place, do you remember?'

'The wood shed?'

'Yes. Make sure you put them back when you're finished.' She pauses. 'Is there anything else you want to talk about?'

There's a long silence. Just as Julie starts to speak again he interrupts.

'No. Not right now, Jules. Once I get a chance . . .' He doesn't complete the sentence.

'But there is something, I can tell.'

'Thanks for this, Jules, I'll call you, right? I owe you.'

'Take care. Call me.'

'Yeah, sure. I will.'

He hangs up before he says anything more.

In the streets below an ambulance races down Upper Duke Street towards the docks, the blue lights flashing and the traffic parting before it like corn in the wind.

God save me. Someone save me.

Please.

13

Berlin, October 9th

'OK.'

Sebastian Gottlenz hangs up and looks blankly at the office wall.

'Shit.'

It's been thirty-six hours since he sent Schneider and Menckel to England. When they didn't get back on schedule he waited as long as he could before making the call but it couldn't be postponed forever. The phone call he's just finished was from the contact in Amsterdam – the guy who'd taken the Merc across from Zeebrugge. In a few short sentences he tells Gottlenz what had happened. None of it is good news.

Gottlenz sits back in his chair and runs a hand back and forth across his bald head. Thirty-eight, trim, wearing rimless glasses and a neat goatee, Sebastian Gottlenz looks every centimetre the middle-ranking Berlin accountant that he is. A partner in an accountancy firm operating in an eight-storey office block just off *Karl-Marx Allee*, he is married with two young kids and drives a two-year-old silver SLK.

What Gottlenz doesn't resemble is the secretary of one of Europe's most vicious and fastest growing neo-Nazi outfits, *Kolumne88*. A Berlin-born hate group, Gottlenz has been with them since the beginning and is a true believer. Using cash supplied from sympathetic donors – many more than most would believe – and an effective fund-raising machine built around warehouse parties that double up as de facto rallies, Gottlenz and the *Kolumne88* hierarchy are fashioning something that resembles a paramilitary organisation. There are already weapons stashes in Berlin and training camps masquerading as political conferences held in remote country areas.

With everyone – mostly – looking at the Muslims, *Kolumne88* and others are slipping under the radar. The far right had been seen as a joke by many in the law-enforcement community; a knuckle-headed throwback to Hitler and other discredited clowns. But in Berlin and Munich and Hamburg, the right is rising. A new dawn. Germany's Intelligence agency the *Bundesamt für Verfassungsschutz*, the BfV, keeps an eye on their movements but *Kolumne88* and their ilk are not dangerous enough yet to warrant the cascade of funds spent watching the Islamic fundamentalists.

Gottlenz, ever creative, ever crafty, and with an eye on impressing those who pull his strings, also runs a lucrative sideline matching up his soldiers as mercenaries for hire. Not in wars but in crime. He has found a synergy between the right and the Berlin criminal underground. If he's honest with himself Gottlenz sometimes finds it distasteful dealing with these people. They are often foreigners and sometimes – especially with those from the Balkans – possibly Muslim, but it is a necessity of business. For a couple of years, things have been progressing well.

Until the arrival of his biggest headache, another true believer and one with deep pockets and deeper ambitions.

Gottlenz's headache is a respectable pillar of society who, through their own interlocking connections to *Kolumne88*, had come to Gottlenz with a juicy proposition that promised, and delivered, a steady income stream for relatively little outlay. At first the relationship had been nothing but good. Gottlenz delivered the muscle and the pillar of society paid. The coffers of *Kolumne88* continued to swell.

Gradually however, Gottlenz had found his interactions with the new arrival decaying – his role becoming increasingly more subservient, deal by deal – their desire for a steering hand on the *Kolumne88* tiller increasing with every euro until it has reached the state it is in now.

If it was simply this new arrival who was the problem, Gottlenz could deal with it. But the new voice has muscle behind it in the alliance with Felix Hoffen, one of *Kolumne88's* key personnel, and the organisation's primary enforcer. It is Hoffen who Gottlenz now has to call. Outwardly at least, Hoffen's new 'colleague' is one of Berlin's most respected individuals with a lot to lose if anything goes wrong.

It is they who should be the ones most nervous about the screw up in Liverpool, not Gottlenz.

Yet it is Sebastian Gottlenz whose fingers shake as he taps out the number.

14

Helsby, Cheshire, October 9th

When Frank drops back to his flat at Mann Island on the docks to pick up some gear the place feels airless and cramped. He's never really liked the flat but now it has all the charm of a dole office waiting room and Frank's glad he'd called Julie about the barn: if he's going to stare down eternity then he needs a better environment than this black box. He needs somewhere to raise his spirits, not lower them. A refuge. A bolthole. The barn isn't a long-term solution but since there may not be any long-term, it will do for now.

Frank stuffs a few items into a holdall, grabs his laptop and phone charger and locks the door behind him. The happy thought occurs to him that he'll never set foot inside the flat again.

He takes the tunnel under the river and heads south on the 53. It's a short journey to Cheshire but even so he can feel a tiny fraction of the tension in him ease as he puts the city behind him. He feels disengaged from the events of the day, as if they're happening to another Frank Keane. Shouldn't he be doing something medical? Isn't there a procedure for this stuff?

The answer comes back loud and clear: he's on his own. That, he is sure, will be the lesson for today. His cancer is his and his alone. How he deals with it – *if* he deals with it – will be up to himself. There are no rules for this. You cope or you don't cope. You die or you don't.

Frank has no way of knowing which category he'll fall into so, for now, getting in the car and going to Cheshire will do for today. He'll do some more serious thinking tomorrow.

The barn, an old wreck picked up for a song and renovated by Julie's parents, stands up on a rise above Helsby. The reason for the place being cheap isn't hard to see. Beyond the sloping garden, about four miles away at the foot of the valley, lies the oil refinery at Ellesmere Port. The vast industrial complex sprawls along a stretch of the south bank of the river spitting fire from slim steel towers and breathing out plumes of steam that drift west towards the Welsh hills. Most people think it's an eyesore but Frank kind of likes it, especially at night. Blade Runner on the Mersey. He's even got a soft spot for the tang of diesel in the air.

In a Tesco's at Helsby he stocks up, trying to shop like someone with cancer would shop. Whatever the fuck that might be.

He buys fruit and organic juice. Muesli. When he finds himself putting an economy bag of quinoa in his trolley, a substance about which he only has the sketchiest idea, he gives up and heads for the alcohol. He's not a boozer, not really, has seen too many decent cops fall by the wayside over the years, but if there was ever a day that demanded strong drink, this was it. Thirty minutes later he emerges from the store with a fully-laden schizophrenic trolley. Half healthy shit; half booze, junk and DVD's.

The key is right where Julie said it would be. Frank unloads the Golf and gets the wood burner going. With that lit, he turns on some of the lamps, clicks his phone into the music dock and lets Van the Man breathe some life into the place.

Frank pours out a glass of red and stands at the window watching the lights at Ellesmere Port and thinking about the times he'd been here with Julie. Good times, he supposes. Nothing dramatic, just good. The sort of times you don't think about until circumstances suggest it's Red Rum to a dead donkey you'll never experience anything like that again.

He puts down his glass and looks at his watch. Not even four.

What do people do when they have cancer? Read? Watch *I'm A Celebrity*? Take long meaningful walks in the woods?

Frank wanders aimlessly through the barn, looking out of each window. Outside in the big oak, the branches already mostly bare, hundreds of crows argue as they settle in for the night. Frank watches them for a while and then drains his glass. He takes it into the kitchen but, as he's reaching for a refill, changes his mind.

He can't just sit around getting pissed. He remembers there is a hotel nearby with a pool and gym. Healthy stuff.

Thirty minutes later Frank is hitting the treadmill hard. He can't help but run hard, pushing himself until he is struck by the stupidity of trying to sweat the fucking thing out. Frank jogs another fifteen minutes and switches to the weights room. There's a heavyweight bag there and he spends twenty minutes going through his regular training routines. Spent, he heads for the pool.

The water feels good and he has it almost to himself for a while. Then as the clock passes five-thirty the place starts to slowly fill. Six or seven women fresh from a class drop into the water and Frank drags himself into the spa.

There is already an old boy in there and he nods as Frank sits down awkwardly on the opposite side.

'Hard day?' says the guy and Frank's tempted to tell him everything. That would be something. Other than Searle he has told no-one.

'You have no idea,' he says, and before the old boy can start yakking, Frank puts his head back and lets the bubbles go to work.

When Frank opens his eyes, the old boy has been replaced by the women from the pool. The spa's full. A couple of the women smile vaguely in his direction and Frank wonders if he'd been dozing. He rubs his face and blinks, tuning out the chatter. Just as he's thinking about getting out he feels a hand brush against his thigh. A few seconds later, the hand is back and this time it remains. Frank glances to his left and sees a woman next to him. She's not looking in his direction, is in fact engaged in deep conversation with another woman. She is around thirty-five, pretty, in good shape. He looks away and the hand strays onto his thigh, one finger lazily stroking up and down.

When a manicured nail starts probing under the leg of his shorts, Frank stands and, doing a good impression of a startled gazelle, lurches from the pool, slipping on the tiles as he escapes. Tottering towards the changing rooms he hears laughter behind him. He doesn't look round.

15

Berlin, October 9th

'Can't you leave work behind for once, Ilsa? It's Friday night.'

'What?' Ilsa Bruckner doesn't look up. Her phone vibrates as they are getting into the cab and, squinting in the shadows, she is trying to read the message when Dieter, a sleekly-dressed, forty-something fund manager at Deloitte Berlin she'd been introduced to at a cocktail party a month ago, pipes up. Without her reading glasses she tries to focus on the words on the screen but it's difficult with the great pompous lump booming away in the background like a flatulent bear.

'You seem –'

'Jesus Christ, Dieter!' Ilsa Bruckner looks up from the phone and glares. 'Can you just keep quiet for two minutes? Please?'

'I'll take that as a "no", then.'

Dieter Patz looks up and sees the driver's eyes regarding him in the rear view mirror. It's hard to tell from the back but there is, Dieter is sure, more than a trace of disgust in the set of his shoulders. The driver is Turkish and Ilsa, Dieter would bet, does not fit the driver's view of ideal womanhood. If truth be told, she doesn't fit his own, but she's a smart piece, the sort of woman a man in his position should be seen with.

Dieter glances over and sees that Ilsa too is looking at the driver. She turns to Dieter and raises an eyebrow as if catching her partner in some sort of anti-feminist discussion. Which, Dieter supposes, she has done in a way. As happens often when he's in Ilsa's company he feels like a small boy caught stealing.

'What?' says Dieter but Ilsa doesn't reply.

Instead she turns and looks out of the window thinking about her phone message. The traffic is heavy and, although they don't have far to travel, progress can be slow at this time on a Friday evening. For a minute or two there is only the faint tinny hiss of the cabbie's ethnic radio station.

Then Ilsa speaks. 'It's not your fault, Dieter,' she says. 'You can't help it.'

'Help what?' says Dieter. He makes a deliberate effort not to glance at the driver.

Ilsa makes a circular gesture with her left hand. 'Being such a windbag,' she murmurs.

The driver coughs and they turn onto *Friedrichstraße*.

Now it's Dieter's turn to look out of the window.

'Don't sulk,' says Ilsa.

'This can't go on, Ilsa. Not like this.'

Ilsa wants to hit him. Was this idiot brought up on a diet of TV soaps? Does every single word from his great shiny red face need to be quite such a clunking cliché? *This can't go on?* Jesus.

Instead of hurling her phone at him she puts her hand on his sleeve. 'We'll talk over dinner,' she says, softly. Getting angry might bring on another of her headaches and she can do without that. Just get through this evening and then Dieter Patz can be quietly dropped for someone else, someone quieter.

'We're going to the opera, Ilsa. I wish we *were* going to dinner. It's bloody *Wagner*, for Christ's sake. We'll be eating at midnight.'

'Food's over-rated, Dieter. We'll get something, don't worry. And this is one of the short ones.'

The car pulls in across the street from the opera house. While Dieter pays the fare Ilsa dials voicemail. Dieter's face clouds as he comes around the front of the car and sees Ilsa on the phone.

'Friday,' he mouths and Ilsa holds up a single finger and turns away. She listens for a few seconds before hanging up and putting the phone back in her bag. Just as she moves towards Dieter she freezes, the hairs at the nape of her neck rising.

Someone is watching her, she's sure of it.

This is a feeling she has been getting more and more frequently in recent weeks. Paranoia induced by overwork? Or something else?

'Ilsa. *Come on.*'

She looks back along the busy pavement, her eyes darting through the well-heeled crowd streaming into the opera house but there's nothing she can see. Still looking over her shoulder she walks slowly up the steps and into the theatre, a familiar throbbing beginning somewhere deep inside her head.

Maybe Dieter is right. Maybe she is working too hard.

16

Liverpool, October 9th

Heading for the accident on the Dock Road, Harris and Magsi pass Frank's flat at Mann Island, the monolithic black box wedged like a piece of discarded builder's rubbish between the redbrick splendour of the Maritime Museum and the graceful white lines of the Cunard Building. As far as Harris knows, Frank's been living in his one-bedder since his split with Julie last year.

Harris can't stand the building and averts her eyes whenever she can. She'd shared a bed there once with Frank and for the briefest of moments there was a flicker that things might have turned out differently. But they hadn't, and what might have been something became just another drunken fumbled hookup between colleagues: something to be filed under 'mistake' and placed in a drawer with a busted lock.

Magsi puts on his blues and nudges through the knot of vehicles around the crash site. He and Harris step out into the rain and put on raincoats. There's an argument going on near the traffic lights between a big cop in bike gear and a small group of firemen, medics and civilians. Three other uniformed cops are standing a few metres away from the group looking like they don't know which side of the fence to sit. There are a couple of tow trucks standing by and a Granada TV van parked across the street is filming the congestion.

'Your mate?' Harris gestures towards the bike cop as they walk across the wet tarmac.

'Yep.'

'I hope he knows what he's doing,' says Harris.

'He's a good guy,' says Magsi.

Harris looks unconvinced, although blocking a street of this size for this length of time is ballsy, she will say that for Magsi's biker pal.

As they draw near the argument subsides.

'DI Harris,' says Harris to the bike cop. 'MIT.'

'PC Halloran, ma'am.' Halloran nods to Magsi.

'Alright, Mags,' he says.

'I hope you know what you're doing,' says Magsi.

'Can we get moving?' says one of the firemen. 'We've been here too long already.'

'Just wait a few more minutes, alright chief?' says Harris. The fireman looks like he's about to reply but decides against it. The two medics start talking again.

Harris holds up a placatory hand and drags Halloran to one side. 'What's the story? You know you're making the news, tonight, right?'

'I know something funny when I see it, DI Harris,' says Halloran. 'It's probably easiest to show you.'

He walks towards a shape covered by a rain jacket. Halloran bends and Harris squats down beside him. Halloran lifts the jacket enough so that Harris and Magsi can see the dead girl but not enough so that many gawkers can.

'Naked?' says Harris.

'That's one of the weird things,' says Halloran. 'But if it was just that I would have let them take her. I've seen bodies get stripped in crashes before. They don't end up completely naked. Not usually anyway. There's this too.'

He points at the girl's wrists. They are a bloody mass of ripped flesh and shredded skin.

'Could the injuries have happened when she was thrown from the vehicle?' says Magsi.

'Looks off to me,' says Halloran. 'I haven't seen that before. Not in a crash.'

He stands and points at the crumpled Mercedes. 'She was in there. Came through the windscreen right in front of me when it hit the transporter. She wasn't conscious.'

'You could see that?'

Halloran nods. 'I was close, ma'am. She wasn't conscious.'

'Dead already?'

'That I couldn't say.'

Stepping carefully around the blood on the tarmac Halloran shows them the driver in the Merc. 'This one ate the steering wheel. Died on impact.'

Magsi blinks. He's seen plenty of bodies but Halloran's daily dose of gore gives him a hardened carapace that Magsi has yet to achieve. Harris inspects the driver dispassionately. 'I'm still not seeing it,' she says to Halloran. 'I mean it's odd, right enough, but I'm still not getting why you want us.'

'It's all in the back. I just wanted to show you the crash first so you can understand the mechanics of the thing. I called DS Magsi because of what's round here.' Halloran takes them to the rear of the vehicle and opens the doors.

Inside is a jumbled mess but the key items can be seen clearly. There are IV drips, medical materials. Duct tape. Plastic sheeting. There's a trolley of the sort used in hospitals that's been almost cut in half by the crash but looks new, expensive. Dangling from the side rails of the trolley are two broken plastic ties. Shreds of skin and spatters of blood are clearly visible. Lying in the corner, his neck at an impossible angle is a young, blonde-haired man.

'The crash sent her straight through the dividing window and on through the main windscreen,' says Halloran. He points at the dead man. 'This one collided with the back of the cab.'

'She'd been strapped down to the trolley,' says Harris, her voice hard. 'The impact ripped her free.' Harris turns to Magsi. 'Get the SOC team down here immediately. And sort out some more traffic backup. This is going to take time.'

Magsi moves a few steps back and begins talking into his phone.

17

Berlin, October 9th

As they're taking their seats, Dieter, stray crumbs from the peanuts he'd snatched from the theatre bar still salty on his lips, tells Ilsa that where they are sitting is just about the same seat that Hitler had occupied on his frequent visits to the Opera House.

'Of course with all the renovations, things have shifted around a bit but the acoustics and the general surroundings would not have altered much.'

Bruckner smiles politely but is glad she is saved from further small talk by the proscenium lights dimming and the orchestra beginning to play. She can do without Dieter's plodding conversation and is rapidly coming to the conclusion that she can do without Dieter full stop. He's right about one thing: this can't go on. This will be their last date.

Settling back in her seat Ilsa dislodges a microscopic speck of dust from the cuff of her jacket and lets the waves of sound wash over her.

Parsifal. Not, perhaps, the best loved of Wagner's works but certainly – to Ilsa Bruckner's ears at least– one of his finest achievements. In the dark, without Dieter's inane chatter, she is free to think clearly for the first time since opening her eyes that morning. Sometimes it seems that everyone wants a slice of her. And, for the past two years, complications piled upon complications. All her own fault of course for over stretching.

Midway through the third act Ilsa feels her phone vibrate inside the bag on her lap. She slides it out and, shielding the light carefully with a cupped hand – the opera audience regarding light pollution from phones as a capital offence –risks a look at the screen. Next to her Dieter is fast asleep.

Ilsa Bruckner replaces the phone, leaves her seat and slips out of the auditorium, her movements are economical and unobtrusive.

In the highly decorated corridor that runs across the back of the stalls, the sounds from inside are muted. Ilsa finds a deserted spot and takes out her phone. This matter can't wait any longer. If she's honest with herself, she should have attended to it before now.

An elderly usher, standing halfway down the corridor, wags an officious finger and frowns.

'*Nach draussen gehen!* 'he hisses and points to the stairs.

As the first wave of her migraine rolls in, Bruckner raises an apologetic hand to the usher before walking down the stairs and out into the cold Berlin night. She tightens her thin jacket around her shoulders and presses redial. While she waits for the call to connect she massages her temple. The headaches have been getting worse recently.

18

Helsby, Cheshire, October 10th

Frank wakes with a hangover and – for a few sweet seconds – amnesia, before the gut-churning horror of yesterday comes rushing back in, as welcome as an incense-swinging Pope at Hampden. The mantra that has been Frank's internal soundtrack since he stepped out of Medavoy's surgery resumes, the medic's coal-black words reverberating in an endless despairing loop.

Cancer. Biopsy. Malignant.
Cancer. Biopsy. Malignant.

He lies for a time without moving, cradling his headache as carefully as a newborn infant, relishing the momentary relief the physical pain gives him from the diagnosis. He stares at the beams running across the ceiling and, for the first time in his life, considers suicide as a practical option. Not for long, and not with any sense that he would ever act on the idea, but there all the same. It's a notion that he knows will return and that scares him. Not that anyone could blame him if he did take that route.

The bleak direction his thoughts are drifting in prompt him to swing himself out of bed and into a long, long shower. When he comes downstairs he makes coffee and toast and sits at the kitchen counter trying to keep them down. By nine he knows he will survive the day and he resolves not to repeat the binge of last night. After the day he'd had, after the humiliation at the hotel, the evening at the barn had been spent getting steadily drunk to *Astral Weeks* and crying. There had been lots of crying. Some yelling too. Frank hopes none of it was overheard. From now until the biopsy he will proceed as if the result is a certainty. He will be able to get the operation and he will survive. There is no other way forward.

He spends most of the morning trying to get some order into his existence, to normalise this madness. His first task is dealing with the fallout from yesterday's emails. From the one he sent Searle detailing the money given to him by Dennis Sheehan there is the expected suspension, indefinite, pending investigation. Searle dances around it – lots of talk about the need for allowing complete transparency to all avenues of enquiry in order to blah blah blah – but the gist of his newspeak is that he's given Frank up to Milner at Lupus.

Frank doesn't blame Charlie. What else can he do? It's a surprise not being called back in for a 'chat' right away but Frank guesses this is simply the start of Searle's campaign to distance himself from any potential fallout. Searle only mentions the cancer in an oblique reference to hoping that Frank is looking after himself. Occupational Health have sent him back a standard form to complete. Nothing personal in it at all. Frank completes the details for OH and emails it back. He sends emails to Harris detailing some points of existing MIT cases that she might not be aware of. The bureaucratic minutiae prove oddly comforting, perhaps because it suggests an ongoing system, something that will continue to operate. Being part of that machine means that you are alive.

Frank's phone chirps several times during the morning but he lets the calls ring out Two are from Harris and one from an unrecognised number. He's not in the mood for conversation. He finds he's rubbing his temples compulsively, as if he can massage the tumour away.

By twelve the hangover has receded. Over a sandwich and instant coffee he decides he won't have anything to drink today. Booze won't get him past this. Exactly what will, if anything, he has no idea. Alternative medicine? Witchcraft? Scientology? Nothing seems likely to give him what he wants.

Frank's disease has a decent survival rate but, he learns through the oracle of Google, once past a certain stage it's something of a lottery. The word *aggressive* crops up repeatedly. Frank feels his stomach cramp up. Staring out of the window he sees the first signs of evening creep into the sky and once again feels the seductive pull of suicide. It would be so easy. So simple.

He has the pills right here.

19

Berlin, October 9th

Kriminalkommissar Anna Ziegler orders a beer from the waiter in the black pants and crisp white shirt and turns back to the window. The bar's an upscale joint and there are still some opera lovers slinging down a last glass before crossing over to *Unter den Linden* for tonight's performance. Judging by the pained expressions on a few faces perhaps 'lovers' isn't the correct term. But this is the Berlin bourgeoisie at play, or what passes for play in that world and Ziegler guesses that attendance at the opera on a regular basis may be compulsory. She doesn't know. She's never been part of the chattering classes but past experience of waiting for Ilsa Bruckner means she does know at least one thing about opera: it takes a shitload of time before the fat lady eventually stops singing.

Ziegler's already put in a nine-hour shift at the *Landeskriminalamt* – the LKA – Berlin's State Criminal Police Office. This is on her own time and has been on and off for almost two years. There are now many more times when Anna Ziegler thinks Dreschler and the rest of the LKA office might be right. Perhaps she is obsessional. But each time she tries to disengage, back comes the thought that tonight might be the one where she lands the fish.

Or at least gets a bite.

Talking of which...

Ziegler opens the menu and, despite the eye-watering prices, orders a meal. She'll have time.

20

Berlin, October 9th

'It's me,' Bruckner says when the call is answered. She listens to the reply which is long and detailed. Outwardly she is calm but can feel the familiar pressure building. This migraine will be one of the bad ones.

'We will need to speak further about this,' she says. 'You understand?'

'Yes. I am sorry.'

'Sorry is pointless. I will talk to you in person soon. In the meantime I expect you to put this mess right. I have standards.'

'We are looking at the best way to fix it. Believe me.'

Bruckner doesn't reply. She ends the call, puts the phone back into her bag and stands for a moment looking up and down the street.

Sitting in the shadows of the linden trees on a cold bench on the other side of the wide street, Anna Ziegler picks up her camera and focuses on Bruckner, her silk dress shimmering under the lamp light above the lobby doors. Ziegler gets a couple of good shots off before Bruckner turns and heads back into the warmth of the theatre.

Ziegler puts down her camera and looks at it for a moment before leaning forward on and resting her chin on her hands. She can feel the hurried meal in the cafe lying on her stomach. Next to her on the bench is a small notebook bulging with notes from previous evenings like this.

'This is stupid.'

'Sorry?'

Ziegler glances up to see a passerby, a woman in her sixties, tired-looking but with a round, kindly face.

'Nothing,' says Ziegler, flushing a little. 'Been a long day.'

'Are you OK?' asks the woman gently. 'This place is too dark to be sitting alone, you know, my dear.'

'I'm safe. Thanks, anyway.'

'You know, you can't be too sure. Lot of immigrants around the parks at night.'

Ziegler flips out her ID, her smile freezing into a scowl. 'I'm a cop. I'll manage.'

'Well, if you say so.' Huffing, the frau potters off down *Unter den Linden*, glancing suspiciously back at Ziegler in the shadows.

Ziegler watches the woman disappear and sits back heavily against the bench. She puts her things in her backpack and walks to her car. Enough. She's finished with this nonsense. It's time to forget about Ilsa Bruckner, stop time-wasting and get back to doing her real job.

21

Helsby, Cheshire, October 10th

A dog barks and Frank twitches out of his oddly reassuring suicidal daydream. He glances over toward the painkillers on the kitchen counter and then looks away. He feels loose, a drifting balloon and about as substantial. He can quite easily imagine a world without Frank Keane. We all die, right? Why not now?

Frank rubs his hands over his face and feels the afternoon stubble. He'd read somewhere that your hair and nails kept growing for a time after you die. Or was it your nose and ears?

Outside, through the window, a neighbour is moving at the end of his garden, a dog sniffing among the vegetable patch. Frank has a dim memory that Julie is friendly enough with the guy. Bernie? Is that his name? Frank vaguely recalls speaking to him once before at a barbecue Julie's folks put on when they first bought this place. A big, rough-arsed Scot made good.

Spooked by the direction his thoughts had been taking, Frank puts on his coat and walks down the garden in the late afternoon October light trying not to look too desperate. The breeze is blowing from the south and is rich with loamy country smells, the petrol tang temporarily absent. Ellesmere Port and the refineries could be a million miles away.

As Frank approaches the dilapidated wooden shed squatting at the low boundary fence separating the two properties, a Glaswegian voice cuts the serenity like a chainsaw.

'Ye fuckers! Cunt! Aw, fuckin' hell!'

As the invective increases in both volume and intensity, the boiler gauge heading for the red, Frank stops, sure that Bernie must have company. Judging from Bernie's tone the argument will end in violence.

Frank turns back towards the barn. A casual chat with the neighbour is one thing but butting in on a local argument is another. He has only taken a couple of steps when the temperature of the discussion goes up a notch.

'Bastard! Ye wee twatting red bastards!' There is the sound of wood splintering.

Frank, reluctantly a copper again, turns back to the shed.

'*Cunts!*' screams Bernie. 'Fucking thunder cunting bastard shitwad *twat!*'

'OK,' says Frank, rounding the corner of the shed. 'Can we just . . .'

Bernie, an enormously fat man with a shaven head whose age is almost impossible to tell, wearing an ancient-looking tweed jacket over a hooded sweatshirt, dirty Liverpool FC track pants and a pair of what can only be described as hob-nailed boots, is savagely stomping his plants into a tangled mess of bamboo canes and greenery and fertilizer-filled gro-bags. A languid dog watches placidly from the sidelines as the Govan Godzilla, spewing inventive profanities at machine-gun speed, rampages through a tomato Tokyo. A punted plant pot sails past Frank's shoulder, closely followed by a splintered bamboo cane with a whole plant still attached, the small clods of earth trailing behind like debris from a comet.

The horticultural holocaust continues unabated until Bernie's dog spots Frank and erupts in a frenzy of barking.

Bernie's red face swings in Frank's direction and instantly relaxes into what seems like a genuine smile. He doesn't look remotely embarrassed at being interrupted mid-blitzkrieg.

'Oh. Hi.'

Bernie steps out of the carnage, kicking out savagely at a couple of plants still clinging to his leg. He mops his brow with one hand and gestures wearily at the devastated vegetable patch with the other. 'Tomatoes,' he growls, managing to imbue the word with several extra consonants – *toomarrratooz* – and more venom than a canefield snake. Narrowing his eyes, he points a chubby finger at Frank's chest and looks at him suspiciously. '*You* ever try to grow fucking tomatoes?'

'No. Not really.'

'Well then,' says Bernie, breathing heavily, grudgingly mollified by Frank's apparent tomato virginity, 'don't, is what I say. Break your fucking heart, tomatoes will.' He looks back at the garden, his expression that of a post-combat Tommy contemplating Flanders. When he speaks next his voice is choked with an impossible, haunting regret. 'They are such cunting things.'

Frank is unsure of the etiquette when faced with this combination of raw emotion and horticulture so he holds out a hand. 'Frank Keane,' he says. 'We met here a while back.'

Bernie shakes Frank's hand. 'Aye, so we did. Bernie Palmer.'

Bernie nods at the dog. 'This is Smitty.'

Smitty whose parentage lies somewhere between a collie and a labrador, wags his tail at the sound of his name and Frank pats his head.

'You bring the wife?' says Bernie. 'Haven't seen her for a while. Lovely woman, Jenny. Absolutely lovely.'

'Julie. And we're not together anymore,' says Frank. 'We split up.'

'Fucking *bitch!* Christ on a stick, they're all the same, hey, the back-stabbing sluts? What did she do? Get off with another bloke? Or was it a woman? They do that sometimes.'

'No. We still get along,' says Frank. 'Otherwise why do you think I'm here?'

'See,' says Bernie, slapping his palm against his head with such force that he actually staggers backwards a step. 'Kath – the wife, you won't have met her – she's always on at me about doing stupid shit like that. Motor mouth talking without thinking as per fucking usual. Of *course* you'd no be here if she was being a bitch. Jesus, I'm such a dumb twat sometimes. Sorry, Phil.'

'Frank.'

'Aye. Frank.'

There is a short pause and the two men turn back to contemplate Bernie's path of destruction. Bernie wipes his brow again with the back of his sleeve and shakes his head sadly.

'Don't ever be tempted to start growing the things,' says Bernie. Any residual embarrassment from their last exchange seems to have evaporated. Frank is getting into the rhythm of Bernie's world.

'No,' says Frank, 'no, I won't.'

'Break your fucking heart.'

'Yes, you mentioned that.'

Bernie glances back towards his own house. 'You fancy a wee drink?'

'Yeah, sure.'

Instead of moving to the house, Bernie steps across to a small shed leaning against the stone wall. He pushes open the door and flicks on the light. A bare bulb spills warm yellow light out into the garden. Bernie rummages amongst the clutter and produces a plastic bottle filled with liquid and hands it to Frank. The hand-written label reads 'POISON!!!!! DINNAE FUCKING DRINK! SPECIALLY NOT YOU, RIGBY!!'. Bernie offers no explanation as to who Rigby might be.

Bernie dives back inside and emerges from the shed with two reasonably clean china mugs, one of which he hands to Frank.

'It's malt. Good stuff,' says Bernie, taking the bottle from Frank. 'Not weed killer. I widnae give you weed killer, honest injun.' He inclines his head towards the house. 'I'm not supposed to drink too much. *She –*' and this word is spat with absolute heartfelt venom – 'doesn't like me drinking. We only got married a couple of years back. Still sort of a work in progress.' He winks at Frank as he pours whisky into the mugs. 'Nae drink? I don't think so. No-one tells Bernard J Palmer when he can and can't have a wee dram. No fucking way. A man's gotta be king of his fucking castle or what's the fucking use, eh?'

He sits down heavily on an upturned wooden crate and tilts the mug to his lips.

'I think Kath's coming,' says Frank, looking at the house. Bernie almost falls backwards off his perch, the blood draining from his face.

'Only joking,' says Frank holding up a calming hand. He raises his mug and takes a tentative sip. The liquid tastes like it should which is a relief. Judging by the chaos in Bernie's shed Frank wouldn't have been surprised if it had turned out to be weed killer after all.

'Sweet Mary Mother of God,' says Bernie. 'That nearly finished me off.' He clinks his own mug against Frank's. 'Don't do that again, y'hear? Kath's a whirlin' terror when she gets going and no mistake. Terrifying. I spose I had it coming after that guff about your ex but I've had about as much excitement as I can take for one night. I'm supposed to be walking the dog too so no doubt I'm in line for a royal bollocking for that.'

'I'll take him if you like, Bernie,' says Frank. 'If he'll come with me. I fancy a walk.'

'Aye, no sweat.' Bernie tops up his mug. 'Smitty'd go with any soft cunt if there's a walk at the end of it. No offence.'

'None taken.'

'I mean, I'd go like a shot but there's one or two things to clear up round here.' He lifts a dog lead off a nail on the back of the shed door and hands it to Frank. At the sight of the lead, Smitty starts barking.

'You know where Delamere Forest is? Smitty loves it over there. Shut up, Smitty!'

Frank nods. 'I know the way.' He hands back the mug of malt to Bernie. From the house comes a woman's voice.

'Bernie! Bernie! Keep that dog quiet!'

'You'd best scoot,' says Bernie. 'It's gonna get ugly.'

22

Berlin, October 9th

In the restroom off the main lobby, Ilsa Bruckner splashes some
water on her face and tries to calm down after the phone call. She
dabs her face with a paper towel and touches up what little make-up
she wears. When she's finished she drinks a glass of water, takes a
painkiller, and checks herself in the mirror. Once she is sure her
expression is serene, her pale skin even in colour, she steps back into
the lobby and heads up the curving stairs to the first floor stalls.

The usher who chased her outside earlier stands impassively in a
curtained alcove. He doesn't look at Bruckner. From the auditorium
comes the sound of bells tolling as the first scene in Act 3 staggers
towards a conclusion.

Ilsa Bruckner takes a few more steps across the richly-patterned red
carpet and then halts, brought up short by a sudden sharp pain in her
temples. She pauses and pinches the bridge of her nose between
thumb and forefinger. A thin, whining sound is building somewhere
inside her head, a sure sign of the migraine to come. For a second she
wonders if she is about to pass out. After the day she's had she
wouldn't be surprised. Her migraines follow stress like birds behind a
tractor. She turns back to the restroom, her hand scrabbling inside
her bag for her painkillers.

'No phones allowed,' says the usher, his stubby finger lifted already
in admonishment. 'I already told you. Don't you understand?'

'What?'

'No phones, I said.' He shakes his head a fraction, his face pinched
with annoyance.

Ilsa Bruckner hesitates, drops her head wearily as the migraine hits hard and grimaces, before looking up and regarding the usher coldly. She takes another step towards the man and lifts something from her bag.

'It's not a phone,' she says, her voice hard. 'See?'

23

Helsby, Cheshire, October 10th

Frank's grateful that Bernie doesn't suggest accompanying him on the dog walk. He goes in one direction, stepping over the fence with Smitty on his heels, while Bernie heads the other, trudging back to the house to face the wrath of the already legendary Kath. As Frank nears his car he hears raised voices from the house and this time is sure it is a two-way conversation, although it's Bernie who's doing most of the listening.

Smitty jumps into the back seat and Frank pulls out of the drive heading west for Delamere Forest. The dog puts his head out of the window and lets his ears blow in the wind. Frank glances over and shrugs. What the hell. He slides his own window down and hangs his head out in the cold afternoon air trying to feel what the dog feels. Beneath him the tires beat out a rhythm on the road and the whisky is warm in his veins. The thought of crashing makes him want to laugh for some reason and then he does, uncontrollably. Frank keeps his head out of the window and lets the wind excuse any tears.

24

Berlin, October 9th

His feet are killing him. He's too old for this work now. Much too old and much too tired.

Wagner is always hard work, the miserable bastard. The expensive insoles Astrid had given him last month don't seem to have made a speck of difference. Otto Leutze just wants to finish the shift and get home to the television and his chair. He leans back against the theatre wall, feeling the bass notes of *Parsifal* rumble against his spine. The sensation isn't unpleasant but Otto feels guilty about enjoying anything while he's at work so he straightens and walks down the corridor for the twentieth time since the interval. There's a chair tucked around the corner in one of the utility rooms but that pig Guzman frowns on it being used during a performance. Naturally, Guzman himself spends the evening with his own fat manager's arse perched comfortably on a nice leather office chair watching porn.

Leutze checks his watch. The Barca game's on later and he's looking forward to putting his feet up and drifting off. Otto's a football nut and should, by geography, support Hertha Berlin, but he finds himself increasingly repelled by some of the younger supporters' fondness for a dark period in the club's past. He'd tried going to a couple of games but the atmosphere put him off. Better to watch Barca or Bayern from the safety of your armchair.

Leutze sees a shape coming up the stairs. One of the opera lovers. A classic *spieber* from Mitte or Charlottenburg, she's already been on Otto's radar for trying to use her mobile phone. As she passes, Otto avoids eye contact until he sees her reaching into her bag once more.

'No phones allowed. I already told you. Don't you understand?'

'It's not a phone,' says the woman. 'See?'

Leunze looks down, puzzled at the object the woman is holding. It is a short-handled, razor-sharp hunting knife which she rams deep into his gut and leans in close, her mouth to his disbelieving ear.

'Sie verdammt dreckiger Jude.' Bruckner hisses the words, pulling the blade upwards as she speaks, her free arm wrapped around Otto's neck to brace herself.

Even through the shock and pain, Otto registers the scent of her expensive perfume thick in his nose and the softness of the skin on her arm against his own. He wants to say something, something incredibly important, but his words are gone. She has killed him and he knows it and he wants to ask why. Otto makes a gurgling sound, his eyes locked disbelievingly on hers as the knife is pushed expertly and precisely into his heart. All sensation leaves Otto Leutze and he drops onto the thick carpet, his killer guiding his body as he falls.

Ilsa Bruckner, gym-rat strong, drags the dead man into the alcove and places his body behind the long red curtain. She wipes his blood from the knife on the man's uniform and checks her own dress for splashes. Satisfied she is clean, and that the body is invisible from all but a thorough search, she replaces the knife in her bag and steps back into the empty corridor. What blood there might be on the floor is masked by the red pattern. Unobserved, Ilsa walks confidently through the auditorium door back into the darkness and the swelling music, slipping into her seat next to the dozing Dieter, her headache gone like smoke on the breeze.

25

Liverpool, October 9th

The dead girl from the crash has no identifying paperwork. No tattoos, nothing. Harris's first act in the investigation is to try and shift her up the pathologist's list. Viner, the new guy, proves more amenable than Ferguson and agrees to move some things around. While he busies himself examining the bodies Harris instructs DC Caddick to start putting together the file, digital and paper on what they are calling the White Van Case.

After stopping at the crime scene to speak to Harris, DI Theresa Cooper has been put to finding what she can about the girl. She'll start that process with the hospitals and the clinics, sieve through missing persons and, later, use the media.

But they all know that the key to this is probably not going to be the dead girl. It's the driver and his passenger. Here they have more to go on. There's the vehicle to start with and Harris gets Magsi and Rose to check the records. Harris also begins the process of ordering forensics on the two dead men and on the Mercedes. She calls Searle to clarify her position. With Frank out of the picture, permanently or temporarily, Searle officially gives her the nod.

'All yours, DI Harris,' he tells her over the phone. 'And I want you to speak to the press later. I'll send Pete Moreleigh over to give you a hand. They're flapping like a clutch of chickens about the road closure. Be handy if it was open before five.'

Harris knows why she's being picked out and it has nothing to do with opening the road before rush hour. Moreleigh from the Media Unit could do that job but Harris knows that having an articulate, good-looking black officer in front of the cameras will do no harm to

Searle's own CV. Liverpool's spotty record on policing and black police numbers needs every bit of help it can get. Searle's one of the good guys though and Harris doesn't blame him too much for using her skin colour like this. She's a fast learner. A black Chief Constable of Merseyside. A black, *gay* Chief Constable. Now that was worth playing along for.

It's almost three now and the southbound carriageway outside the Liver Buildings has been sealed off since nine. There are three police haulage vehicles preparing to take the damaged cars away. The transporter will be driven to the inspection yards. Traffic are dealing with the congestion problems and the SOC team has been over the scene twice. Photography has been done and Harris notices the pathologist office van has taken the bodies while she's been organising.

She notices Halloran, the bike cop drinking a coffee and talking to one of the traffic coordinators and walks over.

'We're just about finished here. You can get things moving again when you're ready.'

'Thanks, ma'am,' says the coordinator. 'I've been getting my ear chewed for the last two hours.'

Harris smiles and turns to Halloran. 'Good work,' she says. 'We'll probably need another statement from you tomorrow. See if you can think of anything you missed.'

'Will do, ma'am,' says Halloran. He takes a step closer so that only Harris can hear him. 'I was thinking of having a drink at the Pumphouse a bit later. Settle my nerves. Do you fancy coming along? Discuss the case?'

Harris blinks. 'I said you did good work, Halloran, but you're not a miracle worker. Which is something you'd have to be for that line to get a result. Now fuck off before I put a note on my report. Cheeky bastard.'

'I had to ask,' says Halloran. He shows no sign of being even momentarily deflated by the rebuff. 'You can't blame me for trying, ma'am.'

Harris gives him her best cold-eyed stare but as she turns away she can't stop a small smile arriving.

Her phone vibrates. It's Searle. Or Searle's secretary, at any rate. He wants to see her.

Harris pockets the phone and tries to concentrate on the job in hand but she can't keep the smile off her face because she knows what Charlie Searle's going to say.

MIT is hers.

26

Liverpool, October 15th

Thursday morning in Fazakerley Oncology and a breeze is blowing south of Frank Keane's bare arse. So is this is how it begins? The slow transition from the living to the dead, from an individual to a patient, from 'Frank' to 'the deceased'.

Frank had always thought for him it would come quickly in a crash, or maybe a nut with a gun, the way it had almost happened in America. Yet sitting in the waiting room Frank knows that this is the reality of decline and death for most and, probably, for him. Clipboards and institutional green paint. Tired medical staff itching for the end of shift and the grinding indignity of giving yourself up to an indifferent machine.

Or maybe they're not tired.

Maybe that's just Frank's take on it; his own preconceptions coming to the fore, bile rising in direct relation to the self-disgust he feels about his own body betraying him. Looking around the ward it doesn't look tired. It's a new building and the staff move briskly. They look smart, like they know what to do. Which is something. Frank tries to relax. He'll have more of this to come. If he's lucky.

He's dressed – if that's what you can call it – in a short, washed-out green robe with no back and with a file containing his notes on his lap, and is sitting on a cold plastic seat, his backside picking up Christ knows what from the multitude of bare arses that have gone before. No-one else in the room seems to mind. They are all older than Frank, many of them by several decades.

'Urine fer bipsy like, la?' says a phlegmy voice in Frank's ear.

He turns to see what looks like a reject from a Peter Jackson casting call gurning up at him.

'What?'

'Are yer in fer a bipsy, like?' Gandalph's midget father looks insanely happy to be here. He waves his own beige file like it contains the Golden Sandal or whatever the fuck it is in those movies. Frank always hated that dragons and dwarf shit and takes an instant irrational dislike to the old man.

'A biopsy?'

The hobbit beams. 'Yeah, a bipsy. Mine's me fourth. Can't get rid of the fucken' stuff.' He leans back, beaming. 'Mr Howard says it's a medical miracle I'm still alive.'

Frank doesn't ask who Mr Howard is and the hobbit seems to assume he knows. Frank guesses he's the consultant but it's entirely possible Mr Howard will turn out to be the hobbit's neighbour.

"Mr Howard's the consultant,' says Frank's new friend after a minute of silence. 'In case you was thinking, like. Top man is Mr Howard.' He lowers his voice conspiratorially and bends in closer to Frank, his breath stale. 'They call 'em *misters* the top blokes. Better'n doctors.' He sneers over the last word as though once you had experienced the rarified air of a consultation with Mr Howard, mere doctors were somewhere on a par with call-centre workers, or toilet attendants. '*Doctors*,' he hisses as though to emphasize the point. 'Get a *mister*, that's the ticket, chief.'

Frank looks desperately towards the reception window where two staff are chatting about a television show. Shifting his position so that his back is slightly turned towards the hobbit, Frank picks up a newspaper and reads about the road crash three days ago. There's a quote from Em Harris and Frank wonders why MIT is involved in a traffic incident. He looks up to see the hobbit walking towards the bathroom, his saggy grey arse cheeks wobbling as he walks. Frank's chin sinks down onto his chest. This can't continue. He will do what's needed but Frank knows that if he keeps coming here, keeps letting them lump him in with everyone else, with *the sick*, he will not survive this disease.

There must be alternatives. Options.

And then the penny drops.

A son of the state since birth, it's never before occurred to Frank that he can *buy* himself out of this. Watching the old man's rear end disappear through the toilet door Frank decides exactly what he'll spend the twenty-five million on: looking after himself.

Before that, though, comes this. The bastard biopsy. As the day chugs on Frank is processed, prodded and pricked. He's moved from waiting room to ward and back to waiting room. Questions are asked and answers received. He sees an impressive array of doctors and nurses and orderlies and students and is asked the same questions all over again. Finally, around two in the afternoon, he's prepped and prone on the gurney being wheeled down to theatre, his fears dulled by opiates. He's told no-one where he is and as the fluorescent lights flick past overhead on the trundle through the rubberised corridors, he regrets the decision. Whatever happens in the theatre – during 'the procedure' – is a crossroads where most of the roads lead to a dead end. Literally. There should be someone with him.

'Alright, love?' asks a woman in scrubs as he slides in feet first. She's holding a clipboard and has a face mask over her nose and mouth. Frank doesn't know if she's a nurse or a doctor.

'Yes, I think so,' he manages to say. Despite himself, his voice wobbles. The woman leans in closer and pats his hand.

'My name's Alison, love. I'm the theatre nurse. The most important one in here and don't you forget it. We'll be quick and clean. Your blood type's not helping. Mr Wilson had to use all his powers of persuasion to scrape together enough to get us over the line. It's a good job you don't need a kidney. Mr Wilson will be doing your procedure today, love. He's good.'

'A mister,' says Frank and smiles. He sees Alison's name badge hovering in front of him as she adjusts something behind his head. 'Alison McDowell' it reads.

'That's right,' says Alison. 'Mr Wilson.'

The anaesthetist is strapping a drip line to his arm. Frank looks in his direction.

'We're going to send you to sleep, Frank.' The guy has a Welsh accent. Frank tries to crack a joke, something about sheep but he finds he can't so he smiles and nods. He can feel the panic rising but it is at a distance, like a bad thing happening to someone else. The Welsh guy starts talking to Alison as more people come into view. Frank hears a soft whining sound which mingles into the buzz of the operating theatre conversation and then he hears nothing.

27

Berlin, October 10th

Ilsa Bruckner sits at the kitchen counter underneath a long skylight reading the *Berliner Morgenpost* over coffee. The sound of the rain on glass overhead is pleasant. Ilsa likes rain. It's cleansing. Yesterday's headache is just a memory.

The *Morgenpost* contains the usual and her mouth tightens as she reads the latest catalogue of Berlin criminality and filth. A couple of years ago she attended an exhibition in the *Deutsches Historisches Museum*, just a short stroll from where she is now. Trumpeted as some sort of liberal landmark in German culture instead of yet another dose of spineless left wing hand-wringing, the intent of 'Hitler and the Germans' was to remind Berliners of their complicity in the rise of fascism. Invited to recoil, Ilsa instead had thrilled at the images of Hitler standing in places familiar to her. She loved the children's school books decorated with swastikas, Mickey Mouse in SS uniform, allegiance pledges to The Fatherland. There were photos of smiling Berliners wearing the deaths-head badge with *pride*.

Glory days.

Now, when reading the papers it is impossible for her to forget that outside, the streets of her city are awash with the detritus and debris of Africa and Asia and Eastern Europe. Everywhere she looks there is hypocrisy and flatulence, weakness and immorality.

The limp-wristed middle classes, content in their tree-lined enclaves, whine like little bitches about human rights and donate to Sea Shepherd and Greenpeace while sending their children to all-white fee-paying schools. The politicians, sleek and fat on euro money, pander to the lying Arab in the White House preaching multicultural claptrap and selling the strategy of only bombing the *bad* negroes, the ones who won't keep the oil flowing. The workers, the traditional rich soil for the Nazis, continues to offer the best pickings but apathy is the enemy. Television and junk food and beer keep most of them pacified. Meanwhile an impoverished brown tide is lapping up against the citadels of the West and threatening to swamp the civilised world. It is intolerable. It will not be tolerated.

But, for Ilsa Bruckner at least, there is one shining ray of illumination in all the socialist murk: if it had happened before it could happen again.

Hitler has not been forgotten. Everywhere she looks, *der Fuhrer* is there. In books, in magazines, on TV and online. This fresh fascination is dressed with a veneer of repulsion to allow the population to indulge because the truth of it is that Hitler sells, Hitler is big business, Hitler is a brand that's making a comeback and the political landscape is shifting. Candidates once considered extreme are getting elected to mainstream office across the globe. The incomers, the immigrants, are being countered by a rising swell of public outrage on the streets of London and Madrid and Berlin. And, just like in '33, this resistance is a phenomenon of the common man. Germany needs a fresh start and down in the shitholes of Marzahn, Neukoelln and Lichtenberg, where the immigrants are breeding like rats, that's where the new right is making a stand before it's too late, before the sand niggers place a mosque on every corner and the burka on every daughter of Germany. In her work, Bruckner knows first-hand that sometimes the only way to save the patient is to cut and cut again until the parasite in the host is exterminated. Life and death rendered simple: kill or die. Hitler knew this instinctively and his genius lay in convincing Germany of this truth. It is not acceptable for upstanding patriots to do nothing while the country is swamped by niggers, queers, addicts and communists. These are the tumours and the new right is the scalpel. If everything goes well with the project a cleaner society is just around the corner. The people will be forced into action.

Ilsa becomes aware that she is breathing heavily. She turns back to the *Morgenpost*.

There is no mention of the dead man at the opera. As she suspected, he may not be discovered until later today, perhaps longer. She sips her coffee and checks off the difficulties facing any possible investigation. She doesn't know for an absolute certainty that there will not be a problem but she is confident that unless she is very unlucky, this will turn out to be the case. There are no witnesses and no motive. Without motive an investigation cannot make easy progress. And, if by some chance someone from the LKA does come sniffing, her record and reputation are spotless. A skilled surgeon, no money troubles, no obvious vices and with no history of violence, it would be a brave policeman who tries to pin something like that on someone like her. Ilsa Bruckner is careful to keep her Nazi leanings under strict control. Only a few people know how extreme she is, how violent, how greedy for power. No-one will be coming.

She puts down the newspaper and focuses attention on something important: what to do about Gottlenz. It had been his calls last night about the screw-up in England that had put her in such a bad mood last night. In some ways, she thinks, it is Gottlenz who is responsible for the usher's death.

A lesson must be handed out, that is clear. Bruckner depends on absolute fear to control her operation and Gottlenz must be punished. Someone must be. Bruckner pours herself another cup of coffee and moves across to a more comfortable chair in the sun lounge to think the thing through. As with everything she does, when it comes to this other existence she leads, her decisions are an odd combination of detached logic and bloodthirsty rage.

Gottlenz. How to send a message with real meaning? How to convey the exact level of retribution? Bruckner's long fingers drum idly on the steel surface. She is doing this when Dieter walks into the room.

'Good morning,' says Bruckner. She smiles a smile as cold as Vladivostock in February. Ilsa wants this man gone, but not before she'd made certain he has nothing to say about last night.

'Coffee?'

'No thanks,' says Dieter. He walks across to Bruckner and kisses her lightly on the cheek. 'I have to go.' He smiles but Bruckner sees a flicker of something familiar in his eyes.

Fear.

Immediately, she is on alert. Did he know something? Her mind begins to run rapidly through possibilities of killing Patz and how best to dispose of his corpse.

'You OK?' she asks.

'Of course.'

'Have I done something to upset you?' Bruckner takes care to remain serene even as Dieter walks towards the apartment door, fastening his tie as he moves. Inside, her blood is screaming. She tells herself: this man is not the usher. This man has been seen with her, has some history, a connection. The taxi driver, the opera audience, people in her building, colleagues, have all seen them together. Besides, what Ilsa sees in Dieter's eyes may be nothing. The risk of killing outweighs the benefits. For now.

'Maybe you were a little . . .rough? In the bedroom, I mean?'

Ah. So that is all it is. Bruckner feels her shoulders relax. 'I am so sorry, Dieter. I thought you wanted . . .' Bruckner lets the words trail off and puts her hands up in supplication. 'A miscommunication.'

She vaguely remembers her fingers round his neck at one point but it really was nothing. Not compared to when she truly allows herself to let go.

Dieter will have to be eased quietly from her life but not just now. He still has a function to serve as possible witness to her innocence. She will keep him until then.

Ilsa stands and shrugs apologetically, allowing her gown to fall open. 'I actually do not prefer that kind of thing. I thought it was your taste.' The lie comes easily. 'Call me?'

Dieter smiles, and this time there is nothing in his eyes to worry Bruckner.

'I will,' he says, his gaze wandering down her body. Ilsa ties her dressing gown and smiles as Dieter leaves, a happy idiot.

Bruckner stops thinking about him before the door has closed. She turns back to the kitchen counter, picks up her phone and taps out a number and arranges to meet Sebastian Gottlenz at the Berlin Zoo at twelve. She likes the zoo.

28

Liverpool, October 16th

'Mr Wilson. I did your procedure yesterday?'

'Did you? You don't sound too sure.'

The consultant smiles fractionally and holds out a hand. Wilson is a bald-headed man of around fifty, well-dressed in a dark blue suit. He looks fit and has a pleasant, open face.

'Nothing wrong with your mind then. Sharp.'

Wilson radiates absolute confidence and competence. Frank smiles. Maybe the hobbit with the saggy arse had a point. Misters might be better.

Wilson sits on the edge of Frank's hospital bed and flicks through his medical notes. Frank, during his long day of preparation for the biopsy had arranged for the rest of his treatment to be carried out privately. Although Frank uses his own credit card, it is the first purchase he's made with Sheehan's twenty-five million in mind and it feels okay.

The money has resulted in several immediate improvements. The first is the complete absence of bare-arsed hobbits. The second is the notable lack of noise. Frank's sure he's wrong but that's what it feels like.

His residual working class guilt is still reverberating but he thinks he'll cope. That's another thing about getting cancer that he's noticing; your capacity to give a fuck becomes greatly diminished.

'So?' says Frank.

Wilson puts down the clipboard.

'Bugger,' says Frank, looking down at the papers. He can feel his right hand trembling so he makes a fist and folds the fingers of his left over the knuckles. 'That doesn't look good.'

'It's not as bad as that,' says Wilson. 'More a kind of hiatus.'

The consultant looks at him. 'Your biopsy did reveal the tumour to be malignant which is in line with what we expected. It does appear to be aggressive although at this stage we're unable to say exactly how aggressive. Given the rarity of your blood group I'd like to get another opinion about how to proceed. That's what I want to speak to you about.'

Frank can almost feel the cancer eating through his nervous system, a writhing alien octopus coiling its slimy tentacles around his thoughts, his ideas, squeezing the life from him second by second. 'OK,' he says. It's all he can manage.

'I'll get these results over to a colleague of mine in London. With this kind of situation where there is a high risk in any operation it is best to be cautious.' Wilson pauses. 'By the same token we can't wait much longer before we decide whether or not to go ahead.'

'How long? Before we need to do the operation? If we can, I mean.'

'I wouldn't like to leave it longer than two weeks, Frank. Of course, we won't wait that long to get the second opinion. My best guess would be that my colleague will have his thoughts back to me tomorrow, or the day after at the latest.'

'And?'

'And at that point there will be two possibilities. The first is that we need to operate, if you agree, bearing in mind the risk associated with an operation when a tumour is at this stage. The second, I am afraid, is that any operation would be pointless. Then it would be about helping you as best we can.'

'Jesus Christ.'

'It's also worth pointing out that this is all your decision Frank. If you decide you don't want to take the risk of an operation then that is something you'll have to discuss with your loved ones.'

Frank is tempted to say something sarcastic but remains mute. Pissing off your cancer consultant would not be one of his better moments.

'I'll start you off on a drug regime that should help with any pain and keep you feeling chipper. Once we get the opinion back then we can start getting some firm dates sorted out. We'll also be getting some of your own blood off you to stockpile for future ops. One in a hundred million is about as rare as it gets. If you needed a transplant you'd be stuffed.'

'I heard that,' says Frank, thinking of the blonde theatre nurse. 'Silver linings and all that, I suppose.'

Wilson folds his arms and looks at Frank. 'Any questions about my assessment? I know it's a lot to take in so take your time.'

Frank pauses. 'Well, what do I do before then?'

'Keep as fit as possible. Eat well, try and stay positive. Wear your seatbelt.' He smiles sourly. 'No point in going to all this trouble if you kill yourself on the 62, right? believe me, it's happened before. The shock of diagnosis shouldn't be under-rated. You'll stay in here while we take blood and check you've recovered from the biopsy – a couple of days maybe – and then take a holiday. Take some time to digest the situation.' Wilson looks at the bandage around Frank's head. 'And nothing too exciting for a few days at least. OK? Do you have somewhere quiet to go?'

'I'm staying at a place in Cheshire. It's quiet.' Frank has a momentary flash of Bernie Godzillaring his tomato plants. 'Mostly.'

'Good,' says Wilson. He stands and shakes hands again. 'I wish I could have been more definite but it is better to take it steady.'

Once Wilson has left, Frank sits and thinks about what's happened. He is no worse off than he was before the biopsy. There is still a chance.

He should call someone. The medic's seatbelt crack had reminded him of Harris and her traffic case. He reaches across and finds his phone in the bedside table drawer.

DI Harris is in a cross-departmental meeting at Canning Place when her phone vibrates. Discreetly palming it and seeing Frank's ID she texts back that she'll call back in ten minutes. She looks back up and pretends interest in the latest round of budget initiatives being discussed. As she does so she catches a glimpse of a DI from Sefton, a beefy-looking, red-faced man whose name escapes her, sneaking a crafty look at her tits. He smiles guiltily and shuffles in his seat. She catches his eye and smiles. Then, sure he has his attention, and certain that only he can see her, she mouths the words *fuck off*. His smile fades and Harris turns back to the speaker in front of the whiteboard.

Around eleven the meeting grinds to a halt. The tit-ogler makes a hasty, scowling exit and Harris, after a few necessary networking chats finds a quiet spot in a corner of the canteen to call Frank.

He answers straight away. Harris can hear muffled clanking in the background.

'Where are you?' she says.

'I'm in the, er, library,' says Frank. A ward orderly is mopping the floor of his room. She glances at Frank and raises one finger. Almost done.

'The library? Of course you are.'

'Well anyway, never mind all that. How are you?'

'More to the point, how are you?'

'Hold on a sec.'

Frank pauses and waits for the orderly to leave. When he speaks again his voice is clearer. 'I want to meet up. Go over a few things. There are a few things I've been meaning to talk to you about.' He hesitates again. 'Personal things.'

'You didn't answer my question, Frank.'

'I'm fine,' he says. 'Like I say, just some personal stuff going on.'

Harris looks around the canteen. There's no-one within hearing range but she drops her voice.

'Are you in trouble Frank?'

There is a long pause. So long that it's Harris who speaks next. 'Frank?'

'What do you mean, 'trouble'?'

'Jesus, this is Merseyside Police. Everybody's got an opinion on everything. There are rumours going around. About what happened in America. About you. I mean, it's not like you've been saying much since you got back, is it?'

'No,' says Frank. 'I should have talked to you earlier.'

'About what?'

'It's a big subject for the phone. Can we meet somewhere later this week?'

'Of course. Today?'

'Er, no. I can't. Have to be in a couple of days.'

Harris hears the hesitation but resists the urge to quiz Frank further. If she wants him to tell her she'll have to be patient. Frank Keane's not an easy man to push.

'Do you want to come round to my place?'

'No.' Frank's answer sounds too definite and comes too quickly. 'Wait, I know that sounded wrong. I don't want to meet at your place because I don't want to talk in front of Linda. Nothing against Linda but . . .'

'It's OK, Frank. I know what you mean. How about Leaf on Bold Street at four on Saturday? It's a cafe. Can you make that?'

'Yeah, good,' says Frank. 'I'll see you then. And Em?'

'Yes?'

'Don't mention all this to anyone at MIT.'

'I won't,' says Harris. 'I've got a meeting with the Super this afternoon but I'll keep this to ourselves. I'll see you on Thursday. Look after yourself, Frank.'

'Yeah, will do,' says Frank and hangs up.

Harris looks at the phone for a few seconds as if expecting it to provide some of the answers Frank didn't give.

29

Berlin, , October 11th

'You brought your kids?' Ilsa Bruckner looks at Gottlenz with amusement but Gottlenz doesn't feel like laughing. 'Jesus, who brings their kids to a meeting?'

Gottlenz swallows. He looks over to where the twins, three-year-old boys, are watching the polar bears through the glass. Felix Hoffen shakes his head and takes a long pull on his cigarette.

Hoffen, a bear-like figure of forty-five, is one of those men born needing a shave. He's dressed in black pants and a charcoal grey shirt. Bruckner suspects there is Jew blood in Hoffen somewhere but he is so useful that she keeps her suspicions to herself.

Hoffen is the man Bruckner called once she had heard Gottlenz had messed up the abduction. Bruckner is someone who takes care of details. That's getting harder as *Kolumne88* expands and as the roles played by the main players start to become more complex. Gottlenz, who wrongly imagines he has power, is simply a bean counter. In the last year it is Hoffen and Bruckner and one other who make up the primary drivers behind *Kolumne88*. It is these three who have the ambition and calculation to take *Kolumne88* to the next level.

Of the three here today, Bruckner is strategy – she adds venom and concentration to the organisation and a steady stream of cash from her extra-curricular activities at the clinic. Gottlenz is administration and funding, Hoffen the muscle management. Although Bruckner prefers a backseat when it comes to public awareness of her alignment with *Kolumne88*, citing the need for respectability in her professional life, she thinks of herself as being in control. Over recent months she's formed a tighter bond with Felix Hoffen that has strengthened both of their positions and weakened that of Sebastian Gottlenz. In March they had spent the night together although the experience hadn't been repeated.

Now, having Gottlenz walking round unpunished will make them look soft, will make her look soft.

'I had to bring them,' says Gottlenz. 'There was no-one to look after them. Martine is working.'

'Really?' Bruckner almost smiles. 'I know why you brought them, Sebastian. You brought them for insurance. To make it harder for us to punish you.'

'No.' Gottlenz stops himself saying anything else. There is a short silence.

'OK,' says Bruckner eventually. Gottlenz doesn't know what she means. Bruckner turns away from the children and lights a cigarette.

'What happened over there?' As she speaks she blows a thick plume of smoke in Gottlenz's face and looks at the accountant like a patient on her operating table.

Gottlenz, clean-living, a non-smoker, tries not to cough but can't help himself. Bruckner doesn't have to explain that 'over there' is Liverpool.

'It was an accident,' says Gottlenz. He keeps his voice flat. 'Nothing but an accident.'

Bruckner picks a piece of tobacco from her lip and flicks it away. It's cold at the zoo and she tightens her coat. 'An accident.'

Gottlenz glances over towards his children, the word triggering an automatic parental safety response.

'Don't worry,' says Bruckner. 'Hoffen is watching them.'

She starts walking around the curved polar bear enclosure. 'Come,' she says over her shoulder. 'We'll walk while we talk. It's warmer.'

Gottlenz wonders why they didn't meet somewhere indoors but once again says nothing.

'Have you done anything to put this right?' says Bruckner. A small group of school children run past. Gottlenz waits for their noise to fade before replying.

'Yes.' He says, eager to bring the teacher an apple. 'I have people on the ground.'

'What are you, ex-military?' Bruckner shakes his head. '*On the ground.* Jesus. You're a fucking accountant, Gottlenz.'

'We'll find a replacement. Once we have a name . . .'

'We have a name,' says Bruckner. 'Our English partner who found the girl came up with another target. Pure fluke, but no less welcome for all that. He has already identified a replacement. A family member. Same blood type, lives close by.'

Bruckner doesn't mention the complication. Hoffen will have to deal with that later. Gottlenz doesn't need to know.

They are approaching the end of the enclosure and Bruckner halts. She stands looking down at one of the bears, her gloved hands on the rail.

'Beautiful creatures,' she says. 'But deceptive. They might look harmless but they are killers, pure and simple.'

'My guys can get to your replacement inside two days.' Gottlenz tries not to sound desperate. 'It won't be a problem. This thing is nothing. An inconvenience.'

'Did you hear about that crazy bitch who jumped in here a few years back?' says Bruckner giving no indication Gottlenz has spoken.

'No,' says Gottlenz. He's lying, he remembers the incident clearly but doesn't like where Bruckner's going.

Ilsa Bruckner waves a hand at the polar bears. 'Made the news. Jumped right in. She lived but was badly bitten.'

Gottlenz leaves her statement hanging. 'So, should I get my guys to pick up the replacement?' he says, after a pause.

Bruckner turns away from the polar bears and back to Gottlenz. 'Well the customer is waiting and he can't wait very long so I'm sending Hoffen over to make certain.' Bruckner smiles at Gottlenz. 'I don't like disappointing my clients, Sebastian.' Bruckner leans closer to Gottlenz and he is conscious of her proximity. She smells of antiseptic and cigarettes. He wants to lean back but forces himself not to. Bruckner is like no other woman he's ever come across. 'We must show the customer that we are making efforts on his behalf. Atoning for our errors. You see what I'm saying here?'

"Yes, yes. We need to move fast. Get the uh, replacement to Berlin as quickly as possible.'

'True. But we also need to reassure our customers that we are looking after them properly. Tell me, if you were served a poor meal in a restaurant – a rude waiter, inefficient service, that kind of thing – what would you expect to happen if you complained?'

'I don't understand.'

'I think you understand very well, Sebastian. If you complain to the manager he will take steps, perhaps get the waiter to apologise, yes? Even sack him.'

'You're sacking me?'

Bruckner laughs. 'No, I need you, Sebastian. *Kolumne88* needs you. You are still useful.' Bruckner puts an arm around Gottlenz and lowers her voice. 'But we must show that we care about our customers, Sebastian, you see that, don't you? Show them that we deal with problems quickly. Take steps to make sure things like this do not happen again. To do otherwise would be weakness, would show that we are not the strong Germans we profess to be. Your stupidity in sending those morons to make the pickup may have killed our client. *Killed* him. You understand that this is not simply a bad meal, or a hair in the fucking soup, Sebastian? If we hadn't had the fortune to find a replacement my reputation would have nose-dived more than it has already. So someone must take the blame and that isn't going to be me.'

Gottlenz finds he can't speak. He twists around to look at the twins. They are watching the polar bears, happy, Hoffen in close attendance.

'Don't hurt my children.' Gottlenz's voice no longer has any aspirations to calm. 'Please.'

Bruckner lets go of Gottlenz. 'Hurt your children? What a strange idea.'

Gottlenz slumps, relief washing over him.

'I'm not going to hurt your children,' continues Bruckner. 'You are.'

'What?'

'You've seen that movie, *Sophie's Choice*? One of my favourites. Funny. You get to choose which one you will throw into the enclosure. Just like Meryl Streep.' Bruckner makes a small gesture with her hands. 'Except she wasn't at the zoo, but you know what I mean.'

'You're insane.'

'I don't think so.'

'I'm not going to hurt my children.'

'We'll see.' Bruckner takes a step back and waves Hoffen across. He takes hold of the hands of the twins and walks towards Gottlenz and Bruckner. While they make their way over there is silence.

'Both of them,' says Bruckner when Hoffen is within hearing distance. 'Throw them both over.'

Gottlenz grabs Hoffen's sleeve. 'Wait!' says Gottlenz. He is trembling violently.

'You choose,' says Bruckner. 'Pick one and throw him to the bears.'

Gottlenz is crying now. 'Please! Don't do this! I'm begging you.'

'You'll need to wait until the place is deserted,' says Bruckner. 'That won't be long. We're early and the zoo is empty.' She holds Gottlenz's stare. 'You do this or Hoffen here will kill them both. And then maybe you and your wife. This way you get to stay alive and so do most of your family. I think that's more than fair, in the circumstances.'

Gottlenz keeps his head down. This nightmare is not going to stop and he has no faith that fate will intervene to save him. Bruckner gets whatever it is that she wants, and Gottlenz knows his situation is beyond all help.

And what is worse, what is making Gottlenz faint with horror is this: he is going to do it and Bruckner knows it.

'Please, Ilsa,' says Gottlenz. He can't stop his voice breaking. He doesn't know what to do with his hands. He can feel his own core, his soul, whatever it is that makes Sebastian Gottlenz who he is, begin to dissolve.

'It's quiet now,' whispers Bruckner. 'We'll go and wait on the bench over there, Sebastian. Pick one. Throw him over the rail and then we carry on. Business as usual and we'll say no more about it.'

Gottlenz steps to one side and vomits into the bushes. The twins wander over to him, confused and crying. He holds them both tight and watches Ilsa Bruckner and Felix Hoffen walk away.

30

Southport, Merseyside, October 15th

'Charlie.' Mark Milner half stands and shakes Charlie Searle's hand as he approaches the table. Milner indicates the empty chair opposite. 'Thanks for coming.'

'Bit cloak and dagger all this, isn't it, Mark? All this way north for dinner? You left the huskies outside?'

Milner, a sallow Londoner in his mid-forties, tall, dapper and wearing an expensive suit, looks around the Southport restaurant. Through the glass windows the well-heeled walk past along a colonnaded Victorian boulevard in the late evening autumnal sunshine. After the rain of the last few days everyone has come out to play. 'Well it's not exactly the Hebrides.' He smiles. 'But I know what you mean.'

Searle adjusts his chair as a waiter approaches with a water jug. Searle nods as the waiter fills his glass. He orders a glass of red wine and Milner stays with water. Once the waiter has retreated Milner leans forward.

'Frank Keane. Is there something about him we should know?'

Charlie Searle frowns. 'Like what?' Milner's olive branch, in the shape of this lunch, will not extend to Searle giving Lupus the information about Keane's cancer.

'How well do you know him?'

'Listen, Mark, I'm happy to talk about my officers in general terms, and I think we've shown our sincerity in helping Lupus by giving you the information Frank Keane gave to me – voluntarily, I might add – but I'll be buggered if I'll share gossip, or medical records without some official paper trail.'

'Medical?' Milner's expression shows Searle that he'd been barking up the wrong tree thinking that this is what Lupus is after.

'Doesn't matter,' says Searle.

Milner pauses before waving a hand. 'We can come back to that, Charlie. I might want access. Could be important if Keane is dirty.'

'I think that's unlikely.'

'He was Perch's junior.'

'And disliked him intensely. And was fundamental in developing a good case against him'

'Well . . . let's leave that aside for now. The reason I dragged you out here wasn't to see if you could drop Frank Keane any deeper in the shit.' Milner breaks off as the drinks arrive. 'Cheers,' he says.

Milner sips his water and continues. 'The reason I got you here was to see if you could shed any light on Keane's connections.'

Searle shrugs. 'I wasn't aware he had any.'

'Come off it, Charlie. I'm talking about the twenty-five million dollars. I'm talking about what happened in America. I'm talking about how a plod from Bootle ends up with friends in high places.'

Charlie Searle smiles slowly. 'You've been warned off, Mark. Right?'

Milner's expression is unreadable.

'The money?' says Searle after Milner doesn't reply.

Milner sighs. 'Clean.'

'Really?'

'That's what the forensic guys are telling me. It's his money. He can do what he likes with it. The paper chain checks out.'

'Bollocks.'

'Bollocks or not, that's what we have. Keane's money is his.' Milner stops as the waiter approaches to take their order. Once that's done he turns back to Searle.

'But that's not the weird thing, Charlie. At least it's not *the* weirdest. The fact is that you're right, I was warned off. I was warned off by someone with a very big stick indeed. I was told – and, needless to say, there's no paper trail – that Keane is off limits to Lupus. Drop him, walk away, nothing to see. It was the Home Office, Charlie. The fucking *Home Office*.'

'They called you directly?'

'Of course not. They called my boss in London. He called me. Made it quite clear that as far as he was concerned, God had sent down this directive straight from above.'

Searle waits.

'So what I'm asking you,' says Milner, his voice dropping as he leans across the table, 'is this: is Frank Keane a spook?'

Searle's laughs dies in his throat. The events of the last four months have changed his view of his DCI and perhaps Milner's idea isn't as crazy as it first sounds. Whatever happened in Los Angeles had changed Keane.

Searle looks at Milner. 'Honestly?'

Milner nods. 'That would be handy, Charlie.'

'I have no idea.'

Milner looks neither disappointed or pleased.

'So where does that leave the investigation into Keane's money?'

Searle shrugs. 'I don't know, Mark. The money does worry me but Frank brought it in. If he knows he's got this protection then that makes me think it'll all turn out to be kosher. I think it's possible that you might come to that conclusion too. Especially after the intervention from above.'

Milner nods. 'I think you're right. If we got a warning about steering clear of Keane I don't think it'll stop there, Charlie. My gut tells me this is going no further. I know the money Keane's got looks hokey from any angle but he, or whoever pulls his strings, is going to make sure nothing happens.'

'OK, let's accept that'll happen,' says Searle. 'It still leaves the question as to why anyone needs Lupus to back off Frank Keane. Or me for that matter.'

'Ah. Well that is the big question, isn't it?' Milner pauses. 'Where is he, by the way?'

'Suspended. I don't know where he is. I assumed you'd be talking to him but that doesn't look like it's going to happen anytime soon.'

The food arrives and both men eat. For a while the talk is about the food.

'What do you think the money's for?' says Milner. 'Just theoretically. A payoff? A war chest?'

'War chest?' Searle looks up. 'Bloody hell, Mark, what sort of people do you think Frank Keane's involved with?'

31

Helsby, Cheshire, October 19th

It takes Frank a couple of days to get over the sickness following his biopsy. The result of the procedure will be in soon but after Wilson's words Frank isn't expecting a miracle reprieve. He keeps his focus on the idea that the cancer is still operable. Since the original diagnosis he has done a decent job of keeping that flame burning.

Frank spends most of the day following his discharge from Broadgreen sleeping. By Monday he's feeling ansty, and after picking up his phone to call the consultant and then putting it down again, he puts a woolen beanie over his head to hide the shaved patch and dressing from the biopsy and goes next door to borrow Smitty from Bernie. The phone call to Wilson can wait a bit longer. He'd have called if he had news. Wouldn't he?

Judging from Bernie's subdued mood, his paint-splashed shirt and the brooding presence of the mysterious Mrs Palmer in the shadows, Frank suspects Bernie's booze stash in the shed has been rumbled.

'Take as long as you want,' mutters Bernie darkly. 'We're nae going fucking anywhere.' He flicks his eyes towards the house. 'Painting the fucking bathroom. Jesus,' he says with feeling.

'Not a DIY enthusiast, Bernie?' says Frank as the reluctant decorator hands over Smitty's lead.

'What do you fucking think?' says Bernie and closes the front door. Frank hears raised voices in the hallway and scurries away, Smitty at his heels.

They go to Delamere Forest again. Not only because Smitty enjoys it but because Frank does. The outdoors lifts his spirits and there's an idea about that, and about his cancer, that has been taking shape since his biopsy. He resolves to spend some time online later putting some flesh on the bones of his plan.

He parks the Golf down the same side-track he'd parked at on his last visit and heads east following one of the forest walks. He spent some time in these woods a kid, taking the train out from Bootle. It had seemed so impossibly distant to him then despite being less than an hour and one train change from the city. Most of his friends wouldn't make the trip, their street bravado only extending to the city and a couple of adjoining suburbs. The Wirral, and places like Delamere were, to all intents and purposes, as foreign as Istanbul. But Frank and Mal Trotter, one of his more adventurous mates, had come here in the summer, even camped out a couple of times when they turned sixteen.

Today is not camping weather. It's distinctly colder than his last walk with Smitty and Frank's glad he's wearing warmer clothes. At this time of the day he and Smitty have the place pretty much to themselves. After only a minute Frank passes another man walking a dog and they nod without stopping. The man's dog barks and Frank glances back. Through the lattice of the trees, beyond the dog-walker, he glimpses something white moving. It's a car turning around at the entrance to the car park.

For some reason, Frank's not entirely sure why, he gets the feeling that someone inside the car is watching him. From habit he looks for the registration and just catches the last three digits – BHN – before the car turns side on and then drops out of sight heading in the direction of Helsby. It's a Ford although Frank can't identify the type. He shakes his head and turns back to see Smitty standing expectantly with a stick in his mouth. Frank throws and Smitty bounces into the ferns. They walk on and after a few minutes Frank feels the tension in his back begin to ease. The forest gives him the opportunity to reflect on exactly what he's going to do about his situation. 'Situation'. Now there's a euphemism that covers some ground. He has cancer. He has a dubious pot of money weighing heavily on his shoulders. He is suspended, simultaneously weightless and trapped. Something has to give soon. He checks his phone for the thousandth time but there's nothing from Wilson.

Almost two hours later back at the Golf he can see his breath white on the late afternoon air. It's colder up here than in Helsby and he's glad the barn is well-stocked. He'll stay in tonight, do that tumour research he'd been planning. Know your enemy.

Smitty leaps up into the back of the car and flops down, happy but tired. Frank starts the engine and heads back through the darkening forest towards his temporary home.

Bernie's place, despite the inner tensions, looks warm and welcoming when Frank returns Smitty. Through the frosted glass, Frank sees a female shape coming to answer and braces himself to meet the formidable Mrs Palmer.

The door opens. Standing in front of Frank, wearing tight jeans and a white shirt unbuttoned just enough to make it interesting, is the woman who fondled his leg in the spa. She looks mildly surprised to see Frank but nothing more.

'Ah,' says Kath Palmer. 'Now that's interesting.' She smiles.

Smitty darts past her and heads inside the house, his nails tick-tacking along the wooden floorboards. There's no sign of Bernie.

'So you're Smitty's new friend?'

Frank nods. 'Er, yes.' He holds out a hand. 'Frank Keane.'

Kath Palmer takes Frank's hand. 'Always nice to get a formal introduction. I'm Kath.'

'I know,' says Frank. Kath Palmer still has hold of his hand. He pulls away fractionally but she holds firm, her skin warm on his cold hands.

'If you're not doing anything tomorrow, come around for a bite,' she says, smiling. 'It can't be easy. On your own, I mean. We'd have you tonight but we have plans.'

Frank wonders if she knows about his illness. There's sympathy in her face. And then he realises Bernie must have mentioned his split from Julie. That's what she's talking about.

'That'd be good. Look forward to it.'

Kath Palmer releases him, dragging her fingers slowly across his palm.

'It's a date then. Frank.' She smiles at him as he heads back down the path towards the safety of the barn. At the gate he risks a glance and sees that Kath Palmer is still watching him, leaning one shoulder against the doorframe. She waggles her fingers at him and he waves back.

Frank opens the door to the barn and shuts out the predatory neighbour. The last thing he needs is a complication of that kind. Or maybe it's exactly what he needs.

He showers and eats his meal watching the TV. He looks at the processed food on his plate with near disgust. That's something else he's going to have to change. He stops eating, scrapes the remaining slop from his plate and stacks it in the dishwasher. Frank switches off the TV and opens his laptop. He works steadily, researching his disease as methodically as any investigation. He's been at it more than an hour when he looks up from the screen and leans back, the hairs on the back of his neck prickling with some instinctive warning. He looks around the room.

Someone's been in.

32

Berlin, October 11th

'You think he'll do it?'

Felix Hoffen and Ilsa Bruckner are sitting on a wooden bench fifty metres from where they'd left Sebastian Gottlenz holding his children. Bruckner pauses while a family of Asian appearance walk past. She eyes them coldly until they scuttle away.

'I'm not sure. I thought he'd run but now I'm not so sure.' Bruckner looks in the direction of the polar bears and then shakes her head in disgust. 'Go get him before he follows through with it. The little prick is dumb enough to think I was serious. Things might get ugly. We don't want any attention coming our way.'

Hoffen's face doesn't change but it's this kind of amateur nonsense that is causing him increasing problems with Bruckner. If Bruckner thought that this little situation could end with unwanted attention then why the fuck did she set it in motion in the first place? Bruckner's outward appearance makes you think she's careful, precise, but Hoffen knows different. Felix Hoffen has done some things he's not proud of, terrible things, in Angola and Mozambique and before that in Serbia, but at no time has he ever lost sight of the boundaries, even when he was crossing them.

It could even be that it is precisely when he does cross those boundaries that he feels his humanity most. Self-loathing, and the repression of that in the service of power, that is Hoffen's bargain with the devil. He knows that and accepts it for what it is; the reality of his situation.

But Bruckner is something else. Bruckner likes to think of herself as an ice queen but, for Hoffen, she takes far too many chances. The day will come when the confidence and the fervour won't cut it and all this melodramatic shit will vanish like lip gloss on a 3 a.m. pickup. Hoffen is not going to be in his present position when that day comes.

Right now though, the reality is that he has to mop this spill up. Bruckner still holds the financial cards and, for all Hoffen's concerns, he knows that Ilsa is not someone to be fucked with without being very sure of yourself. She is entirely capable of having a secondary source of muscle and Hoffen is enough of a realist to know that for now he must wait. He gets to his feet and walks back towards Gottlenz.

'Don't spook him anymore.'

Hoffen nods but says nothing. Bruckner buys this strong silent bullshit so he keeps dishing it up hot and strong. The surgeon, for all her cleverness, has never bothered to find out what makes Felix Hoffen tick. That will cost her in the end. If all this works then *Kolumne88* will face fresh challenges. Hoffen thinks he will be better placed than Ilsa Bruckner when that happens but the bitch is hard work sometimes. Hoffen thinks of the baggie of coke sitting in the apartment on *Christinenstraße*. He could do with a toot right now. Hoffen only has three vices: cigarettes, coke, and violence and Bruckner provokes the need for all three on a regular basis.

Bruckner watches Hoffen with Gottlenz. The accountant is terrified, and for a moment it looks like he will run as Hoffen gets close, but the big man says something that seems to reassure Gottlenz. There is an exchange and then Hoffen walks back towards the cafe with Gottlenz holding his boys by the hand.

As they approach Bruckner she starts smiling. 'Idiot,' she says, to Gottlenz.

Hoffen sees that Gottlenz, his face ashen, is almost at the point where he will lose his mind. He tenses, ready to step in if Gottlenz goes for Bruckner. He wouldn't blame him. It's what Hoffen would have done the moment she even so much as mentioned harming his children. Hoffen has two of his own living in Antibes, although he takes good care not to let anyone know that information. He sees them when he can and would disembowel any man who threatened his children.

But Gottlenz is not like that. He allows Bruckner to do this thing to him but even a worm like Gottlenz has limits and this is what Hoffen is watching for. He doesn't care about Bruckner – the supercilious cunt would deserve whatever came her way – but they are in a public spot and Hoffen doesn't care too much to have attention directed towards him. Especially not if that attention is by anyone in authority.

The accountant manages a rictus smile, his skin clammy, waxen. The twin boys huddle silently behind their father clutching his hands, their wide eyes fixed on Bruckner. They *know*, thinks Hoffen. Three years old and they already know where the power is and that they need to be still when there is a savage beast close by. Bruckner's red lips are parted showing a row of sharp white teeth. She smiles at the boys but they shrink from her gaze and press themselves closer to their father's legs.

'Yes, you got me.' Gottlenz's words are dust in his throat, his skin wax. Bruckner has broken something inside this man, Hoffen can see this. Maybe that was her purpose all along. Or maybe at some level she genuinely didn't care if Gottlenz killed one of his children.

'Hoffen will go to England. Tell your guys to watch and wait.'

Gottlenz nods. He turns, his movements stiff, and walks away without another word. Both boys look over their shoulders at Bruckner until they disappear from view.

33

Helsby, Cheshire, October 19th

Frank pushes back from the kitchen table and walks slowly round the room looking for confirmation of an intruder. He tries to remember where he'd left the various objects in the room. Was that it? Had something been moved?

He walks to the front door of the barn and starts in the hall. There's nothing obvious there so he turns back to the living room and goes over it as methodically he would a crime scene. He comes up with nothing. In the kitchen he repeats the process but again can't find any concrete indicator that there has been someone inside the barn.

By the time Frank has checked upstairs and come up short he is ready to give it up as an overactive imagination.

And then he sees it.

On the kitchen table is a small anglepoise lamp Frank had moved across from its customary position on a bookshelf. The lamp itself is exactly where Frank had left it – as far as he can remember – but the angle of the shade has been altered to direct light straight down onto the table. Frank stares down at the table. Someone has been using the light to . . . what, exactly? Read?

Frank ponders this for a moment but then it comes to him. Whoever had been in wanted the light to take photographs. They would not have used flash for fear of alerting the Palmers. The table itself is clear of anything other than the lamp. Frank looks at it closely but it yields nothing and Frank begins to wonder about his judgement. What would anyone be taking photos of? And why?

Maybe the angle of the lamp hadn't been changed. Maybe he'd done it and forgotten. It's only a lamp.

Another thought: what if this paranoia is part of the illness? Medavoy had mentioned something about mood swings. And Wilson had warned him about the after effects of the biopsy procedure. Frank tries to think like a cop again but that seems as remote as his childhood.

He sits down in an armchair and looks out towards Ellesmere Port. He tries hard to concentrate but the more he tries the foggier he becomes. He sits like this for a long time. His eyes close.

Frank wakes with a start, unsure of where he is for a moment. His throat feels rough and he knows it's because he's been breathing through his mouth, his head back. He rubs his face with both hands and stretches. As he does he glimpses something on the road outside the cottage that hadn't been there before.

A white car is parked outside the Palmer's house. A Ford.

Immediately Frank is awake. He pulls the blind and heads upstairs. Leaving the lights off he peers through a crack in the bedroom curtains at the Ford. He can't see the number plate or if anyone is inside. The vehicle is pulled in suspiciously tight against a hedge, partially concealing it from view.

The lights are on at the Palmers and Frank sees that their gate is open. If someone wanted to keep a close eye on Frank, taking over the next door property would make sense. With the events of last year still fresh in his mind, Frank knows that there are people out there who are capable of anything. Where drugs are concerned there are no limits. An idea is forming in his mind that his paranoia may not be paranoia. This is about the fucking drugs. The dumb shits in the Ford think he has something to do with the eight hundred kilos of cocaine that arrived in Brisbane and disappeared. Now it looks very much like someone thinks he does have something to do with it and it's entirely possible that the Palmers could get hurt.

It makes a sort of twisted logic he supposes. Frank's crooked former boss at MIT, DCI Perch, had stolen *someone's* drugs. These clowns think that if Perch was bent then the same must be true for Frank.

Frank sits on the bed and tries to work out what he needs to do. His thinking is fuzzy, his back aches and he remembers he hasn't taken his meds. His biopsy scar stings like a bastard. He tries to focus again.

Whoever's next door isn't looking for him to find out where the coke is.

That's one thing. If they needed information from him then they would just come straight in and take him and get it that way. Frank has no illusions he would tell them whatever they need to know. The chilling thing is that he doesn't know, which would only mean that he'd be tortured and killed for nothing.

Maybe that's exactly what's happening now. Maybe taking the Palmers makes it easier for them to take him. They could be coming for him right now. Frank needs to be ready, to make plans but there's no time.

The missing drugs might not even be the issue; they may simply want payback. In these kind of high-end turf wars Frank knows exactly how things can go. Sometimes the guy at the top has to show steel or his authority weakens. Punishment and retribution are currency in this world and logic counts for little. Whoever's in charge might know full well that Frank isn't involved but once someone with real power gets an idea into their heads, once they have decreed something will happen, then something *better* happen.

Caught in the crossfire. Frank's seen plenty of dead bodies who had done nothing more than be in the wrong place. He, and the Palmers, might be next.

His illness, and the money he got from Dennis Sheehan, muddies the waters. Frank has no doubt that an investigation will clear him but that will take time. The chances of him surviving until then, if he's right about the people looking for him, are slim. Frank can't wait while the wheels of Merseyside Police grind away. He'll be dead before the investigation file notes are collated.

'Shit.' Frank stands and paces the room. It's time he stopped reacting and started getting ahead of the game.

He pulls on a pair of trainers and a black hooded sweatshirt. Downstairs he takes a stainless steel knife from the wooden block on the kitchen counter and slips it into the back pocket of his jeans.

Taking care not to make a sound, Frank slips out of the side door of the cottage and heads across the darkened garden to the field beyond. There is enough light from the single lamp post on the winding road that links both properties for Frank to be able to see.

Frank circles around the Palmer's house and approaches the Ford from the opposite direction to the barn. As he draws closer a vehicle passes him and illuminates the Ford. It's empty. And the last three letters on the number plate are PHN. Close enough.

He jumps over the low wall of the Palmer house and moves slowly around the side. There's no sign of Smitty. Frank doesn't know if this is a good or a bad thing. At the back of the house the living room window has the curtains closed but a thin sliver of light reveals a gap. There are noises from inside. Frank edges up to the sill, his adrenaline pounding and pulls the knife from his pocket. He hears a muffled thud from inside followed by a sharp cry of pain. Then another, this time louder and producing a more anguished response. A woman's voice.

Frank leans forward and puts his eye to the gap in the curtains.

'Jesus Christ,' he whispers.

34

Liverpool, October 10th

Harris had been right about the reason for Charlie Searle's call. At nine sharp she knocks on his door and walks in. As soon as she does she absolutely knows that he is going to give her MIT.

'DI Harris,' says Searle. He indicates the seat in front of his desk.

'Sir,' says Harris. She takes her seat, crossing her legs and smoothing out a wrinkle in her shirt. Searle's too smooth a politician to be seen ogling anyone but Harris notices his eyes slide across her chest momentarily before landing once again on her face.

Searle takes a moment to look at Harris for a few seconds without speaking. It's an old trick but one he has found effective. Harris, used to being looked at, waits for the appropriate amount of time to pass.

'How are things down at Stanley Road?'

'Busy, sir,' says Harris. 'As usual. We've got a full slate. The Perch hearing is next week and we've been assisting the investigating team as best we can.'

Searle nods approvingly. With disgraced DCI Perch being ex-MIT, the investigation into his case is being handled by members of the Metropolitan Serious Crime Squad. Outsiders. Searle knows it is a balancing act between co-operation and not washing any more dirty linen in public than is absolutely necessary. That 'as best we can' is what Searle wants to hear. He would never explicitly ask his officers to cover anything up but it's reassuring to know she isn't about to hand over the keys to the laundry.

'Superintendent Milner seems very happy.' Searle's not asking. His reference to the chief investigating officer on the Perch case is for Harris to lodge. She nods.

'What else?'

'We have three dead in a traffic incident yesterday.'

'Traffic?'

'At first glance. Almost certainly the three died as a result of the incident.'

'But?'

'There's a girl with distinct signs of being abducted.' Harris outlines the basics of the case, Searle nodding, his fingers steepled together on the desk in front of him.

'On first sight this looked like a sexual abduction. The girl was naked and she had been strapped to a fairly sophisticated medical setup.'

'What's your take on it? Perverts?'

'Most things point to a random kidnapping. They were on Menlove Avenue, saw the girl and took her.'

'But?'

'Sir?'

'You're not convinced.'

Harris nods. 'No, not completely. The van was sighted by several witnesses parked opposite the Lennon house for almost an hour. That's not uncommon but most tourists usually spend around ten minutes or less. Those doing the house tour don't wait outside and the tours are limited in number. They waited for *her*. Maybe.'

'Go on.'

'And if they waited for her it means they wanted *her*, not a random warm body.' Harris's mouth wrinkles in distaste. 'Which means it might not be just a sex thing.'

'*If* it was a sex thing.'

'Yes, sir, if.'

'And the girl?'

'Nothing positive on the ID as yet. We're working at it.'

'From what you're telling me, this looks random, Emily.'

Harris keeps her expression neutral.

'That's another thing that's troubling us,' she says. 'The driver and passenger. They arrived in Hull via Zeebrugge that morning. Drove directly to Liverpool and took the girl. They both had German paperwork which has proven to be false. The Germans ran fingerprints but turned up nothing. The van was stolen from a clinic in Berlin – The B-Kreuz-Scharmer Clinic – and reported as stolen two days later.'

Harris doesn't mention that this information was new to her less than thirty minutes ago. Rimmer and Corner had been busy on the vehicle and Berlin had come up with the goods with almost ludicrously stereotypical efficiency.

'Why the delay?'

'It was stolen on a Saturday. The clinic closes on Friday and reopens Monday. By the time it was reported the crash had happened. I'll be sending Cooper over to dig around and see what she can get, poke around into the theft of the van. There may be CCTV, something.'

'So that's the plan? Just keep digging?'

'Absolutely. If we can get a positive ID on either of the two men we'll get somewhere.

And once we identify the victim we'll keep working her background until we're certain there's nothing in there that led to her death. That's why I want Cooper in Berlin.'

'Do what you have to do,' says Searle. 'No-one likes an abduction.'

Harris completes her report on MIT's case roster and sits back.

'Have you heard anything from DCI Keane?'

'He called this morning,' says Harris. 'I'm seeing him on Thursday.'

Searle holds her gaze. 'How did he sound?'

For a split second Harris wonders if this is the real reason for Searle's meeting with her. Perhaps he's testing what she knows about Frank's problems. Whatever those might be.

'A bit distracted.'

'OK,' says Searle. He looks down at a print out on his desk. 'DCI Keane is currently on health leave. From what I understand he may not be back. Obviously a diagnosis of cancer is not something that can be predicted with any certainty.'

'Cancer?'

For a moment she wonders if she has misheard. And then feels a quick stab of anger at Frank for not confiding in her.

'Ah,' Searle looks up at Harris. 'I can see he hasn't told you. Which means I should probably not have told you. Not like that anyway.'

He sits back and pauses. Harris can see he is weighing up what to tell her. After a few seconds Charlie Searle leans forward. 'There is another matter regarding DCI Keane. Given what I've called you in for . . .' Searle opens his hands to indicate that they both know the situation. '. . . I think you should know what I know.' He speaks carefully. 'Frank came back from America with more than a bullet wound and a broken nose.'

Harris hadn't known until this moment that Frank had been wounded but she says nothing. Clearly Searle thinks she is closer to Frank than she actually is.

'Sir?'

'He came back with money. A significant amount of money. Millions.'

'Frank Keane's not dirty.' Harris's words come out with no thought. Frank's not dirty. It's something she knows. And then: 'millions'?

'No, I don't think he is either, DI Harris. The money appears to be legitimate fees paid to a consulting company that apparently Keane runs on the side. DCI Keane himself told me about the money. But it's a complication. Officially there's an investigation but I get a strong feeling he will be exonerated.'

Searle looks out of the window and watches two rowing boats knife elegantly across the dark water of the Albert Dock.

'The investigation into DCI Keane will run its course. Of more pressing concern is his diagnosis. He'll be signed off for six months effective today. Our department will, of course, offer him our complete support. And there are other, wider political complications concerning DCI Keane that may have an impact. I'm not at liberty to discuss these other matters.'

Harris tries not to let her curiosity show. Other matters? If the money and a cancer diagnosis aren't the worst of Frank's problems then maybe there is no way back from this. Even stranger, she gets the curious feeling that this 'other matter' has scared Charlie Searle. Something in America? What the hell had Frank been involved with over there? Whatever the answer, it's clear that Searle is conveying a message to her. Loyalty in adversity and support for a sick colleague is one thing but Searle seems to be warning her there is more to come. Harris senses that both Searle and she are swimming in deeper waters than either has been accustomed to.

'So, DI Harris,' says Searle, his tone lighter. 'As you almost certainly knew before you walked in here, MIT is yours, at least for the foreseeable future.' He smiles broadly and makes a note on his diary.

'Peter Moreleigh will organise a press conference about the abducted girl. Best for us to be on the front foot before the press run with whatever they decide. You lead. Don't mess it up, will you?'

Harris gets to her feet. 'Of course not, sir.'

'And when you see Frank, don't be tempted to offer any unofficial help, OK?'

'No, sir.' Harris moves towards the door. 'I'm sure DCI Keane is keeping his head down.'

35

Helsby, Cheshire, October 19th

It takes a second or two for Frank to process what he sees in the Palmer place.

There are four people in the room. Bernie and Kath Palmer and another man and woman. Kath Palmer is strapped face down on a red leather bench in the centre of the room. Naked except for a pair of black high-heeled boots and a blindfold, her wrists and ankles tied in a complicated-looking tangle of rope, she straddles the bench, enthusiastically fellating a nude man wearing a leather cape. At the other end, her back to Frank, a plump woman wearing a tight-fitting rubber dress and thigh-high boots is whipping Kath Palmer's bare arse with some sort of leather paddle. Every stroke elicits little screams of pleasure. Bernie Palmer, wearing leather shorts and a black mesh vest that wouldn't have looked out of place hanging off the back of a Grimsby trawler, is sitting on the floral sofa filming the proceedings on a tiny video camera. Frank knows that as long as he lives he will never get that image of Bernie out of his head.

We've got plans.

Kath Palmer's words come back to Frank just as, from somewhere in the house, Smitty starts barking like the Hound of the Baskervilles on crack. Everyone in the living room with the exception of Kath Palmer looks at the living room window.

Frank runs.

He leaps over the back fence and races for home. Somewhere behind him he hears the door opening and Smitty bounding out. With the dog in pursuit Frank reaches the barn and locks the door behind him. He bounds upstairs without turning on any lights and lies down on the bed, trying to stop the laughter.

36

Liverpool, October 10th

The press call goes well.

Watched by Peter Moreleigh standing over to one side like a mother hen, DI Harris comes across as professional, competent and organised. And it helps that she looks the way she does. After the endless parade of pasty middle-aged male coppers, she stands out, not just physically but in the economical and unhesitating way she speaks. For the first time, Moreleigh considers the distinct possibility that Harris might be headed for high office. Really high. Ever the alert pilot fish, he subtly adjusts DI Emily Harris's place in his complex mental diagram of the ever-mutating entity that is Merseyside Police. Moreleigh is not so lacking in self-awareness as to harbour any serious ambitions to wear the crown himself, but he does see a potential place for him as chief advisor. The hand behind the throne. Junior officer though she ⁻ʳris may be one to keep inside the tent. You never know.

Moreleigh snaps ouʰ   ⁻ and nods approvingly as
Harris neatly sidesʰ   h the incident involving
a young naked ₅ʳ   street outside the Liver
Buildings th   ₁iff of interest from the
nationalₛ   e disgust off her face and
almoₛ

  ₅ʳ   ne steps away from the press
r   ou as and when we have any
ₐ   ₍ and heads back into the throng
of   ₁n the shoulder. This is your world,
thinkₛ   ₃h. But I'm not sure it's mine.

She heads back to MIT and spends the rest of the day working the investigation. So soon after the incident they have plenty of information coming in but little in the way of solid development. Harris expects that to change by morning. One thing that has changed already is the team's attitude to DI Harris. Without knowing how, word has reached MIT that they have a new leader. When Harris walks in there is a round of applause.

'All hail Caesar!' shouts Ronnie Rimmer. That gets a laugh or two but Harris doesn't waste any time on pleasantries.

'Thanks but the appointment is temporary. DCI Keane may be back sooner than any of us expect and I, for one, would love that.'

She sees a few knowing glances flick across the meeting room and wonders if news of Frank's cancer is also common currency. Her expression hardens and the temperature drops perceptibly. News of a promotion is one thing but gossiping about cancer . . .

'Right, enough of that bollocks. Let's get this started shall we?'

Em Harris's first official meeting as the new head of MIT gets underway.

Magsi leads the way with the news that they have discovered who the dead girl is.

'Sarah Coughlan, age nineteen, of Menlove Avenue, Liverpool. A local. Her mother had called the police about her not returning home on the day of the crash. A mate of mine took the mother's statement, finally put two and two together last night and gave me a call this morning. The mother formally identified her at seven this morning.'

There is a small ripple of applause and Magsi smiles. Identification is the cornerstone of any murder investigation and, while Magsi's role in it wasn't worthy of congratulation in itself, the fact is that MIT now have someone to focus on.

'Good,' says Harris. She points at Magsi. 'You and Rimmer take the family. The mother knows you already. Let her do what she has to do but interview her today. She'll be helping the investigation, its only procedure . . . you know the score.'

Magsi nods and sneaks a look at Ronnie Rimmer. 'Fuck you', mouths Rimmer unseen by Harris.

'We have forensics on the sedation,' says Theresa Cooper. Harris had fast-tracked the lab once the consensus was that Sarah Coughlan had been abducted.

'Bloody hell,' says Harris. 'That was quick.'

Cooper shrugs. 'That's private sector I guess.' She looks at the print out in her hand.

'Coughlan had been sedated with a drug commonly used in medical procedures. A benzodiazepine, probably Midazolam. It is fast-acting and induces long-lasting unconsciousness. It is not easily obtainable.' Cooper looks up. 'One of the properties of Midazolam is that it is an efficient muscle-relaxant. It also has amnesiac capabilities.'

'Which ties in with the sexual abduction angle,' says Harris. She drums her fingers on the table. 'I suppose.'

'I usually just slip a couple of Rohypnals into their vodka,' says Ronnie Rimmer. 'Works every time.'

Harris and Cooper turn and glare. Rimmer wilts and holds up his hands in supplication. 'Bad joke,' he says, flushing. 'Sorry, ma'am.'

'Try another "joke" like that, Rimmer,' says Harris, 'and I'll shove your foot so far down that massive gob of yours that you'll be able to kick your own arse. Have you got that?'

She turns away before Rimmer has a chance to say anything else.

'Got anywhere with the supply of this Midazolam, Theresa?'

'I'll be checking that today, ma'am.'

'Good.' Harris looks around. 'Autopsy?'

'Completed yesterday,' says Phil Caddick. 'Viner says it'll be a couple of days before the full report. Bit of a logjam.'

'Bugger.' Harris thinks that Viner's promise may have been premature. She feels let down but doesn't blame him too much. He's new and hasn't yet got a handle on where he fits in the big picture just yet. 'On the plus side, I suppose there is the fact that he's already done the thing.'

'He supplied the material for the drug testing quickly,' says Cooper, as if sensing Harris's displeasure. 'Seems like he knows his stuff.'

'But no word on any sign of sexual assault or of any trauma injuries other than those caused by the crash?' Harris flashes on Sarah Coughlan's body white against the black tarmac. She was alive but unconscious before the crash. Harris doesn't need the autopsy to do anything but confirm that.

'No,' says Cooper. 'She looked clean. Obviously there's no way of telling for sure but there was no bruising or contusions that you might have expected in a sexual assault.'

'We're sure it's sexual?' Scott Corner's first contribution to the meeting causes a small pause in proceedings. Corner's tall, and speaks slowly. A rolled up ball of paper bounces off his head. 'Don't be a dick,' says Caddick. Harris's face too forms into an expression of scorn but she stops herself. Just because the big lad appears dumb doesn't mean he is. It's something she continually has to remind herself of.

'Go on.'

'Well,' says Corner, less certain now he has centre stage. 'I mean it looks like that, don't get me wrong. It's obvious.' He looks uncomfortable now and glances over at Ronnie Rimmer. 'Like Ronnie was out of order with what he said but he might have something. Why didn't these two goons go with the Ro-Ro's? Why all the prep? It seems like a hell of a lot of trouble to go to if it's just a pair of perverts. The van, the set-up, the funny drugs.' He tails off. 'I'm just sayin', like.'

Harris remains silent for a moment. 'I think you're right, Scott.' She points at Rimmer. 'You and Loverboy get stuck into the van. Get it identified. I don't just mean the surface story. Where's the van been? Who owns it? Everything.'

She stands and waves her hands. 'That's it. Go. Do good work.'

'What about the men?' says Cooper. 'The driver and the guy in the back? Viner's doing them later today. Do you want anyone to go?'

Harris smiles. 'I'm going,' she says. 'I wouldn't miss it for the world.'

37

Liverpool, October 10th

Viner, the new pathologist turns out to be an affable, scruffy, slightly chubby thirty-five-year-old with a completely bald head and an air of mischief. He is the anti-Ferguson. Harris warms to him immediately.

She and Viner are talking across the examination table about the dead men in the crash. One of them, the blonde, lies nude, his chest open. Viner's almost completed his work and his assistant busies herself tidying up his handiwork.

'I could have saved you a trip,' says Viner.

'I always try to attend,' says Harris. 'A habit.'

Viner gestures at the dead man and then at the second, older man on the table behind him. 'Both died from impact trauma. I'll be checking for the usual alcohol and drugs but if present they will only be contributory factors. They died in the crash.'

'Sure.' Harris looks at the blonde man's face. He looks peaceful and she thinks about the abduction, about Sarah. She has an urge to slap him. 'Anything else, Dr Viner? Tattoos? Name and address stamped under his tongue?'

'Steve.'

'He's called Steve? That was quick.'

'No.' Viner smiles. 'I'm Steve. But I guess I deserved that.'

'Sorry,' says Harris. Viner waves away her apology. There's something about Viner – Steve – that makes her feel at ease. She wonders if he's gay. He certainly doesn't seem to be giving any of the signals that Harris arouses in most men.

Viner lifts the dead man's arm and twists it round so that Harris can see. 'As it happens, there is a tattoo,' he says in the manner of a stage magician. 'Ta da.'

'What a surprise.'

It is now almost a given that any body under the age of forty will have a tattoo. Most of them are useless but occasionally, as happened with the Stevie White case last year, they do lead somewhere. In a case like this, where ID seems problematic, it can make a big difference.

Harris bends and looks more closely at the wrist. A small line of letters in blue ink is tattooed halfway up the dead man's arm. It looks, at first glance, like something that might be found on a Holocaust survivor.

'Some sort of Jewish solidarity thing?' says Harris.

Viner pulls a face. 'It's not my area but I don't have him down as Jewish.' He points at the dead man's uncircumcised penis. 'Not conclusive I know, but worth saying.'

'He doesn't look Jewish.' Harris takes out her phone and takes a photo of the tattoo. 'Is that racist? To say that, I mean?'

Viner shrugs. 'Probably.'

'IX.XI.MCMXXXVIII.' Harris says the sequence out loud. 'Any ideas?'

'Looks like Roman numerals.'

'Meaning?'

'Could be a date. His mother's birthday. A kid's name. Maybe it's his phone number.'

'Now that would be handy.' Harris sends the image to Theresa Cooper back at MIT with a short message to start digging around and then slips the phone back into her pocket.

'Anything else?' she says.

'No, not really. If there are any surprises then it will be in the toxicology reports. But on the surface these two appear to be exactly what they are: crash victims.'

'Who had abducted a girl in broad daylight.'

'You get the report on her?' says Viner. He moves to the sink and begins washing his hands. Harris follows.

'No, not yet.'

'I asked them to hurry it. It'll be with you soon. Anyway, she hadn't been assaulted. Not sexually, I mean.' Viner lathers soap to his elbows. 'And not obviously. There is always the possibility she may have been forced to do things without leaving marks.'

'Or semen.'

'Or semen, yes.' Viner pulls a roll of paper towel from a dispenser and dries his arms. He presses a floor pedal on a large bin and drops the wadded paper inside. 'You alright to finish up in here, Lori?'

The assistant nods. 'Thanks,' says Viner. He opens the door for Harris and they step outside the examination room. Viner strips off his paper bootees and Harris does the same.

'Back to the office?' says Viner.

'Yes, there's a bit of pressure on this one. And I don't like the idea of someone being abducted.' Harris regards Viner. He's an improvement on Ferguson that's for sure.

'You settling in OK?'

'Yes,' says Viner. 'Always tricky moving to a new gig but I like it so far.' He pauses and Harris senses him building up the courage to ask her something. Here it comes.

'Listen,' says Viner. 'I wonder if you'd like to come round for dinner one night?' He flushes slightly. 'I'm a good cook.'

'Er . . .'

'Oh, and bring your partner. Make it a four? Gareth isn't settling in quite as quickly as I am and I worry. You'd be doing me a favour, DI Harris.'

'Em,' says Harris. 'Call me Em.'

38

Berlin, October 12th

In her office on the second floor of the *Landeskriminalamt* building on Tempelhofer Damm, *Kriminalkommissar* Anna Ziegler leans back and looks out over the tree-lined street below. She remains in the same position for a long time.

Robert Weiss, walking through the shared LKA office towards the coffee Machine, nudges an elbow against Christina Dreschler's shoulder and smirks, jerking a thumb in Ziegler's direction.

'Catwoman looking out for the signal again,' he murmurs, bending his head close to Christina. She can smell his cologne, too sweet for her taste.

'Leave her alone, Robert, for Christ's sake.' Dreschler turns back to her work shaking her head. Weiss shrugs and moves away, still smirking. Dreschler waits until she's sure Weiss isn't looking and then glances over at Ziegler. Weiss is a dick but someone should tell Anna straight. She needs to get her act together before Werner runs out of patience. Working at the LKA is a prestigious posting and Holz likes to run a tight ship. Most of the officers look something like Robert: all business, sharply-dressed, urban. Anna Ziegler with her country origins, shapeless suits and straggling hair, does not do anything to help herself. Being single and owning three cats isn't exactly a fast-track career helper either. Werner would never say it out loud but he's one of those 'family values' people and distrusts any woman without a man. Dreschler herself can't stand him but takes care not to let that show.

Christina Dreschler is still looking at Ziegler when Anna Ziegler turns around and catches her eye. Dreschler flushes slightly and looks away.

Ziegler, her face expressionless, turns her attention back to the email on her screen from a detective working out of *Direktion 2* over at Spandau and tries to control her excitement. The email contains details of a Mercedes van reported stolen over the weekend.

Ziegler flicks back to the email from England that Werner had pushed across to her desk, probably due to her excellent English and, perhaps, her reputation with sex crimes. The email is from the Major Incident Team in Liverpool, England asking for help in a case involving two dead Berlin men and a wrecked Mercedes van involved in what looks very much like a kidnapping with sexual overtones. The email from DK2 confirms that the vehicle reported stolen over the weekend from a clinic in Spandau is the same one used in the attempted abduction in Liverpool.

All of this is good information that Ziegler will send back to Liverpool.

What *is* sending an electric thrill down her spine though, is the name of the clinic where the vehicle had been stolen from: B-Kreuz-Scharmer.

Anna Ziegler takes a large file from the stack on the shelf above her desk. The file is marked B-Kreuz-Scharmer and Ziegler checks that no-one is looking before she opens it. The file is not related to any official investigation. This one belongs to Ziegler alone and she has had her knuckles rapped soundly on more than one occasion when – at least in the eyes of her boss, Werner Holz – interest has crossed the line into obsession.

Now Ziegler flicks through the pages until she finds what she's looking for; the photograph of one of the partners at the clinic.

Looking at the woman she has been pursuing for two years, Ziegler feels a tiny thrill of adrenaline in her legs. The MIT email feels like a golden key to a door she's been pounding on for a long time. Only last night she thought she had given it up for good. And then, this morning, this email. As if someone has sent a sign. It is all Ziegler can do to stay still. She wants to run around the office, shout it out.

She doesn't. Mainly because Ilsa Bruckner is her own personal obsession and is one that has already resulted in an official reprimand,

Ziegler's only black mark in a fifteen-year career. So she closes the file and emails the English police, her heart pounding.

39

Helsby, Cheshire, October 20th

The morning after Frank's semi-accidental interlude as Peeping Tom, he wakes to the realisation that he had committed to dinner with the Palmers. With the images from last night still seared on his retinas, he's not sure he can go through with it. He's still lying in bed trying to think of a decent excuse when his phone rings. Frank looks at the screen before answering. It's a number he doesn't recognise. After dithering for a moment he presses 'answer' but says nothing.

'Frank Keane?' says a woman's voice. She sounds like she's in a hurry.

'Who is this?' says Frank.

'It's Jane Watson.'

Frank tries to recall the name and then sits up a little straighter. Jane Watson is a DCI working the Lupus investigation into Frank's ex-boss, Perch. He'd been introduced to her very briefly by Charlie Searle a few days after his return from America

'Oh,' says Frank. 'Hi. Should I be talking to you?'

'It's the other way round,' says Watson. 'I shouldn't be talking to you, Frank.'

'Come again?'

'Listen, I can't go into all that now. You're off limits, that's all I know.'

'What do you mean, "off limits"? Is this some sort of Lupus thing? Am I being taped?'

'Can you just listen?' hisses Jane Watson. 'For fuck's sake, I'm really going out on a limb here.'

'Sorry,' says Frank. 'Go on.'

'I want this to remain a confidential chat. Is that clear?'

'That depends,' says Frank but Watson is already talking.

'I've been working on you for Lupus,' says Watson. 'And, despite all the cloak and dagger stuff, I know you're clean. At least so far as the Lupus investigation goes. Whatever else you're into that's getting the Home Office involved? That's beyond my scope.'

'Home Office?' says Frank. He feels foggy.

'Jesus. Stop repeating everything I say, won't you? I'm trying to help here.'

'I'm listening.'

'Right. So I think you're clean but we've been warned off so that's not why I'm calling. I'm calling as one cop to another because there's something you should know and I don't like you just sitting out there not knowing.'

Watson pauses and Frank is tempted ask more questions. Instead he remains silent. The woman on the other end of the phone is clearly debating how much information she should reveal and a false move from Frank might shut her up.

'You know we've been digging into what happened to the Australian cocaine?'

'Of course.'

'A source we trust has mentioned that your name had come up as someone who has the goods. Almost eight hundred million.'

'That's not the case.'

'I know that.' Watson's tone is dismissive. 'But that doesn't matter. This source knows you have some significant money from somewhere. Twenty-five million dollars was mentioned.'

'How would anyone know that? Assuming it was true.'

'I don't know,' snaps Watson. 'I just know that they know. You see where I'm going?'

'Not yet.'

'The people this source was with? If our info is right, they're the East Europeans, Frank. As you know, they bankrolled the deal – or much of it anyway – through Keith Kite and the Australians with your own Superintendent Perch watching their arses. With Kite dead and Perch looking at a long stretch, the Eastern Europeans want a body. You know how those guys work. *Someone* has to pay. Even if they know you're clean, if everyone else has a sniff that you might be dirty you could be in the firing line. That's why I'm calling. You could be getting some attention and I don't mean from us. There's not going to be any disciplinary procedure if the boys from Zagreb come knocking. They want a body and they don't really mind which one as long as they can sell it to their network. Someone has to pay and it's you.'

'That's all you've got for this?' says Frank. 'One snitch? That's a lot of "ifs" for me to be making plans for.'

'Whatever you want to do, Frank. From the rumours we have in Lupus about your connections you could just call in your markers and have this taken care of. On the other hand, if you're what I think you are then you deserve some warning. We're all on the same side. And this is a very good snitch.'

'Well, thanks, I guess,' says Frank. 'I mean that, Jane.'

'Take care,' says Watson. 'And if you *do* turn out to be dirty I'm going to mess you up myself. I'm not the forgiving sort.'

She hangs up and Frank sinks back into the pillows and puts his hands behind his head.

The stakes are rising. From what he knows of Watson – which, admittedly, is not much – she is a decent copper. He tries to think of another, more devious motive for her call; something linked to the Lupus investigation, but there's nothing that fits better than her story about wanting to give a fellow cop a heads up on some nasty people heading his way. Frank has done something similar before when he's tipped a colleague. You can never know it will happen, just that it might. If he's got any sense he'll act on Jane Watson's words and assume that she has taken a risk for him. The drug gangs that Frank has spent half a lifetime investigating have to be taken seriously, even if they are barking up the wrong tree about the source of the twenty-five million.

He lets out a long sigh before standing and looking out of the window. He'd hoped that last night's farce might have meant the end of his paranoia but after Watson's call here it is back again in full bloom. And with good reason.

Frank had been planning to spend the day resting but the conversation with Watson changes everything.

He needs some stuff. A different car. A new place to stay.

A better fucking plan.

40

Liverpool, October 11th

Harris gets in to work early. It's a Sunday and, other than a couple of secretarial staff, only Theresa Cooper is there.

'I miss a memo or something?' says Harris. 'Or is it a holiday I haven't heard about?'

Cooper looks up from her desk and glances around the room. 'They're all still on, ma'am, I'm sure, Sunday or not.'

'I know, Theresa. I'm joking.'

Cooper smiles. She almost makes it look genuine. 'Jesus, Theresa, was it that bad? Wait, don't answer.' Harris sits on Cooper's desk and lets her legs swing free of the floor. There's something childlike about the posture, as though her and Theresa are at school, gossiping about boys. Or girls, in Harris's case.

'Any joy on the photo?'

Cooper beams. She holds up a finger and brings it down on a sheet of paper.

'As it happens, yes, ma'am.'

'From the look on your face you've found me a nice fat fish.'

Cooper nods and swivels the sheet of paper so Harris can read it. Instead, Harris shakes her head. 'Give me the gist.'

'The numbers are Roman numerals. IX.XI.MCMXXXVIII. As you knew,' Cooper says hastily as Harris's expression darkens. 'And it's a date. Or at least I'm pretty sure it is. The first set of letters means '9', the second '11' and the third is '1938'. The 9th of November, 1938.'

Harris frowns. 'Is that a big date? Am I supposed to know that?'

'Not unless you were German. That date was 'Kristallnacht'. The Night of Broken Glass.'

Harris shrugs. 'I'm still waiting for the good bit, Theresa.'

'The 9th of November, 1938 was the day Hitler launched a series of attacks against the Jews in Germany and Austria. It was the beginning of the real push towards the concentration camps. The date is famous.' Cooper taps the sheet of paper. 'And that date is used by neo-Nazis in Germany.'

Harris stands up. 'He's a Nazi? Are you kidding me?'

Cooper nods. 'Looks that way.'

'And I thought I couldn't hate that bastard more.' She walks away from Cooper's desk. 'Excellent stuff, Theresa. Get everyone assembled for a meeting as soon as possible.' Halfway to her office she stops. 'Do you know if Rimmer or Corner turned up anything on the van?'

Before Cooper can answer, Ronnie Rimmer comes in, closely followed by Scott Corner. Both of them are holding takeaway coffee.

'What?' says Rimmer as he sees his boss staring at him. 'What's happened?'

'Never mind,' says Harris. 'Meeting in ten minutes. We can go over all this then.'

It takes twenty minutes before everyone is in place. Harris updates them on the neo-Nazi connection. 'I want us to focus a little harder on the Berlin angle,' she says. 'It's clear that there are strong connections to our abduction.'

Rimmer raises a finger. 'While we're talking about Berlin, I got an email back from someone in the LKA office there. The van was stolen from the B-Kreuz-Scharmer Clinic over the weekend but no-one noticed until Monday.'

'We're going to need someone to go over and talk to the Berlin police,' says Harris. She points at Cooper. 'Theresa, you speak another language don't you? It's not German is it?

'Yes, some.'

'Close enough. Get the paperwork sorted with HQ and move anything pressing over to Scott's desk. I think a few days should be enough for a recce. If there are any quick developments I'll get another bod over to help.'

Cooper nods. 'No problem.'

Scott Corner opens his mouth to say something but closes it again.

'Just get a feel for how this looks from their perspective. Talk to the locals and see what you can dig up on the two dead Nazis. If they're both Nazis, that is. If we can get an ID for blondy then the older one might follow.'

'How far should I keep looking at Sarah Coughlan's background?' says Magsi. 'It sounds more and more like she's a random selection and I'm not sure how much use my material is.'

'Keep at it another day or two,' says Harris. 'If nothing turns up, switch to looking at any data Theresa picks up in Berlin. And if she does dig up anything quickly you'll be heading over to back her up, OK?'

Magsi nods. Rimmer and Corner roll their eyes at each other which does not go unnoticed by Harris. Schoolboys. Harris makes a mental note to have a word with both of them later. Better to start her new official regime as she means to go on. If she had a criticism of Frank it's that despite his encouragement of herself and Theresa and other female officers before, he sometimes let the unit drift into something of a boy's club. That's going to change. She finishes up the meeting after some discussion of other MIT cases and heads back into her office.

Her office. It sounds good.

41

Liverpool, October 19th

It's cold when Hoffen steps out of John Lennon Airport but still warmer than the Berlin he'd left behind. He plans to be here no longer than twenty-four hours. Out in front of the terminal he looks at his watch and adjusts it to English time. Almost three. The guys Gottlenz sent in to replace the two who died in the crash have not been told Felix Hoffen's arrival time because that's the way Hoffen likes it. He prefers to get the lie of the land for himself in a new place without being encumbered by complications. Being picked up at the airport by the two morons – which is how Hoffen privately regards most of the *Kolumne88* crew closest to Gottlenz– is not a wise move. Hoffen has stayed alive in difficult circumstances for a long time. He does things a certain way or doesn't do them at all.

He's travelled to Liverpool under a German passport bearing a different name. False though the name might be, the document itself is legitimate, Hoffen buying it through a bent contact at the embassy in Berlin. He has other documentation, all also genuine to corroborate his identity if challenged. So far this has not been required but should it ever come to that, Hoffen knows he can shed his skin more easily than a snake.

In Liverpool, Hoffen also wants to take stock of Bruckner's operation. He has been part of the development of her empire – at least the fundraising, criminal part – but as far as Ilsa Bruckner is concerned, Hoffen's involvement is primarily based on cash reward rather than political conviction.

Hoffen allows her to believe this. Like many apparently clever people, Bruckner works under the mistaken assumption that money will always produce results while Hoffen knows from experience that this approach will only go so far. Bought loyalty is not loyalty. Hoffen is a true believer, just like Bruckner. Where he differs from the surgeon is that he has a better understanding that whatever the new landscape will be after the 9th, it will be one in which Hoffen will be more likely to flourish, not Bruckner. Her Hitler fetishism is almost laughable.

Hoffen admires Hitler only in so much as he achieved power. His failing in over-reaching was unforgiveable. To rid Germany of the Jews, the niggers, the degenerates and then waste it all because he wanted more, like some brat, was foolish.

No, once this all begins to unfold it will be time for a realist to take control and Hoffen is going to make sure that will be him.

For now though, Bruckner is a supply of vital revenue.

Hoffen steps into a cab and texts Gottlenz's contact to meet the following morning. He will message the contact exactly where and when. The choice will be his, based on the knowledge he'll pick up over the next few hours, another reason for arriving unannounced and unseen. The ex-soldier in him likes to prepare, and surveying the combat zone is the most important aspect of any preparation. Not that Hoffen expects much in the way of combat. This is a straight mop-up operation. In and out.

Hoffen uses a throwaway phone which will be destroyed the minute he no longer requires it. He doesn't need Gottlenz's contact for very much but the man does have one important item he has brought in from Germany with the new transport: a gun, Hoffen being far too long in the tooth to even attempt to bring one in himself. One of Gottlenz's boys made the motorbike trip last night and, since Gottlenz hasn't told him otherwise, Hoffen assumes the mule made it through.

He's staying at the Hilton in a room looking out across the docks and the river. The city looks good, better than Hoffen had expected. Hoffen's ideas about Liverpool had largely been formed through images of riots and football hooligans and urban decay. After showering he sits in a chair at the window with his laptop to access the information about the target. Tomorrow night, all things being equal, this mess will be wrapped up and the replacement heading back to Berlin.

At ten, feeling jumpy, Hoffen flicks through the escort agency websites. He orders something blonde from the top end of the listings, pours a scotch over ice and waits.

42

Helsby, Cheshire, October 20th

Frank showers and dresses, taking care not to damage the dressing over his biopsy scar. He takes the medication he's been given and makes a pot of coffee. While he's drinking the first cup he thinks about his meeting with Wilson later. Watson's call has pushed him into bringing forward a few ideas Frank has been kicking about. These ideas mostly relate to his health, to improving his survival chances by spending the twenty-five million – or part of it at least – on a better environment, a trainer maybe, better facilities and faster treatment. Now, assuming Watson's information is kosher, elements of his ideas might need to be changed, starting with who needs to know what. If news of Frank's money from Dennis Sheehan is floating around Lupus, then it can also be floating around somewhere else.

Frank decides not to mention anything to anyone except his consultant.

He isn't in a panic. Last night's S&M farce at the Palmer's showed Frank how acting on impulse could backfire. No, Frank thinks that what he needs is to be vigilant, stay alert and get out of Helsby, out of the area. It'll take a few days, and there are a few items he has added to a mental shopping list that still need to be obtained, but it can be done.

The first item on Frank's list is a gun.

He lifts up his phone and thumbs through his contacts until he finds what he's looking for. He sends a text and, as expected, gets an almost immediate response. The man he has messaged never moves from the same spot during daylight hours. Frank's never seen him anywhere else and has difficulty picturing him outside his domain.

Frank knows there are any number of ways he can get his hands on an illicit weapon. The priority though, is the need to establish credible distance from the source. He'll have to get one from someone on the wrong side of the street but any scrote can get a gun and Frank dismisses buying from an anonymous source. MIT busted a gun manufacturer last year who was distributing from the back of a van around the city, in just the same way vans sold bread and milk and dubious fish. The guy also used fourteen-year-olds as straw buyers to move the merchandise and copped a life term for his cleverness in January.

Another important no-no is that the weapon can not have been used in another crime. If this all goes tits up, as is entirely possible, then Frank doesn't need to have his shiny new gun linked with a double murder in Moss Side. Clean gun means less chance of trouble, assuming that from your perspective 'trouble' comes in the form of the constabulary. For the first time in his life, Frank is seeing cops as potential problems.

He also has specific brand requirements. A Glock, or failing that a Smith & Wesson. Both reliable, both accurate and both easy to use. Frank's no gunslinger and doesn't want something he needs a degree to operate, or that will jam or malfunction at a critical point.

All of which points to buying from a seasoned crook. In this case that's going to be Tiny Prior. Frank's got some dirt on the old bastard and it's time to call in the marker. He's sure Prior will do business. Selling a clean gun to a DCI will be money in the bank as far as Tiny is concerned, upping his leverage hugely in any future dealings with Frank. Information is currency and while Prior's main trade is old-fashioned skimming off the containers coming through the docks, it is information that has kept him untouched for so long. The information he doesn't have is that Frank's cancer has made him less risk averse than he ever thought possible. For Tiny's knowledge to be useful in future, Frank has to be alive and right now he'll trade the chance of a future investigation against going in unarmed against the people coming after him.

Frank has his car keys in hand and is moving for the door when someone knocks. With Jane Watson's warning fresh in his mind,

Frank freezes before he sees a familiar face appear in the small window set into the wooden door.

'Frank?' It's too late to hide, Kath Palmer has already seen him. She smiles through the glass and waves.

Frank opens the door and does his best to mask any guilt from his face.

'Hi,' he says, feeling like an inexperienced actor stepping onstage, a nervous teen on his first date. It's possible that he's blushing.

Kath, Frank is finding out, has a disconcerting habit of leaving gaps in conversations where words should be. So now, instead of saying something appropriately polite such as 'what time is best for you tonight?' or, 'can you bring some booze?' she just watches him and raises her eyebrows slightly. She's smiling a little too in what Frank can only call a knowing way. He tries not to look at her cleavage which, if anything, is a little more décolletage than yesterday even with an outdoor jacket over her shirt. She's wearing what look like the same jeans from yesterday but Frank doesn't mind. They still look good on her. He tries not to think of last night.

'You hurt yourself?' Kath Palmer points at the bandage on Frank's head.

He puts a hand to it involuntarily and then grabs his beanie from the hat stand next to the door.

'Yeah, sort of. It's OK.' It's hardly Noel Coward but it's what comes out. Frank pulls down the beanie.

'Sleep well?'

'Um, yes, thanks. Very well.'

'You got an early night.'

'I did?'

'I noticed your lights were out when our friends arrived.'

'Oh,' says Frank. 'Yes, I was tired.' And then he thinks: I have cancer. I'm allowed to be tired. He almost says this out loud but stops himself.

'Smitty was barking. I thought that might wake you up?'

'No. No, it didn't. Slept like a baby. Didn't hear a thing.'

'Ah, ok.'

She knows. Shit.

In desperation Frank jiggles his keys. 'I'm just off, Kath. Got a meeting. Was there something you wanted to ask me about?'

Kath waits two beats longer than manners dictate and then puts her hand on Frank's arm. 'Don't let me stop you, love. I just wanted to let you know that we have to change our plans tonight.'

Thank Christ. Frank says a small prayer of atonement.

'Bernie's got to go to Spain this afternoon. There's a problem with the villa.'

She doesn't enlarge on who owns the place in Spain but from her proprietorial tone, and her use of the singular, Frank guesses it is theirs.

'Bloody roof or something,' says Kath. Her eyes light up and she holds up a hand like she's just thought of something. 'Listen, we don't have to worry about Bernie. Why don't we carry on without him? He won't mind and it means our night won't be spoiled.'

Frank wonders if he's strayed into a bad porn movie. Next thing you know Kath's twin sister will turn up in a tight skirt and ask to use the phone.

'Ah, I'm not sure when I'll be back to be honest, Kath.' Frank puts on his most regretful face. 'I don't want to let anyone down.'

'Oh that's OK,' she says and again places her hand on his arm, this time leaving it in place and squeezing just a fraction harder. 'I'm sure you won't.' She lets go of his arm but allows her hand to drift across his arm longer than is needed.

For fuck's sake.

Frank steps out and closes the door of the barn. Automatically he scans the road for cars that shouldn't be there and finds nothing. Not that anyone worth their salt would be so dumb as to show themselves. He thinks back to the white car from last night and curses himself inwardly for his stupidity.

'Another time,' he says, and finds he has to actually push past her. Heading for the car, Kath Palmer follows him, her boot heels clacking on the stone flags.

'Enjoy your day,' says Kath and waggles her fingers at him. She turns and walks back towards her house, Frank watching her bottom in the aptly-named rear view mirror as she goes.

43

Liverpool, October 11th

The Beatles were before Magsi's time, way before, so being in Menlove Avenue doesn't mean much. On his way to the Coughlans he walks past the Lennon house aware that he is less than twenty metres from the exact spot where Sarah had been taken. Magsi walks a few houses down and checks the number before knocking.

The door is opened by a man in his fifties wearing the broken expression familiar to Magsi as that worn by the recently bereaved. The man's eyes are ringed with black and his shoulders are slumped. A wave of centrally-heated air tinged with the faint smell of booze hits Magsi. We all have ways of coping. Booze is as good as any.

'Mr Coughlan? Dan Coughlan?' Magsi holds up his ID card. 'DS Saif Magsi? I called earlier?'

Coughlan nods and waves Magsi inside. 'I don't know if we've got anything new,' he says as he closes the door. 'We told the last lot everything we know.'

Magsi pauses at the living room door. 'In here?'

'Yes,' says Coughlan. 'Do you want to talk to Mary?'

'If she's around.'

Coughlan gestures towards the stairs. 'I'll go and get her. Doctor's got her on tablets.' He indicates that Magsi should go through into the living room and he trudges up the stairs.

The house is spotless in that way that always worries Magsi, himself a product of an environment filled with chaos and love and warmth. Even allowing for the death this house feels stuffy and Magsi knows from the file that Sarah had been an only child. What it would be like now for the Coughlans is beyond Magsi's imagination. He wanders around the living room looking at the photos and books and mementos. Sarah features heavily.

Magsi is just about to sit down when Mary Coughlan comes in, closely followed by her husband. Her eyes are raw with grief and she looks to be in about as bad a shape as Magsi has ever seen a victim's relative. This is not going to be pleasant.

'Mrs Coughlan, I'm DS Magsi. I know that this is extremely painful for you but we'd just like to make sure there's nothing we've missed that would help us find out exactly what happened to Sarah.'

Mary Coughlan nods and sits down heavily on the sofa. 'We could get some tea,' she says, absently. 'If you like.'

'I'll make tea.' Dan Coughlan vanishes in the direction of the kitchen.

Magsi turns back to Mary Coughlan. She's looking past him at an image of Sarah laughing, her hair a different colour to more recent images.

'I liked her with dark hair,' Mary Coughlan says. 'Made her look younger.'

'She had a lovely smile.'

Mary Coughlan's mouth twitches at the use of the past tense but she doesn't say anything.

Magsi coughs and looks at the file in his hand without reading a word. 'Now, I know that other officers have already asked you lots of questions but I just wondered if there'd been anything at all you've been thinking about that you might have forgotten?'

'Like what?'

'Any of Sarah's friends you may have missed out from the list.'

'She didn't have a lot of friends. Just a few. Some good ones but no-one really what I'd say was 'close', like. She was quiet was Sarah. Wouldn't harm a fly.'

Mary Coughlan starts crying quietly and has her head down when her husband returns. He looks accusingly at Magsi but Magsi knows just to wait and say nothing. Dan Coughlan hands his wife a cup of tea and she takes a sip.

'It's alright,' whispers Dan Coughlan, his head close to his wife. 'It's alright.'

These are the moments when Magsi feels most like an intruder. He can think of nothing to say or ask. This is a bullshit fishing trip that can only cause pain and Magsi wants it to be over.

Dan Coughlan looks up at the cop. 'It's hit harder because she was just beginning to enjoy herself again. Stupid, but it makes it seem worse somehow.'

'Had something happened to Sarah?'

'Nothing important, not now,' says Dan Coughlan. He looks up at Magsi. 'She had cancer three years ago and it really knocked her sideways. Knocked all of us out of whack to be honest. There were a couple of complications too and she almost died.'

Coughlan clears his throat and Magsi waits.

'Anyway, they sorted it all out, eventually. She was alright. She had chemo and that did it.'

Magsi makes a note.

'Is it important?' says Mary Coughlan, her voice thick. She has a dewdrop hanging from her nose.

Magsi shakes his head slightly. 'Probably not, to be honest, Mrs Coughlan. Just something for the file.'

'You are going to find the people who did this, aren't you?' Mary Coughlan wipes her nose and straightens up.

'Well the two abductors also died in the crash, Mrs Coughlan. Which might turn out to be the only good thing about all of this if you ask me.'

'We didn't,' says Dan Coughlan, his eyes narrowed. 'There's nothing good about Sarah dying. Nothing. Don't be so *stupid*. Jesus Christ!'

'I'm sorry, Mr Coughlan,' says Magsi. 'Of course.'

Dan Coughlan gets up and for a microsecond Magsi wonders if he's going to attack.

'I'll get more tea,' says Coughlan and stalks out of the room.

'Don't blame Danny,' says Mary Coughlan. 'He's trying to look after me when it's him who needs looking after really. He was very close to Sarah.'

There's a note of something in Mary Coughlan's voice that Magsi picks up on but for the life of him he can't define what it is.

'It's OK, Mrs Coughlan. I . . .' Magsi trails off as Dan Coughlan returns holding a mug. He raises an apologetic hand to Magsi.

'Sorry. It's difficult.'

Magsi nods and then looks at the photos on the walls and in the frames, desperate for something to say. The silence in the room is oppressive and Magsi can hear the bass tick of the hall clock. Both the Coughlans look at him, waiting for a question he doesn't have.

'What was she like as a baby?' he says eventually. 'It's just that I can't see any early photos of Sarah.' Magsi smiles, relieved to have asked something.

'Well obviously we don't have any,' says Mary Coughlan, as if talking to a dim-witted pensioner. 'She was four.'

Magsi feels as though he's missed a page somewhere. What does she mean 'she was four'? 'Uh . . .'

'We told you,' says Mary Coughlan. 'Or told the last one. Dan told them.'

'Yes. I think I did,' says Dan. He points at Magsi's paperwork. 'It should be in the file I suppose. Maybe I didn't. It's all been very confusing.'

'Sorry to be dense, Mrs Coughlan,' says Magsi, tapping the file. 'Just what did you tell, or not tell, the officers who came last time?'

Dan Coughlan looks at Magsi.

'That Sarah was adopted, of course.'

'She was four,' says Mary Coughlan, smiling at the distant memory. 'When she came.'

'Do you have any idea about her –' Magsi stops himself saying 'real parents' in the nick of time – 'early years? About her birth parents?'

Mary Coughlan's mouth tightens but Dan leans forward. 'Her mother was – her mother wasn't able to take care of herself. Her father was a married man, that's what we heard. He never made any effort to find her. Neither of them did.' Dan Coughlan's voice hardens. '*We* were her family. You understand?'

Magsi nods and, after a brief pause, continues.

'Do you have any adoption paperwork?'

Dan Coughlan gets up and disappears once more.

'Did Sarah know?' says Magsi. 'She was adopted, I mean?'

Mary Coughlan shakes her head. 'We didn't tell her. She's our daughter. Danny wanted to but I put my foot down. I don't hold with it.' She glares at Magsi. 'And what's it got to do with what happened, anyway? It's not going to bring her back, is it?'

'No. It's not. But we have to look at everything, Mrs Coughlan. Even seemingly unimportant information might be useful.'

Mary Coughlan sniffs.

Dan Coughlan returns holding a cardboard file. He sits down, opens it and starts riffling through the stack of paper.

'What are you looking for?' he says.

'A name would be a good place to start.'

Coughlan hands a thin sheet of paper to Magsi. 'I think that's got most things on there.'

Magsi scans the information and looks for Sarah Coughlan's birth name. Although this information is almost certain not to be important, it is new, and as such will be greeted with interest back at MIT. Sarah Coughlan's biological parents weren't married so there are two different surnames listed. Her mother is listed as 'Audrey Jane Bridge'. As Magsi's finger finds the box containing the name of Sarah Coughlan's father, he pauses momentarily and then shakes his head. Just a coincidence, nothing more.

44

Liverpool, October 20th

It had been Frank's former boss, Menno Koopman – MIT's chief before the reviled Perch arrived – who had introduced Frank to Tiny Prior.

'He's a specimen,' Koopman had said before that first meeting and Koop had been right. Now, as Frank turns the Golf into the Freeport Terminal at Seaforth, he starts to remember that odd meeting.

At the gate he shows his ID to the uniform and breezes in without a murmur. Why shouldn't he? His ID is valid and despite the beanie Frank wears to hide the biopsy dressing, looks every inch a cop. The security guard at the gate doesn't give a shit one way or the other.

Tiny Prior's domain is the cabin of one of the massive permanent container cranes angled out over the Mersey. As far as Frank knows, Tiny Prior has been clocking on at the docks since before the dawn of time. Frank hates heights and the climb to the yellow-painted iron door of Tiny Prior's kingdom not only gets his heart beating faster than he'd like, but takes him back five months to the leap across the chasm at Mount San Jacinto. He clasps the rail a little tighter and is careful not to look down through the latticework stairs. At the top he knocks once on the thick window.

Inside is Tiny, an elderly, lumpy man with sharp eyes set in a crumpled face. He's drinking tea and watching an Everton game on a large TV set hung on one wall of the cramped cabin. Two armchairs occupy most of the rest of the space along with a rich array of Persian rugs, richly-decorated curtains and paintings.

Tiny's glance flicks towards Frank as he walks in but the normally chatty Prior doesn't say anything. Instead he pushes a holdall across a small French-polished table and turns back to the action onscreen.

He's scared, thinks Frank and wonders why. And then it comes to him: he's scared of me. Is it something he's heard or is it just that senior coppers who suddenly require unregistered hardware are to be regarded much as you would an escaped rhino? Frank opts for the second. Tiny Prior may be tuned into the underworld radio but even he hasn't got the skinny on the inner workings of Operation Lupus or Frank's more recent problems with the Bavarians.

'Twelve?' says Frank, and Prior, scowling, puts a gnarled finger to his lips. He nods and points to where Frank should put the money. Frank places twelve hundred in used notes on the table and picks up the holdall. He doesn't look inside. What would be the point? If Tiny tries to stiff him it's not like Frank couldn't find him, is it?

'What's with the silent treatment, Tiny?'

Prior frowns and the lines on his face crumple. 'Can't be too careful,' he mutters.

'You think this is a set-up?'

Prior doesn't say anything for a few seconds.

'Jesus,' says Frank. 'It's embarrassing you even think that.'

'I heard stuff.' Prior blurts this out and looks surprised at himself. He even puts a hand to his lips; an involuntary pantomime gesture.

Frank too is surprised. Not because of what Tiny Prior has said but because Prior never gives away information. Ever. Even saying he'd heard things is useful information that someone has been talking about Frank.

He's scared, thinks Frank and that thought, in turn, scares Frank.

'What, exactly, have you heard, Tiny?'

Prior's eyes are back on the screen.

'Playin' well, hey?' he says without looking at Frank.

'What have you heard, Tiny?' Frank puts a bit more steel in his tone and this time Prior does look in his direction.

'That you'd turned, Mr Keane. Gone into another line of work. Like your last feller.'

'You heard I was bent?' Frank finds it hard to keep the anger from his voice and Prior holds his hands up in supplication.

'No, Mr Keane. Never bent, not you.'

'So what am I supposed to have turned into? And who told you this?'

'I'm saying nothing, DCI Keane. I shouldn't have said anything. I don't want to get mixed up in . . . all that. Whatever it is.'

Frank opens his mouth again but Prior stops him.

'No. Take the box and go, Mr Keane. Keep the money, too.' He pushes the twelve hundred back across the table. 'None of this happened.'

Frank looks at Prior but says nothing. He leaves the money where it is and picks up the holdall. Prior remains fixed on the TV. After a second or two Frank steps back out into the petrol-tainted breeze coming off the river and descends, gingerly clutching his purchases, back down to terra firma.

45

Berlin, October 19th

Although she'll never know it, Theresa Cooper departs Liverpool for Berlin on the same plane that Felix Hoffen arrived on an hour and a half earlier. To her surprise, when she exits baggage claim at Schönefeld there is a dark-haired woman waiting for her in Arrivals holding a sign with her name.

'Theresa Cooper?'

'Yes.'

The woman holds out a hand which Cooper shakes. 'Kriminalkommissar Anna Ziegler. I will be your liaison in Berlin, yes?'

'I have a liaison?' Cooper's tone is playful.

'Yess. Naturally. Zis vill be me, I zink. It iss as it should be.' Ziegler's tone is puzzled, her face grim. 'You do not vant zis liaison? I can change, ja?'

Cooper makes a note to use less humour. This is Germany after all.

'Of course,' says Cooper. 'I didn't mean to cause any offence.'

Ziegler breaks into a broad smile.

'I'm only joking with you, Theresa,' she says, this time in near-perfect English. 'Thought I'd do a bit of movie German, see how it went.'

'It was . . . very convincing,' says Cooper. 'And I'll try not to make any more stupid assumptions.'

'Oh some of them you can make. Not all of us are like me.'

'Why the pick-up? I mean, I'm glad and all but I could have got a cab.'

Ziegler picks up one of Cooper's bags. 'This way. The car's just across here.'

As they walk across the tarmac Ziegler talks. 'Schönefeld might as well be in the Black Forest. It would take you a long time to get to the city and I thought we could talk about the case on the way. It is one in which I'm most interested.'

Cooper is still mulling this over when they get to Ziegler's car, a modest VW, none too clean on the outside and positively scummy inside. So much for the Germanic tendency to cleanliness. Another stereotype out of the window and I haven't even left the airport, thinks Cooper.

Ziegler picks her way out of the car park and noses the car through a baffling system of highways and unfamiliar signs while Cooper does her best to surreptitiously move some of the debris of cigarette packs, coke cans and junk food cartons gathered in a deep drift in the footwell.

'Just throw it all out of the window,' says Ziegler. 'I don't care.' Then, as Cooper raises her eyebrows, Ziegler smiles and points a yellow-tipped finger. 'Got you again, English.'

Cooper bends and scoops an armful of crap off the floor. She twists in her seat and deposits it in the back where it joins what looks like an avalanche of junk.

'I keep all this stuff in here to put off thieves,' says Ziegler. 'The car cost me sixty thousand euro and Berlin thieves like to steal clean cars.'

Cooper looks doubtful.

'No, really,' says Ziegler. 'Not kidding you this time. For real. This is camouflage. You'll see when we get to my apartment. It's very clean, even if it is a bit small. I had the shower fixed too so you'll be able to clean up once we get back. Or we could share a bath? We do that in Berlin, you know.'

'What's the name of my hotel?'

Ziegler laughs. 'You're not buying that story? You don't think you're staying at my apartment?'

'I may look stupid,' says Cooper, 'but I'm not. Not completely and not all the time, anyway.' She relaxes into her seat. 'So what's the real reason you picked me up at the airport, Anna? And don't give me any more fake German stuff. I really want to know.'

Ziegler nods. 'OK. Well I think that the first thing you'll find out is that I'm not the most popular officer at LKA.'

'LKA?'

'The *Landeskriminalamt*. My department. The one I work for anyway.' Ziegler waves a hand. 'That's not important. What is, is that I'm not popular because I have a wasp in my hat.'

'A bee in your bonnet?'

'That's it. I have a bee. This has got me into trouble at work, this bee.' Ziegler looks out of the window. 'A whole shitload of trouble,' she murmurs to herself. She turns back to Cooper. 'Never mind that. Do you know anything about Nazis?'

'They bombed our chippy.'

Ziegler raises her eyebrows.

'Doesn't matter,' says Cooper. 'Bad joke. Go on.'

'Everyone knows about the real Nazis, the old Nazis. I have an interest in the new ones. I am part Jewish so you understand how this is for me, right?'

'Of course.'

'Anyway, I've made it something of a crusade of mine to keep tabs on the various right-wing groups. It's not my official role, just something I do. Which is why I get in trouble. Last year, I stumbled across a person who I think is very bad news. I began to follow this person with interest.' Ziegler twists in her seat and rummages in the papers on the back seat, the Audi swerving slightly as she does so. Just as Cooper thinks she'll have to grab the wheel Ziegler finds what she's looking for and swings back. She corrects the car's line and tosses a file onto Cooper's lap.

'This is her.'

Cooper opens the file and sees a photograph of a good-looking woman of around forty in a long evening dress standing outside a grand-looking building. The image has been taken on a long lens and at night but is clear enough.

'I've put together a sheet with the main details and concerns translated into English.'

Cooper holds the translation.

'I still don't understand. What's the connection between this woman and my abduction?'

'She is a partner in the clinic where the van was stolen from.'

Cooper tries not to let her disappointment show. Is that it? Maybe Anna Ziegler's colleagues have a point.

As the LKA officer guides the car through the East Berlin suburbs Cooper turns back to the sheet of paper and begins to read Ziegler's notes on Ilsa Bruckner.

46

Liverpool, , October 20th

DS Magsi takes a grateful lungful of sweet street air as the door to the Coughlan house closes quietly behind him. In the file under his arm are Sarah Coughlan's adoption details.

He walks down the suburban garden path and through the wrought iron gate, each step further away from the house lightening his mood. It had been claustrophobic at the Coughlans and Magsi is glad to head back to the office.

His first act when he arrives is to log onto the MIT system and start looking. Here, in the familiar office, every wall of which seems coated with a thick veneer of world-weary cynicism, his surprised reaction at the Coughlan house to the name of Sarah's biological father seems faintly ludicrous. It's a common enough name but, with Magsi's particular line of enquiry into the case being so arid, he supposes he's looking for any excuse. One thing is for sure; if he hands the information over without doing at least a little independent digging he'd never forgive himself so he plunges in, hoping that once he's scratched this particular itch and come up with nothing, no-one will be any the wiser. With his own need for protective discretion to the fore he works quickly, rattling through the databases, his hands flying, his head constantly turning in anticipation of a bellow of derision from Rose or Rimmer, or any of the other coppers. He feels stupid but follows it through to the bitter end.

Finally though, it isn't the MIT system from which Magsi gets the information he's looking for. Frustrated by the official databases tendency towards concentrating on criminals, Magsi switches to a genealogy site and scores a direct hit inside ten minutes. Magsi leans forward and presses print. As the paper spools through he looks across to DCI Harris's office and wonders how to play this.

Feeling like a schoolboy snitch but without quite knowing why, Magsi knocks on Harris's door. When no reply comes, he cracks it open and sees she's on the phone. He moves to leave but Harris waves him inside and points at a seat in front of her desk. She holds up a finger. One minute.

Magsi sits.

Harris finishes her call and looks at him. 'You got something, didn't you?'

'I did, ma'am.'

'So why aren't you looking happy?'

Magsi hesitates and then slides the sheet of paper containing Sarah Coughlan's adoption details across the desk.

'Adopted?' says Harris and Magsi nods.

'Which is interesting but not relevant. At least not that I know of. And there was something else. Just a stupid thing that I feel a bit embarrassed that I thought it was worth looking at. Felt like I was going behind his back.'

Harris looks blankly at Magsi. 'What are you talking about, DS Magsi?'

'The name of the father, ma'am,' says Magsi. He leans forward and points at the relevant box. Harris looks at it and shrugs.

'So? It's a common enough na . . .' She breaks off mid-sentence and stares at Magsi. 'Don't tell me there's a connection?'

Magsi pushes the results of his genealogy search over.

'*Family Matters*?' says Harris, reading the name of the company. 'Not exactly official, is it?'

Magsi says nothing and waits for his boss to find the right piece of information. When she does she looks up at Magsi, her expression unreadable.

'Sister?'

'Yes, ma'am. Half-sister, to be accurate. I don't know that it means anything but I thought you should know.'

'Yes. You're right.' Harris looks at Magsi. 'Keep this under your hat for a while until I've had a chance to think about how to handle this. Or if we need to handle it. Like you say, it might not mean anything.'

'No ma'am.' Magsi hesitates. 'Do you think he knows, ma'am? About her being dead.'

Harris shakes her head. 'I don't know.' She pauses. 'He might not even know he's got a sister. Had a sister'

She taps her finger on the desk. 'You run along, DS Magsi. I'll shout out once I've decided the best way to proceed.'

Magsi nods, gets to his feet and leaves Harris looking out of the window. She remains like that for a couple of minutes before lifting the phone from its cradle. She calls Charlie Searle's office and while she's waiting for the connection wonders exactly how to tell her boss that Sarah Coughlan is Frank Keane's sister.

47

Berlin, October 20th

Theresa Cooper waits for thirty minutes in the lobby of her hotel for Anna to arrive before losing patience and taking a cab to the LKA office. Ziegler had clearly forgotten or was late. Cooper, who hates forgetfulness almost as much as she prizes punctuality, can't decide which was worse. Now, deprived of her translator and her own German feeling distinctly rusty, she frets for much of the cab ride about how long it will take her to get the information she needs.

It takes her almost an hour to gain access to the building. Cooper's UK police ID and credentials might as well be written in crayon to judge by how seriously they are taken by the jobsworth on the front desk. After a number of increasingly uncomfortable and unsuccessful attempts at speaking German Cooper feels her already thin confidence ebbing away, minute by tortuous minute. In the end she phones MIT and sends Scott Corner to find the German student working in the canteen to translate. Corner doesn't try to hide his glee at her discomfort.

'I thought you spoke German?' he says.

'*Du bist so ein Schwachkopf, Scott,*' says Cooper, her anger increasing her fluency. '*Hol' das Mädchen ans Telefon.*'

'Albanian? Danish?' says Corner but hands the phone over to the student. Cooper can almost hear him smirking.

Ten minutes later Cooper finds herself sitting in a waiting area to one side of the open plan office Anna Ziegler works in. The place appears deserted and a friendly female cop speaking impeccable English tells her that most of the department is at a meeting and will be back soon.

Cooper spends a few minutes catching up on her emails using her phone until a straggle of well-dressed, well-heeled and grim-faced people start walking past her and into the office. With a jolt Cooper realises that they are police officers, not visiting dignitaries. Conscious of her own perfectly respectable but now distinctly dowdy-by-comparison appearance, Cooper tries to attract someone's attention with little success. Finally, after getting the brush-off from three officers, Cooper raises her voice and addresses the room.

'Excuse me,' she says in German, her voice sounding foreign even to her, 'but can someone please tell me where I can find Anna Ziegler?'

Everyone in the office looks at Cooper.

'You are her to meet Anna?' says a man at the nearest desk, replying in English; the ultimate linguistic put-down. He peers at Cooper suspiciously.

'Yes! She is my liaison. I'm an English police officer. She picked me up at Schönefeld yesterday.'

'You haven't heard then?'

'Heard what?'

48

Helsby, Cheshire, October 20th

It's dark by the time Frank gets back from seeing Tiny Prior at Seaforth and guides the car through the twisting lanes towards the barn. The raw afternoon breeze has stiffened into something more and a swirl of leaves flap like bats against the windscreen as he pulls the Golf in some distance down the road.

His phone had beeped while he was at Tiny's. Mr Wilson had called but by the time Frank called back he had gone. A text message had come through: 'call Monday.' Sitting in the car Frank tries Wilson once more but gets the office voicemail. He calls the hospital and after going through a number of operators gets the oncology unit where one of the registrars advises him to wait until Monday.

'If it was very urgent, Mr Wilson would have called us, Mr Keane. Try not to worry.'

Frank pockets his phone, cuts the engine and reaches into the rear seat for the backpack containing the purchases he made in the city. He tucks the Glock in the inside pocket of his jacket and steps out into the night.

There's a thick hedge running alongside the Palmer place which Frank keeps between himself and the barn as he approaches in an overly cautious wide arc. After Watson's warning he's decided that despite the slim chance that the drug guys will come tonight, this is going to be the last night at Helsby. Tomorrow he is gone.

The barn is a blacker stain against the dark and Frank comes at it from the field taking care to keep to the noiseless grass, staying in the shadows all the way. At the back door he tries the handle and finds it still locked. As quietly as possible Frank opens the door and listens for a full minute. There's nothing.

He steps inside and locks the back door behind him before putting on the kitchen light and placing his rucksack on the counter. Frank's back is killing him and he remembers he has some painkillers that, so far, for some vague masculine reason that he would struggle to explain, he has avoided taking. Tonight though, he needs something.

The rest of the downstairs rooms are empty. Frank takes the stairs slowly, keeping his weight out at the extremes of each tread. He's halfway when he feels a warning tremor, some tiny atavistic signal deep inside his instinct memory that something is wrong.

Frank stops, his hand sliding round to the newly-acquired Glock. Frank pulls the thing out, the gun weight in his hand simultaneously alien and familiar. He forces himself to remain still and tries to analyze why he has this twitchy feeling.

And then it hits him.

There's no light showing underneath the bedroom door. And that's a problem because Frank is now as sure as he can be that he left his bedside light switched on. He holds out the Glock in front of him and listens.

There is silence.

Frank, his back to the landing wall, levers open the bedroom door using the end of the gun. He keeps himself to one side, out of any line of fire. With the door open he backs off down the corridor and waits at the end of the landing, standing in complete silence. Something Koop had told him makes him do this. Don't go blundering in. Just wait. Their nerve will crack before yours does. Just give it five minutes.

It's a theory.

The reality is that Frank's nerve cracks long before five minutes ticks by. A car goes past on the road outside and in the overspill from the headlights Frank sees a shadowy figure on his bed.

As scared as he can ever remember being, Frank forces himself forward, the idea of running, and thereby exposing his back, infinitely more nerve-wracking than confronting whoever is in the bedroom.

He goes inside, the Glock extended in front of him, his breathing shallow and his nerve endings wide open.

There's a smell of cologne or perfume that wasn't there before, a foreign scent and he gets a sudden gut reaction that something very bad indeed has happened. He has a sudden flash to last year and Menno Koopman walking into his hotel room to find Keith Kite, a local drug scrote, tied to the bed and gutted like a fish. This feels like it might be something similar. In the few seconds it takes him to locate the light a jumble of potential horrors cascade through his mind.

He fumbles for the switch, the new Glock wavering awkwardly before– finally – he hears a click.

As light floods the room, someone screams and Frank's finger jerks back on the trigger.

49

Helsby, Cheshire, October 20th

The scream comes from Kath Palmer.

She dives sideways across the bed as Frank squeezes the trigger, her naked body squirming across the sheets.

Frank lowers the Glock, his expression one of horror until he realises there has been no shot, no accidental shooting. A hot wave of nausea flows through his gut and he braces himself against the wall with one hand. He had forgotten to take the Glock off safety.

Kath Palmer lies on the floor of the room, the bedsheets gathered against her breasts, staring at Frank in white-faced horror.

'Jesus Christ!' she shrieks; her voice bat-squeak high. '*Jesus fucking Christ!*'

'I . . .' Frank lifts up the Glock to explain but Kath Palmer yelps as the gun comes into view.

'The safety,' Frank says, the words tumbling over one another. 'The safety, it's off. Off. I didn't shoot. I didn't shoot.' Then he's angry. 'What the fuck are you doing? I could have shot you!'

Kath Palmer sinks back on the bed and puts her hands over her face. 'I thought you had,' she says, her voice muffled.

Frank sits down on the edge of the bed and puts the Glock down carefully on the bedside table. 'It's off, Kath. Look. I put it down.'

Kath peeps through her fingers and her body sags. 'Is that thing real?'

Frank nods. He is sweating.

'Why do you have a gun?'

'It's a long story. How did you get in?'

'We have a key. Sometimes we get asked to check something by Mick and Audrey.'

At the mention of Julie's parents Frank shakes his head. There are so many things wrong with this.

'You'd better go,' he says.

Kath Palmer slides out from under the sheets and kneels up.

Frank can't help but notice that she is in great shape.

'I could,' she says softly and Frank knows that he is not going to say no. 'But I'd prefer to stay.' She moves forward on the bed on all fours, her hair falling across her face. When she gets close enough she leans forward and whispers in Frank's ear.

'You saw me last night, didn't you? I know it was you and I don't mind. I don't think Bernie would mind either. But he doesn't know anyway and he's not here and we are.' She kisses Frank's ear. 'It's silly not to.'

'It's been a while,' says Frank. 'And I . . .' He wants to say something about his cancer, about what has been happening, to say something about Bernie and about Julie, but he doesn't. He says nothing and Kath Palmer, breathing heavily, her eyes gleaming, slides her legs around him and kisses him hard.

50

Helsby, Cheshire, October 21st

Three in the morning.

'That the place?'

Ezterhaus, the taller of the two new skinhead morons Gottlenz has sent, nods. 'Yes. He's been there since last week. Took a few days to find him. The place belongs to his wife, or her parents. Something like that.'

Hoffen's not listening. Yak yak like always with these guys. Old women. Why should care about how they found the target? All that matters is the present moment. The target is there and they have to pick him up. This kind of talk is for one thing only and that is so that Ezterhaus can show they have been doing something; to bring Hoffen a bone. Hoffen despairs that Ezterhaus and the other lumbering goon, Neumann, are the best Gottlenz could do on such short notice. But it's useless thinking about it now. They'll have to do.

Hoffen points at the barn. 'You both go in the front door nice and quiet. Get our man parcelled up and call me once you're ready. Clear?'

The two men step out of the van and Hoffen leans out of the window.

'No fuss, OK? Everything clean. In, out, no problem.'

51

Berlin, October 20th

Cooper's in a car with Robert Weiss and Christina Dreschler on their way to the hospital to see Ziegler. Dreschler's driving the big Audi, a vehicle far more luxurious than the workaday Fords that Cooper's used to at MIT. The radio is open to the police call frequency and the intermittent blasts of electronically amplified German provide an atmospheric backdrop to the journey.

Both the LKA officers speak decent English which is useful because as far as Cooper can make out, the German she knows seems to have no resemblance to any language spoken in Berlin. She wants to speak the local language – it's one of the damn reasons she was assigned the job, for Christ's sake – but the hard reality on the ground is that it's faster speaking English. She leans forward to talk now, Weiss half-turning towards her, an arm crooked easily over the back of his seat.

'What happened?'

'A bad situation.' Weiss's expression is grim. 'Anna's place hasn't got parking so she left her car on the street and someone attacked her when she was walking to her apartment. Two men, we believe. Young men with street clothing. White. Prolos.'

"Prolos'?'

'People brought up in bad areas. Places like Marzahn.'

Cooper remembers Ziegler mentioning Marzahn although she forgets the context.

'Were the attackers waiting?' she asks.

'This I don't know. They saw her and beat her very badly. They only stopped because other people came. They ran away.'

Cooper looks out of the window. 'Anna picked me up from the airport yesterday. It was a nice thing for her to do. She didn't need to do that.'

Neither of the Germans reply and Cooper turns back to them.

'You don't like Anna?'

Dreschler looks at Weiss.

'Ask him,' she says.

Weiss grimaces. He says something to Dreschler in German that Cooper can't follow and then turns. 'We are not friends but that does not mean we are enemies. You should know this.' He glares at Dreschler. 'But when *this* happens Anna is police first, yes? You have this same thing back in England, too?'

'Sure,' says Cooper. 'One of your own.'

'One of your own.' Weiss repeats the phrase in a low voice as if committing it to memory.

'Anna can be a difficult woman,' says Dreschler. 'Not just in work but I mean for herself. She is not someone who makes friends easy. She dresses not so good and this doesn't help.'

'Hard to compete in your office,' says Cooper. 'You should see some of the clothes we wear.'

Dreschler doesn't say anything and Weiss looks down at his suit. 'This is how we are in LKA. You must show you take care, show you have authority. It is how it is and Anna does not see that.' He looks at Cooper. 'But do not think Anna's problems are because of clothing. She has ideas about things.'

'Ilsa Bruckner?'

Weiss rolls his eyes. 'She already say this to you? *Schiesse*. Bruckner is her . . .' Weiss snaps his fingers, unsure of the word.

'Obsession?'

'Ja. Her obsession. She's been in trouble for this before. She has idea she is a Nazi, which is bad enough I think. But also she wants Bruckner to be a killer, to be some big criminal. Probably even a terrorist.'

Dreschler says something to Weiss in German in a low warning tone. He makes a dismissive gesture and Dreschler shrugs.

'Anna is Jewish,' she says. 'Which is why she takes such a close interest. She follows Bruckner too many times. And not on LKA business. Just her own time.'

Cooper nods and sits back. These issues are local, they're not part of her information gathering trip. Once she's done her duty and looked in on Anna Ziegler she can get back on track. LKA will assign another liaison officer. The inner politics of the *Landeskriminalamt* are none of MIT's business.

The car moves through the city. Cooper's hopelessly lost but as far as she can judge the hospital is to the north and west of central Berlin. Once they arrive, it is, as expected, clean and with an air of calm efficiency.

Dreschler parks in a space reserved for police vehicles and places a plastic sign on the dashboard. She and Weiss must know the hospital well because they find Anna Ziegler's room easily. She's on the third floor in a small private room just off one of the general wards. Outside, Dreschler and Weiss confer with an Asian doctor for a few minutes before they are allowed in.

The shape in the bed, covered in dressings and administered by a variety of drips and monitors is utterly unrecognisable as the Anna Ziegler who had picked Cooper up at the airport less than twenty-four hours previously. As they approach the bed, Christina Dreschler puts her hand to her mouth and Robert Weiss swears under his breath. He grips the rail of Anna's bed so hard that it trembles. Cooper glances at Christina Dreschler and sees tears in her eyes.

'Jesus Christ,' says Cooper.

Ziegler's face is a swollen, stitch-marked horror show of purple and yellow bruising. One eye is covered with a thick padded dressing and the other is almost closed. A thin slit of white eyeball shows but Cooper can't tell if Ziegler can see anything, or if she's conscious. She has been battered to a pulp.

'Anna?' whispers Dreschler bending close. There's no response. Dreschler brushes a tendril of hair back from Anna's brow. 'Anna?'

Weiss backs off a couple of paces and shakes his head. He mutters something in German. Cooper doesn't need a translator to get the gist.

'Anna?' Dreschler tries again but there's nothing. The green monitor keeps steadily blinking but Ziegler is clearly unconscious.

The three cops stand looking at her for a minute, the only sounds those of the bleeping electronic monitoring equipment and the muted sounds of the hospital through the thick doors.

'Did the doctor say what her injuries are?' says Cooper.

It's Weiss who replies. Even though Ziegler appears to be unconscious he motions Cooper away from the bed and speaks softly. 'I spoke to her physician before we came. She has six broken ribs and a broken nose. Her left arm is snapped in two places and four of her fingers have been broken. Her teeth are smashed and she has lost her left eye. She has a fractured skull and they're monitoring her for brain damage. She has internal bleeding that had to be stabilised and a punctured lung. There is damage to her knee and a lot of deep abrasions and heavy bruising almost everywhere. The internal bleeding is what worries them most.'

Cooper puts a hand on Weiss's shoulder. 'This is terrible. I'm so sorry.'

He nods but doesn't say anything else.

Dreschler straightens up. She takes a tissue from the box on Ziegler's side table and wipes her eyes. Like Weiss, she too says something in German that sounds like swearing.

'I'm going back to the car,' says Dreschler abruptly.

'We'll all go,' says Weiss. He pats Ziegler's shoulder. '*Tschau*, Anna.'

Cooper lifts out her notebook. 'I'm going to write her a note.' She looks at the Germans. 'If that's OK?"

Dreschler nods as she and Weiss open the door. 'You know the way down?'

'Yes,' says Cooper. 'I'll see you at the car. Two minutes.'

The door closes and Cooper moves close to Ziegler's bed. She perches her hip on the edge of the bed and bends to write. Her relationship with the injured woman is slight but Ziegler showed kindness last night. Cooper tries to suppress the thought that if Anna hadn't come and picked her up from Schönefeld then this might never have happened., She knows that thought will come back, with interest. Cooper wants to leave a note she hopes Anna will get a chance to read.

She has just started writing when Anna Ziegler's hand lunges towards her and grips her wrist. Cooper almost screams. She looks at Ziegler and sees movement in her eye.

'Anna,' whispers Cooper. And then, more urgently as Anna's eyes close once more, '*Anna.*'

Ziegler says nothing but her eyes open once more and now her fingers scrabble at Cooper's hand. Cooper experiences a moment of confusion before understanding that Anna is fumbling for the pen.

She places it in Ziegler's hand and holds the pad steady. Ziegler's bruised eye strains to see the pad and then the pen starts to move, the hand holding it trembling furiously and slashing the paper with tiny black marks. Anna's breathing speeds up and she makes a small groaning sound. When the monitor begins to beep Cooper panics.

'Anna I'm going to get the doctor.'

Ziegler shakes a finger – no – and now the pen moves with more purpose, Anna grunting with the exertion. After twenty seconds of almost unbearably intense effort she sinks back into the pillows breathing hard, spent. Cooper finds she has been holding her own breath and she lets out a long sigh. After a minute or two Anna Ziegler is breathing slowly again and her one good eye is closed.

'Anna?' says Cooper but there's no response. Cooper puts a hand on her arm. It's warm. Cooper walks out of the room and finds a nurse. Unable to explain adequately in German, she motions the woman to follow her.

In Ziegler's room the nurse checks the patient. When she has finished she nods at Cooper, gently pushing her towards the door. 'She's OK. But you must go. She is tired.'

In the corridor outside Cooper looks at her notepad. Amidst the flurry of pen marks are two distinct words.

Oper Tod.

52

Helsby, Cheshire, October 21st

Frank wakes with a jolt in the unfamiliar bed, lifts his head from the pillow and tries to figure out what woke him. He's not sure what time it is but it's still dark. Maybe three? He listens for a few moments but the house remains silent.

Kath Palmer's asleep next to him, a thin bar of weak moonlight through the blinds striping the s-shaped curve of her hip under the sheet. She snores gently. Frank keeps his head lifted for a moment before relaxing gratefully. His back feels as stiff as it's ever been but there's a lightness in his shoulders that he can only put down to getting laid for the first time in months. Jesus, that had felt good.

He breathes out slowly, running a tape in his mind of some of the highlights from the night. Guilt, as obvious and permanent as the gargoyles on a cathedral, makes a customary appearance but for now he's happy enough to push that down into a dusty drawer of his over-worked psyche. After what Frank had seen through the window two nights back, Bernie Palmer could not be described as a shrinking violet when it came to experimental sexuality. In any case Kath's genuine, unbridled appetite makes any amount of post-coital guilt worth it. Frank can't remember being with anyone with a more straightforward desire.

He swings his legs out of bed, pulls on a pair of sweatpants and a t-shirt and moves across the bedroom before turning back to pick up the recently acquired Glock. Frank tucks the weapon into the back of his pants and pads across the landing to the bathroom.

He feels slightly ridiculous as the weight of the weapon drags his waistband south.

Inside the bathroom, he leaves the lights off and relieves himself as quietly as he can, pissing against the side of the porcelain. When he's done, he pushes open the door with one hand, the other tentatively rubbing the still shiny scars stretched across his shoulder. Four months back he'd found himself the unlikely central player in a US black ops fuckup and had taken three bullets from an Israeli Micro-Tavor assault weapon that almost cost him an arm. Instead he'd been patched together so expertly at an off-grid US medical centre that now all that remained was a hot dull ache.

As he leaves the bathroom Frank turns towards the stairs and finds himself looking straight down the business end of an ugly Glock attached to a large man silhouetted in the light coming from the bedroom. This guy is tall, with short blond hair and from the steady way he goes about his business, and the fat silencer sitting on the end of the barrel, Frank guesses he's done this before.

Behind the gunman is a second figure standing next to the bed looking down at Kath who has the good sense to stay quiet. She holds the sheets tight across her chest, her eyes fixed on the scene in the hall. The second man lets his gun dangle easily, confident that the sight of it alone is enough to control the woman in the bed. He is dark-haired and reminds Frank strongly of the McGinn brothers, high-rolling drug locals that Frank's MIT unit had put away early last year.

Was that what this was about? Payback?

Without moving the Glock from Frank's face, the gunman on the landing pulls a phone from his hip pocket and thumbs a number. While he's waiting for an answer he and Frank stare at each other without expression, the only sound the hum of the fridge from the kitchen at the foot of the stairs.

'*Ich hab ihn*,' says the man into the phone '*Ja, kein Problem. Bring' den Wagen zum Haus. Alles ist cool.*'

Frank is surprised by the language and changes his mind about this being local. There's not a big German connection in Liverpool. Frank switches his suspicions to his recent jaunt to Los Angeles. Maybe Dennis Sheehan's using European muscle to get his twenty-five million back. Second thoughts. Could be that Sheehan's decided he wants to keep the Brits out of this in case of any blowback. Either way, that this thing tonight has something to do with the unasked for twenty-five million dollars that Sheehan gave him for services rendered seems the more likely option.

Still, the gunman's nationality seems like an unnecessary complication that doesn't sound like Sheehan's style. If Sheehan wanted Frank to give the twenty-five mil back he only had to ask. At least that way it'd save Frank the trouble of explaining it to Charlie Searle. Right now, surviving to do that explaining is looking less likely by the second.

Frank looks over to Kath.

'You OK?'.

Kath nods.

'We'll be fine. You're doing fine.' He tries to sound convincing. Kath's a good woman and she doesn't deserve this.

'Never mind her.' The gunman snaps his fingers. 'Hey, look at me.'

Frank turns his eyes back to the gunman.

'You are Frank Keane?'

'No.'

The gunman starts to speak and then stops short, Frank's answer surprising him. He takes a small step towards Frank and smiles, lowering the temperature several degrees in the process. His face is so close that Frank can smell his breath. A smoker.

'You're Frank Keane.' This time Frank can hear the German in the guy's voice.

Frank shakes his head. 'Not me. You've made a mistake.'

The gunman is maybe ten years younger than Frank, somewhere around the thirty mark. He raises a hand and Frank, expecting a blow, braces himself. Instead, the gunman turns towards the bedroom and nods. The second gunman lifts his gun, puts the muzzle to Kath Palmer's temple and squeezes the trigger. There is a muffled boom and the side of Kath's head explodes in a spray of blood. Frank hears himself moan and he darts forward as she slumps sideways, her eyes still looking right at him, dead before she hits the pillows. Frank spins towards the gunman in the hallway and is pistol-whipped backwards. He slams against the wall and now the muzzle of the gun is pressed hard into Frank's forehead.

'Don't move unless you want me to give you an extra eye. Not a fucking centimetre. Understand, Frank?'

'You didn't have to shoot her. I hardly knew her. She didn't –'

'Quiet,' says the gunman. 'You already fucked up once tonight. Don't do it again.' Behind his shoulder Frank sees the second man come closer and look at him. He glances back towards the bedroom and raises his gun.

'Oops.' His accent made the 's' into a 'z'.

'Come,' he says to Frank. He gestures to the stairs. 'Let's go.'

Having a weapon, Frank knows, gives people a false sense of security. Often this is because they are unused or unwilling to use the gun if required. This doesn't apply here. Frank has no doubt that given a chance, the man in front of him will pull the trigger again. Frank notices the man never lets the muzzle of the gun leave Frank. All of this is bad news but doesn't stop Frank preparing to attack.

In training exercises, MIT officers are drilled in maintaining distance between a suspect and your weapon. Time and again, the mantra of distance had been stressed. Even ten metres is often enough for a suspect to close in on an officer. Frank's proximity to the gunman is a chance, an edge that Frank knows is the only card he has left. Once he allows himself to be taken there is no way back.

Here goes nothing.

Frank moves his hands to his head and rubs his eyes. His voice cracks. 'Don't kill me. Please. I don't want to die.'

The man in front of him relaxes fractionally. He's seen plenty of men cry before and it's always a good sign. It means they will do as he demands.

'Don't worry, we need you breathing,' he says and waves the gun from side to side as if to swat an annoying fly.

It's enough.

As the barrel swings marginally off line Frank lunges forward and slams into the guy's gun arm pushing it awkwardly against the banister. There is a crunching sound and the gunman howls. His broken fingers are still wrapped around the gun they are useless. The gunman in the bedroom steps back looking for a clear line to Frank but there's too much movement in the confined space.

Without pausing to think, Frank jams his finger against the trigger of the Glock and starts shooting. A bullet hits the gunman in the bedroom square in the throat and sprays the walls with blood. The guy drops, a confused expression on his face as he falls. Frank takes a good shot to the kidneys and he buckles, almost losing his grip. As the guy draws his arm back for another punch, Frank drives an elbow into the guy's nose, breaking it instantly. The German staggers back, his left hand cupping his ruined nose. Frank smashes the man's gun arm down once more on the wooden bannister rail and now the guy drops the Glock which cartwheels through the landing rails and down the stairs. Frank takes a quick step forward and head butts the guy. The contact isn't good but it's enough to unbalance the big man at the top of the stairs. As he teeters on the brink, Frank kicks him in the knee using the ball of his upturned heel to achieve maximum impact. Something snaps and the German falls, screaming, down the wooden stairs. As he hits bottom Frank hears another sound. Without ever having heard anything like it before, Frank knows instantly that it is the sound of a neck breaking.

Outside Frank hears a vehicle engine gunning up the hill towards the barn. Frank runs to the bedroom where Kath is lying half in and half out of the bed. The back of her head is gone. On the floor next to the bed is the man who shot her. Without thinking, Frank kicks the dead man in the stomach. *Fuck*.

Outside, tyres crunch on gravel.

Frank grabs the backpack containing the items he'd bought in Liverpool and a pair of trainers from under the bed. He sprints downstairs, vaulting the German at the foot of the stairs and bangs hard into a wall. Frank feels blood trickling onto his brow from the dressing over his biopsy scar and wipes it away with the back of his arm.

There are headlights outside and Frank swings away from them towards the back door. At the last minute he changes his mind and turns into the utility room at the side of the property. Here there is a door which leads into a small walled courtyard. Frank's betting whoever's outside hasn't spotted this exit.

As he steps through the door into the courtyard he glances over his shoulder towards the kitchen door and sees it start to open. Frank carefully closes the utility room door and, as quietly as possible, steps onto a bin and over the wall. Out here he's fully exposed. He drops low to the grass and runs hard for the small copse of trees thirty metres away, feeling the grass and soil beneath his bare feet expecting a bullet at any moment.

He doesn't look back.

53

Helsby, Cheshire, October 21st

Hoffen is in the driving seat of the van parked just off the road on the tail end of a farmer's gravel track waiting for the call. He sits patiently for a few minutes and then, right on time, the screen lights up and there's Neumann telling him to come in for the pick-up, everything as planned. They have the target.

Hoffen starts the engine and almost immediately hears gunfire so close to him turning the key that his first thought is that the noise was a backfire. Then he replays the sound and knows. Shooting? Why would anyone worth their salt need to shoot? Go in, grab the guy and roll. Instead, now he has this shit to deal with, whatever *this* turns out to be. He puts the van back into neutral and waits, his hands on the wheel, the engine running, cursing inwardly at the stupidity of the men he'd sent in to pick up the target.

No matter what's happening in there he needs to hear from Neumann again before he moves. His phone sits on the dash, the screen black.

In his heart of hearts Hoffen knows that the pickup is now probably fucked. Either the target is dead or the target is gone. Hoffen hopes that, of the two outcomes, it is the second. Better to have the guy alive and running than lying in there with a bullet in him.

If he's alive, Hoffen will find him. Dead, they have a problem.

The phone rings once and then goes silent as Hoffen hears another shot and then one more. He swears and turns the van towards the barn. In normal circumstances he'd have driven off leaving Gottlenz's idiots to fix whatever was going on inside there. Instead, he's going to have to take some unnecessary risks.

He pulls up in front of the barn, picks up the Uzi from under the passenger seat and heads to the back of the house. At the kitchen door he waits for a second sensing someone moving around. He steps inside, turns on the kitchen light and moves across the stone floor to the stairs.

Neumann is lying in the small hallway at the base of the stairs. He looks dead. Hoffen is about to move on when Neumann groans and opens his eyes.

Hoffen bends down and places the Uzi on the floor. He grips Neumann's head and twists violently. There is a soft popping sound and now Neumann is dead. Hoffen has no intention of leaving behind an injured witness and the chances of getting Neumann back to Berlin without being stopped are zero. It had to be done.

Hoffen wipes Neumann's blood off his hands on the dead man's jacket, picks up the Uzi and gets to his feet.

Upstairs he finds a dead woman on the bed and an equally dead Ezterhaus on the floor.

Jesus Christ. What a fuck up.

Hoffen steps across to the back window and sees the faint shape of a man running fast towards a copse of trees silhouetted on the horizon by the Ellesmere Port lights.

Hoffen walks downstairs and heads out towards the black trees.

54

Helsby, Cheshire, October 21st

Frank makes it to the woods without getting a bullet in the back.

The foliage is thick and heavy, the welcoming shadows black. Frank embraces the darkness like a friend, burrowing deeper and deeper into its velvet embrace, ignoring the stones and sticks that jab his unprotected feet.

He blunders about thirty metres in and stops, his breath ragged. If anyone is chasing him the last thing he wants to do is attract attention, so he tries to slow his breathing. His first instinct – to run – might not be the best option regardless of how attractive it appears. He could be heading straight into more gunmen on the other side of the trees. Frank has no way of knowing how many of these fuckers are out there. They might have been waiting for the guy in the barn to flush him out like a beater raising a reluctant pheasant.

Conscious of his white skin against the darkness he scoops up handfuls of earth and, feeling foolish, rubs the dirt over his face and arms. He scrabbles into the running shoes. Having something on his feet gives him a little more confidence. He shelters behind the trunk of a tree and looks back towards the barn. He remembers an item he'd got from Prior and rummages around in the backpack. He lifts out a slim black waistcoat made from a strange fabric. It's a bullet proof vest – the world's lightest. Frank had seen the company CEO, a tall Anglo-German guy, on YouTube getting shot by a 9 mm Glock at point blank range to prove the efficiency of the fabric and that had been good enough to make the purchase. Prior had also added a stab vest made by the same company but Frank decides the bulletproof will be more likely to be needed. If they get close enough to stab him he'll be dead anyway. Frank cinches the Velcro vest tight around his waist. If nothing else it makes him feel better. His head is hurting which makes Frank remember his bandage showing white. He carefully peels it off, hoping the biopsy wound has stopped bleeding. The cold air feels good against his scalp and there's no more blood. Frank's not sure that rubbing soil into the fresh scar would be recommended by his doctors but it can't be helped. If he gets shot in the next few minutes then having a clean biopsy wound won't mean a thing. Dead is dead.

For a few minutes nothing happens. It's clear that no-one locally has heard the gunshots. Julie's parents place is reasonably isolated and the Palmer house is empty. Frank feels another sharp stab of guilt at the thought of Kath Palmer that he knows he'll be feeling until the day he dies.

Which could be much sooner than he'd like.

If the events at the barn show one thing it is that the people coming after Frank are deadly serious. This is not going away any time soon.

A car engine starts up in the lane at the front of the barn and Frank watches as a dark-coloured van heads down the road that circles around the woods. Frank follows the headlights as much as he can before they drop below a rise in the ground. Maybe the guy is gone? Or, more likely, he is going to come at Frank from the other direction.

Frank waits.

Five tension-filled minutes later there is movement from the direction of the barn and Frank sees a shadowy figure, backlit by the lights from Ellesmere Port, walk slowly up the path, carrying a heavy-looking object in his left hand. The man moves slow and easy, someone comfortable in his work. A faint smell of petrol drifts towards the copse.

The guy circles the cottage splashing liquid against the walls. At this distance Frank can't hear anything but the smell's getting stronger by the second. When the container is empty the guy pauses and stands for a minute, listening. He lifts something from a pocket. Frank sees the flare of a match.

The man in the shadows tosses the match onto the floor and steps away from the barn.

With a soft *whoomp* the fumes ignite and then, rapidly, the gasoline. In seconds the barn is an inferno. Illuminated by the flames, Frank sees the guy take a gun from his coat and head straight towards him.

Frank wants to run but the thought of the van circling back around the copse keeps him still. If, as he suspects, there is another gunman it makes sense that he'd be behind the woods. Which would mean that Frank is trapped.

The shooter walks steadily across the grass, his shadow dancing in the light from the blaze and heads directly towards the trees. There's a confidence that suggests he's done this sort of thing before. It's not a comforting thought.

Frank settles his breathing as best he can and stifles an almost overpowering urge to cough.

The guy keeps coming. If there is a second guy Frank can't see him and he weighs up the odds of making a run for it.

Instead he keeps still, willing his eyes to adjust more quickly to the shadows. There's some light from the house fire but this far into the woods little of it creeps through.

The trees run up and over a rise before dipping down towards the road about three hundred metres away. Frank again tries to measure how far he has to run to get there, but he decides against it. With a possible fourth gunman around it's too risky. He'll have to think of something else.

Frank's attacker also stops and waits. A patient man. Someone less professional would have blundered straight in. This guy knows that waiting for movement or noise is the best strategy.

And then, from the house comes an explosion as the fire reaches a gas canister in the kitchen. The shooter is momentarily silhouetted as he looks back towards the burning house. Taking advantage of the distraction Frank swings himself up into the branches of a tree and wedges himself as best he can in the centre of the foliage, the backpack on his shoulders. The tree is easy to climb but Frank still makes enough noise for the gunman to hear. He turns towards the woods with real purpose.

Frank holds himself still, lying along the thickest branch. Prey has three options. Run, fight, or hide. Frank is gambling all on the last.

The shooter's close now, moving more slowly as he gets nearer to where he heard the noise and Frank presses his face closer against the bark, closing off all distractions. Everything is reduced to a simple thought. Remain concealed or die.

The guy's four metres away and about a metre below Frank. He's carrying a stocky-looking gun with a short barrel. Even in the darkness, to Frank's eyes there's something vaguely military about the weapon.

Minutes pass; Frank's not sure how many. The shooter is prepared to wait. Above him on the branch, Frank's muscles begin to tremble with the strain of staying motionless and with the cold. It might be only October but this is the north.

The two men wait in the darkness in complete silence.

Then, in the distance blue lights flicker through the trees and the shooter watches for a few seconds before pushing on through the woods away from the barn. There's no sense of panic at the imminent arrival of the emergency vehicles. Frank stays where he is.

The flashing blue lights are closer now, almost at the turn up the hill and the shooter has gone. There are headlights moving away on another road and Frank wonders if that is the van. He has no way of telling but he drops down from the branch and watches the barn burn, aware that he has arrived at a crossroads. The old Clash song runs through his head. Should I stay or should I go? After a minute he pulls out a windcheater from the backpack, puts it on over the bullet proof vest and starts moving away from the burning barn.

There's nothing for him back there except trouble. If someone's putting this much effort into trying to kill him, the problem isn't going to go away on its own.

On the top of the hill, the first emergency vehicle reaches the fire just as the roof falls in. By that time, Frank has made the road. He puts one foot in front of the other and heads for the motorway knowing that back there in the barn a line has been crossed. In more than twenty years as a cop he's never killed anyone.

Now he has. What's bothering him is that he doesn't care.

55

Berlin, October 21st

Ilsa Bruckner is at home when her phone vibrates on the bedside table. It goes off before she can reach it. Sleep-fogged, she reaches across and looks at the caller.

Hoffen.

Bruckner gets out of bed and shrugs on a dressing gown while she waits for Hoffen to call back. She won't call him. Failure isn't something she thinks about, but she prefers it this way just in case she's ever sitting on the wrong side of a police interview table.

She has a full surgery tomorrow and knows that with this disturbance she will struggle to get back to sleep. In the circumstances, she has no option. With Hoffen in England, Bruckner can't afford to leave anything to chance. The client needs the donor kidney and needs it soon. With so much riding on the income she's supplying to *Kolumne88's* project there's no room for drama.

Bruckner switches on the light downstairs and fills the coffee pot. Her phone buzzes once more while she's waiting.

'This better be good news,' says Bruckner.

She listens as Hoffen talks.

56

Berlin, October 21st

Weiss and Dreschler are both talking on their phones when Cooper gets back to the car and neither of them stop when she arrives. They are still talking as they drive away from the clinic. The notebook containing Anna Ziegler's words feels radioactive on Cooper's lap and the longer she waits to tell Weiss and Dreschler, the more awkward the situation becomes; at least in her own mind. For no reason she can easily define, Cooper feels guilty about what happened in the hospital and the seconds tick by one after the other without her finding the right moment to tell the Germans. In the end she just lifts out the notebook, flips it open at the right page, leans forward and places it on Robert Weiss's lap.

Weiss picks it up and stares at the page blankly as Dreschler looks over, her eyebrows raised. Weiss says something to the person on his phone and hangs up. Dreschler does the same.

'Anna wrote this,' says Cooper, pointing at the spidery letters. 'Back there, after you'd gone.' To her embarrassment and anger she feels herself blushing. 'I started writing a note. She grabbed my hand and asked for the pen.'

'She spoke?' says Dreschler. 'No. Surely not.'

'*Warum spricht sie mit Cooper?*' Weiss says, looking at Dreschler who shrugs.

'Can you speak English?' says Cooper. 'If you're going to talk about me. I can understand some things. I don't think she targeted me particularly.'

'No?'

'I think it was the pen,' says Cooper. 'She took hold of the pen.'

'And then you made her write?' Weiss's expression is neutral.

'I didn't *make* her do anything.' Cooper puts a little iron in her tone. 'She wanted to. All I did was help.'

'Is she still conscious? Why not tell us straight away? She could give us information.'

Cooper shakes her head. 'I don't think she can. Not now anyway. She exhausted herself writing the note so I got a nurse in and she checked Anna. She's asleep.' Cooper looks at both LKA officers, this time with some heat. 'And *this* is me telling you *now.*'

'We can go back,' says Weiss but Dreschler shakes her head.

'Theresa says she is too tired. Call and get a uniform in there in case she wakes.' Dreschler points to Cooper's notebook. 'This is what she wanted to say.' He looks at Cooper and nods. 'You did well. I'm sorry if I am too hard.'

'That's OK,' says Cooper.

Weiss takes out his phone and speaks rapidly in German. When he has finished Cooper taps the notebook.

'These words, what do they mean? I should probably know but I don't.'

'*Oper* is opera. *Tod* is death.'

'Does that mean anything to either of you?'

Dreschler and Weiss exchange the sort of glance that can only happen between lovers or close colleagues. Cooper gets the impression in this case it's the latter not the former and that some sort of complex signal has been exchanged. 'No, not really,' says Weiss. Dreschler says nothing.

Cooper doesn't ask the question she wants to. It's obvious that both LKA officers know more. She doesn't feel annoyed; she may very well have done the same with a German officer in Liverpool. Through the window Cooper catches a fleeting glimpse of the Brandenburg Gate as the car crosses *Unter den Linden*. It's a forceful reminder that she is in a foreign city with a job to do that does not include getting involved in a localised assault. The attack on Anna Ziegler and the words on the notebook are none of her business.

Back at the LKA office there is a palpable sense of energy inside the building and Cooper knows that this is connected to what happened to Ziegler. As soon as they arrive Weiss slips away to a briefing leaving Dreschler to give Cooper a temporary berth.

'You might as well use Anna's desk,' says Dreschler. 'You will be gone by the time she gets out.'

Neither of them acknowledges the possibility that Ziegler may never return to the *Landeskriminalamt.*

Dreschler casts a glance over her shoulder. 'I have to go to the briefing. I'll be back soon and we can start. Perhaps you can make a schedule for me of what you want today?'

'That's fine. Thanks.'

Dreschler departs with a brisk nod and Cooper sits down and puts her bag on the floor next to the chair. She slides her laptop out and is placing it on the desk when Dreschler returns with a slim file.

'This is what we have on the vehicle.' Dreschler hands the file to Cooper. 'It is not much and is in German but I will help you with anything you don't understand when I get back.'

When Dreschler has gone, Cooper sees that almost everyone in this office has disappeared too. With a fellow officer so badly beaten everyone wants to make themselves useful. Cooper's heart sinks. Her own improbable chase after information on the stolen Mercedes van seems silly by comparison. Cooper reminds herself of Sarah Coughlan and sits upright in the chair. She opens the file and tries to make sense of the pages. Inside a minute she knows it is impossible. She needs Dreschler.

Cooper drums her fingers on Ziegler's desk. She opens her laptop and tries to find the Wi-Fi link without success. Blowing out her cheeks she sits back and folds her arms. This trip has the feel of a complete waste of time. Without firm ID on the two abductors she doubts she'll be able to gouge anything useful out of Berlin.

Her gaze drifts back to the various items on Ziegler's desk. Stacked files, a stapler, a coffee mug. On the pin boards that form an L-shape on two sides of the desk, Ziegler seems to have assembled a blizzard of post-it notes, street flyers, official-looking letters along with far too many images of cats for Cooper's liking. One small newspaper clipping, half-hidden under what looks like a recipe, catches Cooper's eye. A black and white image of a grand, colonnaded building has the headline: *Oper Tod.*

Cooper leans forward and takes the pin from the clipping.

At first, she can translate little of the story but, after a few painstaking minutes and the use of an application on her phone, she has the general drift. The story is the discovery of a stabbing victim at the *Staatsoper*, Berlin's opera house, just over a week ago. Otto Leunze, a man in his sixties and a casual employee of the opera company, stabbed in an apparently random attack during a performance of *Parsifal*, his body concealed behind curtains.

Cooper takes out her notebook and makes notes of the location, the name of the victim and the relevant dates and times. She replaces the clipping where she found it, unsure of what to do next. There seems to be no reason for Ziegler to have passed this information on.

Cooper takes out her own file on the Mercedes van and reads it while she waits for Dreschler to return.

57

Helsby, Cheshire, October 21st

Frank has found out that he is capable of fighting. Capable of killing.

Back there in the barn, without thinking too much about it, he had killed before being killed. He had always thought that if that time ever came that it would bring with it a tidal wave of guilt. Instead, he feels nothing about the dead men. They made a choice and they must have known there was risk involved.

Kath Palmer is quite another matter.

With these deaths a line has been crossed and Frank's not sure he'll ever be able to step back over to the other side. Right now, as he puts one foot in front of the other and heads along the narrow, high-hedged side roads towards Runcorn, his old self sloughing off like discarded snakeskin with each yard he puts between himself and the crime scene, Frank's not sure he wants to. The killing of the two intruders have focused his attention. Jane Watson's warning it turns out, has teeth. Someone really is after him, someone serious and Frank's status as a suspended cop isn't going to help much.

The system's not going to fix this. This is not going to be handled the official way. Not by him at least. Persuading the authorities to swallow Frank's version of events will be too hard, even for MIT. The bodies in the barn will be investigated and he may well come under suspicion. The best outcome, the one he's hoping for, is that one of the dead will be assumed to be Frank. It all depends on the ferocity of the blaze. If it has reduced the bodies to ash then it is possible that the causes of death may be impossible to discover, the identities of the victims lost.

If the forensic search is anything but perfect they may not find the bullets. They will, almost certainly, find the remaining weapon and Frank curses himself for not taking it. The fact that it was arson will tell the investigators at least one person is still out there.

The question is: will they think it's him?

The answer is: probably not. Not at first and not without motive. He knows that Charlie Searle will prefer the mess at Helsby to be sealed in a neat box called 'unsolved'. He will have no appetite for digging deep if he suspects the end result may point the finger at one of his officers. When Menno Koopman was set up for a murder he didn't commit he ran and then changed his mind. But there is one big difference between the Koopman situation and it is this: Koopman didn't kill anyone and Frank did. Self-defense for sure, but he doesn't fancy explaining the illegal Glock. Coming on top of the twenty-five million from Sheehan it doesn't look good.

There's another, more urgent, reason to drop out of sight and that is that the arsonist did not have the look of someone who would be easily scared off. He, or someone like him, will be back and he'll be back with more people. Frank could look for protection but he's encouraged witnesses plenty of times and some of them got buried, eventually. If these guys are who he thinks they are, if they want someone badly enough, they'll get them so that idea is shelved.

The third thing is that he needs to start getting better. He needs to begin taking the fight against this disease seriously, to start battling the parasites inside him as well as those on the outside. Becoming embroiled in some drawn out legal saga won't help. He needs to be selfish, needs to get out of town and use the money to help himself. The question is: how does he drop out of sight and still be able to follow through with the fight against this tumour?

And, as soon as he's posed the question he knows the answer. He knows exactly how he's going to be able to drop from view and still be able to get the treatment he needs. It's risky but he can't see any other option.

Half an hour after cleaning the dirt off his face as best he can and sticking his thumb out on the slip road to the M56, Frank picks up a ride from a refinery truck out of Ellesmere Port.

'Where you heading?' says the old boy leaning out of the driver's window.

'North.' Until the guy asks, Frank hadn't been sure of which way he is going but north feels right. 'Scotland, maybe.'

'I can take you to Carlisle. That's about as far as I go.'

'Cheers,' says Frank and hauls himself up into the passenger seat. The driver holds out a hand. 'Harry.'

Frank shakes his hand. 'Tom.' Even he notices the hesitation before he gives the false name but the driver doesn't react.

'OK,' he says, 'Tom,' and pulls the truck back onto the road.

As the road unwinds under the wheels of the oil truck, and he puts some distance between himself and the carnage at Helsby, an idea begins to form. The old boy likes to talk but not too much. Frank gets time to think. They listen to the radio and talk football and the truck driver doesn't ask anything personal. At a service station just south of Carlisle Frank switches rides and gets a lift from a nervy businessman in a Beemer who, despite the baby seat in the back – or maybe because of it – makes a cack-handed attempt at seduction. Frank gives him the salesman the bad news about his sexual orientation and the guy takes it well enough. He drops Frank in the centre of Glasgow and drives off quickly.

At an electrical store Frank buys a laptop and iPhone, glad he'd stashed a couple of grand in the emergency backpack he'd assembled in Liverpool two days ago. He gets fresh clothes at an outdoors specialist: a long-brimmed cap, some t-shirts, a flannel shirt, a thick fleece jacket, some hard-wearing khakis and a pair of waterproof, lightweight hiking boots. He wishes he'd bought these items a few days back and used his credit cards but he hadn't thought he'd need this stuff so soon. The purchases use up a chunk of his remaining cash but, if what he has in mind works, that won't be a problem for too long.

After the experience in the Beemer, Frank decides to change his transport and takes the train north to Inverness through a quickly darkening Scotland. He buys a first class ticket, partly for the comfort, but primarily in order that he'll be left alone. He washes and changes in the station toilets and emerges a new man, another hiker heading to the Highlands.

Ten minutes later the train slides into the station and Frank sinks back into his seat. He keeps his cap pulled down and the collar of his fleece turned up. He stares out of the window and watches the grim outer suburbs of Glasgow slowly give way to the brooding hills and lochs. He takes a beer and a sandwich from the waiter whose accent reminds him of Bernie. Frank swallows some painkillers as dessert and tries not to think about Kath Palmer. He can save that particular level of guilt for another time.

By the time he arrives in Inverness it's half six and pitch-black. The town feels colder than Frank would have thought possible. By comparison, Cheshire was Antigua. He pats himself on the back for buying some warmer gear. Outside the station, just across the river, he stops at the first big-sized chain hotel he sees. He needs access to communications and a smaller place won't cut it. The hotel is a large one, American-owned. Anonymous.

The only hitch is his lack of a credit card.

'I was robbed,' says Frank to the receptionist. 'Some bastard stole my car. I'd left my stuff inside.' He fishes his remaining money from his pocket and peels off three hundred. 'This'll cover things, I'm sure,' he says.

'I shouldnae really,' says the girl. She glances around the room and then leans a little closer across the desk. 'You're supposed to have a credit card. For charges to the room, that kind of thing.'

Frank takes another fifty and slides it across. 'Not everyone, right?'

The girl hesitates and then snakes out a hand to scoop up the note.

'Ye can fill in the details when ye have them, OK?'

In his room Frank showers but doesn't shave. With a towel wrapped around his waist he sits at the small desk and lifts the laptop from its packaging. After some false starts, he logs onto the hotel Wi-Fi.

It doesn't take him long to find the number he's looking for.

Loder Industries.

58

Berlin, October 21st

After the attack on Ziegler, LKA is in overdrive and Cooper's request to visit the B-Kreuz-Scharmer Clinic is downgraded to somewhere south of zero on the priority scale. Dreschler and Weiss have no time to spare and Cooper would prefer not to go there without her liaison. She knows she'll only get one decent pass at the clinic so she decides to wait for Dreschler and Weiss to get something going on Ziegler. Cooper understands. Back home, the last thing she'd be interested in if one of MIT had been beaten as badly as Anna, would be baby-sitting some foreign cop chasing a stolen van.

Which means Cooper has time on her hands. After an hour doing little at LKA she takes Ziegler's Bruckner file and heads out of LKA.

Her first call is at the Opera House. After a heated exchange with the spectacularly uncooperative woman in the manager's office, during which Cooper threatens to bring in the LKA, she is eventually granted access. Ten minutes in and she's not sure it was worth the trouble. She sees the auditorium and the spot where Otto Leunze was found. There is nothing left there to indicate what happened. There are no personal items at the Opera House belonging to Leunze, no indication of his employment other than on payroll files. The CCTV footage has already been taken by LKA and Cooper knows from Weiss that it revealed nothing. Rapidly losing confidence in this as a source of information she shows Bruckner's picture to a couple of maintenance people and draws blanks.

Outside she gets a taxi to Otto Leunze's apartment. She calls ahead and manages to speak to the widow. Cooper's not sure if she made her meaning clear, so when she presses the apartment buzzer she's interested to see what happens.

Otto Leunze's widow, Hanna, turns out to be a small-boned, dark-haired woman in her early sixties, who is pleased enough to see Cooper despite the English police officer's creaky German. She shows Cooper up to the second floor apartment in a shabby suburb to the east of the city. Smiling, Hanna Leunze indicates an armchair in the apartment's main living room, crowded with books and bric-a-brac and dominated by a massive flat screen television which has been draped with a lace tablecloth.

'Sit, yes?'

Cooper sits, yes and Hanna Leunze mimes drinking from a cup.

'Tea?' says Cooper, in German. Hanna smiles. Her eyes are red but she looks like she has already made some mental adjustments after the loss of her husband. Cooper's met other fatalistic widows like this before; often religious.

'Yes, tea. Good.' Hanna Leunze leaves Cooper and heads for the kitchen. The sound of cups being rattled comes through the open door.

The Leunze apartment, although small and crowded enough to be claustrophobic, every centimetre of wall space hung with photographs and paintings, every windowsill and side table groaning with knick-knacks, is clean and tidy. Cooper looks across at a well-worn Laz-E-Boy armchair facing the TV and can almost see Otto. The only photograph in the file Dreschler grudgingly handed her of Otto Leunze shows a younger man wearing a suit, the image taken from someone's wedding. A pair of faded tartan slippers are lined up next to the chair waiting for an owner who will never wear them again.

When Hanna Luenze comes back in with the tea, Cooper is looking at the slippers and glances away, embarrassed, as if caught stealing. I am stealing, thinks Cooper. I'm stealing her memories of her husband. That's what we do.

'Thank you,' she says as Hanna hands her a china cup.

'So,' says Hanna, taking a seat on the small sofa and settling into a corner like the missing piece of a jigsaw, 'what can I tell you?'

Cooper and Hanna Leunze talk for a while. Cooper shows Hanna Ziegler's photo of Ilsa Bruckner, she has never seen her before. There is no connection between the Leunze's and Bruckner, no illnesses that took them to Bruckner's clinic, no secrets that Hanna is aware of, no gambling, no links with *Kolumne88*.

'*Kolumne88?*' says Hanna. 'They are Nazis. Is it likely Otto would have anything to do with Nazis?' Hanna indicates a yarmulke on a side table. 'We are Jews.'

Cooper packs away the file and gets to her feet. There's nothing in this. Ziegler's obsession is just that. The idea that Ilsa Bruckner killed Otto Leunze simply because he was Jewish – and did it during a performance, in full view of anyone who happened to be passing – was too much to contemplate. For that to have happened the woman would have to be a complete psychopath.

59

Inverness, Scotland, October 21st

Loder Industries are one of the most powerful private organisations in existence. Their influence stretches out from the base in Texas in a direct line through Washington and from there to the rest of the world. Construction, communications, security. These are the foundations of a multi-billion-dollar empire with one man at the very top of a very profitable tree.

It's this man that Frank Keane is calling from the hotel in Inverness. A man who owes Frank one last favour.

Of course, he doesn't get through. But he does, after three attempts, manage to speak to a buttoned-up kind of guy in the main office.

'I'd like to speak to Mr Sheehan.'

'I'm afraid Mr Sheehan is unavailable.'

'Tell him Frank Keane wants to talk. Tell him it concerns Ben. Do you have the number I'm calling from? It's in Scotland. Inverness.'

'Yes, but I really don't think . . .'

Frank hangs up. The guy on the other end won't be able to *not* pass the message higher. It's the American way. Just the chance that Sheehan might want to speak to the caller is enough. Someone is going to call back.

Two hours later the phone rings.

'Mr Keane?' This time it's a woman.

'Yes.'

'I'm checking you're there. The person you asked for is unavailable. Do not call again. Your business with him is concluded.'

'Tell Sheehan it's all going to be in the papers tomorrow about Ben. Everything. And I mean the quality papers, the kind his investors read. He needs to speak to me.'

Again, Frank hangs up. This time his heart is beating noticeably faster. Sheehan's not someone you want to be fucking around with.

This time there's only six minutes before the phone rings.

'Mr Keane.' It's Dennis Sheehan, no question. There are clicks on the line. Keane doesn't know if that's because the conversation is being recorded, or if it's being scrambled. Or simply because Dennis Sheehan is calling from a jet. Or the moon. 'I didn't think I'd ever speak to you again. I'm hoping that this isn't what I think it might be.'

'Which is?'

'A shakedown.'

'No, it's not. And I apologise for the deception. This has nothing to do with Ben.'

There is a short silence from Sheehan. 'Go on. You have one minute.'

'Some people tried to kill me.' Frank pauses. 'I need something from you. It will be the last thing I will ever ask.'

'This *is* a shakedown .'

'I don't want any more money but I do need two things from you. If you tell me you can't do it then that's that. I'm not making a demand. I'm asking as a favour.' Frank lets that hang. Both men are thinking the same thing: Frank Keane almost lost his life stopping Sheehan's psychopathic son slaughtering hundreds of innocent people.

Sheehan still owes. It's a good card to call in. Frank's silence is worth more than the twenty-five million.

'What do you want?'

'Someone tried to kill me. At first I thought it was you but it's related to something else. They burnt down my in-laws place with three people inside and there's a fair chance that you are the only person alive who knows I'm not dead. I'm placing trust in you and assuming that you are an honourable man.'

'Go on.' Sheehan's voice is like distant thunder.

'I lost everything in the fire. These are the things I need. I need a new passport, a British one. A genuine one in another name, I don't care what. I want some supporting documentation to back up that passport. I want the twenty-five million you gave to me to be assigned to that new name, right down to the company details and I want the investigation into the fire in Helsby to –'

'Helsby?'

'Where these people tried to kill me. I want that investigation to conclude categorically I was one of the victims. Can you do that?'

Sheehan doesn't reply. A few seconds pass and Frank wonders if he's conferring with someone. He gets an image of an assistant shaking his head, no.

'Yes,' says Sheehan. 'We can do that. Anything else?'

'I need a credit card attached to the account you set up. And I need them right here in Inverness as soon as possible.'

'That's it?'

'No. I need full, identity-protected access to the specialised US Air Force medical facilities at Lakenheath.'

'I thought we'd fixed your wounds?'

'I have cancer. I may need an operation and until I'm sure no-one is coming for me I'd prefer to stay off-radar. They'll need all my medical records.'

'Cancer? You are having a time of it, Mr Keane. OK, Lakenheath it is. I'll see what I can do.'

Sheehan pauses and when he speaks again his tone has changed. 'You are an interesting individual, Mr Keane,' he says. 'We may be in touch.'

The line goes dead. Frank doesn't know what he was expecting from Sheehan but the guy doesn't waste any time on social niceties.

He lies down on the bed and turns off the light. In the darkness Frank considers the distinct possibility that Dennis Sheehan will simply call in a cleanup crew and take him out. It's something that may be more appealing than handing over the passport.

Frank's gambling everything on the phone call.

He closes his eyes and wonders if they'll ever open again. Thinking about it he finds he doesn't really care one way or the other. He just wants to sleep.

60

Liverpool, October 22nd

Harris could simply call Charlie Searle to give him the two items of information that land on her desk on Thursday morning except that this news is the kind best passed along face to face. She calls ahead and discovers he's attending a symposium on anti-terror legislation at the Hilton just across the street from Canning Place.

Searle, in full uniform, is coming out of a conference room at the hotel with two other brass when Harris spots him. Searle sees her and holds up a hand, indicting for her to wait while he finishes chatting. After a minute or two the boy's club breaks up and Searle walks across, a quizzical look on his face.

'Apologies, for the interruption sir,' says Harris. 'I know you're busy here.'

'These things are vitally important, DI Harris,' says Searle, his voice sharp. 'I'm detecting some sarcasm in your tone.'

'Absolutely not, sir.'

Searle motions to a couple of armchairs facing the window and the two of them sit.

'It must be something bad,' he says. 'You've got that look.'

'It is, sir. Three things.'

'Spit them out.'

'One is that there may be a political angle.'

Charlie Searle raises his eyebrows. 'Oh?'

'The dead men? One of them was a Nazi. Probably.'

'What?'

'A neo-Nazi. He had a tattoo.'

'Don't they all? Jesus.'

'This one said "9th of November 1938". It's a German extremist group.'

'OK. But that's not why you're here.'

'No, sir.' Harris pauses. She should have started with the news, not waffled on about Nazis. As if in agreement, Searle consults his watch.

'The second thing is something one of my DS's turned up, sir. DS Magsi. I had him digging into the abduction victim's background. A bit of a dead end in all honesty but he came back with this.' Harris hands over the sheet detailing Sarah Coughlan's background.

Searle looks annoyed. 'Just tell me what he found, DI Harris.' He glances at his watch. 'I'm a little pushed for time.'

'Sarah Coughlan was adopted. Her biological parents are both dead but DS Magsi discovered that Sarah Coughlan was related to one of our officers.'

'Oh?'

'She was Frank Keane's half-sister.'

Charlie Searle sits forward, rests his elbows on his knees and knits his hands together to support his chin.

'What?'

'Sarah Coughlan's biological father was listed as Michael Keane, Frank Keane's father. DS Magsi talked to the adoption people and Sarah Coughlan's biological mother had given her up for adoption when she was three years old. What the story is with Keane's father and this child we don't know. Both Frank's parents are dead.'

'Has Frank ever mentioned a sister?'

Harris shakes her head. 'Not to me.'

'Get him in,' says Searle, his expression grim. 'DCI Keane needs to talk to us whether the Home Office likes it or not.'

'It's entirely possible, likely even, that Frank doesn't know Sarah Coughlan is dead. He may not even know he has a sister.' Harris rewinds Searle's last statement in her head to make sure she'd heard correctly. Home Office?

'There's not much that gets past Keane,' Searle murmurs.

'That's not everything, sir. The main reason I came here is the news I got half an hour ago.' If Searle's going to go ballistic this is going to be where it happens. 'In the light of the Sarah Coughlan information I thought it best we speak to Frank – to DCI Keane – so I called him. He didn't answer so I called his ex. She told me he's been staying at a barn her parents own in Cheshire.'

'I thought he had a flat in town?'

'Maybe he wanted a change of scene?' She pauses and Searle motions impatiently for her to continue. 'Anyway, I called the place at Helsby and got no reply. This morning I heard from Cheshire Police that the property DCI Keane was staying in was burnt to the ground last night. Almost certainly arson.'

'What?' Searle pulls his chin down and peers up at Harris. '*Arson?*'

Harris nods. 'Looks that way.'

'Keane's OK?'

'There were three bodies in the building, sir.'

'Three? Is he one of them?'

Harris shrugs. 'From what I understand they are so badly burnt that the pathologist will struggle to identify their sex, let alone anything else. I heard that there's no sign of the next door neighbours. It's possible that they and DCI Keane are the victims.'

Searle is shaking his head from side to side. 'Christ Almighty, what a fucking shambles.' He gets to his feet and Harris follows suit follows as he paces across the lobby. 'It won't be us handling the investigation. That will obviously be the Cheshire lot but I want you to keep me fully informed of any developments. And, until we know otherwise, we're regarding this as a tragedy for DCI Keane.'

'Tragedy?'

Searle looks at Harris and she sees the steel under his politician's skin. 'I'm almost hoping they *do* find Keane has been barbequed.' Searle leans a little closer and drops his voice. 'Because if he isn't – and given Keane's recent record I strongly suspect he most definitely isn't dead – then he has more than a little explaining to do, don't you think? And if DCI Keane has some explaining to do then it follows, as surely as sharks follow ships, that *I* will also have some explaining to do and that particular steaming pile of crap is something I think we all want to avoid. Right?'

Searle moves to go and then turns back, his face twisted in fury. 'And if you hear so much as a word from Keane I want to know immediately, DC Harris. I don't care if it's a text, face-to-face, or if the slippery bastard communicates using semaphore, pigeon post or fucking smoke signals. If he's out there, tweeting, blinking, winking or farting, you tell me first.'

Em Harris watches Searle, the chameleon, rejoin the conference attendees, a warm sincere smile in place, his hand clapping someone on the back. How do you do that? Harris heads for the lobby thinking about Frank, not sure if she should be grieving or starting a case file.

61

Berlin, October 21st

'Who is this guy?'

There's a tone in Hoffen's voice that Bruckner doesn't like. A hard edge to his words.

'What?'

'The pick-up in England. He killed two of Gottlenz's men. Shot one and broke the neck of another. These men are not good soldiers but they would be tough enough to deal with a civilian. This pickup is not a civilian. I ask again, Ilsa. Who is the target?'

'Gottlenz supplied the name from the usual source. He didn't say anything about the target except name and address. You know how it works. The data source identifies the target and Gottlenz sees to the pickup. I assumed everything would be as normal. You were supposed to be the insurance, Hoffen.' Bruckner puts vinegar into her tone. '*You're* the one who has messed up. It is not good.'

'I did mess up. This is true. I messed up by not doing this myself from the start. I messed up by not bringing my own team. I messed up by not doing my homework. We should have researched this target, spent some time getting it right.'

'We don't have much time! Not even two weeks. The client needs the kidney for his treatment and we need his money if we are to finish this on schedule. No donor, no payout. We are already cutting it fine on the timing. We need this donor at the clinic and we need him there soon. The client does not have much time and he is a very demanding man. He will go elsewhere soon. If he can.'

'Can he?'

'It's possible,' says Bruckner. 'There are one or two clinics like ours.' She speaks as though the clinic is her own personal property which Hoffen knows is not the case. Other than a bent anesthetist and a security guy who turns a blind eye for a slice, Bruckner does all the dirty work herself.

'I spent some time today digging into this man, the one in England. He's a cop, Ilsa, did you know that? Detective Chief Inspector Frank Keane. High-ranking. And, worse, not just any cop, this one seems to know his stuff. He managed to kill two of our men. Now, despite my personal opinion of the quality of our recruitment, killing two armed goons isn't a bad effort. It wouldn't surprise me if he turns out to have some sort of military, or even intelligence, background. Do we really need someone like that sticking his nose into what we're doing? There is less than a month to go. Are you out of your tiny mind?'

Bruckner is silent for a short time. Hoffen can hear her breathing heavily. Both she and Hoffen are aware that something is changing in the dynamic between them. It is something to do with Bruckner's ambitions and Hoffen's skills. She is impatient to get Keane and Hoffen is the only one who can deliver him.

'We need him,' she says in the end.

'He's that rare?'

'There are almost no available donors in this precise blood grouping. Believe me, if we could obtain it without doing this we would. Money isn't the problem for our client. It is time and availability. He pays for us to provide the donor and save his life. We have to have Keane so we can harvest his kidney. That's it. We have a schedule.'

Hoffen again senses the ground shifting beneath their feet. With the clock ticking, Bruckner, for all her ice-queen posturing, is not adjusting as quickly as someone with field experience would. If the project is to be seen through to completion Hoffen will have to take control.

'I'm calling it now, Ilsa.'

'Don't forget who you're talking to, Hoffen.'

'I won't. Be quiet for once and listen. You are not General Brückner. You are a doctor. You should have concentrated on that. You could sit back and watch money roll in but that was not enough for you. That's OK, you want things to change in Germany and you have the hots for that old-time Nazi stuff. I don't care about that, about what little schemes make you tick. For all I care you could sit around wearing Hitler's underwear and singing the Horst Wessel. What I care about is results, about bringing in money and about what that money can help *Kolumne88* achieve and about the power we can access. It is only what we can achieve *after* we do this thing that I'm interested in, understand? Everything else is secondary. Everything. Your sideline has been useful, I won't deny that. We get the name, we make the pickup, you do your part and the movement gets the big cash. And without that cash the project stalls.'

Hoffen pauses and then speaks with a hard edge.' And then you decide to go after a fucking cop.'

'I didn't know he was a cop. Gottlenz was handling that.'

'Gottlenz handled nothing,' Hoffen says. 'Christ Almighty, his men couldn't even drive properly! So far this fundraising scheme has cost four men their lives, not to mention the two women. It is out of fucking control, so this is how we are going to arrange things from now.'

'Are we?'

'Yes. The first thing is that, although I really don't want to, we do have to complete the job. If this target is on the loose for too long it will start interfering with the bigger picture – remember that, Ilsa? – so I will complete the job using my own men. Mainly the men I fought with in Serbia and Angola. Real soldiers, not these posturing children Gottlenz supplies. It will cost more – not all of them are believers – but we *will* find the target and bring him back to Berlin. For this I will be partner in the enterprise. Fifty fifty. You take care of the medical side, get your money from the client and split it with me. I do the delivery and security.'

For a moment, Bruckner hesitates. She has clearly underestimated Hoffen. It is not a mistake she will make again. She is already thinking of the best way to kill him.

'Very well,' she says. 'This is acceptable. If you bring the target here, intact, we will proceed as you say.'

'I will call when we have him.'

Hoffen hangs up and Bruckner puts down the phone. As well as dealing with that greasy half-breed she's going to have to talk to Sebastian Gottlenz and express her disappointment in the strongest possible terms.

62

Inverness, Scotland, October 22nd

There are raised voices and Frank, peering down through the stair rails, watches his mother sitting on the edge of a wooden chair, a cigarette dangling from her thin fingers. His father is pacing the room, his own hands making small, nervy movements. In the blue light from a muted TV screen they flutter like caged birds and throw shadows across the walls.

'When?' Frank's mother's voice is hard, but before his father can reply he glances up at the boy. Frank's mother follows the direction of her husband's gaze. She turns her face and Frank can see mascara tracking down her cheek.

'Frankie?' she says. 'Frankie?'

Frank wakes up.

Given the circumstances, he's going to call that a bonus.

The images of his mother and father are still there but fading, like a story with a punchline you can't remember. The dream leaves him feeling disoriented and queasy, as if he has been caught spying. There's something important about his mother's tears, something Frank has seen or heard, but the information is too slippery to be retained.

In the flat northern light seeping through the thin curtains, there is a gnawing sense of hopelessness already there at the edges of his consciousness. Depression, the red-eyed monster in the shadows, is waiting for the right moment to emerge. Frank's been catching longer glimpses of the beast whenever he stops moving so he fights off the rising wave of cold panic about his cancer and swings his legs out of bed, a nasty, aching sensation in his back. All this running around, all this bullshit with guns and killing. It's ridiculous. It has to stop, at least for a while. He rubs his eyes and feels the grit. When he opens them again, stretching his arms as he does so, he sees a plain white package sitting on the hotel room table that hadn't been there last night.

He stands and approaches the package on the table as if it is an unexploded bomb. How it appeared in his room is almost as disturbing as anything that has happened during the last week. They don't call them spooks for nothing.

Inside the package is what appears to be a completely genuine British passport in the name of 'Tom Machin'. The issue date is today. There is a recent photo of Frank where it should be. Inside the passport is a credit card in the name of a company called 'MK Consultants'. The bank the card it is attached to is American. The final item in the package is a bundle of documentation backing Frank's new identity: a UK driver's license, a laminated pass for a medical centre in London together with a detailed letter of introduction to a cancer specialist. There is a printed note attached to this letter which reads 'this will work better than Lakenheath'. There is a sheaf of company information about MK Holdings.

Frank checks the time on the clock next to the bed. It's almost nine in the morning. Which means that Sheehan had put this together in a little under twelve hours.

It's impressive, even when you have seen the power before. To see it in action here in the far north of Scotland is almost beyond belief. Frank has no doubt at all that the rest of his requests have been actioned. He tries not to think about any future bill that might come in from Sheehan.

He showers and dresses in the clothes he'd bought yesterday. He'll buy more today, along with a few other items. His biopsy wound is now more a scar but is still noticeable. Frank makes a note to keep wearing hats. There don't appear to be any ill effects from the violence.

He orders room service breakfast and opens his laptop, logs onto a real estate website and starts searching.

By the time his breakfast has arrived Frank has found what he's looking for.

He wolfs down his food and calls the agent.

63

Berlin, October 22nd

Dreschler says little on the way to the B-Kreuz-Scharmer Clinic and Cooper gets the idea once again, loud and clear, that the liaison with Liverpool is not something the German cops regard with anything that could be confused with enthusiasm.

Whatever was discussed in the LKA meeting remains sealed and Cooper doesn't ask. It's time to get to the task in hand even if, after Anna Ziegler's beating, both Dreschler and Weiss don't want to be there.

The clinic is part of a sprawling medical centre occupying a corner site off one the main streets in Spandau, to the west of Berlin. Cooper, whose only knowledge of Spandau is through half-remembered history lessons, associates the place with Rudolph Hess. This leafy suburb doesn't seem right.

Dreschler parks in the almost full car park. Most of the vehicles are expensive; lines of black and silver Audis, Beemers, and Mercs gleam in the hazy winter sun; a well-heeled clientele. Inside, that impression is reinforced. The thickly-carpeted lobby, littered with designer chairs and lamps, positively hums with money. It's a long way from Walton A&E on a Saturday night thinks Cooper.

At the main desk which serves all the various clinics within the building, Dreschler shows her identification and asks for the maintenance division. She's directed through two sets of double doors and along a corridor to the maintenance office tucked away down a flight of stairs near the back of the complex.

'Herr Atay?' Dreschler addresses a short middle-aged man of Turkish appearance wearing blue overalls, spectacles and sporting a spectacular mustache. The man shakes his head and points across to another man seated behind a desk who, on first glance, appears to be his identical twin. Then Cooper sees that the appearance is superficial. Both men are of similar build, appearance and race and both have thick black mustaches.

Atay stands when he sees Dreschler and Cooper. He bows slightly and invites them to sit. Dreschler has called ahead so Atay knows what this is about.

'We called as soon as we knew the vehicle was missing,' he says. 'Right away.'

'We understand,' says Dreschler. 'The clinic is closed over the weekend, is that right?'

'Can you translate back for me?' says Cooper. 'I'm picking some things up but not everything.' Her accent brings a quizzical look from Atay.

'Of course,' says Dreschler. She repeats her question and then turns back to Atay. 'So...?'

'Yes, all weekend. So on Monday I open and see that a van has gone. I called right away.'

Dreschler nods and translates back to Cooper. 'And you and your team look after the whole of the B-Kreuz-Scharmer Clinic?'

Atay's co-worker who has been listening unapologetically, smiles. 'Yes. That's right. Whole place!'

'You must not mind Mesut,' says Atay. He taps the side of his head. 'He is an almost total imbecile.'

'Very funny,' says Mesut. He turns to Dreschler. 'Do you need to speak to me too?'

'Possibly later. After we've talked to Herr Atay.'

Mesut nods and wanders off into a backroom store.

'Can you show us the vehicle compound?' says Cooper. Now the three of them are getting into the rhythm, the back and forth translation is becoming easier. Cooper finds she is losing some of the rust.

'This way.'

Dreschler and Cooper follow Atay through a supply area and out through a set of sliding metal doors into a concrete area the size of a tennis court on which are parked three identical white Mercedes vans and two white cars. This area backs onto a service road and is winged by a three-metre high wire fence. A wire gate leads to the service road.

'You get many break-ins here?' Cooper is looking at the surrounding buildings.

'No,' says Atay. 'This area is very safe, very good.'

'No previous thefts of the vehicles?' says Dreschler. Atay shakes his head, his expression dark.

'No! We look after everything very well.'

'Yet this vehicle was stolen,' says Cooper, directly, the confidence in her German growing now she is working on the case she has been sent here to pursue.

Atay nods. 'Yes.'

'And the vehicles. None of them have the clinic name on them. No logo?'

Atay looks puzzled. Cooper's German is too patchy to follow everything so Dreschler rephrases the question.

'The vehicles are used by all the different clinics in here. And sometimes patients do not like having an ambulance at their home.'

'Was the gate damaged?' Dreschler's tone is flat. This is turning into a bullshit trip. There's nothing here she can use.

'Yes, they break gate, Take the vehicle. That is all.'

'What about the doctors?' says Cooper. Next to her she senses Dreschler stiffen.

Atay looks puzzled. 'Doctors?'

'Do you see any of the doctors? Do they come here?'

'Maybe one, two time, if they have lost something. But no, not so much.'

'How about Dr Bruckner?' says Cooper. 'Do you see her?' At the mention of Bruckner she hears Dreschler make a small exasperated noise. Cooper doesn't catch her eye.

'I don't know the doctors,' says Atay. He looks across at Dreschler for support, perhaps sensing her discomfort at Cooper's line of questioning. 'I work in maintenance. The doctors work upstairs. And they don't use the vehicles. This is for nurses, patients. Or delivery maybe.'

Cooper asks a few more questions but there's little more that Atay can give her that helps in any meaningful way. She takes some photos of the yard and the vehicles to pad out what seems increasingly likely to be meagre findings for her report.

On the way back to the car Dreschler is silent for a few minutes. As they reach reception she turns to Cooper. 'What was all that about Bruckner? Did Anna tell you something back at the hospital?'

'Look, I'm not trying to step on anyone's toes here.'

'What?'

'I don't want to get in your way. It was just something Anna showed me. Not long after I arrived.'

'Her file on Bruckner?'

'Yes.'

'Jesus.' Dreschler stops as they reach the car park. 'That damn file. She is . . .'

Dreschler lets the sentence trail off, unable to express her frustration. She looks at Cooper and holds her gaze. 'Anna Ziegler has a problem with this woman. I mean a real mental problem, you understand? She has zero evidence of any criminal activity by Bruckner. Zero. Our boss put an official reprimand on Anna's file before about her behaviour.' Dreschler looks up and waves a hand at the clinic. 'Tell me why a transplant surgeon would risk all this to do whatever it is that Anna thinks she is doing? It is ridiculous. She wants to drag you into her world because all of us are sick of it. Anna has become an obsessive.'

'Because she's Jewish? I'd say that gives her the right to take an interest.'

'Like me, you mean?' Dreschler's voice is hard. 'Being Jewish does not mean you get to be judge and jury. We have a system, perhaps like the one you work in, back in your own country. Checks. Balances. Anna is stepping further and further outside this system and it is not right, Theresa. Those words she wrote on your notebook? She thinks this Bruckner killed the man at the opera. She has no evidence, no motive, nothing. It is a fantasy of a woman with too many cats and time on her hands.'

They get into the car and drive in silence through Spandau back to the city.

Every word Dreschler says rings true with Cooper. This is none of her business and Ziegler, from the little she knows of the woman, is the very definition of a loose cannon. The best thing that Cooper can do is to complete the file on the vehicle theft and hope that an ID comes in from either of the two abductors.

Then go home.

64

Inverness, Scotland, October 22nd – Long Carraig, Scotland, October 25th

By mid-morning the deal is done. It will take three days for it to be rushed through the system, Frank waiving all legal checks and balances to hurry things along. He pays premiums to the agent in Glasgow, to the lawyer he hires online and to the seller.

He wants a bolthole and he wants it quickly. Twenty-five million dollars isn't as much money as it used to be. But it's more than enough to help a man disappear.

If they can find him, Frank figures he has a few days before the men who tried to kill him in Cheshire try again, but Frank's not planning on giving them that long. Once he gets confirmation that his purchase is secure he takes the credit card into Inverness and buys a new set of clothes and all the necessities. Back in the hotel he packs everything into a holdall and checks out. Until his new place is ready he'll keep moving. There's no harm in being careful.

Using his new identity he takes a flight to Amsterdam. There is no problem with his passport at either end. He stays quietly in a hotel on the fringes of Amsterdam for three days until an email confirms his purchase is ready. Frank heads back to Schiphol and takes a flight to Newcastle.

In Newcastle he finds a hotel and spends the day finalising arrangements for the new place online. He scours the internet for news about the barn but although there are some local reports about the blaze there's nothing that mentions bodies. He's not sure why this would be and is tempted to call Harris. He doesn't.

In the morning he gets breakfast while he waits for businesses to open. At a second hand dealership in the city Frank buys a car. A low-mileage auto Hilux with GPS. He pays for it using the MK Consulting credit card. Since Frank himself has never heard of the company until three days ago, he calculates that it is not going to be spotted by anyone trying to find him. From now on he only pays for things by cash or using the MK card. Anything with his real name on is left unused.

By lunchtime Frank has driven most of the way across Scotland stopping once at an out of town supermarket to buy supplies. Around two, he pulls up at the dock at Mallaig, a small coastal town west of Fort William. It's freezing, the sky already darkening and snow drifts gently down to dissolve on the surface of a glassy sea. Frank gets out of the Hilux and stretches, drinking in the crisp air.

At the bar of the Marine Hotel facing the harbour he orders a whisky – what else? – and waits. He doesn't have long. Five minutes after arriving the door opens and a man wearing an oiled Berghaus jacket and woollen beanie comes into the pub. He looks at Frank Keane who is, apart from the barman, the only occupant.

'Mr Machin? Tom Machin?'

It takes a second for Frank to remember this is his name for the foreseeable future. The man asking is younger than he expected, no more than a kid, really. He's small and wiry and his face looks like he spends a lot of time outdoors.

'Yes,' says Frank. He extends his hand. 'You're Calum Finn?'

'Aye.' Finn sits down on the wooden chair across from Frank. He pulls a padded envelope from his pocket and hands it over. 'All the details are in there, Mr Machin, just like you asked. Keys, everything.'

Frank takes the envelope. 'Thanks. You like a drink, Calum?'

Finn shakes his head. 'No, not for me, thanks all the same.' He glances out of the window. 'To be honest, if we're going to get you across we'd best be going. The weather's no too bad but I don't like to be on the water after dark. And we got some early snow.'

Frank drains his glass and stands. 'Let's go.'

At the dock Frank points to the Hilux. 'The car alright there?'

Finn nods. 'Aye. I'll put it in the boat shed when I get back. You got any gear?'

'Just some stuff in the back. Some groceries and a couple of bags.'

Finn opens the door and takes the box without being asked.

'That the lot, Mr Machin?'

Frank picks up the two holdalls and follows the kid along the harbour wall to a small, sturdy-looking inflatable boat moored between two trawlers. Finn steps down easily onto the deck, puts down the groceries and turns to help Frank only to find him already aboard.

Finn gets behind the controls mounted near to the stern and starts the engine. He leaves it idling in neutral while he casts off. He moves fluidly with the natural grace of someone who has been doing this all his life.

'Me da's,' he says as he pulls the boat into open water jerking a thumb at the bigger of the trawlers. 'Not too many trips these days, but...'

'How long will this take?' says Frank, raising his voice as Cal Finn guns the engines. The boat is rounding the harbour wall. Past the protective stone the swell is larger.

'Half an hour, mebbe,' shouts Finn. 'Good sea today. Don't get too many of these.'

Frank, sitting with his back to the bridge, braces himself against the roll of the boat, enjoying the feel of the snow on his face. The air could be bottled. Finn plugs in his iPhone to a cable on the wheelhouse instrument panel and hip-hop blares out of speakers.

'Ye don't mind?' he shouts over the engine roar, leaning out and smiling so politely that Frank doesn't have the heart to object.

'I love a bit of old school.' Finn smiles. 'N.W.A. Feckin' brilliant, man. There's a wee bit of swearin' in some of them. Lots of *muthafuckas*, that kind of thing. That OK?'

Frank nods, smiling. Something he hasn't done much of in the last week.

Finn, reassured, turns back to the wheel, his head bobbing to *Straight Outta Compton* and for a time there is only the noise of the engine, the sound of water passing below the bow and the sound of angry black America circa 1988.

About twenty minutes after leaving Mallaig, Finn switches off the music and gestures towards a grey shape looming through the snow. He pulls back on the throttle and the boat slows.

'There she is.'

The island is much larger than Frank had expected from the images he'd seen. It's a long piece of land, maybe eight hundred metres by two hundred, lying in the protective lee of a finger of coastal mainland which stretches around from the north. It's shaped like a teardrop with a craggy headland at its southern tip rising to thirty metres at the highest point.

Finn pulls the boat around a rocky outcrop and kills the engine at a snow-covered wooden jetty. He steps out and ties up while Frank steps out behind him.

Finn lifts out the box of supplies and makes a move along the jetty.

'Wait,' says Frank and the lad stops. 'I think I'd like to find everything myself.'

'It's no trouble. And you might need some help with the generator, finding out where everything is.'

'I'm fine.' Frank smiles but he's firm.

'No problem, Mr Machin,' says Finn. He puts down the box. Frank takes five hundred pounds from his pocket and hands it to Finn.

'What's this?' The kid is instantly suspicious. He might be a country boy but he's not completely green. 'I don't want money from yer. I mean, I do, like . . . but not. Ah, you know what I mean.'

'I'll be here a while, Calum,' says Frank. 'I'd like to be able to call on you to get me stuff from time to time.'

Finn holds out the money. 'You don't need to give me that much Mr Machin. We can pick ye up anytime the weather's fine.'

'I know,' says Frank. 'But I'm a rich man, Calum. An eccentric rich man.' He looks directly at the kid. 'The money's my invisibility cloak. Anyone asks about me? I'm not here, is that OK? If it helps I can tell you that I'm completely legitimate. I just like my privacy.'

Finn nods. 'Aye, sure.' He pockets the cash and shakes Frank's hand.

Frank watches him leave through the thickening snow, Tupac Shakur's *California Love* just hitting its stride before fading as the boat disappears around the headland.

Alone, Frank turns and walks up the jetty to look at the wee treat he'd given himself using the Sheehan money: the island he'd paid four and a half million dollars for back in Inverness.

65

Liverpool, October 22nd

'The body is definitely Frank,' says Charlie Searle. 'And that's a direct quote from the Cheshire Coroner's Office autopsy report. No doubts. The other two bodies remain officially unidentified although the woman is very likely to be the wife of a neighbour, Kath Palmer. The husband was called in Spain but with nothing to ID he's not going to be much use but it doesn't take Sherlock Holmes to work out it's her. There's nothing on the other man.'

Definitely Frank? Harris struggles to compute the information. It's not possible.

'They're sure?'

'No question. DNA match, everything. It's done. Frank Keane tragically died at Helsby.'

Searle sounds like he's preparing a press release. Maybe he is, thinks Harris.

She has more questions but as soon as she starts speaking Searle cuts her off. 'I'm sending an email package across now with all the details,' he says. 'If you don't mind, DCI Harris, I'd prefer it if you read that first before we talk further. I'm out most of the day but will be in reach later.'

Harris puts down the phone trying to organise her thoughts. Despite being half-expected, the confirmation that Frank is gone still comes as a shock.

And there's something else.

Searle hadn't said a word about the blood relationship between Frank Keane and Sarah Coughlan. The message is this: you handle it, and you take the responsibility. Harris gets the distinct impression that how she manages this aspect of the case will define her MIT career.

Searle's call is twenty minutes before the morning briefing at MIT. Harris downloads the information and sits at her desk sifting through it and pondering the best way to give the team the news. She tries not to think about Frank the man. That will come later in the privacy of her own home. In here, she has a job to do.

Coming into the main office she sees Ronnie Rimmer first. 'Is everyone here?' she asks. Rimmer nods.

'I think so, ma'am. Only DS Cooper missing from those rostered on.'

Harris nods and takes her seat at the head of the central table as the last few people filter into the room. Most of the choice seats are taken by the DS's with the DC's crowded wherever they can find a space. Harris waits a few beats for what conversation there is to fade and then leaves them waiting a little longer as she gets her thoughts together. After what Searle has told her she knows this is a pivotal moment for MIT.

'Before we get to the general business there's some information I have been given a few minutes ago that you need to hear.' Harris looks slowly around the packed office. 'Superintendent Searle called me to tell me that one of the bodies in the fire at Helsby has been identified as being that of Detective Chief Inspector Frank Keane.'

Harris waits for any comments but there are none. A few of the team exchange glances or look down at their hands. There isn't a sound in the room.

'As one or two of you may already know, DCI Keane was on indefinite medical leave. To save any rumour-mongering it seems that this blaze has nothing to do with DCI Keane's health. From what I know the fire was started deliberately by someone outside the building. The investigation will be handled by Cheshire MIT and the SIO, as I understand it, will be DI Nick Mercer. We will give DI Mercer all possible help with his investigation.' Harris looks around the room. 'There will be no misguided attempts to protect DCI Keane's reputation because there's nothing that needs protecting. DI Mercer is working on the assumption that DCI Keane is a victim of a revenge hit left over from the Stevie White case. As such we will be working closely with Cheshire MIT on that angle, bearing in mind that the investigation is theirs and, although there is clear crossover, it will remain theirs.' Harris points to two of her officers. 'DS Blake and DS Reece will be our co-ordination point for this investigation and will report directly to me.'

Harris looks at her notes and then at the meeting. 'Any questions about that?'

There is a short silence before DI Blake raises a hand. 'The other bodies? Any ID on them?'

Harris shakes her head. 'No, not as yet.'

'I heard one was a woman,' says Scott Corner.

'One of the bodies is female,' says Harris. Anticipating Ronnie Rimmer's testosterone level rising she fixes him with a cold stare but his face betrays nothing except shock at the news. Even so, Harris can't help giving him a small warning.

'You have a comment, DC Rimmer?'

'No, ma'am.'

'Good. As I say, complete co-operation with Cheshire MIT.' Harris pauses again. 'In the circumstances we will not be having any memorial drinks or anything of that kind until the dust settles. This is direct from Superintendent Searle. Obviously I'm powerless to prevent you having an independently arranged meeting at 7 p.m. tonight at The Phil but officially there's nothing from us until Cheshire have reported.' Harris glances over at DC Magsi. While the news about Frank is sinking in she knows that there is more she has to tell them. Harris gestures to Magsi, standing over to one side.

'I'd like DC Magsi to speak about some potentially key information he has turned up.'

Magsi looks uncomfortable but he speaks clearly. 'It's a bit complicated,' he says. 'But I did a bit of digging into Sarah Coughlan's background. It turns out she's adopted.' Magsi coughs. 'And here's where it gets weird: Sarah Coughlan was DCI Keane's half-sister.'

'Fuck off!' The words are out of Ronnie Rimmer's mouth before he knows it. He holds up an apologetic hand. 'Sorry ma'am.'

'That's alright, Ronnie,' says Harris. 'It was more or less my reaction too, to be honest.'

'There's no chance this is a mistake?' says Peter Wills.

'No,' says Magsi. 'No mistake.'

'But this is huge,' says Blake. 'Am I the only one who can see that this establishes another line of enquiry into DCI Keane's death? Does Cheshire know?'

Harris shakes her head. 'No, but I'll be speaking to DCI Mercer after this meeting to pass that information along.'

Magsi holds up a hand. 'I already did that, ma'am.'

'OK, good.' Harris glances at Magsi and then back to the room. 'The overlap complication we have is that while the Helsby deaths are Cheshire's responsibility, the investigation into Sarah Coughlan's death is ours.'

'Which means a joint investigation?' says Blake.

'Correct.' Harris stops short as she realises that this might be exactly what Charlie Searle wants. The crafty bastard has put Harris at the centre of the decision. If it goes wrong, if Harris turns up uncomfortable information, then it is she who will carry responsibility, not Searle. Harris wonders if her ambition is taking her out of her depth and wishes she could talk to Frank.

Harris shifts in her chair and leans forward. Enough with the self-examination.

'Clearly we're going forward looking closely at this information. It may be a complete coincidence but I'm assuming that's not the case. Disregarding our knowledge of DCI Keane, what we have is a brother and sister meeting violent deaths in quick succession. I'm happy for DCI Mercer and his team to look at the potential drug connection. What we're going to do is take the relationship between Keane and Coughlan apart. Saif, Phil and Steve, that aspect of the investigation is yours. You'll report directly to me, the DI's are already spread pretty thin. While we want to nail the people who took Sarah, and possibly killed DCI Keane, we have to be conscious of looking after the full caseload. I've emailed all the DI's to meet with me after this meeting breaks up and we'll go point by point over what else is happening.' Harris looks around the room. 'I just wanted to tell you the bad news together and to make sure we focus on fixing this one. I want it very badly. OK, unless anyone has anything to add, it's time to get moving.'

As Harris gets up from her seat a DS called Dave Flynn raises a hand. 'Excuse me. Ma'am?'

'Yes?' says Harris as everyone turns to look at Flynn. He is a relatively new addition at MIT with an earnest manner about him which, together with his watery eyes and slack mouth, has the unfortunate effect of making him look somewhat simple. He is the only MIT officer with a mustache. Harris can't recall ever speaking to him directly.

'I was thinking we might just have a moment's contemplation for DCI Keane's passing.'

Flynn, Harris now recalls, is some sort of happy clapper. One of those non-denominational pop-up churches; all cardigans and guitars and tambourines. She'd seen him once in Church Street appropriately enough, preaching to the Saturday shoppers with his serious-looking children and dowdy wife in tow along with half a dozen other God-botherers. Harris had slipped past, careful not to be spotted.

'Perhaps we could all pray,' says Flynn. 'And hold hands.'

There are audible sniggers but Flynn seems utterly impervious. Harris sees Rimmer stuffing his knuckles into his mouth.

'I think if DCI Keane were here I could guess what he'd say to that suggestion. But I'm more polite than Frank so I'll just say 'yes' to the minute's silence and a big 'no' to holding hands. If something like that got out we'd have to close the shop.'

'Should I say a few words?' says Flynn.

'No, Dave,' says Harris. 'I think we can manage.'

Flynn drops his head and closes his eyes and most of MIT follow suit. The first few seconds of the developing silence are interrupted by someone's mobile, hurriedly muted. 'Sorry', says a whispered voice. Then there is just the traffic surf from the road outside as the room of cynic's mark Frank Keane's passing. As the seconds tick by, Harris changes her opinion about Flynn's suggestion. The silence makes her think about Frank properly for the first time that morning. It's Harris who breaks the silence.

Afterwards, and after the briefings with the DI's, Harris sits in her office and wonders why, despite Frank being a friend and colleague and, briefly, lover, she doesn't feel his loss more intensely. It takes a few minutes before the answer comes back.

It's because, despite the pathologist's confirmation, Charlie Searle's phone call and the minute's silence, she doesn't believe for one minute that Frank Keane is dead.

66

Berlin, October 22nd

The boys roll around on the cream rug, the soundless TV playing a cartoon in the background. Outside it's quiet and inside the apartment are the sounds of domesticity; small voices, plates clattering.

'You're not yourself, Sebastian.' Eva's voice comes in from the kitchen where she's cleaning up after the evening meal.

Gottlenz, watching his boys in the living room, one fist propping his chin, tries to put some sincerity behind his answer.

'I'm fine, Eva.'

Eva Gottlenz peeps through the open doorway and shakes her head but doesn't push it any further. Sebastian's been like this for days. Never the most demonstrative of men, he now sinks into these almost catatonic states too often for her liking. She finishes putting the dishes into the washer and moves across to where the children are playing on the rug in front of the TV.

'Bedtime,' she says, her voice a sing-song, smiling at the protests.

'Leave them a little longer,' says Gottlenz as Eva bends to pick up one of the boys.

'They're too tired, Sebastian. They've been up longer than usual.' She scoops up the nearest boy and leads the other by the hand. Both are already bathed and wearing pajamas. 'Say goodnight to Papa.'

Gottlenz leans forward and grabs the boys as they pass. He kisses them both on the cheek and holds them tight. 'Goodnight.'

He watches them walk the few paces to their room and sits watching the closed door for a few minutes. He can hear Eva's low voice reading to them. Gottlenz's head swings slowly from side to side; an unconscious movement.

As silence slowly descends, he pulls himself up out of the armchair and walks across to his computer. He logs on to his bank – the private fund, the one no-one but he knows about – and checks the balance. His accountant's mind makes the calculations and he nods to himself. He closes the connection, switches off the computer and checks his watch. There is still no sign of Eva finishing with the boys. Gottlenz walks into the small hallway of the apartment, puts on his coat and pulls a woolen beanie down over his scalp. He picks up his car keys and slips out without saying anything to Eva. She won't ask about his movements. She's learned not to. The apartment is one world and out there, where Sebastian operates is another and Eva likes it that way.

It's cold outside and Gottlenz wraps his coat tighter as he walks the few metres to his car, a Passat, that most narcoleptic of vehicles. He heads east towards Marzahn, the heater on high. A cold front is moving in.

67

Long Carraig, Scotland, October 25th

From his Inverness hotel room, Frank had shelled out a touch over three million pounds to buy twenty-five acres of pristine Scottish Island from a thirty-something DJ needing quick cash to fund the new joint in Ibiza. Three mill isn't as much as it used to be but, besides the lump of rock itself, the money buys a low-slung converted crofter's house with grey stone walls thicker than a Glaswegian Tory's skin and in much better condition. It buys a jetty, two slipways and a boat house. It buys CCTV cover and electronic security that wouldn't be out of place at Guantanamo Bay and it buys a shiny black helicopter, complete with hangar, thrown in to sweeten the deal. If he has anything to say about it, Frank's vertigo means he'll never get into the chopper, but he feels a cheap buzz just thinking about owning one.

The island, a slender finger of stone extending into the Atlantic, is called, with dust dry Scottish accuracy, 'Long Rock' – *Carraig* in Gaelic – and is the perfect bolthole to prepare for the battles to come. And, if those battles don't come, if there is no operation, no chance of recovery, then Long Rock is a good place to end up.

Frank bought the place through MK Consulting via an agent in Glasgow, expediting the sale by adding on a hefty bonus for early completion. As far as the agent is concerned – and the same goes for the law – *Carraig* is owned by a Belgian company as a tax shelter. The selling DJ couldn't care less who bought just so long as the dough showed up in his account. And, unless Dennis Sheehan suddenly decides to hold a press conference about his arrangement with Frank

– an event about as likely as a starving lawyer waiving a fee – then the trail leading to the island is closed.

With Cal Finn out of sight and sound, Frank climbs the winding path from the jetty to his new home. He opens the heavy wooden front door and turns on the lights, his fingers finding the switch as naturally as if he'd lived there for years. It's warm inside; the agent said he'd make sure the place was in a condition for occupation and he has been as good as his word. Frank's learning fast that money makes people pay attention. He dumps the box of supplies in the kitchen, takes out a small bottle of Laphroaig and slips it into the pocket of his jacket.

The snow is falling more heavily now, an early taste of the winter to come. Frank pulls his beanie down over his ears and winds his scarf around his neck. With the silver light fading, and the temperature falling fast, he steps outside to inspect his new kingdom. Standing with his back to the stone house, warm orange light spilling out onto the snow-speckled grass, Frank looks across to where the grey-white sky bleeds gently into the charcoal ocean and experiences a moment separate from himself. Everything that has happened and will happen is temporarily forgotten in the perfection of the moment. He's not a man given to poetry but if he died tomorrow he will at least have had this.

He contemplates the view for a time and then as the chill enters his bones, laughs, reminded of something from a few years back. One of the guys from the unit, Billy Pierce, had retired early and bought a place in the Lakes. Top of the fell looking down the valley to Ullswater. Perfection. Wordsworth bottled, the whole bit. Piercey living the dream. Frank and three of the lads had driven up for the weekend and arrived on a perfect July morning. Billy, the proud landowner, a Kirkby boy made good, took them to the garden to show them the view – *his* view – and they duly gazed out at the beauty below, genuinely dumbstruck. After a minute, Tony Tucker let out a long sigh, patting Billy on the back. 'That's incredible, mate,' he said. He turned back to the view savouring it once more. 'Gets fucking boring after a while though. Any chance of a brew?'

Tucker might have kept quiet here though.

The house is set on the highest point of the Island. Frank's not expecting unwelcome visitors anytime soon but if he gets them, the island is a good one to defend and difficult to attack.

To the south, the island is thickly wooded along its more sheltered eastern shore. On the west, the side facing the open ocean, the land is harsher and drops away sharply to the ocean. The trees are bent against the wind, their hunched posture the result of a hundred thousand storms coming in from the west.

There's enough snow on the ground now for Frank's boots to squeak a little as he presses down. Behind him, foot prints run in a straggling line, just visible in the dying light. Frank walks slowly, taking pleasure in every step, feeling every iced wine breath being drawn down into his lungs. He feels as alive as he ever remembers feeling and, with each squeaking step, he feels more and more as though he has found home.

He glances over his shoulder. The house lights appear brighter now as night draws in and Frank drops towards the tiny curving cove of pebble and rock cut like a notch into Carraig's northern tip. It's the only beach on the island, nothing visible from here except endless flat water the colour of a gun barrel. Snowflakes drift into the waves and dissolve. At the shoreline, Frank takes out the malt whisky, unscrews the top and raises the bottle to the sky.

'To you, Kath,' he says and drinks. With the malt hot in his throat he replaces the bottle in his pocket and picks up a black stone from the ground. He weighs it meditatively in his hand and thinks about Kath Palmer and how he killed the two men at Helsby and how little guilt he feels. He thinks about the cancer and throws the pebble into the black Atlantic. West of here is South Uist, invisible now in the gloom, and then nothing until you get to Newfoundland. This is a pure place, clean and sharp and good.

Tomorrow Frank begins fighting back.

68

Liverpool, October 23rd

The Happy Clapper's not looking too happy now. When DS Flynn suggested marking Frank Keane's passing in some way, Harris reckons that getting hammered at The Phil was probably not exactly what he had in mind. In the end, Flynn scarpers less than an hour in.

Harris watches him slip away and almost wishes she could do the same. She can't though, not the boss, it wouldn't be right.

Ronnie Rimmer, as expected, is leading the proceedings. Half-cut already he is at the centre of a tight cluster of MIT personnel in the backroom. They're swapping Keane stories and steadily becoming sentimental: a Liverpool trait that Harris finds simultaneously compelling and nauseating. At funerals or wakes it can become unbearable. So far, everyone is just the right side of mawkish but it won't be long before some gonad starts blubbing.

It won't be me, thinks Harris. For more than one reason.

Siobhan MacDonald, one of Frank's old protégés who has travelled back for the wake from the wilds of London is sitting next to Harris. There's a new urban sheen on Siobhan that Harris can't help being a little envious of; the subtext being the superiority of a capital posting, even one a rank or so below her own. Not that Siobhan is saying anything that could be interpreted as patronising. It's more that Harris notices the small details of her clothing and the comfort Siobhan has with the unfamiliar place names.

'To Frank,' says Siobhan, raising her arm. The women touch the rims of their glasses together.

'I suppose it's alright to call him 'Frank' now?' says Siobhan. 'Still doesn't feel right.'

She drinks and shrugs her eyebrows.

'Frank won't mind,' says Harris.

'I don't know, DC Harris. He was always a stickler for formality from the junior ranks.'

'I'm sure we can make an exception. And you can drop the 'DC Harris' bit too while you're up here, Siobhan. Makes me feel like your mother.'

'OK, 'Emily,' says Siobhan.

'Em.'

'Em.'

Both of them look across to Rimmer's group as they cheer about something, the noise levels rising minute by minute. If they start singing 'You'll Never Walk Alone' or 'New York, New York', I'm off, thinks Harris, no matter what it looks like.

'How's the case going?' Siobhan says. She leans forward and props her arms on the table. Harris, seeing a pool of spilled wine edge closing on McDonald's sleeve, picks up a beer mat and wipes it away. Siobhan glances down, amused.

'OCD,' says Harris, apologetically. 'Or something like it.'

'The case?'

Harris drops the wet mat back on the table and sits back. 'Which one? Frank's?'

Siobhan nods.

'Well it isn't our case, or at least not completely. We're in a joint investigation with Cheshire MIT. The bodies were found in Cheshire but there are apparently clear links with our investigation into Frank being targeted by a drug gang involved in the Australian thing.'

'They don't think that . . .?' Siobhan lets the question fade, unwilling to say the words out loud. Harris shakes her head.

'No. Not really. I mean there's an internal enquiry going on from Lupus but Frank's not dirty. I don't think they think he's dirty either, to be honest. There are things that point away from that, not least that Frank has been open with them. Stuff that happened in the US raised questions but, as far as I know, no mud has stuck to Frank.'

Harris doesn't mention Frank's illness. If Siobhan knows about it, or has heard anything, she doesn't raise the issue.

'Rosie mentioned something about a weird family thing connecting Frank to something else.'

'The abducted girl? Yes. Frank's related to her.'

'A sister,' Rosie said.'

'I'm surprised he didn't send you the sodding case file. Jesus.' Harris looks over at Steve Rose, his young face flushed with booze and bonhomie. If Rosie wasn't already pissed he'd surely feel the lasers burning into his skull. Harris turns away dismissing Rose with a wave of her hand. Coppers have gossiped since the dawn of time. It is written thus and Harris has as much chance of stopping it as she has juggling eels. Besides, who is she to judge Rose? Isn't gossiping exactly what she's doing now with Siobhan? She takes a drink and turns guiltily back to the conversation.

'Yes, a half-sister.'

'And Frank never knew? He died without knowing?'

'Apparently.' Harris takes another drink. She's starting to feel a little teary herself but exactly why, she isn't certain. She doesn't like the feeling.

'Saif found out,' says Harris. 'You won't know him but he came in to help with the Williamson Tunnels thing and we kept him on. He's good. Like you.'

'It's none of my business,' says McDonald.

'But?'

'But this thing is a real mess.'

'Oh, cheers, Siobhan. Like I don't know that.'

'That's not what I mean. You've got Frank dead and you're working on the assumption that it's drug-related.'

Harris nods. 'There's a lot of evidence to suggest that. I talked to Jane Watson at Lupus and she hinted they'd had intelligence that Frank may have been targeted.'

'Because of the Perch case?'

'Yes.'

McDonald pauses. 'So why do I get the feeling that you don't buy into that theory, Emily?'

'I don't?'

'No. You don't. You can say the words all you like but we've worked together, remember? Superintendent Searle has passed this parcel along to you and if you're left holding something nasty at the end of it then it'll be you that gets the blame, not him.'

'Isn't it always that way, Siobhan? Don't tell me it's different in the Met?'

'No. It's not. Worse if anything. But what I mean is that you're being given a very complex case. Lots of possibilities, lots of threads moving around all over the place. At least, that's what it looks like from the little I know.'

'You're right. It is very complicated. I don't get what you're driving at.'

'I'm trying to give you an outside point of view.' McDonald takes a sip from her glass. 'You don't remember when Menno Koopman was at MIT, do you? He was before your time.'

Harris nods. 'But I met him last year.'

'He used to say something that stuck with me.'

'Here we go.' Harris rolls her eyes. 'More Wisdom of Koop.'

McDonald smiles. 'I think it might help.'

'Go on then. What did The All-Seeing Dutchman say?'

'Follow the money.'

'What money? There's no money.'

'There's always money, Emily. Or sex. Or blood. Or all three. What I mean is this: maybe stop worrying about what's going on below the surface, or what's happening upstairs and just start investigating the simple things. Who benefits? What if the drug people aren't the ones behind Frank's death? The fact that Frank is related to the abducted girl is just about the only real piece of evidence I've heard so far. That and the connection with Germany. There's the evidence chain. Everything else is pie-in-the-sky. Surely Frank Keane's sister is the key to this. Someone wanted her and someone wanted Frank dead. The two have to be connected, right?'

Harris opens her mouth and then closes it again. Her instinct to bite back is over-ruled by the very pertinent point that Siobhan is on the money. Or blood.

'Theresa's in Berlin now,' says Harris. She's not looking for a reply and Siobhan says nothing. Harris nods to herself. Over near the bar she hears Steve Rose launch into song.

'When you waaaaalk . . .'

As the rest of the group chime in, Harris has to raise her voice so that Siobhan can hear her. 'You think?'

Siobhan nods. 'Follow the link between Frank Keane and Sarah Coughlan.'

Harris peers at Siobhan and puts a hand on her shoulder. 'When did you get to be so good?'

'I moved south,' says McDonald. 'Big city girl now.'

'Fuck off,' says Harris and waggles her glass. As Siobhan heads for the bar Harris listens to the singing and thinks about the conversation.

Blood. It's all in the blood.

69

Long Carraig, Scotland, October 26th

At eight the first morning, Frank's out running just as it gets light. He swings open the double doors and shivers pleasurably in the cold Western Isles air. He hits 'play' on his music and hears the familiar horn riff and then that testifying Belfast voice starts up as Frank leaves the house to jog down the incline north towards the sea through the frosted grass. *Man I feel so good tonight. Man I feel so good tonight.* Four minutes and fourteen seconds of pure undiluted affirmation of being alive. Frank hasn't got a religious bone in his body, but here and now, with Van Morrison riffing on the call and response, he feels as close to spiritual as he's ever been. *Baby I feel so good.*

Long Rock – his island – unwinds beneath his feet as he runs and another song kicks in, the applause of recognition bringing a smile to Frank's face. Van gets him up and out and running, the little Belfast miseryguts channelling fuck-knows-what from fuck-knows-where and coming up with gold. *I feel aaaaaaalright. Gee-El-O-Are-I-Ay* .

Frank runs relays from the house to the beach and back again for an hour. After showering he eats breakfast overlooking the ocean and rests for an hour. Late morning he spends trying to get the satellite internet connection working. After several abortive attempts he manages it. The afternoon is spent researching what he can on the events in Helsby. He makes an appointment to see the specialist Dennis Sheehan has given him. Since Helsby, and despite his sorrow at Kath Palmer's death, physically he feels wonderful. He makes plans to pick up more items for Long Rock when he goes to London. The evening is a quiet one. He thinks about contacting Em Harris but doesn't. No-one, other than Cal Finn knows where Frank Keane is right now and as far as he's concerned, Frank is Tom Machin. Frank watches some TV, cooks a steak and drinks a couple of beers. He's asleep by eleven.

Something wakes Frank with a jolt and he opens his eyes to complete blackness, his heart pounding, a sheen of sweat on his skin. Night on Long Rock is total. He can hear wind buffeting the house and the electronic hiss of the surf. He reaches under the pillow and slides the Glock out before propping himself up on an elbow. He cocks his ear to pick up on any sound that doesn't fit to be ready for whatever is out there. He presses the light on his watch. 3.12 a.m.

There's nothing. Frank waits for fully five minutes before sinking back into the pillows, wary, but relieved.

He has just closed his eyes once more when a sharp stabbing pain shoots through his skull making him gasp out loud.

Sweet Jesus.

Frank drops the Glock and hugs his knees to his chest. He curls into the foetal position, his breath ragged, his heart jackhammering against his ribs and sweat drenching him in an instant.

Pain of an astonishing intensity sweeps through Frank like a tsunami, overpowering every rational thought, reducing him in a finger snap to a mewling animal streak of tissue and nerve endings. For two or three minutes he rocks back and forth in a tangle of damp bedclothes. Gradually the agony subsides enough for Frank to roll off the bed and, crab-like, inch his way to the bathroom. He vomits into the pan and leans against the cold porcelain, shivering before vomiting once more.

After a couple of minutes Frank gets to his feet and props himself up at the basin. He looks at himself in the mirror and recoils. The old man in the mirror is ghost-white, his skin clammy, his dark eyes ringed with red. Flecks of spittle and vomit cling to his chin and his hair looks thin, plastered to his head. For the first time since the diagnosis Frank can see the dread creature he will become. It's in there waiting for the old Frank to shed his skin. There's no gunman coming for Frank, no gangster, no thug, no bogeyman. No monster will be coming for him tonight because the monster's already here. Right inside him.

70

Liverpool, October 24th

The day after the wake at The Phil, with Siobhan McDonald's words still reverberating, Harris is about to call Theresa Cooper from home when Cooper calls her.

'Sorry to call on a Saturday, ma'am, but I think I need more time here.' Cooper launches into a rationale but Harris cuts across her.

'It's fine, Theresa. I agree. I want you to do more digging out there.'

'You do?' Cooper finds it difficult to keep the surprise from her voice. Even in her most optimistic moments she hadn't expected DI Harris to roll over quite so readily.

'We've been treading water, Theresa. We need to go back to basics and trace anything that you can find in Berlin that has a bearing on Sarah Coughlan. Did you get anywhere with the van?'

Cooper outlines her visit to the clinic. It doesn't sound like much.

'That's it?'

'I know,' says Cooper.

'Nothing else?' It's hard for Harris to keep the disappointment out of her voice. She knows how hard it can be to make any sort of progress when the victim is random – and you can double that for anything working in tandem with a foreign force – but until Theresa had spelled it out Harris realised she had been hoping for more.

Cooper hesitates before replying. She's been weighing up how much of the Anna Ziegler story to tell DI Harris.

'There is another possibility,' she says.

'Go on.'

'My liaison here? Anna Ziegler, works for the LKA – the *Landeskriminalmt* – was attacked last night.' Again Cooper hesitates.

'Spit it out, Theresa,' says Harris. 'Is it related?'

'That's hard to say, ma'am.' Cooper details her encounter with Ziegler and the reaction of Dreschler and Weiss.

'And this opera business? How on earth could that be connected to Sarah Coughlan?'

'That's pretty much what the Germans think, ma'am. The only connection is Ziegler's thing for a doctor at the clinic. The same clinic the van was taken from. Dr Bruckner.'

Harris senses something and sits up a little straighter. 'This Bruckner. What's your impression of him?'

'Her. And I haven't met her yet. The LKA aren't fond of me poking my nose in. Anna Ziegler was already on a reprimand for following Bruckner. From what Dreschler and Weiss tell me it amounted to stalking.'

'A woman? Shit.' Harris pauses but Cooper says nothing, sensing that her boss will have more to say. She's right. 'And this opera thing?'

'I don't know just yet. Should I look at it?'

'Yes. If there's nothing coming out of the van angle – and it doesn't sound like there is – then get stuck into whatever's available. If this Ziegler had the hots for Bruckner as no-good, and you're there looking into the clinic then I think it's legit for you to spend some more time and resources looking at her claims.'

'And the LKA?'

'Never mind the Germans, Theresa. If you have to upset them that's OK. This is our case, remember? Step on any toes you need to and follow the line of this investigation wherever it takes you. I'll clear things at this end and try and get some more manpower to you if I can.'

Harris tidies up some details with Cooper and rings off. She slumps back on the bed and then abruptly gets up.

Ten minutes later when she's making tea in the kitchen her phone rings. It's Cooper again.

'Theresa,' says Harris. 'Forgot something?'

'Anna Ziegler died. Christina Dreschler just called me.'

'Jesus.'

'Dreschler gave me the clear impression that it would be best if I left.'

'Do not leave. In fact, I want you to go hard on this, Theresa. There are too many people connected to this clinic dying. Don't tell the Germans anything before you speak to me. I'll call you in an hour once I've spoken to Superintendent Searle.'

'About what, ma'am?'

'About me coming over to help.'

Harris hangs up and calls Searle before thinking better of it. She'll have more chance persuading him face to face. If she can find him.

71

Liverpool, October 24th

'No.'

In the end she'd found Searle in his office, Saturday or not.

'"No"?' Harris hasn't yet sat down and now she remains standing. 'What do you mean?'

'It seems clear enough, Emily. You can't go to Berlin. The answer's no.'

'It seems unreasonable, sir.'

'Sit down, DI Harris.'

Harris takes a seat and Charlie Searle removes his glasses. He rubs the bridge of his nose and places the spectacles on his desk.

'Getting so I need these things all the time,' he says, smiling. 'One of the downsides to becoming older, Emily.'

Harris looks like she's about to say something but Searle raises a finger to stop her.

'No, my turn, DI Harris, don't be greedy.' Searle taps two fingers on his arm. 'The pips mean I get to decide. When you have these things then *you* get to decide. That's how it works.' Searle smiles. 'I'm not being an arse, Emily. In fact I'm being generous in explaining. You don't get to go to Berlin because you are in charge of MIT. And, before you start squawking about Frank Keane being allowed to go to America earlier this year I'd like to suggest that that would be a strong argument against you going. I don't want another Frank Keane incident. He only went over there on an MLAT, Emily and look at what happened there. A complete balls-up.'

'Was it?' Harris leans forward. 'We never really got told what had happened to DCI Keane out there, sir. What did happen?'

Charlie Searle purses his lips. 'Good question.' He looks as though he's about to say more but instead he closes his mouth abruptly. 'No. You can't go.' Searle pauses. 'I'm not losing another head of department on some foreign jolly. Send someone else. Someone smart. No-one who's going to embarrass the department. Not Rimmer or any of that boy's club.'

'I'll send DC Magsi, sir.' Harris hides her disappointment at being denied the opportunity to go to Berlin. She has no expectation that it would have been, as Searle put it, anything resembling a 'jolly', but after her chat with Theresa Cooper she's getting the sense that the answer to Sarah Coughlan's death lies in Germany, not Liverpool. Frank Keane's relationship with the dead girl? Follow the blood, Siobhan had said at The Phil and the blood trail is pointing to Berlin.

'Magsi? Not very experienced is he?'

'He'll be fine, I'm sure. Cooper's very good, and she sticks with it, but DS Magsi has a bit of flair about him.'

'OK, fine. That's your business, Emily. I'll approve Magsi.' Searle picks up his pen and Harris knows the interview is over.

'That's fine, sir,' she says, getting to her feet.

'Terrific.' Searle is still smiling. 'Oh, and Emily?' he says, as Harris nears the door.

'Sir?'

'Let this be the last time you come in with something like this. One of the downsides to getting a promotion like yours is that it should be you making these kind of executive decisions, not me. Just because Frank Keane fancied himself as a bit of a Clint Eastwood that doesn't mean you should do the same. Magsi should have been sent without this cozy little chat. Despite my cuddly exterior, I'm not your fucking favourite uncle, is that clear?'

'Yes, Superintendent Searle. As crystal.'

Searle pauses, sucking the end of his pencil. He leans back in his chair and looks at Harris. 'Actually . . .' he says.

'Yes, sir?'

'On second thoughts I'm not approving DC Magsi's travel to Berlin. I'm being too easy with you. You should have figured this out without coming in, DI Harris. I don't like being played and you've just tried to do exactly that. I won't have it. Give Cooper a few days to sniff round and then pull her back in. I shouldn't be having to make these kind of field decisions but you're forcing me into doing it. OK?'

Harris nods. 'Of course, sir.'

'Excellent. Now go.'

Harris closes the door and waits until she's in the car heading back to MIT before she starts screaming.

72

Berlin, October 24th

The drive from his apartment is a short one and the traffic is light. Sebastian Gottlenz arrives at his destination a little after nine. He parks on the main street and walks two blocks back towards the sports hall tucked away behind the stadium. He doesn't think he's under surveillance but given the circumstances he keeps to the shadows and takes a long way round. As he gets close he can hear the bass thump of thrash metal from fifty metres away. Apart from the cars and the neon signs here and there, this could still be Cold War-era East Berlin. Some of the concrete buildings look as if they are made from cardboard and every centimetre of spare wall is coated in a thick patina of graffiti.

The venue has been hired; a regular booking, one that comes across Gottlenz's desk every month for payment. It was Gottlenz who negotiated the rental, dressing up *Kolumne88* as a cultural organisation. The landlord didn't give a shit; he is fully aware that *Kolumne88* bore as much resemblance to culture as a late-night kebab does to a Michelin-starred soufflé.

Outside, the small car park is jammed and a knot of dark-clothed men talk and smoke. The level of violence in the atmosphere is palpable. As Gottlenz approaches, three young men drift out from the pack and come to look at him, their expressions set and posture aggressive.

'Relax,' says Gottlenz when he gets close enough. 'It's me.'

The outer security parts and a hand opens the hall door. Gottlenz feels a wave of heat and noise rush out to greet him. One or two people look at him interested in why such a square would be here.

Those in the know look away or nod respectfully. The ignorant or the uninitiated glare as they do at anyone. Gottlenz doesn't say anything. His visits to the frontline are irregular and this visit is unplanned.

Gottlenz walks along a short corridor towards another set of double doors. Inside the bar off the main hall a band is playing. They are so loud that it is all Gottlenz can do not to put his hands to his ears. At the front of the small stage where the crowd are jammed together most tightly Gottlenz sees hundreds of shaven heads moving to the music. The place is packed solid with more than five hundred in for the fundraiser. Metal music and a slate of cage fighting. It's a combination that's been bringing in a steady income stream for *Kolumne88* and tonight is no different.

The organisation makes good money from these events but it's small beer compared to the donations from individuals. Ilsa Bruckner is the biggest contributor and the one most closely linked to the guts of *Kolumne88*. Without her drive and money, Gottlenz knows, they would be in a much weaker position and would not be able to contemplate the undertaking ahead. That doesn't stop him hating her.

At the very back of the bar standing amongst a group of men older than most of the audience, Gottlenz finds the man he's looking for; Gunther Lamm, the one who'd made contact with *Kolumne88's* partners in this project. As he approaches, Lamm, a middle-aged man with prematurely greying hair, moves towards him and gestures for them to go outside. Talking in here is an impossibility. He guides Gottlenz through two sets of fire doors until they find themselves in a small, stinking service area at the back of the warehouse. When Lamm closes the outer door, the throb of the music drops to a muffled bass that seems to make the floor vibrate.

'I'm surprised you can still find us, Sebastian,' says Lamm 'I haven't seen you at one of these for months. Too busy with your friends uptown?'

'Something like that, Gunther.' Gottlenz rubs his ears. 'Jesus. That noise is unbearable in there. I don't know how you stand it.'

'Gets them fired up.' Lamm lights a cigarette and sits down on a low concrete wall skirting the garbage bins. 'So, what's the occasion?'

'I need the name.' Gottlenz looks at Lamm. 'There's been a change of plan.'

Lamm looks up and regards Gottlenz coolly. 'A change of plan? I hadn't heard about that.'

'This is you hearing about it.'

'I dunno, Gottlenz. This doesn't seem right. That side of things is being taken care of by us. You suggested that the details should be kept separate in case of trouble. Shouldn't there be . . .'

'A memo? An email? This isn't the *Deutsche Post*, Lamm. This is *Kolumne88*. We're Nazis, remember? And last I heard, I was secretary. It's been cleared with Hoffen. You know Hoffen's been the one dealing with this end of the operation. He told me the person I need to speak to would be here tonight. Now give me the name.'

'What name?' Lamm stands again but Gottlenz holds his ground and Lamm can see there's been a change in the little man. Although Lamm has no physical fear of Gottlenz he knows that the accountant is one of the big three. And, since Lamm is unsure of Gottlenz's relationship with Felix Hoffen, he's going to tread carefully. Nobody wants Hoffen on the opposing side.

'You know exactly what name and you know that I'm not someone you want to be on the wrong side of, Lamm. I know you were meeting the contact tonight.' Gottlenz leans in to Lamm and lowers his voice. 'Now give me the name of the person making our fucking bomb.'

73

Liverpool, October 25th

They haven't had anyone round for a while and Harris can see that Linda is enjoying herself at the prospect of new blood. Harris knows herself well enough to see the streak of puritan and seeing Linda happily busying herself in the kitchen she makes a note to try harder in future.

'Jesus,' says Linda, looking up from the stove, a wooden spoon in hand. 'They're not vegetarians are they?'

Harris shakes her head. 'No, I don't think so, Linds.'

'We should've checked.'

'Mmm.' Harris is tapping the screen on her phone, checking her messages before Steve Viner and his partner, Gareth, arrive. It's almost two weeks since her invite and Harris had almost cancelled several times in the intervening days, especially after the last run in with Charlie Searle. Only Linda's insistence had kept the dinner alive and now Harris is glad, not least because of the chance it gives her to quiz Steve Viner.

'Em? Em?'

Harris looks up, suddenly aware that Linda had been talking and equally aware that she hadn't been listening.

'What? Sorry.'

'I was asking if you were still OK with this? What with . . . you know.'

You know.

'Frank?'

Linda nods but doesn't look at Harris.

Harris lifts her glass and takes a mouthful of red wine. She doesn't reply straight away. The final path report on the Helsby bodies had come in that afternoon and although Harris had scrutinised the findings very carefully, the document had left her with more questions than answers about Frank's death. She's about to say something to Linda when the doorbell sounds.

Steve Viner looks different outside work. Younger and thinner. His partner, Gareth, an English teacher, turns out to be a funny and entertaining guest. The time passes quickly and Harris feels a small thrill of satisfaction every time she sees Linda laughing, the wine bringing colour to her pale skin. It's going to be a good evening and reminds her that they need more of them.

After dinner, Linda and Gareth clear the plates.

'Go,' says Linda, shooing Em out of the kitchen. 'Talk to Steve. Get all that work crap out of the way.'

Sprawled across the sofa in the living room, Harris congratulates about the report on Sarah Coughlan.

'Thanks,' says Viner. 'Always good to get decent feedback when it's a new job. I was very pleased with that one.' Viner blushes. 'Not that I should get pleasure from someone's death. Especially someone so young.'

Harris waves away his discomfort. 'You know what it's like, Steve. You have to take victories when you can. It's your job.' She raises a glass and Viner does likewise.

'Still,' he says, 'it might have been worse, I suppose.'

Harris cocks her head. 'Oh?'

'I just meant that Sarah might not have had all that long. If things hadn't worked out.'

'What do you mean?'

Viner's hand stops, his wine glass halfway to his mouth.

'Her illness.'

Harris feels foggy.

'Obviously you read the report?' says Viner. 'Coughlan's toxicology?'

'I'm sorry, Steve. I read the report but I don't remember it having anything in there about Sarah Coughlan being ill.'

'What?'

'Nothing.' Harris holds up her glass. 'I know I've had a couple but there was nothing in there.'

'Bollocks,' says Viner and Harris sees Linda and Gareth look up. 'Coughlan was taking a number of drugs as part of her recovery. I listed them.'

'Recovery from what?'

'Cancer. She had had cancer. I put it all in there.'

Harris looks like she's about to say more when she catches a warning glance form Linda. She sinks back, holding up her hand in apology.

'Sorry, Steve,' she says. 'I probably misread something.' She looks at him. 'It'll be me, not you, OK?'

'OK' says Viner. He takes a drink, the skin on his neck mottled red.

Harris dips the rim of her own glass in apology. 'I *am* sorry, Steve. Really.'

Viner sits up a bit straighter. 'OK, move on. It's easily checked, right? Now, ask what you want to ask and we can start talking about something important again.'

'I don't know what you mean.'

'Again, bollocks. Since we got here you've been desperate to get me alone and talk about the Helsby bodies, right?'

'Yes.'

'You know we didn't do the report?'

'Of course.' Harris leans in closer. 'That's why I wanted to pick your brains.'

She glances across the room but Linda and Gareth are deep in a conversation about books, both of them having a thing for Neil Gaiman.

'I don't like it,' says Harris. 'The report. Have you seen it?'

'Why would I see it?'

Harris shrugs. 'Don't know.' She waves her hand. 'Anyway, that doesn't matter.'

'So what's bothering you? Cheshire do good work. From what I know. Which, admittedly, isn't much.'

'It's not the science,' says Harris. 'It's the scenario. Three bodies, all unidentifiable. All the report really says is that there were two men and one woman. No dentals, nothing.'

'Intense fire can do that. I heard there was a propane bottle inside the property?'

Harris nods. 'That's right.'

'The heat would have been increased by that. If petrol had been used on the bodies that would also have rendered identification more difficult. It was arson, right?'

'Yes. And petrol was used. Or an accelerant of some sort. But I've seen a few deaths by fire – in fact we investigated one last year – and I can't recall one which had such destructive results in terms of the condition of the body.'

'It all depends on the circumstances,' says Viner. 'When a body is in a fire it melts, basically. The fat in the body acts as a fuel supply and can reduce the bones and tissue to ash. Think of what happens during cremation. The heat ignites the skin, the flesh, everything.'

'Teeth?'

'At the right temperature everything is destroyed.'

'But it's not common, right?'

'Well, yes, it is, to be honest, Emily. I've seen a number of cases where the body is degraded so much that it is not initially recognised as being human. If the fire in the barn had an explosive element then that would have further degraded the forensic situation. Let's say the fire made considerable inroads on the bodies and was then subject to the propane explosion, the effect would be to shred what remained of the carbonised bodies. There may have been considerable co-mingling of tissue . . .'

Viner breaks off. 'Sorry,' he says. 'I got carried away with the technical details. I forgot for a moment you knew one of the victims. Keane, was it?'

'Frank Keane,' says Harris. 'My boss.' Her eyes flick over towards Linda who looks up quickly. Despite being apparently engrossed in the Neil Gaiman chat, Linda still finds time to register the mention of Frank and Em's tiny hesitation before the word 'boss'. In the moment that she and Harris lock eyes a wealth of information is exchanged. Em's one night stand with Frank. Linda's revenge acid attack.

Harris turns back to Viner. She wonders how much of the subtext he had registered.

'Sorry,' says the pathologist.

Both of them are quiet for a moment. Then Viner leans forward. 'That's not it though, is it, Emily? That's not why you're antsy about the report.'

Harris shakes her head and reaches for the wine bottle. She tops up Viner's glass and then her own.

'No,' she says. 'I'm ansty because I don't really believe the body at Helsby is Frank Keane.'

'Ah.' Viner leans back against the cushions. He takes a sip of wine. 'OK. That kind of response is fairly typical. You should know that. Friends and family consistently resist the facts. From what I know, one of the bodies in the barn matches Frank Keane in terms of size. And the circumstantial evidence is pretty compelling. It was his place – or it was where he was staying – and the woman is likely to be the neighbour. She's missing. On the balance of probability I'd say that's pretty compelling. If I was making a bet I'd say they were in a relationship.'

Both Gareth and Linda have stopped talking, aware that the other conversation in the room has taken a deeper turn.

'And the other man?' says Harris.

Viner shrugs. 'One of the arsonists?'

'Two arsonists? How many arsonists work in pairs? Come on.'

'That's your area, Emily. I'm just making suggestions.'

'OK.' Harris slumps back against the cushions. She holds up her hand in a gesture of surrender. 'I know what I sound like.' She raises her wine glass for inspection. 'Blame this.'

'Amen,' says Gareth. 'I'm always getting too carried away when I'm having a good time.' Gareth drains his glass and holds it aloft. 'To good times!'

Harris sees Steve shoot him a look that contains gratitude and knows that she's been badgering the pathologist.

'Are you sure you're not getting *too* carried away now, Gareth?' says Viner but his tone is warm. 'You don't do hangovers, remember?'

'It's my funeral,' says Gareth and reaches for the bottle.

'Can I come?' Linda lifts her glass as Gareth pours. She looks at her partner but Em isn't listening. She's thinking about something Gareth said.

It's worth a try.

74

Berlin, October 24th

The air is thick with testosterone and violence and heightened sexuality. The mostly male audience wear dark clothing and strong cologne. The few women present are, mostly, accessories. Hardcore plays over the sound system.

If extremism could be bottled it would smell like this.

Gottlenz leaves Lamm outside and moves through the crowds clustered around the bar. He heads for his seat, a spare, near the back, no ticket required. The boys on the door tonight wave him through with a respectful nod. Unremarkable as he is, Gottlenz has juice here.

Even keeping to the back, Gottlenz knows some of the more knowledgeable in the crowd can still pick him out as easily as if he was painted orange. The thought is not comforting.

Despite the shabbiness of the venue there's nothing amateur about the event.

There is serious money up for grabs tonight and a drunk crowd who have bet heavy. The rules are simple: anything goes. Both fighters are contained within an octagonal cage. They fight barefoot and wear light gloves.

Kolumne88 take the gate, the bar and collects on the betting action. It's one of many mechanisms that keep the funds flowing into the hidden accounts that Gottlenz controls. The money is good but it's not enough for what Bruckner, Gottlenz and Hoffen have planned. For that last tranche the assumption they've been working under is that they need Bruckner's cash supply from the forced donor operations at the clinic to remain flowing. It's this assumption that

Gottlenz is about to challenge. What he's doing isn't a change of emphasis in the *Kolumne88* ranks.

It's a coup.

The first bout lasts less than a minute and results in one of the fighters being stretchered away, still unconscious, blood dripping from a shattered eye socket. A guy with a mop and bucket cleans up the canvas and, accompanied by an animal roar and a fresh blast of thrash metal, the lights dim in the auditorium as the main bout gets ready to start.

A white spot hits the back of the auditorium and the fighters and their entourage leave the dressing room. Led by two blondes in gold bikinis and hi-cut shorts, the two fighters dance to the ring. One is bare-chested while the other, a black guy, wears a long silver dressing gown with the hood up. Both men rotate their heads and arms as they walk. To Gottlenz, they look indestructible: walking knots of pure muscle and energy and he wouldn't like to meet either of them in a back street without full body armour, a loaded Uzi and half a dozen of Lamm's foot soldiers. As they reach the ring and step through the cage door, howls of abuse are hurled at the black fighter. The choice of ethnicity is carefully orchestrated. Gottlenz knows the receipts go up if *Kolumne88* puts in a couple of ethnic fighters. It also boosts the betting –although it doesn't pay to have them win too often. At a fight last February there had been a near-riot when a black fighter beat one of Marzahn's own favoured sons.

A fat man wearing a dinner suit introduces the fighters over the sound system as the trainers and physios fuss around. Gottlenz watches the white fighter with cropped blonde hair, wearing red and black shorts, impatiently swat away a hand extended by his trainer. She is a slender, serious-looking, dark-haired woman wearing a white t-shirt and loose Adidas track pants. She steps back, her expression unreadable as the MC finishes the announcements and the fight starts.

The audience rises and despite himself Gottlenz feels his own pulse quicken. As tawdry as the event is there's no denying the frisson of Neanderthal excitement as the two men close in on one another.

It is brutal.

The white guy cops it for the first few minutes. He's not as tall as his opponent but although that doesn't seem to matter much in a boxing arena, in here it does. Whitey is taking a pasting and the crowd don't like it. With howls of hate swirling around the warehouse, the black fighter closes in on his opponent. The white guy tucks in his arms, surviving, just. His larger and quicker opponent has a longer reach.

And then, as though a switch has been flicked, the fight swings back his way. There's a slowing in the bigger man's moves and the crowd sense the change. Now, roared on by the crowd, the white fighter is up on his toes as he moves out of range before darting back inside to deliver a short jab to the chin. It doesn't connect cleanly but it rocks the black guy backwards. The crowd rises and whoever is in charge of the address system plays a sound effect of breaking glass.

Suddenly there's a real fight on. Sensing he is losing momentum, the black fighter redoubles his efforts but this time encounters real resistance.

'Fuck the nigger up!' The shout comes from a man at Gottlenz's elbow. His face is flushed and his expensive shirt spotted with sweat. He turns to Gottlenz. 'Fucking niggers.'

Gottlenz nods but says nothing. He has no time or sympathy for ethnics himself but also finds it difficult to raise himself to the levels of red-raw hatred in the warehouse. For him the struggle is ideological, not racial. It is bigger than that. *Kolumne88,* Gottlenz believes, are fighting for control of Germany and hatred of minorities is simply the fuel for the fire. If truth is told, Gottlenz finds the type of people he represents to be coarse creatures he would sooner not be around. Circumstances dictate that he needs them. *Kolumne88* needs them.

The round finishes and the bikini girls clamber into the ring as the fighters are attended to. The white fighter's physio keeps her head down as the girls saunter past. Her attention is all on her fighter.

The rest of the fight goes the way Gottlenz expects. After the early onslaught in round one, the white fighter starts strong in the second. Within a minute his opponent is bleeding profusely from a vicious cut underneath his right eye. If it had been a boxing match the thing would have been over but this is something else. Towards the end of round three the black guy goes to the canvas. His opponent straddles him and, to a rising cacophony from the baying crowd, lands a series of bone-crunching punches directly to his face. After a long time, much longer than Gottlenz would have liked, the referee finally intervenes and the fight is over.

Gottlenz slips out of his seat while the attention is on the brightly lit ring and heads for the dressing rooms.

At the door leading backstage two *Kolumne88* goons stand aside as they recognise Gottlenz. He walks past them with a nod and waits outside the dressing room for the winner.

Then the auditorium doors swing open and the corridor is filled with noise and people. The blonde fighter passes Gottlenz. He smells of sweat and liniment and blood, happy in his victory, his eyes shining. Close up, he's smaller than Gottlenz had thought but even more intimidating. There's a brief moment when the fighter's eyes catch Gottlenz's and then he is gone, his trainer close behind. Two or three more people go inside and the door is closed.

Gottlenz waits a few minutes and then follows them.

The fighter is sitting on a massage table stripped to his jocks with a long towel wrapped around his shoulders. His physio is working on his fingers while he talks to a smartly-dressed East European guy who Gottlenz knows is the manager. As Gottlenz comes into the dressing room, the conversation halts. The fight guys are outsiders. They don't know Gottlenz from a plate of schnitzel.

'Who's this guy?' says the fighter. He and his manager look at Gottlenz. 'Press?' His voice is soft but there's no denying the man's power.

Gottlenz shakes his head.

'Then fuck off,' says the manager. 'Or did you want to ask Jens on a date?' He and the fighter and another couple of men in the room laugh.

'I've come to talk,' says Gottlenz.

'Didn't you hear me?' says the manager, his voice taking on a harder tone. 'Jackie boy don't want to talk to anyone right now.'

'That's ok,' says Gottlenz mildly. 'It's not Jack I want to talk to.' He turns to the trainer who looks up from her task. 'It's Fräulein Lehmann.'

75

Long Carraig, Scotland, October 27th

The episode in the night scares Frank so much that he makes some adjustments to his plans to see the specialist. He can't wait a moment longer, and, with twenty million still sitting in the MK Consulting account, he doesn't have to.

Online he finds a helicopter charter company and arranges to be picked up, his fear of heights laughable now in the face of the real horror eating away at him from the inside. At ten Frank is at the hangar waiting, his bag slung over his shoulder. Eight minutes later the Bell 206L-3 Longranger descends from a sunless sky and lands like a dragonfly on Long Rock.

The pilot steps down and greets Frank who says little, keeps his cap brim down. The pilot stows Frank's bag, checks the flight plan and they rise into the air. Frank sits in the back, silent and watches the ocean rushing past below as they head south. The pilot is used to rich people with attitude; he keeps quiet, does his job. With the memory of last night's pain fresh in his mind, and the threat it could come back at any time, Frank can't get to the specialist quick enough. His skin feels papery, his bones dry and brittle and Frank folds his arms tight across his chest as if that will stop himself crumbling into dust and blowing away on the wind.

76

Berlin, October 24th

Gottlenz paces the corridor outside the dressing room for forty minutes before Angelika Lehmann has finished with her fighter. When she does emerge, carrying a holdall and wearing street clothes, her head covered by the hood of a black sweatshirt, she walks straight past him without any sign she has seen him. She pushes open the double doors and disappears.

Gottlenz hurries after her. Inside the auditorium he sees her walking towards the exit, ignoring those among the crowd who look her way. This is not a good environment for a woman but Lehmann gives off an almost palpable air of indifference. Gottlenz increases his speed and catches up with her as she crosses the wasteland to the front of the warehouse.

'Angelika,' says Gottlenz when he is a few paces behind her. 'Wait.'

Lehmann turns and looks at him.

'Are you a cop?' she says. Her voice has a pronounced Berlin accent, so much so that even Gottlenz, a Berliner himself, has trouble understanding some words.

'No,' says Gottlenz. 'I got your name from Lamm. I'm his . . . controller.'

Lehmann looks around. 'I have no idea what you're talking about.' She turns and starts walking.

'Angelika,' says Gottlenz. 'Angelika!'

Lehmann stops once more and walks back to him. She gets close. 'Fuck off,' she hisses. Her gaze is intense but Gottlenz can hear the muffled fear lying below. He leans in close and drops his voice.

'I'm not a cop. The bomb is my idea, Angelika. Mine. Do you understand what I'm saying? If I know about the bomb I'm either a cop or who I say I am, right? Who else would know?'

Angelika Lehmann shakes her head, the movements small and quick. 'Are you out of your mind?'

Gottlenz holds up his hands. 'Maybe,' he says. 'There's been a change of plan.'

'We can't talk here,' says Lehmann.

'No.'

'Meet me in thirty minutes at the Cafe Istanbul on *Rhinstraße*. Opposite the rail crossing.' Lehmann makes a move to turn and then stops. 'If you're not who you say you are you won't leave that place. Understand?'

Gottlenz nods and Lehmann walks away.

Cafe Istanbul turns out to be a brightly-lit, bare-bones joint in a dingy concrete strip of closed shops. It faces a wide strip of rubble-strewn wasteland that separates the road from the rail track. Gottlenz parks the car and sits watching it for five minutes knowing that he is at a crossroads. Then the image of his children at the Zoo comes into his mind and he steps out of the car.

There are around fifteen people in the cafe, all of them dark-skinned. Few of them look up as Gottlenz enters. He orders a coffee from the waiter and takes a seat at a table near the back. There is no sign of Lehmann. Gottlenz drinks his coffee and tries to control the twitch in his leg. He spills a spoon of sugar across the formica table-top and the man cleaning plates behind the counter glances over before returning to his task.

After twenty minutes Lehmann comes into the cafe. She shakes hands with the man behind the counter and walks across to Gottlenz.

She has changed out of her sports gear and is wearing a fitted black leather jacket over jeans. Gottlenz can't tell if she's wearing make-up but it looks like she might be. Her hair is pulled back and tied in a ponytail. Her nails are short and unpainted. She wears boots with a small heel.

'Just so you know,' she says and points towards a large man sitting at a corner table. Gottlenz nods. 'That's fine.' He gestures at his glass as the waiter approaches. 'Drink?'

'Water.' She speaks directly to the waiter, not Gottlenz. 'Still, no ice.'

While she waits for her drink, Lehmann looks at Gottlenz. Her expression is neither warm nor cold. This woman knows how to remain within herself.

The waiter reappears, places a glass of water on the table and retreats. Angelika Lehmann takes a sip and places it back down. 'OK,' she says. 'Tell me what it is.'

'I was wondering if you were going to come,' he says.

Lehmann ignores the statement. Instead she flicks her eyes to the door. 'I'm here to hear what you have to say.'

'There is a change in funding.'

'What do you mean?' Lehmann pulls back. 'The funds are not coming?'

'They will come,' says Gottlenz. He leans forward. 'The difference is that now it is me who will be paying. Directly.'

'Why?'

'That doesn't matter.'

'Have it your way.' Lehmann glances over at the big man in the corner but doesn't move off her seat. She looks back at Gottlenz and lowers her voice. 'Tell me what you want.'

'I have a change of structure to our deal,' says Gottlenz. 'From here this is just between us.'

'Alright,' says Lehmann. 'Do you want to cut to the chase and tell me what it is you want? And please don't let this be some weird stalking shit.'

'I want to headhunt you,' says Gottlenz. 'This is a job offer of a kind. The project remains as it is but with one big difference: you and your people report to me, not to *Kolumne88*.'

'I have a deal already. Why should I change to you, at this stage?'

'Because after tomorrow there will be no funding other than that coming from me.'

'What's going on?' says Lehmann. 'A take-over? No, wait, I don't want to know.' She taps a finger on the table. 'I'm sorry,' she says after a few seconds. 'I'm not interested. For all I know you're wearing a wire and, if that's the case, then I'm just humouring someone who is stalking me.'

Gottlenz makes a small gesture of dismissal. None of this stuff matters now. The how and the why and the what are all mixed. The only thing he knows is that the project must go forward and that Bruckner must not be part of it. Whatever he must do to make that happen, he will do.

'Fine, I thought you might say that. So I brought this.'

Gottlenz reaches inside his coat and retrieves a thick envelope. He pushes it across the sugar-starred table. The paper makes a tiny grinding sound against the crystals.

'A completion bonus,' he says. 'A loyalty bonus.' He fixes his eyes on hers. 'There's a quarter of a million Euros in there. Take this and the project becomes mine.'

Lehmann is silent.

Gottlenz remains still. There is no sign on his face that contained in the envelope is every cent he owns. No sign that he is gambling everything on this push.

'What am I supposed to do with this?' she says eventually.

'I really don't care,' says Gottlenz. 'As long as the project is ready on time and I am the one who hears any information first. You either do this or you don't.' He leans forward and taps the envelope. 'This is the message to take back to whoever you work with; I am now your point of contact. I now supply the funds. From now until completion you report to me. Is that clear?'

'I report to no-one. This is a commercial transaction.' Lehmann pauses. 'But when I have information to give then it doesn't matter to me which of you lunatics I speak to, it is all the same to me.'

She reaches out a hand and takes the envelope. There is a mobile number written on it and Gottlenz taps it as he pushes himself up from the table.

'Call me,' he says and walks from the cafe without another word. Outside, he gets into his car and drives a few hundred metres. Then, quite suddenly, he swerves towards a dark patch of shadow under some scrubby trees, opens the door and is violently sick.

77

Berlin, October 25th

Mick Lydon's not the sort of person that people pay any attention to. On the small side, well-dressed without being flash, his hair mid length, conservatively cut. He has an open face, friendly enough but with no outstanding features. He looks like someone who might work in a bank. Someone's dull dad.

Lydon runs a small electronics firm with a bare bones office and well-equipped warehouse on an industrial estate outside Watford. Lydon's a family man – PTS meetings, school runs, birthday parties, the whole thing. He's doing what he can in a difficult market. In reality he makes less than a quarter of his money from this. The rest comes from two other lines of business. One stream of cash comes from the porn sites he controls which specialise in sailing as close to the legal wind as possible. It is one of these that he is looking at now when his phone vibrates against his leg.

Lydon checks the caller ID. As soon as he sees the number he answers and then turns his eyes back to the screen.

'It's me,' he says. His voice is soft.

'I have a job,' says Felix Hoffen. 'Rush work. And the target's a pro.'

'OK,' says Lydon. 'Wait a second.' He puts the phone under his chin and lifts a pen and notebook from his breast pocket. 'Go on.'

'His name is Frank Keane. A cop from Liverpool. I want him.'

'OK.'

'Alive.'

'OK, sure. Give me what you have.'

Lydon listens as Hoffen talks. In the background he can hear street sounds, traffic, horns, an unfamiliar siren.

'This is going to cost,' says Lydon.

'Just find him. Don't worry about the fucking bill.' Hoffen talks about the logistical needs once Keane is found and Lydon makes notes.

When Hoffen finishes, Lydon hangs up and stares at the girl onscreen for a few seconds before closing the site with a click. He leans back in his office chair and breathes deeply, a predator catching the scent of blood on the wind.

78

Berlin, October 25th

Felix Hoffen finishes his call to Lydon and places the phone back on the table. It's almost three in the afternoon outside a corner cafe on *Kurfürstenstraße*. He's drinking thick sweet black coffee and smoking the English cigarettes he bought at John Lennon Airport. He likes this place. The dark wood walls and soft lighting inside remind him of his grandparents' apartment in Munich, a lifetime ago. He'd rather be sitting inside, soaking it all up but cigarettes force him to huddle at a table under the almost bare apple trees. That's OK, it feels clean out here and the sharp air helps him think.

The conversation yesterday with Ilsa Bruckner had been one that had been coming and, now it is out of the way, Hoffen feels happier with the situation. He has spent the past hours putting the operation back onto a professional level. Taking it out of the hands of an amateur was the right thing to do.

He blows out a long stream of smoke and watches it coil up into the cold grey sky. Under the table his leg bounces in an unconscious rhythm as he goes over the strategy he's just put in place. Until Keane is found there's no point in sitting around in England. The story Hoffen had given Bruckner about bringing in his own soldiers is true but what he hadn't mentioned was that he wouldn't be calling them in yet. The reason for this is simple: as good as they are, Hoffen's guys can't bring back anyone if they can't find them and, he suspects, Frank Keane will be a tricky find. Hoffen's soldiers will wait until Lydon gets the job done. Hoffen is confident Lydon will do the job. He always does. Bruckner doesn't need to know the details.

Hoffen finishes his cigarette and lights another from the stub before checking his watch. The call isn't his only piece of business that afternoon. He looks up and there, right on time, is Angelika Lehmann. Coming so soon on the heels of his conversation with Bruckner, her call is more than interesting. The dynamics of this situation are shifting and so are the players.

Lehmann sits down at the table opposite him without saying a word.

'I'm here,' says Hoffen. 'What is it you want?'

Angelika Lehmann leans forward and starts talking. She talks urgently for a few minutes while Hoffen listens closely. What she has to say is of great interest.

79

Liverpool, October 26th

'Brando?'

'Brando, mate, I'm telling you.' Magsi takes a slurp of coffee and looks out across the water towards the Liver Building. 'Voice like nails down a blackboard. The kid was only two or something.'

'What was she like? The mother. Yummy mummy?'

'What do you think, Ronnie? She was a fucking supermodel.'

'Really?'

'Don't be a dick. If she's got a kid called Brando, it's ten to one she's a council house slapper with an arse like a rhino.'

'She might have been a looker,' says Rimmer. 'How do you know?'

Magsi tunes them out. The woman he's talking about, no more than a girl herself, had been good-looking enough, even with a stack of curlers piled high and the usual sheen of orange make-up, the thickness of which indicates the class system in the city as sharply as being branded on the forehead. He feels sorry he mentioned it now as a stab of guilt hits home. She can call her kid whatever she likes. What business is it of his? Having a knob-jockey like Ronnie leering over her, even from an anecdotal distance, makes Magsi feel dirty, complicit in Rimmer's relentless quest for sex.

'What's Madam got us doing this afternoon?'

'What?' The conversation has veered back to work. Magsi looks at Ronnie. 'Don't call her that. I don't like it.'

Rimmer catches Steve Rose's eye. Rose is with Magsi on this one: despite his lapses into laddishness, he doesn't like calling Harris by that name either. It's not like calling DCI Keane, 'Roy'. That had few negative connotations, at least for the MIT team. 'Madam' has something of the schoolyard about it. Disloyal. Dumb.

'We're interviewing the husband this afternoon,' says Magsi. 'You already know this.'

'Which husband?' says Rose.

'Can't see why it's a two-man job, like,' says Rimmer, cutting across Rose's question, his face January bleak.

'The dead woman in Helsby. Kath Palmer.'

'Can't you do it?' says Rimmer. 'I've got paperwork.'

'We've all got paperwork, Ronaldo,' says Rose. 'Jesus, look at the gob on you. You're only driving to fucking Cheshire in a fucking nice warm car, not patrolling Kandahar at dawn.'

Rimmer looks like he's about to say something and once again stops himself just in time. From the leery look on Rimmer's face Magsi guesses it would have been something relating to Islam.

'I'm only messing,' says Rimmer. 'There are a couple of things I want to ask Bernie Palmer.'

'Oh? Like what?' says Magsi.

'You'll have to wait, Mags. Been doing a bit of digging of my own.'

Magsi glances at Rose and the two of them smile. Ronnie Rimmer comes out with so much horseshit he could fertilize Kew Gardens.

'Bit of a dark horse, DCI Keane,' Rimmer says. Magsi and Rose look at him blankly.

'Oh fuck off. Stop acting like a pair of virgins. We all know Roy was knocking a slice off her. I'm only saying what you're all thinking.'

'Fair enough,' says Magsi. The interview with Bernie Palmer isn't likely to reap much in the way of information and he's finding it hard to produce much enthusiasm for the task, especially as it involves schlepping over to Cheshire with Rimmer in tow. He hadn't piped up in the briefing but he's also somewhat puzzled by Harris sending them both.

'How about you?' he says, looking at Rose just as he stuffs the remains of his pastry into his mouth.

'The girl,' he says through a mouthful of sugar and crumbs. 'Again.' He chews frantically for a few seconds. 'Pointless. She's a random. A sex thing.'

Magsi's still thinking about that last word from Rimmer after they leave Costa and head across to his car. On the face of it, the big tit sounds like he has a point. Surely Sarah Coughlan was a random pickup, a warm body selected by the two Germans as casually as a shopper checking a rack of apples? The sexual element can't be overlooked. The girl was naked when the accident happened, she had no connection – so far – with either of the Germans. She was young and vulnerable and almost everything points to a sexually motivated abduction. Just because it's what Ronnie Rimmer thinks doesn't make it not true.

The only trouble with that line of thinking is that Magsi doesn't believe it for a minute. From what they can gather from CCTV, the Mercedes did not cruise the streets of south Liverpool looking for targets. MIT have the van coming off the M62 and from there, driving more or less directly towards the Coughlan house. There are a couple of cameras situated on roads nearby that would be far easier locations for an abduction but the Merc never drove down either. Magsi had to hand it to Rimmer on the CCTV. He'd put together a convincing patchwork of images that trace the van almost from the point of entry to the city up to Menlove Avenue. It had been too much to hope that there would be footage of the abduction and so it had proved. The last image of the Merc is of the crash, taken from a camera mounted on the Cunard Building.

With all things considered, Magsi leans towards the view that Coughlan was directly targeted. He knows too, that while this line is one that has yet to gain real traction inside the department, there are a number of officers who feel the way he does. DI Harris, judging by her assignment of Rose to continue digging on Sarah and her readiness to send Theresa Cooper to Berlin, is one of them. Sarah was picked up because she was Sarah Coughlan.

The big question, the one that none of them have the answer to, is what was so special about her?

80

Liverpool, October 26th

Charlie Searle's just about to head out to lunch when Karen buzzes through from the outer office that there are people in to see him.

'I don't have an appointment now do I?'

'No. But they . . .'

Searle hears a muffled exchange in the background and then Karen is back on the line.

'Perhaps you ought to see them, Superintendent. They mentioned the Home Office.'

Karen has been with Charlie Searle for three years and he knows she is good. If she thinks he should postpone lunch then it probably is something he should be doing.

'Them?'

'There are two gentlemen, Superintendent.' Karen pauses. 'A Mr Smith and a Mr Jones.'

'You're kidding.'

'No, Superintendent.'

'Well send them in, I suppose.'

Searle hangs up as the door opens. Two men walk into his office. Both are smartly dressed, of middle height, around forty years old. One of them smiles, steps forward and offers his hand.

'Mr Smith. Thank you so much for seeing me at such short notice, Superintendent.' His voice is pure drawled Oxbridge, several notches up the class pole from Charlie Searle's own rugger-bugger tones.

Searle shakes the man's hand and glances at the second man. 'Mr Jones, I suppose?'

'Exactly.' Smith smiles. 'You have it.'

Searle looks at the man in front of him. 'Smith and Jones? Really?'

Smith shrugs. 'It doesn't really matter.' He makes a small dismissive gesture. 'They'll do for the moment. We are in a city that prides itself on its humour after all. Tarbie. Doddy. Craig Charles and John Bishop. Comedy gold.' He smiles at Searle who remains impassive. Smith's smile stays in place a few beats longer than it should. It's Charlie Searle who looks away first.

Behind Smith, Jones lifts a slat in the office window and looks out bleakly at the city.

'Christ,' he mutters, shaking his head. He lets the white plastic snap back into place and wanders across to an L-shaped sofa in the corner of the office.

'Er . . .' Charlie Searle isn't often lost for words but he's finding this encounter difficult. The visitors have an ability to generate uncertainty.

'Are you going to sit down?' says Searle. He indicates the chairs. 'We have seating for special visitors. Only primitive construction naturally, but we do our best.'

Smith smiles and sits across from Charlie Searle's desk, crossing one leg over the other and straightening the creases in his trousers. Jones takes a seat on the sofa, his back to the wall.

Searle looks from one to the other and shakes his head. 'Does this routine work?'

'Indulge us, Superintendent,' says Smith. 'Mr Jones is the strong silent type.' He reaches inside his jacket, lifts out an identity card and holds it out at arm's length. 'Home Office. In a manner of speaking.'

Searle looks at the document. He hands it back and sits down. 'I don't recognise the department.'

'No-o.' The word is drawled. 'You wouldn't have. If you have concerns you can call your Chief Constable.'

'If you don't mind, that's what I'll do, Mr Smith.'

Smith shrugs. 'As you wish.'

Charlie Searle picks up the phone.

'Karen, can you check Mr Smith's credentials with the CC's office, please. Call me when you have the information.' For a few moments there is silence in the office.

'Busy?' says Smith, eventually. He glances over his shoulder out of the window. 'I imagine it would be a pretty active beat. Up here.'

'In 'the north', you mean? Or in Liverpool?'

'Aren't they the same thing?'

'Not necessarily.'

The phone bleeps and Searle picks it up. He listens for a moment.

'Thanks,' he says and replaces it on its cradle. 'OK, you can talk. The CC approves.'

Smith nods.

'Frank Keane,' he says.

'What about him?' Searle sits up a little straighter in his chair. Keane might be dead but he is, or was, one of his officers and Charlie is alert for any implied criticism.

'Relax, Superintendent,' says Smith. 'We simply want to know how his demise has been taken in the department.'

'I don't follow you.'

'DCI Keane died in a fire in Helsby, Cheshire nine days ago. Since then we have been made aware that one of your officers is of the belief that he isn't dead.'

'How would you know that? No, wait, I don't want to know.'

'It's no great secret, Superintendent. There have been two calls – unanswered I might add – to Keane's mobile. In addition, he has been sent two emails by the same person. None of the information in those communications is sinister. It is the fact that they have been made at all which interests us. We wondered if you could shed any light on the matter?'

All trace of warmth has gone from Searle's face. 'I assume the person calling is Emily Harris?'

Smith nods.

'She was close to DCI Keane. She may be experiencing difficulty accepting his death.'

'Are you?'

'Am I what?'

'Experiencing difficulty?'

'Should I be?'

Smith smiles. 'This is getting rather too circular for my liking so I'll say it straight. Have you or any of your officers heard from Frank Keane?'

'How could we? He's dead.'

'Yes.'

Charlie Searle is beginning to feel he's asleep. This encounter has the air of a dream. Not exactly a nightmare perhaps but he feels it could head in that direction.

'Look, what do you want?' Searle leans forward and leans on his desk.

Smith remains silent for longer than is comfortable. 'I don't really know,' he says eventually. 'That's the honest answer, Superintendent Searle. Our department has noted DCI Keane as a person of interest: his experiences and connections in the US earlier this year alerted us.' Smith waves his hand. 'We have various flagging procedures. Boring stuff that alerts us when someone on our files does something unusual. So far we aren't quite sure exactly *how* Keane interests us. Is he one of us? Or something else. You see the difficulty?'

'I'm struggling. You say you already had a file open on Keane?'

'Keane comes back from America with some serious connections. Well, one in particular. He is also carrying – in a manner of speaking – twenty-five million dollars.'

'Which he told us about.'

'That's right.' Smith doesn't expand on how he knows Frank had told Searle and Charlie Searle doesn't want to know.

'When we hear about connections like the one that a humble copper makes out there, we take an interest even if it seems that the connection is at least partly accidental. A file is opened which is usually as far as it goes until something odd happens. Like dying in unusual circumstances. And then receiving calls and emails from people who know he's dead. All of this leaves my department with a problem – which is why we slogged up here this morning. I have to decide if Frank Keane has been killed by 'friendlies' or is involved in something else entirely. Or, indeed, if the chap is dead at all. Then I have to decide what, if anything to do about it.'

'So what is your visit here for?'

'I want you to tell me if you hear anything.'

'Inform?'

'Exactly.' Smith pushes his seat back and gets to his feet. He holds out a hand. 'You have grasped the situation perfectly.'

Searle shakes Smith's hand. 'I thought you spooks could just get any information you want, whenever you want it, with all your digital witchcraft.'

'We wish. No, Superintendent, sometimes we just dip a line in the water and hope for the best.' The handshake complete, Smith moves to the door, Jones behind him.

'If Frank Keane does pop onto your radar, let me know, there's a good chap.' Smith pauses in the doorway. 'We're going back to London from here but could do with a decent lunch before we go. Is that something you can get up here?'

'Food, you mean? Yes, we have food. Along with electricity and running water.' Searle smiles sweetly. 'The best place to eat is just along the street on the corner of Piss Off and Go Fuck Yourself.'

'Sounds perfect,' says Smith. 'Toodle-oo.'

81

Liverpool, October 26th

Despite the smirks from Ronnie Rimmer in the driver's seat, Magsi still calls his mother from the car. A single man, he makes sure he eats with his parents at least twice a week. She asks him to pick up some limes and he gets the smirking Rimmer to detour into a supermarket. Domestic duties taken care of, Magsi and Rimmer arrive at the Palmer house fifty minutes after leaving Liverpool.

As he steps out into the green surroundings, Magsi is struck by how quiet the place is. The unfamiliar silences and damp poetry of the countryside puts him on the defensive.

'Nice and quiet,' says Rimmer. To emphasise the point, he lets rip with a fruity blast. He's the type that always makes a comment following a public breaking of wind and, sure enough, as soon as the bass notes have subsided, out it comes. 'You could hear a sparrow fart,'

'You're not a sparrow,' says Magsi, moving upwind into an area uncontaminated by Rimmer. 'You're a fucking dirty bastard.'

Magsi trots clear of Rimmer's methane and up the neat path towards Bernie Palmer's place. Here the air contains the smell of ashes. Over to the left a tangle of blackened beams is all that the remains of the barn. Magsi doesn't know how Bernie Palmer can stand to be so close to the scene given the circumstances.

Rimmer pushes the door bell and glances at Magsi while they wait. A dog barks somewhere inside.

'Ten to one he's pissed,' says Rimmer.

Magsi doesn't reply.

After ringing again, a shape lumbers into view through the ripples in the glass portion of the front door. The door opens and Bernie Palmer looks at the coppers with Glaswegian distaste. Magsi doesn't think Rimmer's guess was right but there's evidence of a heavy night in Palmer's sagging skin and dark-rimmed eyes.

'Mr Palmer?'

Bernie Palmer nods slowly.

'Aye,' he says, his voice flat. 'You polis?'

'Yes,' says Magsi. 'I'm DS Magsi and this is DS Rimmer. Can we come in? There are a few things we'd like to go over.'

Palmer shrugs and walks back down the hallway. From behind a door comes renewed barking.

'Quiet,' growls Bernie Palmer and the barking stops.

Rimmer looks at Magsi, eyebrows raised.

'We'll take that as a 'yes', then, Mr Palmer,' says Rimmer.

'Take it any fucking way ye want,' Palmer says over his shoulder without stopping or turning round. 'Like I give a shit.' He disappears through a door and Magsi and Rimmer follow him.

Inside the living room Bernie Palmer sits down heavily on the sofa. The giant TV is on but the sound is down. Onscreen is a soap. Palmer looks at it blankly as Magsi and Rimmer take a seat.

'Any news?' says Palmer, still looking at the screen. 'You fellers got any hot leads? Taken anyone in for questioning? Put out an APB?' The last is spoken in tones of venom, the syllables drawn out and then bitten off sharply.

'We're working on a number of lines of enquiry, Mr Palmer,' says Rimmer.

'Oh aye, I bet you fucking are. Nothing like a copper getting killed to get yers all running around like headless chickens.'

'One of which is taking a long hard look at all possibilities. That includes examining if DCI Keane was the intended target.' Rimmer ignores Palmer's statement and puts a bit of bite into his own tone.

Now Palmer does look at the cops. 'You think Kath had hit men after her?'

'No-one mentioned hit men, Mr Palmer.' Magsi leans forward. 'Why would you think that?'

Bernie Palmer makes a dismissive gesture but some of his bile fades. 'I don't know.' He waves a fat hand towards the TV. 'Too many of those alphabet shows, mebbe.'

'Alphabet shows?'

'CSI, JAG, all that shite. You can't move for fucking hit men in those things.'

'This isn't CSI, Mr Palmer,' says Magsi. 'We're just trying to get information.' He pauses. 'I want to ask about your wife. About her relationship with DCI Keane.'

Bernie Palmer glares at Magsi but it's only momentary. He shrugs.

'I didnae know there was one. Not until I was contacted by you boys.'

'In Spain?'

'Aye, we have a place there. Almeria.'

'So there had been no contact prior to . . .'

'Prior to her fucking him?' Palmer shakes his head. 'Only a bit of banter over the fence. Your man took the dog for a walk now and again. I know Kath liked the look of him. She was after getting him round for a bite.'

'And did he?' says Rimmer. 'Come round?'

Palmer shakes his head. 'No. He called and cancelled. Said he had a few things to do.' Palmer looks at Magsi and then Rimmer. 'Kath could be a bit of a flirty thing, to be honest with ye. It may not have been Keane who did the chasing if you know what I mean.' He looks back at the TV but not before Magsi's seen the tears brim in his eyes.

'Can we come back to Almeria, Mr Palmer?' says Rimmer. Magsi looks at him and tries not to let the surprise show on his face.

'What about it?'

'Michael Oakley,' says Rimmer.

Bernie Palmer doesn't move but Magsi can see the tension.

'You remember Michael Oakley, don't you, Mr Palmer?' Rimmer doesn't look at Magsi.

'Name rings a bell.'

'Come off it, Bernie.' Rimmer's voice is sharp now. 'Michael Oakley is someone you know through your building business. Last year he was up in Crown Court on charges of extortion. The man he was charged with extorting was a James Newman.'

'And?'

'Newman owed you money, Bernie. Oakley was trying to recover it when he was pinched. He's an old-fashioned stand-over man. A big guy, lots of muscles and a face like the back of a train.'

'Oh aye,' says Bernie Palmer. 'I remember. It was all a misunderstanding. Michael was acquitted.'

'Michael, is it now? Two minutes ago you hadn't heard of the bloke. And a while back you mentioned hit men. You're connected, Bernie. Well connected.' Rimmer pauses. 'The only thing we have to work out is if those nasty little connections have got anything to do with the deaths. Oh and we know all about your little S&M circle, Bernie. Finding out they've been shagging a couple involved in a murder tends to have a tongue-loosening effect on some people.'

Palmer glares at Rimmer and Magsi.

'I want a lawyer,' he says.

82

Ellesmere Port, Cheshire, October 26th

'No, sorry mate.'

The driver climbs into his cab and hits the ignition. As the big transporter coughs fumes up into the orange-tinted night sky, Lydon shivers. It's five, he's been out here most of the night and so far has come up with nothing more exciting than an offer of a quickie from the driver of a Sainsbury's truck who didn't seem to worry too much about Lydon's snide police ID.

Turning away from the latest knock-back, Lydon tucks his prop clipboard under his arm, jams his hands into the pockets of his North Face and walks across the windy car park to where a white and green BP truck is pulling into a space. Two more, he thinks and then I'll try something else.

He reaches the cab as the driver's stepping down. The man holds up a hand as he approaches.

'Not buying, feller,' he says in a thick Liverpool. 'Too tired.'

'I'm not selling,' says Lydon. He holds up the fake police ID and hands it to the guy.

'What's this all about then?' The driver, an obese man with the air of someone fully focused on a mission to get outside of a full English with all the trimmings, looks yearningly at the warm light spilling out from the transport cafe windows.

'We're looking for someone who might have been looking for a lift in this area a few days ago. He's around forty, middle height, in good shape and speaks with a Liverpool accent. Did you see him?'

'Where's your accent from? London?'

'What's that got to do with anything? Did you pick anyone up or not?'

'No. I don't pick hitchhikers up. Too risky.' The driver looks at Lydon with interest. 'And it's illegal. But you'd know that, right?'

'Thank you for your help, sir,' says Lydon. 'That'll be all.'

The driver nods. 'You don't hear many Cockney coppers round here,' he says and winks at Lydon. 'You know what I mean?'

'Very good, sir.' Lydon steps to one side and watches the scouse gutbucket waddle towards the cafe doors hitching his overalls up over the swell of his giant arse. At the door he turns and looks at Lydon before going inside.

'Shit.'

Lydon stamps his feet and gets back into the Land Rover to warm up. It's a raw day and he's been working the big carpark at the Ellesmere Port cafe since midnight. Judging from his performance with the last guy he's getting too tired.

Lydon sees the headlights from another refinery truck swing off from the road. He waits for the driver to park and leave the cab before stepping out. One last time tonight and then he'll try something else. It's getting risky staying here and the last guy might just decide to give the local police a call.

This driver is older than most, perhaps sixty-five. He looks fresh though. Lydon repeats his story.

'Yes.'

Instantly, Lydon's fatigue is gone. 'You did?'

'Last Friday?'

Lydon nods.

'Yes. Late it was, or early, depending on your starting point. Anyway, it was about this time. Still dark. He looked like a decent enough feller. Maybe a bit down on his luck but I never hold that against anyone. After the years on the road I've put in I can do with a bit of company sometimes.'

'How far did you take him?'

'Carlisle. Or a bit before. Southwaite services.'

'What time?'

'Maybe a bit before eight?'

'Did he say where he was heading for?'

'What's this about?'

Lydon ignores the question. 'Did he say anything?'

'Not much. Quiet sort of bloke.' The driver pauses. 'You're not police, are you?'

Lydon smiles. 'Is that what you really think?' He steps fractionally closer to the driver. 'Because I've just told you I am police.'

The driver looks like he's about to say something but he stops himself. Lydon is still smiling softly but the expression looks off kilter on him. For a moment there is no sound from the traffic, as if time has frozen.

'OK,' says the driver, looking down at the tarmac. 'I didn't mean anything.'

'He did say something else then.' It's a statement from Lydon. There's more here, he's sure. He steps closer to the driver who flinches slightly. Lydon has done nothing, suggested no violence, yet the threat emanating from him is so palpable that the driver of the oil truck is surprised he can't see it coiling up into the cold northern sky. He wants to get away from this man as soon as possible.

'Tom. He said his name was Tom. I thought he seemed OK. Had he done something?'

Lydon nods. 'Yeah. Just 'Tom'? Nothing else?' His voice is sharper now and both men know that this is now a different kind of conversation. There is no pretense now from Lydon that he is a cop. He barks the questions out, demanding answers quickly and that's how they come back, the driver eager to please, to escape. To live.

'Just Tom. He only said it once, that's how I remember. Tom, yeah. My brother's name. So I remembered.' The driver halts, aware he's babbling. He draws a deep breath and then offers more. 'And he mentioned something about heading north.'

'Anywhere specific?'

'Scotland. He mentioned Scotland.'

'Anything else?'

'No, that's it. That's all he said. Tom. Scotland.'

Lydon makes a note on the clipboard and regards the driver for a few seconds.

'OK,' he says eventually. 'That will be all. Sir.'

He smiles sourly at the last word and the driver moves towards the cafe, grateful to be going but unwilling to turn his back on the man asking the questions. Lydon, standing stock still, watches him all the way to the door.

83

London, October 27th

After the helicopter to London, Frank is sitting across from Stevens, the specialist, by one o'clock. Stevens is a man in his fifties with a smooth, glossy look about him and a voice that wouldn't be out of place coming from the mouth of a minor Royal.

'Those are the biopsy results?' Frank nods at the file on Stevens' desk.

'They are, Mr Machin.' The doctor straightens himself and looks directly at Frank. 'There's no easy way to say this so I'm just going to say it. The cancer is inoperable.'

Frank blinks. 'Inoperable?'

Stevens nods. 'I'm really sorry.'

'OK.' Frank breathes out slowly.

'Would you like a glass of water, Mr Machin?'

There's a short delay before Frank remembers that the doctor is talking to him. He shakes his head and looks out of the window. 'Raining again,' he says in a flat tone.

Stevens follows the direction of Frank's gaze.

'Y-es,' he says. 'It is raining, Mr Machin. Look there are . . .'

'It was raining the first time,' says Frank, cutting across the medic without taking his eyes off the London traffic. The scene is a mirror image of the one in the medical centre in Liverpool where he'd been given his original diagnosis. Frank runs his hands over his chin, feeling the new beard prickling his fingers and turns back to Stevens. 'When I got the original cancer diagnosis, I thought that was about as bad as it could get.' Frank smiles. 'But you proved me wrong.'

'I'm sorry.'

'I thought you were the best? That you would fix me up.'

'It's not for me to say if I'm the best, Mr Machin.' Stevens rests his elbows on the desk. 'But I do know my stuff. And sometimes, like today, I wish I didn't. My expertise is telling me that your cancer is beyond treatment, beyond chemotherapy, beyond any surgery. Your doctor in Liverpool – Mr Wilson, was it? – knows his stuff but was, in my view, being overly optimistic in allowing you hope. There are no easy paths in this scenario, Mr Machin, but from experience I can tell you that you are better knowing the truth than working under the mistaken assumption that everything will turn out fine. You can get other opinions I'm sure but I'm rather afraid that the conclusion would be the same. There is no doubt.'

Frank nods. 'At least you're telling me straight.' He coughs and tries to get his voice under control. 'How long do you reckon?'

'Six months. A year, perhaps. No more than two.'

'Six months? Is that a guarantee?'

'There are no guarantees, Mr Machin.'

'Aye. You can say that again.' Frank pushes his chair back from the desk and moves to stand when Stevens speaks again.

'Wait. Please.'

Frank sits down and looks at the doctor curiously.

Stevens has the same look that Frank has seen on a thousand faces across the interviewing table. The look that says the person has information but doesn't want to share it.

'C'mon, spit it out,' says Frank. 'What is it? I'm the poor fucker who's just been handed a death sentence, doctor.' Frank taps his watch. 'I'm on the clock here.'

Stevens hesitates before reaching down and opening a drawer in his desk. From it he pulls out a white package about the size of a shoebox. He puts it on the desk and, using the tip of one perfectly manicured finger, slides it across the polished surface towards Frank as though it's a bomb.

Frank looks at it blankly and then back at Stevens.

'Is this some sort of touchy-feely consolation prize? Because if this turns out to be a box of chocolates or a little book of uplifting poetry I won't be answerable, you know what I mean? I'm in no mood for jokes.'

'It's no joke, Mr Machin,' says Stevens. He licks his lips and Frank can see his discomfort. 'Believe me, I really wish it was.' He looks at the box and then back at Frank. 'I was told to tell you this came from a friend.'

'What does that mean?'

'I don't know.' Stevens lowers his voice. 'I was visited by . . . some people, Mr Machin. They are people who I sometimes get referrals from when specialised treatment is needed for key personnel. Military personnel. Intelligence services. Those kind of people.'

Sheehan, thinks Frank. This is Sheehan.

'You were threatened?'

'No, not in so many words. But I was left with no illusions that I didn't have a choice but to give these to you. There was some unnecessary unpleasantness' Stevens wrinkles his mouth in distaste at the memory. 'It's my medical licence at stake by the way. Just so you know.'

Frank opens the package. Inside, placed in a bed of grey protective styrofoam, are two rows of small glass vials with various chemical words printed on labels wrapped around them. A folded sheet of paper is tucked down one side of the box. Frank glances at it and sees a list containing times and quantities.

'What is this?'

Stevens rotates the box towards him. 'I rather think that these are experimental cancer drugs, Mr Machin. In fact, I know they are because that's what I was told.' He looks back at Frank. 'The people who spoke to me were Americans, just like the organisation that fixed your appointment with me. My guess – and that's all it is – is that these drugs come out of some sort of military or intelligence facility. Perhaps a by-product from a biological site, something like that?'

'Chemical weapons?'

'If you like.'

'And I, what, I take these? Aren't they dangerous?'

'Mr Machin,' says Stevens. 'You're going to die, sooner rather than later. I'd suggest

that you are some way beyond the point at which taking these drugs would represent a long-term risk to you. There's every chance that they won't work and there is also a very decent chance that they will kill you somewhat sooner than your cancer if you let the disease run its course. Of course, what path you take is entirely your choice.'

Frank puts the lid back on the box and places it carefully back into the protective package.

'Then I guess I'll start taking them,' he says.

'It's a simple enough process. A vial a day until all 21 glass tubes are empty. From there your guess is as good as mine.'

Stevens also advises quiet and rest but admits this is more as a general guide than for any medical reasons.

'The fact is that I don't know what's in those vials, Mr Machin,' he'd said. 'I've looked at the labels and they represent nothing I am familiar with. You are stepping into the unknown.'

The unknown.

Frank's getting to know what that world feels like. He's been living in the unknown since his diagnosis. No, for much longer. Since finding Nicky Peters in the tunnels. From that point things became 'unknown' to a degree Frank would not have believed possible if he hadn't lived the experience.

Frank gets a second chopper back north that afternoon. On the flight he keeps the package of drugs on his lap. From time to time he finds his eyes flicking down to the box. He lets the sound of the chopper blades wash over him, his eyes focusing on the tiny diamond-glittering drops of water on the glass of the door window. It would be so easy to keep his gaze fixed there as he opened the latch and stepped out into oblivion but he doesn't. There is the package on the seat next to him for one thing. One last throw of the dice before Frank Keane departs this mortal coil, one more chance.

And at least one more appointment on his old patch before heading back to the island.

84

Berlin, October 26th

Angelika Lehmann moves the phone away from her ear and waits for the little prick to stop talking.

'Do you know nothing, woman? This is not the way to operate in the field. Do you not know that calls can be monitored? Jesus.'

Now Lehmann stays silent because she is biting her lip. Eric Roos, a neo-Nazi zealot with a personality problem – he doesn't have one – has absorbed almost all his 'field craft' from TV, movies and endless hours playing *Call of Duty*. The nearest he's been to a terror training camp before Lehmann recruited him is a hardcore metal hate festival outside Cologne. Angelika Lehmann needed a particular set of skills and she found Roos through her connections to the student nerd groups at Humboldt and Berlin University. Now, six months after Roos's arrival on the project that has consumed her for almost two years, it's hard to take the assumption of power from someone who is no more than a technician – a technician *she* found, handled and instructed. She could point out Roos's continued attendance at neo-Nazi events as being less than discreet. She could suggest that if the calls were being monitored as strictly as Roos thinks they are, they'd already be on a flight to a CIA black site getting the details waterboarded out of them. She could talk about the fact that this 'cell' is a fiction dreamed up by herself and without access to anything resembling an organisation. There is no cell, there is no hierarchy, no holy Aryan mission, no white jihad. Just blood and profit, supply and demand.

She could say all of those things but, with less than eleven days to go, Lehmann keeps quiet. Let the boy think it is he who is in charge.

Let him think he's doing this for the Aryan race or whatever crap floats his boat. He will be dead, one way or another, by the time two weeks have passed.

'Forget all that,' she says. 'It is wasting time. I called to let you know there had been some behind the scenes maneuvering. I don't want you freaking out when the time comes because I didn't tell you some detail. In my view, it makes sense to keep you informed.'

'Your view.' Lehmann can almost see Roos's rat face puckered in a sneer.

'If you are not strong enough to see it through, I understand. It is not for everyone. And our partners would be unhappy.'

'Partners?' Roos's voice is scornful. 'Fuck them. Fucking passengers, every one of them.'

Lehmann wonders just how dumb Roos is sometimes. If it wasn't for his technical expertise – which is admittedly considerable – she would never see or hear him again.

'We need those 'passengers'. We are not big enough to complete this alone. We are too visible for this. I keep telling you. We've been over all of this and we don't need any more complications than we already have.' Lehmann speaks urgently. Despite Roos amped-up right wing beliefs, it is she who is the connection to *Kolumne88*. Being around *Kolumne88* makes her feel dirty but you can't be too choosy about your friends when they pay so well. Lehmann is a pragmatist. A survivor.

'We need their money,' she says. 'It is their money that is opening the doors we need to open and I don't much care where it comes from.' She makes her tone more conciliatory. 'We're close now, Eric, really close. We can't let your good work go to waste. Let me handle the money and you finish your job.'

'Do what you have to,' says Roos and hangs up.

Eric Roos puts the phone back into the pocket of his jacket hanging on the back of the door. He is dressed in blue coveralls and wearing latex gloves. Slight, spectacled and serious-looking, Roos is in his early twenties. His head is shaved completely bald and has an Iron Cross tattooed across the crown.

Roos pulls up the blue paper mask to cover his mouth and nose and approaches the work bench in the centre of the small industrial unit which has been his base since being recruited.

On the bench, lit by three powerful tungsten lamps, is a shallow box made from 6 millimetre MDF. It is exactly 2.38 metres long, 0.95 metres wide and 30 centimetres deep. The box is a smooth grey in colour, the texture and appearance of polished cement. It has taken a lot of trial and error, and many reconnaissance trips to get this appearance correct. One wall of the warehouse is papered with photographs of the intended site and Roos makes constant checks to ensure the accuracy of his creation against the real thing.

Running round the base of the box is what appears to be a grey metal band, 10 millimetres thick and studded with bolts at each corner. In fact, the steel, just like the 'concrete' of the slab, is fake. Like the box, it too is constructed from MDF and paint. Weight is an issue and every effort has been made to keep the slab as light as possible. A lid for the box is propped against a wall, a cotton sheet protecting it from accidental damage. This lid will be the last thing to be put in place once the device is completed.

Inside the box, running around the walls, are arranged dozens of cylindrical metal containers. These are packed with tiny ball-bearings and nails. Several accelerators are positioned at points against the cylinders to ensure maximum velocity on detonation. Although capable of inflicting massive damage to anyone caught in the initial blast, the shrapnel is there simply as a disguise. The main component of the device is something else entirely.

Surrounding the bench is a bewildering assortment of tools and equipment. A camp bed is pushed up against one wall. Since this operation began, Roos has tried to be on site as often as possible, the warehouse door, triple-bolted and guarded by a sophisticated CCTV set-up showing a 360 of the industrial estate on which the warehouse is situated. The location of the construction site is only known to Roos. Even Angelika Lehmann does not know: a deliberate choice by her to protect the project in the event of her being taken before the project completion. She cannot confess what she does not know.

The warehouse is well lit and warm. An industrial-scale fridge is backed against one wall and various plastic containers are stacked here and there. It looks chaotic but to Roos, everything is in its place.

Just as in any laboratory.

On a table close to the door are three weapons. A Glock, an Israeli-made Machine gun, and a shotgun. None of the weapons have ever been fired and, Angelika Lehmann doubted they ever would be.

Asked to approve the purchase of the guns by Roos, Lehmann had hesitated, doubting his capability when it comes to shooting in the heat of battle but she had agreed with the purchase regardless. What did it matter? If it came to a point when guns were required then the whole thing was over. The guns gave Roos confidence and, Lehmann knew, that is what guns are about: to give boys confidence. Boys always need confidence. The trick in this situation was to give him enough to do the job but not enough to get careless. They don't have long now until November the 9th.

85

Berlin, October 27th

The light is painful. Too bright by a long way.

Sebastian Gottlenz shuts his eyes again and feels sleep tugging at him but, instead of drifting off, a sharp pain jolts him awake, this time he keeps his eyes open. Above his head are four circular lights set into a disc. He tries to move his head but can't.

A silhouette appears in his field of view, temporarily blocking some of the glare.

'Sebastian,' says a soft voice, a female. The voice is familiar but Gottlenz finds it difficult to place. His thoughts are sluggish, his responses slow.

'Sebastian.' This time the voice is sharper and Gottlenz recognises its owner.

Ilsa.

'Can you hear me, Sebastian?'

She's wearing a mint-green paper mask over the lower half of her face which she pulls down.

'I don't really know why I'm wearing this, Sebastian,' she says, smiling. 'It's only to stop me giving patients an infection and, well . . . that hardly matters now, does it?'

Why? Why doesn't it matter? Gottlenz wants to ask the questions but there's something wrong with his mouth. He strains to talk but nothing happens.

'Easy,' says Bruckner, bending low and peering at his face. 'You'll damage the stitches.'

What was this lunatic talking about? Gottlenz tries to shout but his lips won't open.

'It's pointless, Sebastian,' says Bruckner. She speaks more clearly, enunciating each word. 'I've sewn your mouth shut. You understand? It's more of a symbolic thing really because the drugs you have been given will probably not allow you to talk, but I hate to see good workmanship destroyed. It'll be best if you just lie back and try not to struggle. I won't say this is going to be easy – because from your viewpoint it most certainly isn't – but there's no need for you to suffer any more than is absolutely necessary.'

Gottlenz feels his bowels loosen as his wits begin to return. He makes a muffled keening sound and tries to get up. His limbs feel like they are made of lead.

'It's no use, Sebastian. You have been injected with 15 milligrams of atracurium. This has the effect of rendering your muscular system inert.'

Bruckner looks at a monitor which is beeping rapidly.

'You need to try and calm down, Sebastian. No point in going to all this trouble if you die on the operating table.' Bruckner smiles and waves a scalpel in front of Gottlenz's face. 'I mean, you're going to die anyway but there is some information I need from you and we can sell some of your better organs. You can regard it as your last meaningful contribution to the cause.'

Gottlenz's eyes move frantically around the edges of his vision. He is naked. He is in an operating theatre and he is completely immobile. That much is clear. What is also clear is that Bruckner knows everything. She knows about his conversation with Lehmann. How she knows he has no idea.

And then it hits him. Lehmann double-crossed him.

This must be Bruckner's clinic but he can't understand how and why he got here. Fleeting images return. He had been to one of the meetings in a flat in Spandau, he can remember that. His car had been parked on the street. He must have been taken there.

'The Führer knew that progress can only be made if emotion is taken out of the equation,' says Bruckner. Smiling, she leans across Gottlenz, her forearm on his chest, her voice low and warm. 'I need to know if you have talked, Sebastian. To find this out I'm going to do things to you. Medical things. These procedures will be very horrible and incredibly painful, at least, I imagine they will. To avoid most of this suffering I suggest you simply give me the answers as truthfully as possible. You can communicate by blinking. One blink is 'yes', two blinks are 'no'. I know you betrayed us, Sebastian. That's not the purpose of this. But I do want to know if that is as far as it went: a stupid plan, but no more. Once I am satisfied that you have not leaked information any further than the bomb-maker I will kill you humanely. Do you understand?'

Gottlenz stares at Bruckner. There are things he wants to say, questions he wants to ask. He wants to see his family, he wants someone to hold him. He doesn't want to be there.

Bruckner moves and Gottlenz feels an excruciating pain in his groin that sends him into spasms. In the reflective surface at the edge of one of the theatre lights he sees Bruckner making an incision in the base of his penis. The monitor linked to his heart rate beeps frantically and Bruckner stands, blood coating the blade in her hand.

'I asked you a question, Sebastian and I expect an answer or I will open those stitches on your mouth and stuff your shrivelled little cock down your throat. Again, do you understand?'

This time Gottlenz blinks. Once. Bruckner smiles. 'Excellent.'

Before she can ask anything else, Gottlenz hears another voice.

'I've had enough of this,' says Hoffen.

Gottlenz rolls his eyes sideways and sees Hoffen push himself off from one of the walls. 'Tell me if you get anything useful. Call me when this bullshit is done,' he says. Hoffen moves out of view and Gottlenz hears a set of doors open and close. As Ilsa Bruckner turns back to the table, scalpel raised, Sebastian Gottlenz feels a cool breeze from the closing theatre doors stir the hairs on his forearm. It is the last faint scrap of pleasure he will ever feel.

86

Liverpool, October 29th

Almost three in the afternoon on a day that already feels staler than a week-old Goodison pie, Rimmer, one arse cheek perched on the edge of his desk, slurping coffee from a red cardboard Costa cup the size of a bucket, is holding court to anyone who'll listen. Two work stations away Magsi tries to tune out the big bag of wind by concentrating on the file stack in front of him but it's like trying to shelter from a hurricane behind a cocktail umbrella. Rimmer's got the Helsby case all worked out and what's eating away at Saif Magsi as he listens to The Tao of Ronnie, is that despite the fountain of bollocks spewing out of the DS's gob, the dickhead has got something with Bernie Palmer.

With corroboration sliding in from Malaga via the Cuerpo Nacional de Policia, the fat Glaswegian's shonky Spanish connections are looking more and more worthy of closer examination with every passing minute. Judging by the rising notes of triumph in Rimmer's endless honking, Magsi's half-expecting a lap of honour of the office before much longer.

It's been a good morning's graft for Ronaldo. He's unearthed three separate stand-over cases involving Palmer in which violence has been used or threatened. It's not like Rimmer's had to do much legwork – pulling up the references is about all it took – but the Scot's 'against' column are getting crowded with actual hard data. All of the cases involve Palmer's company recovering money owed by apparently less than legal means. Although none of the cases on file have resulted in any conviction for the fat man, Magsi can easily see why Rimmer – along with a number of other MIT officers – is liking

Palmer for Helsby. Smoke, fire, etc. blah blah and the eternal copper's truth that if it smells like a horse, looks like a horse and sounds like a horse, then it's probably a horse. Or a zebra, a donkey or a unicorn. Either way, close enough.

Palmer's speedy, and knowledgeable, request for representation on being brought into Stanley Road is another indicator that the Bernie Palmer angle could be fruitful. Magsi and everyone at MIT know that Palmer's bleating for a brief means two things: the guy is bent and the guy has done this before. Bernie had been in the interview room less than six minutes before he gave the interviewing officers the name of his lawyer.

Rimmer, his supply of listeners running low, shifts position closer to Magsi's desk and peers over the divider. 'How's your line going, Mags? Any joy?'

Magsi doesn't move his head. 'Not much.'

Rimmer picks up an old copy of the Echo from Magsi's desk, folded open to the story about Frank's death.

'Surprised we haven't had any reporters calling up about old Blueface,' says Rimmer.

'Blueface?' Magsi, momentarily forgetting his personal vow not to give Rimmer any encouragement, looks up. 'Oh, wait, I see. Because he's Scottish? Braveheart?'

'What else, you tool?'

'I'll give you he's dirty,' says Magsi.

'Gee, Saif, thanks. My parents will be so proud. The haggis-chomper's dirtier than a fucking coal miner who's fallen into a sewer full of nappies.'

'Haggis-chomper?' Magsi doesn't even have the energy to shake his head. 'And listen,' Magsi says, pointing a pen at Rimmer, 'I wouldn't be tempted to give the papers a call, either, Ronnie. She wouldn't like it.' He gestures towards DI Harris's office door but Rimmer doesn't appear to have noticed.

'Add in that his missus was knocking a slice off DCI Keane – did you see her photos? A right sexy piece and 'A' grade- A perv by all accounts. Yum, yum, oh yes please– and we've got enough to take to the CPS already.'

'Textbook policing,' Magsi mutters from his side of the office divider. Rimmer's answer is to lob a rolled up wad of paper at his head and lumber back to his desk.

Rimmer's summing up of the case against Bernie Palmer might be lacking in political correctness but there's no doubting the accuracy of the work. Although Palmer himself can easily prove he was in Spain at the time of the fire, his patchy history of using violent extortion via third parties, *and* the clear motive of jealousy, means that Rimmer could be onto something. The presence of the three bodies, and the lack of anyone in the frame as the killer, represent the biggest holes in any case against Palmer, but Magsi thinks Rimmer will get the go-ahead for more work on Bernie.

And yet . . . and yet . . .

For himself, no matter how forcefully Rimmer tries to jam it down his throat, Magsi can't get behind the idea of Palmer as the hand pulling the strings. That third body in the barn takes some explaining. No matter how compelling the arguments are for Palmer, the third body is a problem if Bernie Palmer pulled a hit on Frank and Kath.

No, from what he'd been told by DI Harris, Frank Keane had made some formidable and determined enemies relating to the Stevie White drug case and it is these individuals who present the more promising line of enquiry as Magsi sees things.

Yet Saif Magsi finds he just doesn't buy into this line very much more than he does the Palmer angle. For him, instead, it is becoming clear that the single shining thread that runs through the events of the past two weeks is Sarah Coughlan.

It is Sarah who had been abducted.

It is Sarah who had been killed.

It is Sarah who has a connection by blood with Frank Keane.

All that can't be irrelevant, can't be a coincidence so Magsi finds it much easier to accept a story linking Frank and Sarah by blood than one that portrays Bernie Palmer as some sort of jealousy-crazed overweight Glaswegian mastermind.

The answer lies with Sarah and Frank. The only problem is finding something that connects them beyond the accident of birth.

Magsi pulls out the initial file on Sarah and clears some debris from his desk. He flips open the covering page and reads it again, trying as best he can to see it with fresh eyes. Tuning out the MIT office chatter he goes through the Coughlan file line by line. He makes notes on a pad next to the file of anything that occurs to him. There's no method other than reading. When he's finished he slides the thinner file on Frank Keane in front of him and goes through the same process. This takes much less time and Magsi makes fewer notes. When he's finished he closes the Keane file and looks at what he has.

It's not much.

Other than the half-sibling relationship there is nothing DC Magsi can see connecting Sarah Coughlan with his old boss.

Magsi leans back and stretches. He looks across to DI Harris's office and recalls walking in on DCI Keane and finding him with tears streaking his face. What had that been about?

Magsi gets to his feet and walks over to DI Harris's office.

'Ma'am?' Magsi raps a knuckle on the half-open door. A tired-looking Harris is on the phone but beckons Magsi inside. He stands for a moment before she points to a chair.

Harris finishes her call and flips open a file.

'What's up?' she says her head bent to the paperwork.

'DCI Keane.'

Harris looks up. 'What about him?' The sharpness in her tone makes Magsi pause but he takes a deep breath and plunges in, outlining his objections to the case against Bernie Palmer and identifying his own line of enquiry.

'And where did that get you?'

'Nowhere. I re-read the Sarah Coughlan file and then did the same with what we have on DCI Keane. Apart from the blood link there's nothing connecting the two as far as I can see. They never met – again as far as we know. So . . .' Saif Magsi stops and looks at Harris. This is the tricky bit.

'What?'

'I was wondering if there was anything DCI Keane may have told you that might help me.' Magsi coughs. 'Personal things. If DCI Keane hadn't been a DCI then I wouldn't have to worry about asking you. As it is, I'm looking at Keane's recent history and there are some holes in it. Blanks, anyway. And those blanks need me to at least make an attempt to fill. What happened in America?'

Magsi has Harris's full attention now. She starts to say something and then stops herself. 'He . . .no, wait. The honest answer is that I don't know, DS Magsi. I haven't been told.'

Magsi can tell that making this admission is painful for Harris. He nods, already bracing himself for the next question.

'I apologise in advance for this, ma'am,' he says and then plunges right in. 'You had a close relationship with DCI Keane during the Nicky Peters case.'

'You need to be careful, DC Magsi.'

'With respect, ma'am, I am being careful. But someone has to ask you and despite most of the office knowing about it, it looks like I'm the only one dumb enough to give it a go. I've come this far so I might as well carry on. There was an incident with DCI Keane in which he was attacked by your partner.'

'What's that got to do with anything?' Harris is openly angry but Magsi leans into the wind and pushes on.

'It's got everything to do with me thinking you might know something about Frank Keane that is relevant to this investigation. Ma'am. If you did have a relationship – and it seems to me that the attack on DCI Keane suggests you did – then it's credible that he may have told you something in private that could help. Someone has to ask you.'

Harris looks out of the window without speaking. Magsi can see the tightness in her jaw line.

'I'm sorry if th . . . ,'

'He has cancer.' Harris turns back to face Magsi. 'Had cancer, I mean.' She breathes deeply. 'Although I don't see it is of much use to your line of enquiry, DS Magsi.'

'Maybe not, ma'am.' He scratches his chin. There's something tickling his memory. Something in the files he's just been going over that relates to Keane's disease but, as quickly as it arrives, it goes again.

'Is there anything else, DS Magsi?'

Magsi waits a beat before standing. 'No ma'am.'

'Than clear off and bring me something I can use. If I hear another word from Ronaldo today I'm going to chin him. Don't let him win this one, Saif. He's wrong about Bernie Palmer. Show me why.'

87

Mallaig, Scotland, October 28th

An empty can of coke bounces off Calum Finn's shoulder and clatters across the quayside. He looks up and sees his father standing below the level of the harbour wall on the deck of *The Mackinaw*, his mouth moving fast. Calum pulls the buds from his ears and the bass in his ears is replaced by the sounds of the harbour: the clanking of metal against mast, the slop of water and squawks from the hopeful seabirds.

'What?'

'Will you stop listening to that rap shite and go and do something useful for once?'

'There's no need to throw things, old feller. You'll put yer back out. Man o' your age should know better.'

'How else am I supposed to get your attention, you eejit? Go on and fetch the long net. The new one. I think this thing's just about had it. And less of that old man stuff.'

Calum waves a dismissive hand and walks towards the sheds where his father keeps the nets. Calum senior's had the new net there for months but, until now, has clung stubbornly to the much-patched old ones. Calum had tried pointing out that he was saving bugger all keeping the new one dry but Paul Finn, like many in this part of the world, isn't a man who can be easily hurried.

Calum swings open the weathered wooden door and goes inside. It's a raw day outside and he's glad of the temporary shelter. The net is stowed on a low shelf at the rear behind the Toyota he's looking after for Mr Machin. Which reminds Calum of the email from Machin. He scoops up the long net and steps outside.

'I'm for going over to Carraig to get the place warmed,' he says when he hands the net down. 'Machin emailed. He's coming back soon and wants the place dry.'

Paul Finn automatically looks seaward, his first reaction at any mention of going out of harbour.

'You could have mentioned it.'

'I just remembered.'

Paul Finn shakes his head. 'It should be ok. You taking the Zodiac?'

'That alright?'

'Sure.' Paul looks up at his son and winks. 'Got to keep the rich feckers happy, son.'

Less than an hour later Calum Finn brings the big inflatable out of the shelter of the harbour wall. As his father had said, the going looks good. Calum guns the engine and the orange hull of the RHIB crashes sweetly through the first big swell.

Intent as he is guiding the small boat through the open water chop, there's no reason at all for Calum to notice the man leaning against the wing of the Land Rover parked on the quay. The man watches Calum until the boat rounds the headland before getting behind the wheel of the Landy and pointing it back towards Mallaig.

On the dockside, Paul Finn glances up from his work and makes a mental note of the Land Rover's plate. He might be too slow to get the new gear on the boat for his son's taste, and his knees have only got a couple of years left in them, but when it comes to who and what and when in *his* harbour there's not a thing Paul Finn misses. He watches the Landy turn in behind The Harbour Lights and park. Ten minutes later Finn looks up from his nets. The Land Rover is still in place at the pub.

Finn takes out his mobile.

'Liam. Paul. You'll have had a wee streak of a man come in your place just now? Probably ordered chocolate soy milk cappuccino or some such shite.'

'Aye.' Liam Slater's Irish voice is wary. 'Man ordered a chai tea. What about him?'

'Chai tea? Jesus Christ, Liam.'

'You can drop that tone, Paul, you gobshite. I like a drop of chai meself. Wouldn't do yourself any harm to try it. Calm you down a bit.' Finn hears the sound of plates being washed in the background. 'Wait a minute,' says Liam.

Finn hears Liam moving to a quieter part of the pub.

'That's better. Now what's up? This feller from the Fisheries or something?'

'No, nothing like that. I don't like the look of him.'

'You don't like the look of him? It's not feckin' Texas, Paul. He's one of those rare birds: a fucking customer. What am I supposed to do, run anyone who turns up past the Paul Finn Committee before I let them in?'

'Maybe. Might not be a bad idea. And you can relax, I'm not coming over all redneck on you. I just got a feeling about him and something our Calum's been doing.'

'The rich feller? On the island?'

'Jesus, who told you? Calum been blabbing?'

'No.' Slater pauses. 'Well maybe just a bit. The lad had had a couple like. He didn't tell us much. No-one else has said anything though, I'm sure of that.'

'No-one else? Did he tell the whole feckin' bar?'

'No, just Jimmy and Bean. The Russian feller. Maybe a couple of others. I can't remember who was in.' Slater pauses. 'He was a bit trollied to be honest, Paul.'

'I don't know why he didn't get up on the karaoke and announce it.'

'We-ell . . .'

'No. Really? He never?'

'No. Just messing with you.' Slater lowers his voice conspiratorially. 'Anyway, what do you want to know?'

'Has he booked in?'

'Aye. Three nights. Says he's a photographer.'

'Bollocks.'

'What he says.'

'Has he got any kit?'

'Kit?'

'Aluminium boxes. Big feckin' cameras. That sort of thing. The stuff that photographer's generally use in their line of business.'

'No, not that I've seen. Could be in the car like.'

'Yeah, maybe. Anyway, what I want is for you to keep an eye on him. Let me know if there's movement?'

'I don't know . . .'

'There's a tenner in it.'

'Deal.'

Paul Finn signs off and pockets the phone. He looks out to the open water. There are big things out there underneath the black water. He's seen them. Pale nightmare creatures that get caught up in the nets from time to time and dragged to the surface.

When that happens you always have to be careful.

88

Liverpool, October 30th

It's amazing what a little professional jealousy can do. The day after his talk with DI Harris, Magsi pulls an early shift and takes the medical records of Sarah Coughlan and Frank Keane apart line by line. Again.

At the end of a couple of solid hours he has nothing. Nothing new anyway.

Magsi pushes himself back from the desk, clasps his hands behind his head and blows out a long sigh. It's still dark outside and he's the only one in the MIT office. His reflection stares back at him from the black, rain-speckled, window. That tantalising connection he'd had in DI Harris's office hasn't, so far, made another appearance. What makes it so frustrating is that he is sure the information is contained in the two files in front of him.

Magsi closes both, pulls up his chair and starts again. As the minutes tick past, the office begins to fill but Magsi sticks to his task. And then, assuming he's remembered it right, there it is, right in front of him.

Magsi sits upright, a thrill of adrenaline making his legs weak. He checks the names again to make sure before lifting the phone and calling Terry Furlong, a uniform in Sefton who Magsi had come up with at the academy. Although their paths had diverged the two remained friendly. It had been one of Terry's stories, gossip really, that had been the memory Magsi had been unable to recall. Until now.

'Last week,' says Magsi, once the small talk is over. 'You were telling me something about a punter who'd been beaten who didn't want to talk. With a girl who looked special. A traffic stop. Remember? You'd pulled him for erratic driving and he was bleeding?'

'Yeah, I know the one. Stopped him on the Dock Road in a big Audi, very flash. Late like. His rear light was out and soon as we saw him we thought we had something. Feller had cuts and bruises on his face. Suit all messed up.'

Magsi looks up and sees DI Harris going into her office.

'And the girl with him?'

'Yeah, that was the thing I was telling you about. She was stunning. Short skirt, really classy but scared looking. No knickers, that was why I told you. When we got her out of the car her skirt rode up and hello Philadelphia! We got them out of the car, put him in the back of ours. Did the breath test, the drug test. Nothing. Checked their stories in case it was a domestic, or she was a hooker, but nothing. She was who she said she was, no priors, solid citizen, worked at a bank. Long-time girlfriend. All that. And both told the same story about the injuries. They'd been out. He'd been jumped in the car park by two guys. The weird thing was that he wouldn't press charges, or file a complaint. We looked in the car for drugs thinking that was it, but it was clean. He was clean too but, yeah, there was something off about it all. Why are you asking?'

'His name?' Magsi closes his eyes and hopes. Please be the one.

Terry tells him the Audi driver's name and Magsi punches the air.

'Cheers, Tez.'

'No explanation?'

'Maybe sometime. Not yet.'

Magsi signs off and hits the databases. Half an hour later, there it is on three A4 pages; the link between Sarah Coughlan, Frank Keane and Berlin.

89

Berlin, October 31st

Saturday morning. Theresa Cooper has been in Berlin over a week but this is the first time she's set foot in the giant consumer palace of KaDeWe. In the packed Kaufhaus des Westens restaurant Cooper scrolls down her screen pretending to read her messages. Ilsa Bruckner is seated less than twenty metres away looking at her own phone and drinking coffee.

Cooper's pretty sure that Bruckner never clocked her while she was trawling through the store but now her Ninja antenna is twitching. It's been twenty-five minutes since arriving at the cafe and she's caught Bruckner glancing in her direction twice in the last ten, her eyes sliding across the room, pausing for a split-second and then moving on. In a red plastic bag on the seat next to Cooper is a hastily bought scarf; something plucked from a rack, but it's only a thin layer of concealment to this half-arsed undercover op.

Cooper's been tailing Bruckner since the woman left her apartment around ten. It's Saturday and so far there has been nothing. Exactly what she was hoping for, Theresa doesn't know, but after Anna's death this is the best she can come up with. Dreschler and Weiss at LKA are giving her frost so this is an independent operation. Even MIT don't know about it yet. Right now it feels like a penance for some unspecified sin. The sin of omission? Certainly Dreschler and Weiss make her feel that she should have revealed the note from Ziegler sooner than she did. Weiss even went so far as to accuse her of harassing Anna.

Bruckner drains her cup and walks away from the table, Cooper's peripheral vision tracing her path through the middle-class crowd, before picking up her own bag and following at a respectable distance. Outside on *Tauentzienstraße* Bruckner, her coat buttoned high on her throat, heads west blinking into the low winter sun. She crosses the wide street at the first intersection and takes a right. Cooper loiters at the corner and through a glass-fronted clothes shop watches Bruckner cross the street and turn into an anonymous grey-white six-storey building.

Cooper hurries after Bruckner. Outside the building is a sign. *Thermen am Europa Center.* Cooper doesn't know what it is so she plunges inside and finds herself faced with a metal-grilled security gate through which, regarding her blankly through the bars, is Ilsa Bruckner waiting for a lift.

With no time to react, Cooper finds herself pushing the rotating gate forward and into the small lobby. She nods at Bruckner but gets nothing back. The two women stand in silence until the lift arrives. Inside there is barely room for them both. Cooper blindly presses the top floor button. If Bruckner exits before then she can always come back down but Bruckner too is headed for the top floor.

The lift judders to a halt and Bruckner slides back the grille. She steps out, Cooper following a few paces behind.

They are in the lobby of what is clearly some sort of spa. The tang of chlorine is in the air and there are posters of various treatments on the walls. Bruckner walks to the reception desk and shows a laminated card to the white-coated assistant who hands her a key and a towel from a large stack on the shelf behind her. Bruckner turns and heads back past Cooper towards a door marked 'Damen'.

Once Bruckner has passed through the door Cooper checks the list of charges and buys a day pass for the whole spa.

'How about a swimsuit?' she asks the attendant.

'No suits.' The woman points to a sign on the wall behind her. 'No swimwear allowed in the saunas, spas or baths. Hygiene, you understand? You can wear suits in the main pool but we don't carry any for rental.'

'Oh. Right. OK.'

Feeling foolish, foreign, English, Cooper gets a towel, sandals and a key and heads into the changing rooms. Each passing moment feels like she's walking further from shore on an icy lake. This is wrong. She's isolated, untethered from her moorings. Cooper could just walk but she thinks of Ziegler's battered face and pushes on.

There is no sign of Bruckner. Cooper finds her numbered locker and undresses, trying to appear as nonchalant as possible. With her towel wrapped tightly around her she finds the entrance to the spa.

Inside the first thing she sees are the showers. Following the lead of an elderly woman in front of her, Cooper hangs her towel on a peg outside and showers, trying to ignore the naked men on either side. Finished, she dries herself and wraps her towel around herself once more.

The marbled main room of the spa houses a large, semi-circular pool which runs into a kind of moat on the outside of the building roof accessed by two small openings at either end. Through the blue-tinted windows Cooper can see steam rising from the open water. Inside, the pool is flanked by several rows of loungers and marble-stepped seats. Further back is a bar and cafe and, on either side of that are a series of saunas, steam baths and plunge pools. Everyone is naked. About half of the pool users are female which helps but, even so, Cooper finds it difficult not to stare.

Cooper leaves her towel on a sun lounger and slips gratefully into the blue water. She dips her head below the surface and swims across the pool towards the outside area. She dives under the plastic curtain that protects the inside portion of the spa from the cold and surfaces, steam rising in a thick white plume from her scalp. It's a curious sensation out here under the silvered Berlin sky, her body warm in the heated water, head tingling in the frosty air. A naked man in his seventies, seemingly oblivious to the cold, his cock shrivelled to a button, his legs hairless, ambles across Cooper's line of vision, heading towards a row of outdoor hot tubs which face the ranks of apartment windows of the building opposite. On the roof to Cooper's left, a huge metal Mercedes advertising emblem turns lazily. There's no sign of Bruckner.

Cooper swims slowly around the glass-fronted pool and dips back inside under the plastic curtain. She remains floating in the pool for a few minutes before plucking up the courage to walk up the pool steps in full view of anyone who cares to look. As far as she can tell, few do. With every passing minute she is becoming more relaxed in this environment.

Cooper wraps herself in her towel, takes a seat on a sun lounger to the left side of the pool and pretends to doze.

Five minutes later a naked Ilsa Bruckner emerges from one side of the spa, places a towel on the lounger next to Cooper without looking at her, and enters the pool. From under hooded eyes Cooper watches Bruckner swim several steady laps. She is athletic, a good swimmer.

When Bruckner leaves the water she is completely unselfconscious in her nakedness. She runs her hands through her short hair, brushing off water, her breasts rising as she does so. She's in good shape, her rangy, loose-limbed runner's frame making Cooper more conscious of her own, rounder, curves. Her pussy is clean-shaven.

Bruckner lifts her towel from one of the loungers and fidgets into her sandals. Walking slowly around the curving edge of the pool towards a set of marbled steps, she wraps the towel around her hair. Outside a sauna door she stops to exchange a couple of words with a hairy-chested man who follows her inside. From the little she could see, Cooper's unsure if the man is a colleague, a friend, a lover, or something else.

She gives it a minute before her curiosity gets the better of her.

The sauna is large and, thankfully, not one of the hottest. Cooper is getting familiar with how this place works and it's clear that there is a routine for most of the regulars, a group to which Bruckner looks like she belongs.

Inside are three people.

On the lowest, and coolest, level, a shaven-headed middle-aged man sits forward on his towel, resting his elbows on his knees, his paunch swelling over his cock and balls. His face is bright red and sweat drips steadily from his chin. He glances appraisingly at Cooper before returning his gaze to the floor. On the second level are Bruckner and the big man. They sit side by side without touching, their backs resting easily against the blonde-wood wall, protected from the heat by towels. Both of them look at Cooper and she nods. Neither Bruckner or her companion nod back. Cooper can't tell if this is personal, or some German thing, or if she's been blown. She unwraps her towel and places it on the lowest level at the furthest point from anyone else in the sauna. As she sits, the middle-aged man gets to his feet and leaves. He says something in German that Cooper doesn't catch.

Bruckner and her companion watch him go and then the guy says something in German to Cooper.

'Sorry,' says Cooper in English,' I don't understand. I'm English.'

'*Sie verstehen gut*,' Bruckner says, her eyes steady on Cooper's.

'What?'

'You understand fine.' This time in English.

'I'm sorry. I'm not sure what you're talking about.'

Bruckner opens her mouth to speak but the man puts a hand on her thigh. 'You English are always apologising. Sorry this, sorry that.' He smiles.

'*Dumme Fotze.*' This from Bruckner. The aggression is clear now, her voice a hiss. Cooper knows enough to translate: 'stupid cunt'. She folds her fist and tenses, ready to move if required. This has gone south quickly.

'*Sei ruhig, Ilsa.*' The guy's voice is a low growl and Bruckner's mouth sets in a thin line but she remains silent.

'Now it is my turn to say sorry.' He smiles again but Cooper doesn't move a muscle.

'You have made a mistake,' says Cooper.

Bruckner mutters something. The man responds and the two turn away from Cooper. Cooper leans back and closes her eyes. It is an act of will to appear unconcerned. She is conscious of her breasts, her nakedness and, above all, her foreignness. She gets to her feet and staggers awkwardly from the sauna without looking back.

90

Liverpool, October 30th

'Let me get this right. Coughlan and Frank have been targeted because they share the same blood group?'

Magsi faces Harris across her desk. In front of her are the three pages of notes Magsi made after his call to Terry. As they talk, Harris slowly turns them.

'Yes, ma'am. Both were type AB, Rhesus negative, NS and Hp1. There are other factors at work also which mean that both DCI Keane and Sarah Coughlan's blood are among the rarest.'

'How rare?'

'As I understand it – and I've yet to get the fine detail on this – it is lower than one in one hundred million.'

'OK. That's rare. And your idea is that Coughlan's abduction was a botched attempt at taking her blood? A vampire fuck-up?'

'I wouldn't put it like that, ma'am. Not vampires. But yes, basically, that's my idea. And when they lost Sarah, Frank Keane was next in line. The blood type might have been an indicator for something else. Maybe they needed DCI Keane's lungs or kidneys. If you have a blood type as rare as that, finding a donor for a transplant could be next to impossible.'

'So they take the donor,' says Harris. It makes sense. Siobhan's words come back to her. Follow the money. Well here's the money all right. Exactly how much a rich man in need of a transplant would be willing to pay, Harris has no idea but she's willing to bet it would be a lot. If Sarah's death was an accident and Frank was near to hand then the events made sense. Assuming they knew Sarah and Frank were related.

'This is where I'm having trouble, Saif,' says Harris. 'If Frank Keane himself didn't know he had a sister, how did these bloodsuckers find out?'

'On the last page of my notes, ma'am.'

Harris flips the pages and then looks up. 'Just tell me.'

'OK. Let's say someone very sick who has a rare blood group needs an operation, a transplant. Their blood is a really rare group, hard to come by and with complicating factors. If they couldn't find a donor through normal channels, and they had deep pockets and an unscrupulous medic, they might be tempted to simply harvest what was needed.'

'Harvest?'

'Yes. An involuntary donor. To make this happen they need someone to notify them when that blood match turns up. Someone presents at a clinic, at a hospital, somewhere where there is a bent doctor, or a nurse, even an administrator. Someone with access to the records.'

Magsi leans forward and taps the desk. 'Sarah Coughlan had been ill. The clinic where she received treatment was the Hemswood Clinic in Liverpool. Her doctor was a Doctor Lucas Medavoy. Medavoy was also Frank Keane's doctor.'

'Ah.'

'Yes, ma'am.'

'That's not all you've got though?' Harris fails to keep the disappointment from her voice.

'No.' Magsi grins. 'This is where it gets really good. Medavoy once worked at a surgical clinic in Berlin. The B-Kreuz-Scharmer Clinic in Spandau. The same clinic that the Mercedes van used in the Sarah Coughlan abduction was allegedly stolen from.'

Harris starts to speak but Magsi, on a roll, holds up a hand, forgetting in his enthusiasm that he's talking to his boss. He's getting to the real meat. 'It gets better. Medavoy was pulled over by a friend of mine a few weeks back on a routine traffic bust. It was that story that got me digging. He was bleeding.'

'This Medavoy you mean?'

Magsi nods. 'Yes. Said he'd been jumped. Wouldn't press charges.'

'And you think, what – he's been punished for non-delivery?'

'I don't know. Maybe. Or maybe it's something tangential. If Medavoy's feeding that kind of information through to an operation like this, there has to be a motivating factor. Maybe he's a gambler? The beating could be related to that.'

'You're stretching.'

'I know, ma'am, but there's something there, isn't there?'

Harris nods. There is something.

'It's good,' she says, 'but it's thinnish, Saif.'

'Less thin if the money's good, ma'am. If there's someone out there who needs that blood and time's running out, then don't you think they'd do anything they could to get hold of it? We've seen crimes committed for less, every day.'

'Why don't they just find someone with the same blood group and pay them? Why go to all this trouble?'

Magsi shrugs. 'Could be technical reasons for that. Sarah and DCI Keaen's blood group was very rare indeed. Paying someone might not have been an option. Maybe they need to keep taking from the donor over a long period? They could be harvesting the donor for months for all we know. Years even. A one-person blood bank.'

'It sounds like a horror movie.'

'We all know that stranger things have happened, ma'am.'

Harris pauses and pinches the bridge of her nose before leaning forward.

'OK. There's enough there. I want you to dig into Medavoy some more. Get me some motivation for serving up Sarah and Frank like that.' Her face wrinkles in distaste. If Magsi's line proves to be accurate then the description of these people as vampires is right on the nose.

Blood. It all comes down to blood in the end.

That, and money. As it always was and forever will be, amen.

91

Helsby, Cheshire, October 31st

Kath Palmer is the first of the Helsby victims to be buried. The funeral takes place on a dry Saturday morning at the Catholic church not far from the Palmer house. It is well attended.

Harris arrives as the coffin is being carried into the church. Bernie Palmer, his head bowed, walks behind the cortege, his massive frame shrunken in grief.

The investigation into the possibility of Palmer's involvement in the fire is stalled. Despite turning over everything, and pulling in a dozen or more of Bernie Palmer's associates, including a couple of solid hits that demonstrated his prior use of stand-over guys, the best they are left with is the strong suspicion that the big Scot is crooked. As Keane himself would have said, that doesn't make him a killer. Given the difficulty of connecting the other dead man in the barn to Palmer, and despite Ronnie Rimmer's increasingly insistent efforts to persuade her otherwise, Harris is coming to the same conclusion. DS Magsi's findings are also pointing her away from Palmer and towards Berlin.

Harris also has the complication that she still doesn't believe Frank Keane is one of the Helsby bodies. It's difficult to get behind a line of enquiry with revenge as motive when you think there's a good chance that the victim is still breathing. Of course, if Frank is alive that doesn't mean that Palmer is necessarily innocent. It doesn't take much imagination to envisage a revenge attack that misses the target. And that line is the one that Rimmer is currently flogging.

At Bernie Palmer's side is an elderly woman who Harris pegs as Kath Palmer's mother. She knows from the case files that Kath's father is already dead and notes Bernie's tenderness in his interactions with his mother-in-law. It means nothing – Harris has seen more than one villain behave like this – but there is something in the way he handles himself that is pushing her ever closer to dropping Bernie as a likely culprit. She sees Bernie glance her way but he doesn't change his expression.

Behind the two chief mourners come the rest of the family and friends, many of them in tears. At the back of the group Harris spots two officers from Cheshire MIT. Harris has met both men before on a course and they exchange nods. They're good officers but their presence makes her skittish. If she's right about the funeral then the last thing she needs is an encounter with fellow cops.

Harris waits until most people are in the church before going inside herself. With her back against the rear wall she remains standing while the service unrolls. Harris has been to too many funerals but when the priest starts delivering the eulogy she pricks up her ears to see how he'll deal with the elephant in the room: namely Kath Palmer's overnight presence in Frank Keane's house. When he gets closest to the issue there is a clear frisson of embarrassment inside the church. Harris sees two or three people bend heads and whisper to their neighbour. In the event the priest delivers a master class in avoidance. Frank Keane's name isn't mentioned.

As the hymns start, Harris slips outside, grateful for the crisp air. Unusually, Kath Palmer is going to be buried in the churchyard. Perhaps the manner of her death persuaded Bernie that cremation would be too painful a reminder. Either way, this is where she is going to lie. The graveyard is full but a kind of annexe has been opened out in grounds to the side of the church, the new grave already surrounded by flowers. Two men hang back at the edge of the graveyard, a bobcat digger on hand ready to complete the job.

The coffin and shuffling entourage emerge from the church in that peculiarly English muffled silence. Harris waits for the procession to pass and then walks in the opposite direction, out of the churchyard. As the mourners follow the priest towards the grave, Harris skirts round the lane that borders the graveyard. She turns right and right again and comes back around the edge of the field next to the extended grounds. By now the graveside service has begun.

Along the edge of the field a line of poplars are set back on the rise of a dry ditch. Harris, pushes her way through the scrubby bushes and finds herself at one end of the trees. From here she has a good view of the funeral service. She begins to walk slowly along the row until she sees a dark-clad figure leaning against the tree that stands furthest away from the church. The silent spectator has his back to Harris as she approaches. Harris is less than five feet away when she speaks.

'Hello, Frank.'

'Jesus Christ!' Frank Keane spins on his heel, his face white with shock. 'You nearly gave me a heart attack.'

'Good place for it.' Harris gestures towards the funeral.

Frank nods. 'Yeah.'

'How are you? You look good. For a dead man. And I like the beard.'

'Thanks.'

'Being away hasn't improved your comebacks. You need to work on them.'

'Yes.' Frank is dressed in cold weather clothes: black boots, olive combat pants and a black zip-up. He's wearing a long-brimmed cap pulled low and is carrying a canvas bag over his shoulder.

'All you need is sunglasses,' says Harris.

Frank touches his face. 'I thought the beard might be enough. Sunglasses could be pushing it. Who wears sunglasses in October?' He scans the area. 'You're alone?'

Harris nods. 'This is not an operation, Frank, if that's what you think. There's no SWAT team hiding in the woods.'

'How did you know?'

Harris glances across to the funeral. 'Give me some credit. I know you. A good Catholic boy like yourself couldn't let Kath Palmer be buried without showing your face. Even if no-one actually sees you doing it. The surprise is that no-one else thought of it.' She flashes on the Cheshire MIT cops and wonders if someone else has.

'I'm not religious.'

'Oh. OK. Then I guess I was wrong and you're not here.'

Frank doesn't respond. Harris can see that the change in him isn't simply the cancer. There's something else. Something different at Frank Keane's core. What that is, she's not sure she's ready to find out. There's a stillness to him that wasn't there before. He looks older too. Not old, just older.

He looks like someone else.

'Maybe someone did think of it,' says Frank, looking round, his phrasing echoing Harris's thoughts so closely that, for a moment, she wonders if she'd spoken aloud. 'You might have been followed. There's a couple of Cheshire boys there.'

'I saw. Are you expecting me to be followed?'

Frank shrugs. 'It's possible. Things have been getting strange. To say the least. Just about the only thing I've got going for me is that I'm dead.' He laughs without humour. 'The weird thing is they've only got to wait. Why go to all the trouble to bump me off when by summer it might be academic?'

'We haven't talked about . . . all that.'

'No, you're right, Em. I think that's what I'm supposed to do, y'know. Talk about it. Talk about 'all that.''

'It might help.'

Both of them turn back to the graveyard and stand in silence for a moment.

'So,' says Frank. 'Where do we go from here?'

Harris shrugs. 'Pub?'

Frank smiles.

92

Berlin, October 31st

'Too hot for you in there, hey?'

The male voice so close to her ear makes Cooper jump. She is in the shower, her eyes closed against the shampoo. It takes her a second to realise the man is the one from the sauna. Bruckner's friend.

'Yes,' she sputters. She rinses her head and blinks her eyes open. The man is looking at her calmly and appraisingly, his big hands lazily soaping his chest and stomach.

'Nice,' he says.

'What?'

'Nice. In here.' He waves a hand to include the general spa. Cooper, standing at right angles to him, sees his cock swing round in an echo of the gesture. She feels the skin at the base of her throat redden. 'After sauna.'

'Yes. Yes, I suppose it is.'

The man reaches out to a handheld shower unit and sprays warm water on Cooper's back.

'You missed soap,' he says, as if rinsing off a naked stranger is normal. Maybe it is, thinks Cooper. The man runs the water slowly down her spine and onto the top of her buttocks before holding the nozzle out to Cooper. 'Unless you want me to finish the rest?'

'No,' she says and takes the shower handle, her finger brushing momentarily against the skin of his palm, both surfaces smooth and soapy. Despite herself, a small charge passes between them and she is conscious that she is breathing more deeply than usual. She gets a sudden image of this scene being replayed in the MIT office and puts some steel into her voice. 'I'm OK.'

Cooper rinses the rest of the soap from her body, her back to the man. As she cuts off the water she turns and looks at him.

'Is this a pick-up?' she says. She tries to keep the disbelief from her voice. Is it possible that her cover is still in place? Perhaps Bruckner's hostility is simple jealousy.

The man smiles. He's a big guy, with a belly on him, but solid.

'If you want.'

Cooper shakes her head and walks out of the showers, almost bumping into Ilsa Bruckner. She looks from one to the other, her expression unreadable.

'Excuse me,' says Cooper and slips out, her heart hammering. Time to go. This was a mistake. Behind her she can hear Bruckner talking in a low insistent voice.

Ilsa Bruckner had tagged the woman the moment she'd stepped into the gated lobby at the *Thermen Am Europa Center*. It was the same bitch who'd been eyeballing her across the tables at the rooftop cafe at KaDeWe, her little red bag of shopping propped against her feet to muddy the waters. That hadn't fooled Ilsa for a second, not in her present state of high alert. The meeting with Hoffen here had been designed to reduce any possibility of observation: what cop would strip naked?

The answer comes back almost as soon as she'd posed herself the question: this one. That Ziegler bitch had been capable of pulling something like this. Maybe this was another Ziegler?

Finding out in the sauna she was English had thrown Bruckner. Tourists did find their way into the spa but with the project nearing completion – and the woman seeing her and Hoffen together – now was not a time to be taking any chances.

In the showers Bruckner gestures to Hoffen.

'Go and see who she is. Do what you have to do.'

Hoffen looks like he's about to argue but then nods. OK. Bruckner's right. It's too close now to let this go any further. He wraps the white towel around his waist and follows the woman into the changing rooms.

Cooper is at her locker putting on her bra when a shadow moves behind her. It's the man from the showers. Cooper takes a step back, her hands dropping instinctively over her groin.

'No,' says Cooper. 'I'm not interested. You shouldn't be here.'

'Maybe.' The man moves forward and Cooper takes another step backwards but instead of attacking her, the guy opens the door to Cooper's locker and lifts out her bag.

'Hey,' says Cooper. '*Hey!*' She darts forward but he grabs her arm, holding her easily while he shakes the contents of her bag to the rubber floor. Cooper twists in his grip but the man rolls with it and forces Cooper to her knees. In the process his towel is dislodged. As they struggle, the man's cock presses against Cooper's chest and she feels him harden.

'Stay quiet,' the man hisses. He turns and presses Cooper flat to the floor, his knee on her back, his weight holding her in place. 'If you scream I kill you, understand?'

Cooper, her head on its side against the floor, nods as best she can, her skin sliding across the wet rubber of the floor. Her attacker's balls are inches from her face as he starts looking through her belongings. She struggles again and this time he presses a hand onto her neck.

'Enough. Stay still.'

Cooper can hear the rustling of paper and then the man goes still.

A card is thrust under her nose. Her MIT identity card.

'*Du bist ein Polizistin?* British? Police? Are you kidding me?'

'No,' Cooper snarls. 'You are fucked.'

The man on top of her laughs. Through a gap under his leg Cooper sees Ilsa Bruckner come in.

'*Sie ist ein Cop,*' says the man. '*Britin.*'

Ilsa Bruckner says nothing before nodding, once. Cooper feels the muscles of her attacker's legs tense and a rush of air as the downward blow connects solidly with her cheek. From a great distance a woman screams and Cooper realises the voice belongs to herself.

After that, nothing.

93

Delamere Forest, Cheshire, October 31st

In the end they don't go to a pub. Too many cameras, too many possibilities of running into someone you've banged up, or talked to across an interview table, or shared a shift with. There's even the distinct possibility of running into the Cheshire MIT team having a post-funeral drink. In the present circumstances that would be more than difficult. Despite the light tone, Em Harris is walking a very high tightrope talking to Frank and both of them know it. The idea of any of this ever getting out to Charlie Searle sends shivers down Harris's spine. It would be the end of her.

'Follow me,' says Frank.

He takes the rental picked up from Manchester Airport west towards Delamere and parks at the end of a track coated with a thick layer of dead pine needles. Harris parks her car next to his and gets in beside Frank, the manila folder in her hand. As she steps inside Frank moves the square canvas bag containing the drugs he got via Sheehan off the passenger seat and stows it in the back. Harris looks at it questioningly but Frank says nothing. Until the contents of the vials are inside him – for better or worse – the box isn't leaving his side. No-one has to know. Not even Em Harris.

'So,' says Harris.

'So.'

There's a silence for a couple of beats and then both start speaking at the same time.

'You first,' says Frank.

'You're not dead.'

'Well spotted.'

'I'm not being a smartarse, Frank. You being alive is a huge problem. For me, I mean. After what happened. Which is probably where I should start. What did happen?'

'In Helsby?'

'And before. You never told me what really happened back in America.'

'Is it relevant?'

'I heard you came back with money. A lot of money. Is that true?'

Frank nods. 'Twenty-five million. Dollars.'

'Right.'

'I told Charlie. Which is why I was suspended, pending investigation.' Frank looks at Harris. 'The money's legit, Em. I didn't ask for it and I don't know what to do with it. At least, wait, that's not true. I *didn't* know what to do with it but I do now.'

'Twenty-five million?'

'Can we leave the money to one side? I don't think it's connected to this and I haven't got time to debate it.'

'What about Koopman?'

Frank shrugs. 'He was shot. His arm. I haven't seen him. I've tried calling but there's no answer.'

'He's back in Australia?'

'I think so. I don't know.'

'OK. Tell me about Helsby.'

'What about it?'

'Well we can start with Bernie Palmer. Rimmer's hot for him as the prime suspect.'

'It's not Bernie.'

'No?'

Frank shakes his head. 'I mean, it could be. But I don't think so.'

'Why? You were fucking his wife.'

'True. But it was more complicated. They had a different arrangement than most.' Frank outlines the events he saw through the Palmer window and Harris laughs.

'Sorry,' she says.

'That was my reaction too. But it's not exactly placing Bernie as an enraged husband is it? The DPP gets wind of that and the case against Bernie's gone. There'll be evidence of past encounters with other couples. Jealousy as a motive isn't going to fly. Bernie's passionate but it's not him.'

'You're very sure of that.'

Frank drums his fingers on the steering wheel. 'The blue pill or the red?'

'What?'

'In *The Matrix*. Neo has to choose between hard reality and the easy sham. Red pill for truth and blue to continue on, oblivious. Maybe the other way round. But you get the point.'

'*The Matrix?* Jesus Christ, Frank, I've already taken the pill.' Harris looks directly at him. 'I'm here. In a car with a dead man. MIT are involved in a joint op investigating your death and I'm head of MIT. I think you know what way I've jumped already Frank.'

'OK. Bernie wasn't involved in the Helsby thing, I'd bet my life on it. He didn't order any hit, no matter what his background suggests. I was with Kath Palmer – just a casual thing, the first time we'd ever been together – and two guys came in during the night. Luckily I was in the bathroom when they came in. I assumed they were drug people. Jane Watson had given me the heads up that Lupus had heard I was on a want list. Someone somewhere decided I was going to cop it for the Aussie drugs thing.'

'Go on.'

'I came out of the bathroom and acted like I didn't know the score.' Frank looks down. 'They shot Kath. I got her killed trying to be clever.'

Harris waits and then Frank pushes on.

'There was a struggle after that and I got lucky. The guy who'd shot Kath Palmer was killed by a stray shot. The guy I was wrestling with fell down the stairs.'

'You killed two of them? Unarmed?' She finds it hard to keep the shock from her voice.

Frank nods. He has no intention of revealing the Glock, not even to Harris. Even though he hadn't fired his own Glock, the possession of the gun puts Frank's actions – seen from a cop perspective – in an entirely different light and Frank's not certain how far Em's new found faith in him will last if she knows he armed himself beforehand. After the news from Stevens in London, Frank doesn't intend to spend what time he has left waiting on remand.

'I ran when the third guy came.'

'A third?'

'Yeah. Big man. Followed me across the field and into the woods. I got away, hitched north.' He doesn't say add any more detail. As with the Glock, Harris doesn't need to know about Long Rock. The island is his bolt-hole.

'And why couldn't these guys be working for Bernie?' says Harris.

'I guess they could. They spoke with accents. They were German. I should have mentioned that earlier. Does Bernie have German connections?'

'German?' Harris sits up a little straighter.

'Yes. Why?'

Instead of answering, she slides the folder across to Frank. As he starts to flick through the contents Harris talks.

'You weren't lucky with the guys who came to Helsby, Frank. Luck had nothing to do with it. They weren't there for revenge or payback. They didn't want to kill you.'

Frank looks up from the file, eyebrows raised.

'They didn't?'

Harris shakes her head. 'They were here to abduct you. They were vampires.'

'Vampires?'

'Sort of.' She reaches over and touches the file. 'Read first and then we'll speak.'

Harris sits back and looks out at the grey-brown forest while Frank reads. The silence in the car is broken only by the turning of the pages. Harris listens to Frank's breathing, wondering if she can hear anything of his disease. They haven't said much about the cancer and she doesn't know if they ever will.

After a few minutes Frank looks up.

'A sister. Jesus.'

'Saif Magsi made the connection. You knew nothing about her?'

'No.' He shakes his head and looks out of the window, away from Harris.

She touches his arm and he flinches.

'It's OK. I never knew her. Fuck. They never said nothing.' His accent thickens as the years slip away. *Dey never said nottin.* Harris knows he's talking about his parents. She stays quiet.

'It would have been alright, y'know? If they'd told me. If he'd told me. I would have forgiven him.' Frank clears his throat. 'Fuck, Em, this thing is bad.'

She doesn't know exactly what he means. The cancer, the sister he never knew, the deaths at the barn, or all of it, and she doesn't have the words to say to him. Instead she leans across and wraps her arms around her friend and this time he doesn't flinch at her touch but leans back into her, his face buried in her neck and although he is silent she can feel him shaking.

94

Berlin, October 31st

'What?' says Cooper.

Her head has been kicked by an elephant. That's what it feels like at any rate.

She hears a German voice in the distance, a woman. Cooper's vision is blurred and all she can see is white. The German woman says something again and now the words swim into focus.

'*Können Sie mich hören?*' the woman says. 'Can you hear me?'

'Yes. *Ja.* Yes.' Cooper nods but the movement sends a spasm of pain shooting across her shoulders. 'Jesus.'

'Remain still.'

'Where am I?'

'The spa? Don't you remember? You are in one of our massage rooms. You hurt your head and must remain quite still, yes?'

'I was attacked. Did you see them?'

'Who?'

'The man who attacked me. Is he still here? I need to speak to the police.'

'You fell,' says the attendant. Her face appears in Cooper's cone of vision. She is in her early thirties and has a pleasant, open face. 'This happens sometimes. Wet floor and people move too fast. A lady saw you and, well, here you are.'

'What lady?'

'She has gone. A doctor lady. She is a member.'

'Ilsa Bruckner.'

'Yes.'

'She was one of them. There was a man with her.'

The attendant shakes her head. 'No, this is confusion. Miss Bruckner told us about you. She saved you. There was no-one else.' The woman says something more in German but Cooper can't understand what she says.

Cooper puts a hand to her head and slowly swings her legs down off the massage table. The attendant starts to say something but Cooper stops her. 'My clothes?'

The attendant points to a chair where Cooper's belongings have been piled.

'You should go to the clinic.'

Cooper lifts her jeans and steps into them. 'No. I need to speak to Detective Dreschler or Weiss.'

'This is something you do. I cannot help more.' The attendant opens the door of the massage room. Through the opening Cooper can see another white-coated woman. She and the attendant exchange glances and then the door swings shut.

Cooper finishes dressing and takes an inventory of her bag. Nothing appears to have been taken. She calls Dreschler but gets voicemail. Next, despite the coolness of their last exchange, she calls Weiss. With Bruckner and the guy from the changing rooms around Cooper wants a cop to pick her up.

'Weiss.'

'It's Cooper. I need someone to pick me up.' Weiss starts talking but Cooper cuts across. 'I've been attacked. The attacker could still be around outside.'

'Where are you? I'll get someone there.'

Cooper's grateful that Weiss doesn't ask too many questions. She gives him the address and signs off. Ten minutes later a uniform cop, a woman, appears in the spa lobby and Cooper follows her down to the patrol car waiting at the kerb. It's dark outside, and freezing. Neither the female officer nor her partner talk much and Cooper is glad to get some thinking time in the back of the car on the journey to LKA.

At the office, despite her call with Weiss less than half an hour ago, there's no sign of him or Dreschler.

'Have you seen Officers Dreschler or Weiss?' she asks at the entrance to the LKA unit. The uniform looks up, frowning, before her eyes flick to the bruising on Cooper's face and her expression softens. 'Are you alright?' she asks in German. 'I can get you to the hospital, let someone take a look. What happened?'

'A long story,' says Cooper and then realises she's speaking English. '*Das ist eine lange Geschichte.*'

'Both Officer Dreschler and Weiss are at a meeting.' She speaks slowly, for Cooper's benefit and gestures upstairs with her thumb. 'Back here in an hour's time.'

Cooper finds Anna's desk and gets out a handful of painkillers she finds in a drawer. The bruising on her face attracts more attention but Cooper keeps her head down. She will only talk to Weiss or Dreschler. This thing is starting to unravel fast, she can feel it. Ziegler was right. Ilsa Bruckner is in this thing deep.

Whatever 'this' turns out to be.

She spends the hour waiting for Weiss and Dreschler writing a detailed account of what happened. When she's finished she emails it to DI Harris and copies Saif Magsi in on the message. After her finger presses send she sits back and waits. She doesn't know what else to do.

95

Mallaig, Scotland, November 1st

A pig of a day. Raw and wet with the biting wind that funnels through the harbour mouth slapping heavy curtains of rain against the stone walls of The Harbour Lights. Inside, Paul and Calum Finn are at the bar working on their second pint and passing the time of day with Liam and a couple of local deckhands. The lads have their eyes fixed on a TV showing an English football match. In one corner the electronic poker machine emits electronic burps at regular intervals while diagonally across the room a party of four damp-looking French tourists regard their microwaved pub food with open horror.

'I bet eating soggy neeps on a wet Scottish Sunday afternoon in November is no how they'd imagined their wee Highland jaunt back in Paris,' says Paul Finn, glancing over his shoulder and smiling. He raises his glass to the table and winks without getting a response. He turns back to the bar. 'Miserable fuckers.'

'C'est la vie,' says Liam. 'And less of the 'soggy' too, big man. Nothing wrong wi' my neeps.'

'By the look of the Frenchies you might need to call The Samaritans, Liam. Or *Les Samaritains.*'

The door opens and Frank Keane comes in brushing rain from his hair. He nods to the group at the bar and orders a beer with a whisky chaser from Slater. While he's waiting he walks over to Calum Finn.

'Can I have a word?' he says.

'Aye, Mr Machin, no problem.'

For a moment as the boy slides off his barstool Frank wonders who he's talking to before remembering that he is supposed to be

Tom Machin. He notices Paul Finn looking at him closely and wonders if he's seen the hesitation.

'What can I do for you, Mr Machin?' says Calum. Frank walks him a few paces down the bar. As they do so Paul Finn speaks. 'He's no going over to the island today, Mr Machin. Too heavy out there.'

Frank raises a hand in acknowledgment without looking round.

'So what is it?' asks Calum.

Frank keeps his voice low. 'I want you to take me to Long Rock. I tried to get the helicopter service to take me out but they won't go up in this weather.'

'So how did you get up here? The Hilux is still in the shed.'

'I flew to Inverness and got a rental. I need you to return that too if that's OK. I'll pay for your time. So, how about it?'

'You heard what me da said, Mr Machin.' Calum glances through the window towards the sea. 'It's getting up out there. I don't blame the chopper boys.'

'It's impossible?' says Frank.

'Well, no, mebbe not quite "impossible."'

'You've got that rigid hull inflatable. That can go out in anything, can't it?'

'More or less. But it wouldn't be comfortable.'

'I'm not looking for comfort, just a ride out.'

'What about me da?'

Now it's Frank's turn to glance at Paul Finn. He turns back to Calum. 'Let me deal with your da, Calum.'

Calum nods but the expression on his face is doubtful. 'You can try.'

'What's going on?' Paul Finn looms into view. 'All looks very secretive.'

'Mr Machin here wants me to take him to Long Rock this afternoon. I said you wouldn't like it.'

'You're right, I don't.' Finn dips his glass towards Frank. 'It's too risky to make a passage today Mr Machin. Sorry about that. Just one of those things. In good conscience I couldn't let the lad out.'

Frank lifts a roll of banknotes from his pocket and peels off three hundred. He presses them into Paul Finn's hand. 'How about you, Paul? Is it too dangerous for you?'

Finn looks at the money and then through the window.

'Now you come to mention it,' he says, 'it does seem to be brightening up a bit.' He drains his glass and smiles at Frank.

'Hey!' says Calum. 'Mr Machin asked me.'

'It is a two-man job right enough,' says Paul Finn, his eyes never leaving Frank's.

Frank peels off another hundred.

'And you must be keen like.'

'I'm keen, Paul,' he says, 'but I'm not green. Take me to Long Rock or give me back the three. If it's a no, then I'll go in the morning.'

Fifteen minutes later Frank's in the Zodiac heading out of Millaig harbour. The single bag he's got with him has been wrapped in a bin bag and stowed in the waterproof compartment. Frank wishes he was in there. Despite the heavy weather gear he's been loaned, he's chilled to the bone before they've rounded the headland, his stomach somewhere up around his tonsils as the boat lurches through the swells.

'No' as bad as I thought,' says Paul Finn standing at the controls looking for all the world as though he's still leaning on the bar at The Lights, his only concession to the weather a thin yellow oilskin which he leaves flapping behind him in the wind. Finn says something else that Frank doesn't catch.

'What?' Frank can hardly hear anything over the noise of the Zodiac engines and leans nearer to Paul Finn.

'I said, that anyone stupid enough to come out on a day like this must be running from something.' Finn pauses and looks at Frank as the rain bounces off his face. 'Mr Machin.'

Frank doesn't reply. He thinks back to the man in the Land Rover he'd seen watching them leave the harbour. Finn's no fool and he knows that Tom Machin is about as real as Harry fucking Potter but he's got one thing wrong.

Frank's not running. He's waiting.

96

Berlin, November 1st

'What are you playing at? Are you out of your fucking mind? The woman was in a public *spa*, you imbecile! Do you and that drug-munching gorilla get off doing this kind of shit? Jesus! Fucking amateurs!' The words are spat out in a controlled fury, each one articulated clearly, the endings bitten short, the consonants cracking and the sibilants hissing as if this precise articulation is the only way the caller can retain any control. He paces the office, the phone close to his mouth, his movements agitated, spittle flecking the screen of the phone.

'Are you two fucking each other?'

'Me and Hoffen? Of course not.'

'So why the spa? That's a very cosy arrangement.'

'We can *talk* in the spa. That's why we chose the location. We are not imbeciles. The spa meant that we could talk without being observed.'

'But you *were* being observed! By a fucking English cop! The one who came to check on the van from *your* fucking clinic. The same van that was operated by the two cretins Hoffen sent.'

'I told you, Hoffen did not send them. Gottlenz did.'

'Then he needs to go.'

'He's gone. It's been dealt with.'

'What about your customer?'

There's a pause before Bruckner replies. 'The donor is still required.'

'And how do you propose to deliver this donor? You haven't exactly been successful so far, Ilsa. Four dead so far is it?'

'Hoffen assures me he has someone in place who will deliver. Believe me, we need the cash. If Keane isn't in Berlin inside a week then I'm probably dead anyway.'

'And the cop in the spa?'

'We think you should take care of that.'

'Oh, you do?'

'Yes.'

The caller starts to speak and then stops himself. Bruckner's idea makes sense. The Brit has ID'ed Bruckner from the spa records and has a solid description – although no name as yet – to identify Hoffen. It may be best if this particular loose end is cleaned up in-house.

'You're right. I'll take care of it. Just get the donor, get the fucking money and get this project to completion.'

Bruckner hangs up without another word.

In his office on the sixth floor of the *Landeskriminalamt*, Robert Weiss pockets his phone and smooths down his hair. He steps across to the mirror on the wall and checks his face to see if he looks flushed. Talking to Bruckner often makes him angry.

97

Berlin, November 1st

Theresa Cooper is in a bathrobe, a towel wrapped around her head, and looking in the mirror at her damaged cheekbone when there's a knock on the hotel door. She bends to the peephole and sees a familiar figure standing in the hallway. She takes the chain off the door and opens it.

'Come in,' she says. 'What's with the hat?'

Robert Weiss steps into the hotel room wearing a fat-brimmed Russian hat jammed low on his head and a black parka with a high-cowled neck; a combination that hides most of his face.

'It's cold outside,' he says, as he steps across the threshold. He closes the door behind him with a gloved hand and follows Cooper into the hotel room. Inside he notes the curtains are closed. Good. One less detail to worry about. The TV is on, the sound low, tuned to an English-speaking news network. Cooper has her back to him, oblivious. It will be easy.

He'd taken the back service entrance into the hotel and, as far as possible, avoided any CCTV cameras. In the deep front pocket of his parka is a long-bladed hunting knife lifted from a crime scene in Neukoelln a few months ago. He'll drop the blade in the river once he's finished with Cooper and burn his clothes out in the woods. The service pistol on his belt won't be needed.

'How are you doing?' he says in English. There's something in his tone that makes Cooper look up from the minibar where she's lifting out a half-bottle of white.

'I'm how you'd expect me to be,' she says. 'Bruised and pissed off. I'm funny like that when someone attacks me in broad daylight and no-one gives a shit. Other than Christina maybe.'

'Yeah?' Weiss isn't paying attention. He's looking for Cooper's phone; the one he'd called her on ten minutes ago. He'll need that once this is over. 'Good.'

Cooper pours out a large glass of wine. 'Do you want one?' she says.

Weiss doesn't answer right away and the pause lasts so long that Cooper cocks her head on one side. 'Are you OK?' she asks.

'Yes. I'll have a drink. I'm fine. I just came to see how you were. We weren't very sympathetic at the office and I feel bad about it so . . .' He lets the sentence trail off, aware that he is babbling.

Cooper pours him a glass, her back to Weiss.

Now, he thinks. Now, before she turns around. His hand reaches into his pocket and finds the handle of the knife as Cooper finishes pouring.

Now.

Weiss starts to lift the knife from his pocket when from behind him he hears the sound of the toilet flushing. He pauses, the hand in his pocket still on the knife. After a second or so the bathroom door opens and Christina Dreschler steps out. She looks at Weiss, puzzled.

'Robert?'

'What are you doing here?' The question is blurted out. Even to Weiss his tone sounds off. He notices, too late, a bag that must be Dreschler's lying next to the coffee table, an outdoor coat draped over the armchair, a third glass half full of white wine half-concealed behind the TV.

'I came to check on Theresa,' says Dreschler. 'After she left the office I had a chance to think about it and I wasn't happy about our response. She's going to stay at my place tonight. We can't risk her being attacked again and I thought she'd appreciate some family life. Some normality.'

'Right.' Weiss brings his hand out of his pocket and unzips his parka. 'I thought the same. Something similar anyway.' He smiles, his emotions once again under control. With Christina here he'll have to postpone the business with Cooper. Tomorrow. Yes, tomorrow will work.

98

Berlin, November 2nd

Almost ten in the evening.

A week to go.

Gunther Lamm, driving the van painted in the markings of the Berlin council workforce, swings a right onto *Charlottenstraße* and then left onto *Krause*, zig-zagging through the tourist crap clustered around Checkpoint Charlie, coming at the target from the south, the same direction as the local authority depot. The streets are relatively quiet.

Despite the cold Lamm is sweating. He surreptitiously wipes his brow with his sleeve so as not to alert Ecklenberger, the *Kolumne88* muscle next to him in the passenger seat to his nervousness. Like Lamm, Ecklenberger wears a yellow hi-vis padded vest over the dark blue counterfeit council uniform. In the back of the van are three more *prolos* just like Ecklenberger, all in council duds. They sit swaying on the wall benches, fake bored eyes fixed on the big, plastic-wrapped grey box on the pallet in the centre of the van floor, the bravado back in the warehouse long since subsided into nervy silence.

'Caps on,' says Lamm, twisting in his seat and pointing at his head like these guys can't understand simple sentences. 'It will reduce your identity on CCTV. Keep your heads down as much as possible. Try not to face the American Embassy often. That place is alive with cameras.'

One or two of them mutter and Lamm suppresses the urge to get violent. They place the caps on their heads. All of the men in the van carry guns inside their padded jackets although they are there more for comfort than practicality. If this trip goes wrong, in this location, then they are finished, it's as simple as that. Even Lamm doesn't believe they could escape if shooting starts.

Eighty metres behind, Angelika Lehmann is in the passenger seat of a beige-coloured Nissan driven by Felix Hoffen.

'Too close,' says Lehmann.

Hoffen shakes his head a fraction but drops back without a word. They are only a few hundred metres away from the target. He and Lehmann are only there to observe. If they are already under observation themselves, then none of it really matters. It is what it is. Hoffen knows from experience in the field that once the battle is underway then, no matter how meticulous your preparations have been, events can change quickly. How you react to those changes is what separates the amateur from the pro. He looks over at Lehmann. So far, at least, she is handling herself well.

There had been tension at the warehouse when they were leaving. Tonight was the first contact between the muscle of *Kolumne88* and Lehmann's 'team'. Hoffen had been surprised to find that the team consisted of precisely two: Lehmann herself and the ridiculous wannabe technician, Roos. While Lehmann had been quiet enough Roos had been openly hostile. It had taken the combined efforts of Lehmann and Hoffen to bring things down to an acceptable level.

Angelika Lehmann had greeted the *Kolumne88* group at the door holding an automatic. Although Hoffen had expressed amusement he noticed that she had handled the weapon comfortably, only stowing it in the waistband of her jeans when satisfied the *Kolumne88* contingent were on the level.

The internal squabbles in *Kolumne88* which had resulted in Sebastian Gottlenz making his stupid power bid, followed by his rapid and painful disappearance, had, naturally enough, rattled Lehmann. Hoffen didn't blame her for being antsy. She'd be fine. Roos, well that was another matter.

For her part, Angelika Lehmann is enough of a pragmatist to accept that with profit comes risk. As the day's tick closer to the 9th, Lehmann finds herself more and more running on automatic. This part of the deal is the part that contains the most risk from her point of view. Too many people involved for her liking, too many possibilities of loose lips letting something slip.

'Pull in over there,' says Lehmann. She points at a car park off *Getrud-Kolmar Straße* and Hoffen pulls the Nissan up in a space under a tree. He kills the lights and they look across the diagonal to where Lamm has slowed the van. He bumps up over a small kerb and parks off-road at the corner of *Hannah-Arendt Straße* and *Cora-Berliner Straße*. The van is pointed nose first at an open sloping square on which are set row upon row of concrete obelisks, almost three thousand of them, each at a different height, some no more than the level of a kerbstone while others, those at the centre of the square, are over three metres tall. From the angle that Lehmann is looking at it, the place looks like a modernist cemetery.

'You know what this place is, right?' says Hoffen.

'What?' Lehmann is peering through the windscreen watching Lamm unlock the back doors to the van and the rest of the *Kolumne88* men emerge. 'Of course I know. You people paid me to make the device and oversee installation, remember?'

'No, not there. This car park, I mean.'

Lehmann glances over at Hoffen. 'What?'

'This car park. It's where Hitler died. His bunker was here.'

'I don't care about Hitler.' She turns back. 'You need to concentrate.'

'Relax,' says Hoffen. 'This is going to take some time. If we're blown then we're blown.' He points across the open square at a blocky white-grey building running along the northern side. 'Uncle Sam'll have the cameras on them now. There's nothing we can do except hope they haven't already been tipped. The plates of the van will have been checked already against their database.'

'The plates are legitimate. The papers are legitimate. There will be no problem.'

'Then we are fine.'

He pauses. 'And I don't care about Hitler either.'

'I thought you people were mad for him?'

Hoffen gestures towards the square. 'They are. It's not my thing. My interest in *Kolumne88* is more opportunistic, you understand? It's just strange that they sited that thing there, just across the street. Or maybe that was why?'

'Be quiet.' Lamm, watched by two of the team brings the wooden pallet containing the plastic-wrapped grey box out of the van on a low-wheeled gurney. While he's doing that one of the *Kolumne88* team is talking to a man in a blue uniform, clearly some form of security. Papers are inspected.

'C'mon, c'mon,' mutters Lehmann. The jobsworth in the square is taking forever looking at the fake paperwork. Lehmann knows the papers will check out because they aren't forgeries: the job has been logged onto the council system and fully itemised and docketed. There should be no problem. The team are there – at least according to the official paperwork – to do a legitimate repair job. Every stamp has been stamped and every box ticked. It had cost a bundle and now this guy . . .

'They have to be careful,' says Hoffen, placing a hand on Lehmann's shoulder. 'It'll be fine.' Lehmann glances at Hoffen's hand and he removes it without comment. 'Maybe they usually get a familiar crew, maybe this guy knows someone at the council, who the hell knows? If our guy holds it together, if the paperwork holds up, we're in.' Hoffen shrugs. 'If not, then I'd get the car started and hope your exit strategy works.'

'There should be no problem. Why is he taking so long?'

'Wouldn't you be taking your time?' says Hoffen. 'If you were working security at the Holocaust Memorial?'

99

Mallaig, Scotland, November 2nd

Paul Finn's phone vibrates against the moulded casing of the control panel when he's on his back under the fuse box in *The Mackinaw's* wheelhouse fiddling with the wiring. By the time he gets himself upright the call is gone. Finn checks the number and presses redial.

'Paul,' says Liam Slater.

'Liam. What is it?'

'Your boy's been in the bar a couple of hours.'

'Aye?'

'Well he was talking a blue streak to the feller you asked me about? The Englishman? Land Rover guy?'

'What about it?'

Liam hesitates. Paul Finn has a temper on him and sometimes he isn't fussy about that whole not shooting the messenger thing.

'Spit it the fuck out, man.'

'Like I said, Calum was in here sinking a few with the Englishman. They seemed pretty friendly and all so I didn't worry anything about it.'

'So?'

'So they were talking like and then they left.'

'Where'd they go?'

'How the fuck should I know? They left. But the reason I'm calling is that Harry Taft just came in and said he'd seen your Calum with the guy.'

'Taft's nothing but an old woman.'

'Aye, sure enough. But listen, Paul, here's the thing: Harry said he saw them both heading through the harbour. On the Zodiac like.'

'Tonight?'

'Aye. About twenty minutes back. Like I said, that's why I'm calling. It's no weather to be heading out tonight.'

There is a short silence.

'Paul? You OK?'

'It's alright, Liam,' says Finn.

'Should I call the Coasties?'

'No,' says Paul Finn already stacking his tools back in the box. 'I'll sort it out.'

100

Liverpool, November 2nd

DI Harris pauses at the threshold. Charlie Searle might have been right when he forced her hand by sending Theresa Cooper to Berlin but now, with Cooper having been attacked and with Cooper's positive identification of Ilsa Bruckner – someone linked to the Sarah Coughlan abduction – Harris believes she has a solid case for raising the temperature level and pushing the Super again. Still, as she raps a knuckle on Searle's door, she knows she'll be in for a fight.

'I'm looking for you to support an EAW, sir,' she says once she is seated. 'I'd go over to serve it.' The EAW– European Arrest Warrant – is fast becoming the *modus operandi* for European Union criminal cases. Harris knows it's a stretch to issue one for Ilsa Bruckner but it's worth a try as an opening gambit. The EAW's are almost exclusively used to bring back absconding Brits for trial in the UK, so Searle is unlikely to approve. Harris's thinking is that if he knocks back the EAW he may be more likely to sign off to let her go and take a look around for herself.

'She's German, DI Harris,' says Searle. 'An EAW isn't going to do it. And it certainly won't convince the Germans.' He holds up a hand to stop Harris replying. 'Even if she were a UK national I don't think the evidence would be strong enough.'

'A serving police officer has been attacked, sir. DC Cooper identified Ilsa Bruckner.'

'She identified Bruckner as being present.' Searle taps the papers on his desk. 'There's nothing in here that could be construed as demonstrating a clear involvement with the attack on Cooper. Even Cooper doesn't say this woman laid a finger on her. The spa didn't treat it as an assault and Cooper herself admits she was following the woman on nothing more than dubious evidence. Didn't the liaison officer get a warning about exactly this sort of behaviour?'

'Anna Ziegler?' Harris nods. 'Yes, she did get a warning. She ended up dead. I'd say that was a pretty solid warning, wouldn't you?'

'Don't push it,' growls Searle. 'I don't take kindly to that sort of nonsense, Harris. Frank Keane found that out on a couple of occasions and I've already been cutting you slack. I spoke to Berlin this morning.' Searle makes it sound as though he addressed the entire city. 'Officer Weiss told me that Anna Ziegler was the victim of a random street attack. There is nothing to suggest that Ziegler's death is connected to our case. Even if she's onto something with this Bruckner link we aren't the ones best positioned to connect the dots. Weiss and the LKA will do that and I've no doubt they'll do it well. The days of us acting like John Wayne are gone, DI Harris.'

'John Wayne?'

'Very funny. Generation gap noted. Don't do it again.' Despite the rap across the knuckles, Searle's voice is sympathetic. Christ, thinks Harris, are things as bad as that? 'Listen, Emily, it's early days in your job but I need to see you acting with more responsibility than you've been showing.'

Harris summons up all her resolve to return the serve. Inside, she is jelly.

'With respect, sir, I think I have been showing responsibility.'

'How's Frank doing?'

Harris looks up quickly. 'Sorry, sir?'

'Keane. How's he doing?'

'DCI Keane is dead, sir.' Harris remains very still. Searle fixes his eyes on her long enough for Harris to get the message. The sympathetic tone he'd adopted only a few seconds ago is gone so fast that Harris wonders if she'd imagined it.

'Oh, right. Of course he is.' There is a moment's silence. Searle sits back in his chair and taps his fingers on the arm of the chair. 'I think you need to consider very seriously how far you want to push this investigation, DI Harris.'

'Are you asking me to back off, sir?'

'Not at all. Apart from being a cliché – don't you hate it when they do that in the movies? All that 'you've gone too far, this time, Connor' stuff – it would be most unprofessional for me to ask you to step away. But – purely theoretically, you understand – if it transpires down the line that Frank Keane isn't playing a fucking harp on a cloud but is instead still happily down here sucking oxygen along with the rest of us mortals, then it could be very tricky indeed for anyone who has had contact with him. On the whole, the Force doesn't take kindly to coppers who pretend to be dead. It makes them nervous. And anyone who makes the mistake of talking to one of these zombie coppers falls into the same category. It's a career killer.'

This time it's Harris's turn to remain silent.

'You went to Kath Palmer's funeral,' Searle continues.

'Is that a question, sir? Yes, I did go to the funeral. I went to see if I could pick up any useful information. Standard practice.'

'And did you? Get any useful information?'

'I saw enough, sir. Nothing worth reporting.'

And there it is. The great shining lie out in the open, just as Harris suspects Searle was angling for all along. Deniability. Searle's personal insulation. Now, if it ever emerges that Keane is alive Searle can point to Harris's lie as proof of his own innocence. The worst that can be laid at his door is promoting a maverick officer. Despite this, Charlie Searle looks down at the desk as if Harris has just vomited on his files. He looks up and inclines his head a fraction.

'That's alright then. If there's nothing to report from the funeral then I'm happy.'

This is how it works, thinks Harris. However, Searle knows about Frank – and she's ninety percent sure that he does – whether that's through someone following her, or a random sighting, or, as she thinks likely, a simple calculated guess, the fact that he is talking about it at all gives her the dizzying sensation that the ground is shifting beneath her feet. The other thing that hits her is this: Searle doesn't give a rat's about her being honest. What he cares about, what really gets him over-heated, is protecting the department, protecting himself. Under the ice, under the steely charm, he is telling her something here.

He's telling her to keep quiet.

Telling her to keep her head down.

Telling her to stick to the story no matter what the truth of it is. That way we might all come out of this intact.

'And Berlin?' says Harris. 'I could go there on an MLAT.' Following on from Searle's slippery discussion of Frank's mortality, her Trojan horse plan of offering up the always doomed EAW as a precursor to getting him to agree an MLAT now seems thinner than a supermodel's pizza tab. Charlie Searle actually laughs.

'Like DCI Keane trotting off to America? I don't think so, do you? That didn't work out too well, did it?' Charlie Searle closes the file. 'Look, Emily, I'm not unsympathetic to this. I'd like nothing more than to nail the scrote who got DC Cooper but she is on German soil and has a thin case at best. A case that is already compromised by a lack of anything approaching evidence and by a prior harassment charge against Cooper's contact. The best people to collect that evidence are the officers on the ground. German officers. They're always banging on about how bloody efficient they are. Or is that racist?'

'Perhaps, a little, sir.'

'Well, racist or not, let's give 'em a chance to prove it. Ziegler is one of their own. Do you think they're going to just sit back and do nothing? If Ilsa Bruckner is involved let them make the solid connection. We can come in then and, if required, apply for extradition on the Coughlan case. Get Cooper back here, where she belongs. OK?'

Searle picks up a file from the stack at his elbow and puts on his reading glasses. He bends to the file and then looks up over the rims at Harris. He smiles bleakly and moves his eyes towards the door.

'So that's a "no", then? Sir?'

'Correct,' says Searle, his eyes down. 'Pull Cooper back from Berlin. Immediately. I want her on a plane today.'

As Harris closes the door to Searle's office she lets out a long breath. She's not sure if it's tension about being refused permission to go to Berlin, or relief she still has a job. She has the sense that she is out on a high-wire strung between two tall buildings, too far to go back, too scared to move forward. The lie she told Searle a few minutes ago about not seeing Frank Keane does not sit well with her. It's a mistake. She puts one foot in front of the other and heads back to Stanley Road, her course of action decided.

It's too late to stop now.

101

Berlin, November 2nd

'What was his problem?'

Ecklenberger watches the security guard walk away as Lamm returns to the van.

'Nothing.' Lamm keeps his head down and his voice low.

'It didn't look like nothing. What was it?'

'Just nitpicking.' Lamm stares at Ecklenberger. 'Stop talking. We're in. You need to keep talk to a minimum. We don't know what sort of listening devices they have. Understand?'

The guy gives Lamm the obligatory death stare but nods. 'Let's get this over with.'

Lamm presses the accelerator and the van moves into place nearer the target.

They leave one of the crew at the van, the rear doors open while the rest of them take the equipment towards the centre of the memorial. The device is on one gurney, ladders, toolboxes and arc lights on another.

'This is it.' Lamm, who has been counting the slabs, halts at the one Lehmann has identified as the optimum placement. It stands exactly two metres above ground, and thirty metres in from the northwest corner where the van is parked. Near to the top of this slab are several noticeable cracks in the otherwise smooth concrete. Dotted here and there in the Memorial are signs of repair on similar problems; the cracking slabs reinforced by steel banding wrapped around the block and painted the same colour as the concrete.

It had been the cracked memorial slabs that had given Lehmann her idea.

Posing as a maintenance crew, they will slide a fake slab top containing the bomb into place. The bomb/box will cap the slab, the metal banding masking the join. It will become impossible to spot by anything other than an intensive search. The cracks that the crew are supposedly here to reinforce will be temporarily filled. The pungent drying cement will also help mask the device from the sniffer dogs.

Mobile arc lights and a generator are put in place. Lehmann wants maximum noise and light. To use covert ops in this environment would be useless. With the sensitivity of the Memorial being accentuated by the proximity of the US Embassy, the Brandenburg Gate and the *Bundestag*, every movement here is monitored and risk-assessed. Better to hide in plain sight.

With the throb of the generator drowning out any possibility that their conversation can be eavesdropped, the crew move quickly. The grey box prepared so lovingly in the warehouse is unwrapped and hoisted into place, the process hidden from the Embassy by a blue tarpaulin. The men move carefully. Despite Roos's bland assurances that the detonation cannot take place without the remote trigger, the bomb is handled with extreme care. Roos is not the one out here on display.

Lamm checks his watch and glances up and down the corridors running through the ranked slabs. Down here the memorial is a maze.

In the Nissan, Angelika Lehmann also checks her watch.

Next to her Hoffen nudges her elbow and nods towards a small knot of passing drunks who have stopped to gawp at the repairs. A patrol car pulls up at the kerb and the drunks start moving. The cop inside remains at the kerb looking at the activity on top of the slab. Hoffen feels Lehmann tense.

'Move,' mutters Lehmann. 'Go.'

They wait, the patrol car stationary. They can see the cop's head turned, the peak of his cap pointing at the bombers.

Lamm, his hand to his face, glances over at the cop car and then turns back to the crew. 'Keep working,' he says. 'Don't look over.'

Time crawls. An eternity. Lamm finds it difficult not to keep checking the patrol car. He can feel the weight of the gun against his chest. Despite the cold he is sweating still.

'They're going,' mutters Ecklenberger. Lamm feels tension flood from his body and has to work hard to prevent his legs shaking.

As the cop car starts moving, the crew start hauling the box containing the bomb on to the top of the slab. It is heavy and as they start lifting one corner knocks heavily against the slab.

'Careful!' Lamm heaves and the box slides up, over the centre of gravity. One of the goons guides it into place. At this moment, with the patrol car moving past the intersection, Lamm can't believe that they haven't been blown. Lifting this box into place is so obvious, so stupid. Previous repairs surely didn't look like this? And yet, they are not spotted. They wear hi-visibility vests. They have lights and generators and papers. Everyone looks at them but no-one sees them. The woman was right.

In the Nissan, Lehmann and Hoffen watch the patrol car swing left and then left again, circling the Holocaust Memorial before accelerating right towards Brandenburger Tor.

'How much longer will it take?' asks Hoffen.

'Not long,' says Lehmann. 'A few minutes.'

With the device fitted over the slab, they smooth the cracks with concrete filler. Ten minutes later Lamm switches the generator off.

'How's it going?'

The voice appears from nowhere and it is all Lamm can do not to jump. The guard has come from nowhere.

'They don't normally do it like this,' he says.

Before Lamm can reply Ecklenberger leans down from his position on a ladder and holds out a cement-tipped trowel to the security guard.

'Dive right in, friend,' he says. 'Because I didn't know there was a fucking expert checking up on us and I'd be happy to have my feet up watching the game instead of being out here freezing my fucking balls off.' He shakes his head and turns back to the slab muttering. 'Everyone's a fucking expert.'

The guard takes a step back and looks at Lamm. 'What's up with that guy? Jesus.'

Lamm rolls his eyes and taps the side of his head. He bends closer to the guard.

'Between you and me, brother, he's a nut.'

'I heard that.'

Lamm smiles and the guard shakes his head.

'Ten minutes and we're done,' says Lamm to the guard's retreating back. He doesn't turn around. Once the guy exits the corner, Lamm lets out a long slow breath and makes a note to buy Ecklenberger a beer. That took balls Lamm didn't think the guy had.

'Let's get moving,' he says and Ecklenberger nods.

They are inside the van in three minutes.

'They did it,' says Lehmann. 'We're in play.'

'Looks that way.'

'Let's get moving.'

'Stay here a while. If they are under observation there's no reason for us to get pulled too.'

Lehmann sits back, twitchy. Hoffen's right but it's difficult resisting the urge to get away.

'The other half of your team,' says Hoffen. 'He's cleaning?'

Lehmann nods. Roos should be eradicating all trace of the cell from the warehouse. There had been some talk of torching the place but Lehmann had nixed that. Too risky. A fire meant authority. An investigation. If this thing is going to work then she has to believe that BfV, the *Bundesamt für Verfassungsschutz*, Germany's elite anti-terror group, will not find the warehouse before the 9th of November. After, then things will be different and the warehouse not so important. Even so, if Roos does as she has told him, he will strip everything from the building. The lease, through a complex series of holding companies established by Angelika Lehmann in preparation, has the warehouse until the middle of next year. 'I'm taking care of it,' she says, her eyes scanning the square for any sign of law enforcement activity. When she turns back to the fake slab top she finds she can't pick it out.

'And what about cleaning the personnel?' Hoffen's voice is a growl.

'He can be trusted.'

Hoffen shrugs. 'No he can't, and you know it. If he gets pulled into a CIA black site then the information will follow quicker than you can say 'Guantanamo'. From what I saw your guy won't last a second. I'm not telling you your business but . . .'

'That's exactly what you're doing.'

'But you need to think about tidying up the loose ends.' Hoffen faces Lehmann. 'And have you considered that he might be thinking the same about you?'

Hoffen starts the engine. 'Like I said, I'm not telling you your business.'

'Are you following your own advice?'

Hoffen shakes his head. 'If I was, why the fuck would I tell you about it? You might have some brains but you're operating in a different world now.' He thinks about Bruckner. Lehmann and her share some characteristics, one of which is the belief that people act in predictable ways. What Hoffen knows is that that sort of thinking only holds true in peacetime. Under pressure, in the field, things change. Adaptability to conditions is all there is.

It's the reason why he will kill Lehmann once the bomb explodes.

No loose ends.

102

Long Carraig, Scotland, November 2nd

Here goes nothing.

Sitting at the kitchen counter at Long Rock, Frank checks the printed dosage guide and snaps open the protective packaging on a hypodermic. The package had been sitting there for almost twenty-four hours while Frank tried to find a reason not to try the drugs. In the end the tick-tock of the kitchen clock had pushed him into action.

He pushes the needle through the rubberised cork on top of the first of the vials and carefully draws eight milligrams of clear fluid into the barrel. Without exactly knowing why, he flicks the glass tube with a nail and inspects the contents as if expecting to see . . .what, exactly? Air bubbles, that's it. Air bubbles are bad. Frank holds the hypo to the light and checks. The liquid is clear. He presses the plunger a little to fill the needle then, quickly, before he has the chance to think about it, inserts the spike into his arm. It hurts more than he imagined it would.

Frank places the empty hypo on the kitchen counter, picks up an antiseptic swab from an open pack and presses it onto the fat droplet of blood oozing from his arm. He holds it for a few seconds and then presses a plaster onto his skin. He can feel his lungs moving inside his chest and is aware of his heartbeat although he's not sure if this is a result of his illness or simply that he's listening more closely to what his body is saying. Frank leans back, looking at his reflection in the mirror on the kitchen wall. He's not sure what he expects to see. Wolverine? The Hulk? Lou Reed? Instead, it is his own face that stares back, the skin a little tighter on his bones perhaps, the eyes deeper and darker than they were a few months ago maybe, but still recognisable as Frank Keane.

Next to the cancer drugs and medical paraphernalia on the countertop is the file Harris gave him after Kath Palmer's funeral. Frank's read it from cover to cover a dozen times in the twenty-four hours he's been back but he's no nearer making sense of what's been happening than he was the first time he went over the material. He's compartmentalised Sarah's existence as a half-sibling for now. That particular sack of snakes can wait until, or if, he gets through this.

What's left is this: someone is willing to pay large sums of money to get hold of Frank. Frank had been reluctant to let go of the notion that his pursuers were in the drug trade. Despite the ferocity and the violence of the events so far, the notion that it is 'only' drug dealers who are chasing him fits in so well with Frank's experience that it is almost comforting. He knows the drug world inside out, understands the motivations, the demented rationale and the psychotic capitalism at its heart. It is a simple business. But Jane Watson's intel that he is not being targeted by drug gangs, added to the information coming from Berlin, places Frank's predicament in a less certain world. What does he know about Berlin? Why was Theresa Cooper attacked? What is the link between Sarah Coughlan – Frank still can't think of her as his sister – and all of this? In all the madness of the past few days he has had precious little time to reflect on the news Harris had given him in Delamere Forest. Frank's never been much for family life. He and Julie never had so much as a dog to look after and the idea of kids gave him the heeby-jeebies. How Julie had felt, he wasn't so sure, but in any case that all turned out to be an impossibility for her. Now he's got a sister? *Had* a sister. Christ.

Frank picks up the folder and starts reading again in the hope that repetition will yield something he'd missed. Some minutes pass in silence and then, from across the open plan room, a red light blinks on the security console set into one wall.

The security set-up on Long Rock is one of the reasons Frank bought the place. Small, flat screen monitors show the front entrance to the house, the rear entrance and the laundry room entrance. Another shows the outside of the garage and hangar while a fifth shows the jetty. It is this monitor which is indicating activity.

The milky green night vision image of the dock from a camera mounted on a metal gantry shows Cal Finn tying up the Zodiac.

Calum finishes tying the boat and stands, waiting for a moment. Frank wonders exactly what the boy is doing and then he sees a second figure walk into view. Frank's stomach lurches as he sees the gun in the man's hand and knows in that instant that he has made a mistake. Getting the boy off the island hasn't put him in safety.

It's put him slap bang in the firing line.

Calum starts walking towards the house, the gunman a few paces behind as Frank tries to work out how to stop another innocent going the way of Kath Palmer.

103

Berlin, November 2nd

At eight in the morning the Holocaust Memorial security shift swaps over. Holtz, the night chief, signs the docket and hands over to the day crew.

'Anything?' says Christian Boehne, the day chief. Holtz, the hood of his big yellow Jack Wolfskin parka already up in preparation for the raw Berlin morning outside, shakes his head and jerks a thumb at the activity roster. 'Some maintenance. All in there.' Boehne, a thirtysomething Dresden blow-in is the last thing Holtz needs right now. Breakfast is calling. Holtz murmurs something as Boehne, his outdoor coat still on, slides the clipboard holding the log towards him across the desk. As Boehne bends his head to read the details, Holtz follows the other two night security guys through the door.

'Maintenance?' murmurs Boehne, scanning the entries. 'I didn't see any scheduled maintenance until after the 9th.' He looks up but the office is empty. 'OK,' murmurs Boehne, flushing. 'And fuck you too.'

Frowning, he looks to the CCTV monitors. DeWaltz and Gunnerson, the Swede, are running through the security prep in the museum housed below the memorial. Boehne opens the computer and checks the numbers on the maintenance log with the council database. After a few moments he leans back. The maintenance assignment numbers match. He checks the slab co-ordinates and remains seated, his fingers drumming on the desk. There will be a security sweep in three day's time and more in the days after and Boehne doesn't like leaving anything to chance.

After a moment he gets to his feet and heads outside again, picking up a Maglite torch from a rack. It's still dark although the memorial is well lit by the street lights. Deeper into the slab canyons however, the shadows become murky. Boehne counts off the rows heading west from the security office and then north. At Block 1178 Boehne can smell the fresh concrete. He switches the mag on and sweeps the beam around the new metal of the reinforced banding, the cracks the maintenance crew repaired showing as still damp concrete. In a few days they will be invisible.

Boehne checks the ground around but can find nothing to complain about. He shrugs and walks back towards the office.

On the top of Block 1178, securely sealed from heat imaging detection by a protective inner skin of plastic and aluminium, sit eighty kilos of high explosive, around which are tightly packed over four thousand ball bearings. This lethal payload is merely the delivery system for the main threat squatting at the edges of the device: four sealed tubes of hydrogen cyanide compound.

There is a sick poetry to Roos' choice of chemical. In a previous incarnation, a hydrogen cyanide mixture invented at the Kaiser Wilhelm Institute for Physical Chemistry in Berlin in 1922 was used to exterminate more than a million people in the concentration camps of Dachau, Auschwitz and Bergen-Belsen. The brand name of this Berlin-made poison was Zyklon B.

On the 9th of November, during a commemorative service at the Holocaust Memorial designed to counter the date being commemorated by neo-Nazis, Angelika Lehmann and *Kolumne88* will unleash Zyklon B on the innocents once more. According to the security roster, Boehne will almost certainly be one of the victims.

104

Long Carraig, Scotland, November 2nd

A few minutes before midnight, Frank reaches a hand up to kill the lights and stops himself with his finger on the switch. One of his very few advantages is the gunman's apparent lack of awareness about the CCTV cameras. A light going off suddenly might tip him off.

Leaving the house lights on, Frank runs to a large utility room off to one side of the laundry. From a metal-doored cupboard on the wall he takes out the Glock and checks it is loaded before he returns to the security monitors. With luck he can get a clear shot before anything is said. After Kath there's going to be no attempts to be clever.

The screens show no sign of the boy or the gunman. Then, just as Frank is about to take a look outside, they come into shot at the back entrance to the house. Frank sees Calum glance up momentarily at the camera, his face stricken.

Frank, his nerves vibrating like piano wires, opens the front door but doesn't leave. Instead he steps inside a darkened alcove off to the side that doubles as a cloakroom and tries to slow his breathing. He allows himself one long exhalation and then stays quiet, the barrel of the Glock raised against one side of his face, suddenly calm.

There is movement.

Frank can't see it so much as sense it: a displacement of the air, the soft scuff of sole on wood, a creak, a shadow.

'Frank.'

It's an English voice, a Londoner.

'Frank Keane,' says the guy once more. The tone is almost gentle. 'Let's get this done.'

There is another, metallic, sound. The sound of a gun being cocked.

'I'll shoot the boy, Frank.'

Frank hears Calum make a small involuntary animal noise, somewhere between a cry and a plea. Scared.

Frank steps out of the alcove, the Glock held steady out in front of him as he moves around the corner and into the main room. On one side of the kitchen island stands the gunman. He is a man around thirty-five years old with bland features, wearing dark-coloured combat pants and a thick waxed jacket. In his right hand he has a gun which is pressed to the head of Calum Finn.

'Drop your weapon,' says Frank. 'Then get down on the floor.'

'You sound like you've said that before, Frank,' says the gunman. 'But it's not going to work here. When I said I'd hurt the boy, it wasn't an opening gambit, it was a statement of fact.' In a single smooth motion, and before Frank can react, the gunman lowers his arm and shoots Calum Finn in the foot. The boy screams and starts to fall before the gunman grabs him by the collar and hauls him upright again. He rams the barrel of the gun hard into Finn's open mouth.

'Now, for the last time, put the fucking gun down, there's a good chap.'

Frank lowers the Glock to the floor. 'Leave him alone.' Please God don't let this boy go the way of Kath Palmer. Please let him live. Please give me a chance to kill you, you miserable motherfucker.

'Slide it across,' says the gunman. Frank kicks his gun across the wooden floor and it comes to rest against a leg of one of the bar stools. The soft-spoken gunman drags Calum Finn around the kitchen island. Dropping the boy to the floor he bends and picks up the Glock.

'See to his foot,' he says to Frank. 'His squawking's giving me a headache.'

'The stuff's in the bathroom,' says Frank. 'Medical kit.'

'Let's go.' The gunman gestures, following Frank down a corridor. Frank finds a green nylon medical kit in the cabinet and, closely watched by the gunman, returns to the kitchen.

'Sorry, Mr Machin.' Calum gasps out the word as Frank kneels. His face is ghostly, his skin clammy and he is trembling.

'Quiet, Cal,' says Frank. 'Let me get this tidied up.'

'Machin?' says the gunman. 'Is that what you're calling yourself?'

Frank says nothing.

'Jesus.' Calum's voice is close to hysterical. 'This fucken hurts, man.'

'Not like on the video games, eh?' says Frank, smiling calmly. 'I'll have to get your boot off, OK? See what the damage is. You OK with that?'

Calum nods.

His boot is tight and Frank has trouble getting it loose, each blood-slicked fumble and fruitless twist of the leather producing a sharp spasm of pain. When eventually it eases free with a quick jolt, Calum screams again, his hands balled into fists.

'That's the worst of it, son,' says Frank. He pulls away shreds of Calum Finn's sock. The bullet has entered the foot on the soft, fleshier part on the right side and passed through leaving a gaping, ragged wound pulsing with blood. It's messy but Frank thinks he might be OK. Frank glances up at the gunman. 'He needs medical treatment.'

The gunman leans across and looks briefly at the boy's foot. 'He'll live,' he says taking a phone from his pocket and thumbing a number.

'Lydon,' he says. There is a short silence and then: 'I got him.'

Lydon looks down at Frank. 'No, I don't think there'll be a problem. I can get him to the mainland and you can pick him up. Make it somewhere not too far. I don't want him on my hands too long.'

Frank, his hands slick with Calum Finn's blood, wipes them on his jeans. 'Take me and we'll drop the boy on the mainland,' says Frank.

'I need him for the trip back, anyway. It's too choppy out there.' Lydon points at the medical kit. 'Get him strapped up. Quick, I don't want to be in Jockland longer than absolutely necessary. And clean him up. He looks disgusting.'

'Fuck you,' hisses Calum.

'Easy,' says Frank. He takes an antiseptic pad and puts it over the wound. Calum cries out and Frank winds a crepe bandage tight around his foot. While he's busy Lydon stands and watches. Frank's been here before, in Helsby, but this guy is different. The Germans had been sloppy but Lydon is in another category. His posture is alert and the muzzle of his gun hasn't left Frank.

'Finished?' Lydon jerks a thumb at the door. 'Let's get moving.' He gestures at Frank. 'Get back over by the kitchen.'

'He needs help,' says Frank.

'Get away from him,' says Lydon.

Frank moves to the kitchen counter, his eyes scanning the surface for weapons.

'There's no knives, if that's what you're looking for, Frank.' Lydon shakes his head and waves the gun at the boy. 'Get up, Braveheart.'

'I'm going as fast as I can, you English prick,' says Calum. The words come out staccato as the boy braces himself against the pain from his foot.

'Don't,' says Frank but the boy has lost it.

'You can shoot me again, you English motherfucker.'

Lydon takes a quick step forward and swipes the barrel of his gun savagely across Calum Finn's face. His head whips back and a long bloody streak opens up under his right eye. Calum turns back defiant only for Lydon to lash out again. This time, Calum is rocked back to his knees, blood dripping to the floorboards. He spits and several teeth come out. Lydon stamps down on his wounded foot. Calum Finn screeches in agony and Frank darts forward.

'Leave him!'

Lydon pulls Frank's Glock out of his waistband with his left hand and extends his arm at Frank.

'Back off.' Lydon jabs the automatic in his right hand towards the boy. 'Now. Can we all please just start doing what I say? Finish with all the hero bollocks and just obey orders. Easy.' Lydon looks at Frank. 'Stand him up.'

Frank gently gets Calum upright and they stand looking at Lydon. Cal Finn holds a hand to his shattered jaw and says something to Lydon through a mouthful of blood.

'I'd prefer you to guide us back, son,' says Lydon, 'but I reckon we can manage without you.' He pulls the slide back on the top of the gun and slides a bullet into the chamber before pressing the muzzle against Calum Finn's head. 'So, for the last time, you whining little Scottish cunt, start improving your manners, or I will put a bullet in you, understand?'

'Wait.' Frank takes a half-step forward and then stops as, over Lydon's shoulder, he sees Paul Finn steaming in fast from the open front door holding a shotgun by the barrel.

Lydon, too late, senses something and starts to swivel, but Paul Finn, his expression savage, is already moving too fast. The big man closes the space between himself and Lydon and smashes the butt of his shotgun hard into the gunman's face with a sickening crunch of breaking bone and cartilage.

The Londoner's face explodes in a shower of blood and snot and smashed teeth. He crashes drunkenly into a chair. As he slides to the floor, Paul Finn whips the shotgun round in one fluid movement and rams the muzzle roughly into Lydon's eye. Vibrating with barely suppressed fury the fisherman stands over the prone figure, his gnarled finger hard against the trigger.

'Put a bullet in my son, will ye?' Paul Finn is screaming. He leans down on the shotgun pushing it hard into Lydon's face. 'Not such a big man now, eh? Ye fucken London arsewipe!' Finn whips the shotgun round again and drives the butt hard into Lydon's ruined nose. Ignoring the screams, Finn swings the gun back into a shooting position, thumbs the hammer and steps over Lydon, the twin barrels inches from his head. 'Ye're a dead man, Londoner. A dead man.'

'Don't,' says Frank quietly. 'Don't do it, Paul.'

For a moment Paul Finn doesn't move. The bleeding mess on the floor looks up through a mask of blood and makes a small sound.

'Shut the fuck up.' Finn jabs down again, the muzzle of the shotgun breaking more teeth and producing another moan from Lydon.

'Da.' Calum's voice is soft.

'It's alright, Cal.' Paul Finn holds up a hand, palm upright. 'I'll sort this out, son.' He looks at Frank blankly for a moment as if he's forgotten he's there and then speaks without warmth. 'Not a word from you, OK? I'll do it or I won't do it but whatever happens it'll be on my say so, not some Englishman telling me.'

'I'm a police officer, Paul,' says Frank.

'Is that right, Mr Machin? Then maybe we should call the police and see what they have to say.'

Frank says nothing.

'No? Did nae think so. Fucken police, my arse.'

For a few seconds the only sound in the room is Lydon's ragged breathing and the wind coming off the black Atlantic through the open front door.

'Get up,' says Paul Finn. He stands and gestures at Lydon with the gun. Slowly, like a man underwater, one hand to his face, Lydon pushes himself upright. He starts to say something but the effort proves too painful. He leans forward and blood drips to the floor through his fingers.

Paul Finn turns to look at his son, the shotgun never leaving Lydon. 'Can you move?' His voice is soft when he talks to the boy.

'Aye, I think so, da.' Calum hobbles upright, wincing. He braces himself against the kitchen counter keeping his damaged foot off the floor. The boy looks at Frank. 'I'll be OK, Mr Machin.'

Frank nods. He reaches over the counter and hands Calum a roll of kitchen paper.

'Get something and tie his hands behind his back.' Paul Finn is speaking to Frank. 'I don't want him trying nothing on the way back.'

Frank finds a couple of bungee cords in one of the kitchen cupboards. He moves to Lydon, pulls his arms down and wraps the bungee cord around his wrists. Lydon staggers and Frank hauls him back to his feet. Finn's instruction to tie Lydon has reassured Frank.

'Take him to the jetty,' says Finn. Frank grips Lydon by the back of his jacket collar and moves to the front door. Behind him, Paul Finn puts an arm around his son and follows.

In the dark, Lydon slips twice on the way to the dock. As they get within sight of the jetty Frank sees Paul Finn's fishing boat tied up next to the inflatable.

Finn places Calum gently next to one of the wooden posts on the jetty and steps lightly into the trawler. He puts the shotgun down flat on a pile of nets and turns to Frank. 'Pass him over.'

Frank moves the bleeding man to the edge of the dock and guides him across the pitching gap between the boat and the water.

'He's going to kill me,' says Lydon, his voice thick, the words sliding across broken teeth and flesh. He locks eyes with Frank. 'Don't let him kill me. You're police. Don't let him.'

'Who sent you?' Frank says in a low voice.

'What?'

'You heard. Quick before I let him take you.'

'Hand him up,' says Paul Finn. 'Get moving.'

Frank reaches into Lydon's jacket, lifts out his mobile and slides the phone into his own pocket.

'I don't know who sent me,' says Lydon. He is crying. 'I don't.'

'You're lying.'

'I'm not! I've done a couple of things for this man before. Found people. That's what I do. But I don't know who he is.'

'Now!' Paul Finn leans over the edge of the trawler and prods Frank's shoulder with a finger made of steel. Frank keeps hold of Lydon's arm for a moment and then let's go. Let Finn take him and do whatever he wants. Why should he do anything about this piece of vermin? Lydon, or someone like him, killed Sarah. And, despite Paul Finn's violence, Frank's not sure he's got it in him to kill. And Lydon was lying to him about not knowing who sent him, Frank would bet on it.

'All yours,' says Frank.

Paul Finn pulls the gunman aboard and pushes him to the floor.

'Now Calum,' says Finn.

Frank helps the boy aboard. Paul Finn settles his son inside the wheelhouse. The sea is getting heavier by the minute and the trawler scrapes against the buffer tyres lashed to the side of the jetty. Finn starts the engines and then comes back to the side of the boat.

'You can use the inflatable in the morning. The sea's not too bad tomorrow. Leave it tied up somewhere on the sea wall and we'll make sure it gets taken care of.' Paul Finn raises a finger and points it at Frank's chest. 'Your business with Calum is finished, is that clear?'

'What are you going to do with him?' Frank points to Lydon, huddled on the deck, blood pooling around his head.

Paul Finn doesn't reply. Instead he points at the mooring ropes. 'Cast us off.' He turns to the wheelhouse and makes a circular gesture. Calum starts moving the trawler backwards, freeing up slack on the lines. Paul Finn looks at Frank again. 'This is over for us. I should never have let Calum work for you.'

Frank lifts off the heavy coil of rope and passes it across the gap.

'The hospital will want to know how he got injured. There'll be questions.'

As the boat moves into open water, Paul Finn picks up the shotgun and holds it loosely by his side.

'He's not going to any hospital, Machin. There'll be nae questions.'

'Don't, Paul,' says Frank but there's no conviction in his voice and the words are swept away on the wind. More disturbingly, Frank finds he doesn't much care if Lydon lives or dies.

Finn, moving as only someone with a lifetime on the water behind them can do, turns away, bends to check on Lydon and then steps into the wheelhouse. He props the shotgun on a sill and leans into the instrument panel.

Lydon, lying awkwardly on the pile of nets looks at Frank as the distance between them increases. The trawler leaves the shelter of the small harbour and heads west through the darkness the dip and roll of the boat increasing in the bigger swell. From the jetty Frank watches the white line of the boat's wake, waiting for Finn to calm down and reconsider, to swing the trawler to turn south towards Mallaig, but it doesn't happen. The boat stays on a westerly course through the deep black waters of the Atlantic until its swaying lights are swallowed by the night.

105

Kietz, Germany, November 3rd

Two parked cars on a late night gravel road.

'Was this absolutely necessary?'

'Just get in.' Weiss leans across and opens the passenger door of his car for Ilsa Bruckner who has just stepped out of her Audi. She glances at Hoffen sitting in the back seat, his expression unreadable. Bruckner, her arms plunged deep into the pockets of a thick winter coat, looks like she's gargled battery acid. Her breath rises in a white plume which wraps itself wraith-like around her head before dissolving into the cold black night.

'We could have done this in town. It's freezing.'

'Then get in the fucking car, Ilsa. Do you think we'd have got you all the way out here if things weren't serious? We have a big problem.'

Bruckner gets in and closes the car door. 'Is this yours?' she asks Weiss as she looks around the interior. 'A Skoda? Does the heater work?'

'It's a pool car. And you might have been better not using your own. BfV are all over us, Ilsa. Almost certainly because of your stupid run-in with the English cop, the woman.'

'I thought you were dealing with that?'

'We are.'

In the back seat, Hoffen stirs. Bruckner turns to see him dab a finger of coke onto the back of his hand and snort.

'Jesus, Hoffen.' Bruckner shakes her head and looks out at the blackness.

It's almost two in the morning. They are parked down a track leading nowhere about an hour east of Berlin and a spit from the Polish border.

'Has anyone been sniffing around, Ilsa?' says Weiss, shifting in his seat to face Bruckner, his leather jacket squeaking as he moves. One side of his face is lit green from the dash, one side in shadow. 'Anything we should know about?'

'Of course not. Don't you think I'd have told you?'

'And your client?' Hoffen leans forward and puts his elbows on the back of the front seats. Bruckner can feel his breath on her neck. 'What does he think about the non-delivery?'

Bruckner scowls but Hoffen can see the fear in her eyes when the subject of her client is raised. 'He is being patient,' says Bruckner.

'Does he know anything about us, about the project?' Hoffen sniffs wetly and Bruckner wrinkles her nose in distaste.

'Don't be ridiculous. Why would I tell him anything about this business?'

Hoffen doesn't reply but Weiss leans in a little closer.

'And you're sure you weren't followed here? No-one knows we're meeting? You didn't mention it to that guy, what's his name? Dieter. You didn't say anything to Dieter?'

'Dieter is no longer around. No-one knows anything. There is nothing connecting me with you. You can relax, OK?'

Weiss turns forward and looks straight ahead out of the windscreen. In the backseat, Hoffen moves forward, loops the garrotte over Bruckner's head and pulls back in one smoothly savage movement. The wire bites deeply into Bruckner's flesh and she scrabbles frantically at her throat, her feet banging against the dashboard.

Weiss steps out of the car and walks a few paces away to wait for Hoffen to finish. The vehicle rocks and bangs for twenty, thirty seconds and then is still. After a short pause Hoffen steps from the car, winding the garrotte into a coil. He slips it back into his pocket and hands Weiss the keys to Bruckner's Audi.

Weiss moves the Audi twenty metres back down the track while Hoffen takes a can of petrol from the boot of the Skoda. The vehicle isn't a pool car. It had been stolen in Berlin three hours ago and the plates switched by Hoffen for those of a legitimate scrapyard junker.

In the unlikely event of being pulled on the way out here the plates would cover it.

Hoffen splashes the petrol around the Skoda and, stepping back, puts a match to the fumes. Hoffen walks to the Audi as the fire gets a hold on the Skoda and gets in. He looks back to see Ilsa Bruckner's profile silhouetted through the dancing flames for a second or two and the Skoda explodes with a dull whoomp.

Bruckner's fate had been sealed the day that Gottlenz tried to recruit Lehmann. The cash he'd handed over meant that Bruckner's importance receded rapidly. *Kolumne88* no longer needed the income from Bruckner's donor. Closing that line of enquiry felt good. Too many complications.

Weiss drives towards the main road. They'll dump the Audi back on the outskirts of Berlin and pick up their own cars which have been left parked behind an auto shop owned by *Kolumne88*. Weiss knows this killing has zero chance of coming back to bite them. Bruckner's gone.

106

Berlin, November 3rd

The 9th of November this year has been looming large for many people in Berlin and for different reasons. As usual, the Central Council of Jews, in tandem with representatives from the main religious organisations of other denominations, the trade unions and civil liberty groups form the largest of the interested parties. The rally to mark the dark days of 1938's *Kristallnacht* is set to be one of the largest. With the worrying rise of the neo-Nazi's, the committee is making a big push this year. Numbers in excess of twenty thousand have been spoken about.

Kolumne88 themselves are taking as many fellow travellers as they can. For obvious reasons they haven't promoted the anti-Jewish protest as widely as they might have done. Hoffen, Bruckner and Gottlenz had all agreed that while it was desirable for there to be *Kolumne88* casualties, there is no reason to be stupid about it. After the bomb they'd need as many hands as they could muster. Some dead, to provide plausible deniability, but not so many that they'd be light-handed in the aftermath. This bloodletting will push the debate to the right. Hoffen has been encouraging the production of fake Islamist materials in the days and weeks before the bombing. *Kolumne88* will claim no responsibility. An Islamist attack on a Jewish memorial sends a message to Israel especially if, as both Hoffen and Lehmann fervently hope, there are casualties from the embassy: several diplomats will be there, along with representatives from the *Bundestag* and the UK Embassy, just around the corner in *Wilhelmstraße*. Most of the EU countries will be represented. There will be a satisfying body count amongst the opinion formers.

The rest of the interested parties belong to one of two groups: the media and law enforcement. Both view the Holocaust memorial rally with the same level of enthusiasm. Which is to say, practically zero. Both need to be there, both need to do their homework and both would rather be somewhere else. The chances of a newsworthy terrorist incident are slim although many of the journalists are secretly hoping for trouble of some sort. The Memorial rally is a target but it's soft. As with the attacks by Lashkar-e-Taiba in Mumbai in 2008, the Moscow subway attack in 2010, and the 2005 London bus bombs, the target here in Berlin is not connected to the military, to the police, to the intelligence services. It's not an embassy or a seat of government. It is not a 'hot' issue. Not here. There is a limit to the amount of protection BfV and the *Grenzschutzgruppe 9 der Bundespolizei* – the police anti-terror arm, better known as GS9 – can be expected to provide.

But the Memorial is still a target so BfV run through the standard operational measures. Sweeps of the area, collation of intelligence, liaison with the LKA, with the Transit Authorities, with the City Council. None of these measures find anything they should be overly concerned about. There'll be more sweeps, more measures taken in the next days.

The 9th will be fine.

107

Long Carraig, November 3rd

Lydon's phone only has one number on it; the last call he made while he was in the kitchen. In the early hours, Frank, sitting in a chair in front of the big window, looks at the string of digits on the screen – something tangible, something real, a ticket to the show – and feels the familiar tingle at the base of his spine he always got when a case started to peel open.

Was that what this was? A case? MIT seems a long time ago.

He presses redial and listens to the ringing tone. Someone answers on the second ring.

'Ja?'

The voice is deep and quiet. If whoever answered was asleep the voice doesn't betray it. Frank checks his watch and makes the quick calculation; 3 a.m. in Germany. He says nothing in reply, hoping for more, but after a few seconds the line goes dead. Frank holds the phone and, after a short time, it rings. He presses 'answer' and puts it to his ear, saying nothing. Whoever is calling says nothing. Frank stays quiet and, once again, the phone line goes dead. There's no point in calling back. There will be no answer this time. With luck, the caller may think Lydon is having technical difficulties and keep the phone.

Frank puts Lydon's phone on the arm of the chair and picks up his own. He should be feeling exhausted after the day he's had but he is alert. He wonders if it's the drugs. He dials a number and it rings out, goes out to voicemail. He hangs up and redials immediately. This time it is answered.

'Hello?' says Harris, her voice sleep-clogged and irritable. Frank realises that she doesn't have his latest number.

'It's me,' he says.

He hears tiny movements and imagines Harris sliding out of bed to go into the living room. There is a muffled exchange of words and Frank knows she's telling Linda to go back to sleep. When she comes on the line again her voice is sharper but she keeps it hushed.

'It's late,' she says. Frank's pleased to see she hasn't spoken his name. It's an outside bet that someone's listening in but given the circles Frank is moving in these days it's a wise precaution.

'I know,' he says. 'I need a trace on a number.'

Harris starts to object and then stops herself. Frank can almost hear her internal dialogue. In for a penny. 'Go on,' she says.

Frank gives her the number he's just dialed. 'It's German,' he says. 'Most likely. And I'd lay odds on it being in Berlin. Keep it off the system if you can.'

'It'll take time,' says Harris. 'If I can get it.'

'Try,' says Frank. 'It could be important and I don't know how long I've got.'

'You're going there, aren't you?'

'I'll call,' says Frank and hangs up.

108

South Uist, Atlantic, November 3rd

The weather had eased faster than Paul Finn expected. Now, two and a half hours west of Mallaig and ten nautical miles past South Uist, out in the deep channels, *The Mackinaw* rises and falls on a slow even swell. The rain, which had fallen steadily since leaving Long Rock has petered out to nothing.

In the wheelhouse, Calum Finn, his wounds cleaned and dressed, sleeps heavily, sedated by the sleeping pills his father had given him. Paul Finn would take Cal into the hospital in the morning with the story of a trawler accident. They would believe him: worse things than this happen at sea.

Paul Finn lets the engine idle and allows the trawler to drift on the current. Checking that Calum is unconscious, he leaves the wheelhouse.

'Wake up.' Finn kicks Lydon's leg and the Londoner groans. Exposed to the rain, he is soaked through. He rolls, wincing with the effort, to look up at the man standing over him. Lydon's face is a mess. He tries to speak but nothing comes out.

Finn reaches down and hauls him upright.

'Can you swim?' asks Finn.

Lydon's eyes are suddenly open wide.

'N-don't,' he says.

'Can you swim?'

Lydon nods. Tears start streaming down his face as Finn pulls him towards the stern of *The Mackinaw*. The Londoner twists violently but his strength is gone and he is no match for the big trawlerman who handles him as easily as a fish.

At the stern, Finn halts. He lifts a knife from his belt and Lydon flinches. Finn spins him round and cuts through the cords at his wrists. Lydon turns to face Finn and makes a feeble effort to fight. Finn puts out a huge hand and pushes Lydon hard in the chest sending the Londoner flying backwards.

Lydon's feet slither on the wet deck, his landlocked legs unbalanced, his hands finding nothing as he hits the low rail and tumbles over, his fingers scrabbling at empty space. For a moment he is conscious of the black sky above and *The Mackinaw's* lights swinging crazily across his vision before he hits the icy waters of the Atlantic and slips below the waves. For several long seconds there is complete blackness.

Sputtering, the cold already sending shock waves through his body, sea water stinging his nostrils, Lydon surfaces. He twists to see *The Mackinaw* already four or five metres away.

'Wait!' screams Lydon. He flails madly at the water but his clothes are too heavy, his movements too slow, the water bone-cold. As his mouth and nose fill with water he can feel the Atlantic pulling him down into the unimaginable depths below and he voids himself.

'No, please, no!' Images of great sea creatures feeding on his flesh spring into his head. Lydon bursts up through the surface, spluttering and coughing.

Finn watches him for a few seconds and then walks back to the wheelhouse. Lydon manages to swim a metre closer, two metres, the stern of the trawler rising and falling with each stroke. Three metres, four, and then the engines start and *The Mackinaw* slides away from Lydon.

'I didn't . . . I don't . . .' Lydon is saying words without knowing what he wants to say. There is so much, so very much and the lights are moving away. After twenty seconds the trawler's lamps are impossibly distant and Lydon is alone in the great, featureless, merciless, impassive ocean. Sobbing, he watches *The Mackinaw* disappear from view between each black swell as it turns east towards land.

Lydon thinks of his wife at home, he thinks of men and women he has killed, or delivered for killing, and he is sorry. His body will never be found. His time is done.

109

Long Carraig, Scotland, November 3rd

A drum roll of rain against the glass jerks Frank awake. He swallows, his mouth dry, and looks at his watch. Almost seven forty-five. Although still dark outside the sky is beginning to lighten. He stretches, once again feeling a lightness in his joints that he hadn't known was missing. He pushes himself upright and puts on some coffee. While it starts to bubble he sets out his injection paraphernalia ready for the next dose, due soon. Last night's drama has the feeling of a hallucinatory dream. He tries to suppress the thoughts about the danger he'd put Calum Finn into by bringing him into this savagery and, to his surprise, finds that he can. Maybe it's a side-effect of the drugs. If so, Frank's glad. He could do with a break.

As he's pouring the coffee his phone rings.

'It's a Berlin number,' says Harris without preamble. 'It belongs to a Felix Hoffen. I'm sending you the information I have via email. It's all I can get on short notice.'

Frank knows that to get this Harris must have gone straight into Stanley Road after his call. She's been working all night.

'You'll brush sand over the tracks, right?' he says.

'Already done,' says Harris. 'We didn't talk. My phone is going into the river this morning.' She still hasn't said his name.

'Thanks,' says Frank.

'Be careful,' says Harris. The warmth in her voice almost unmans him.

'I won't,' says Frank.

110

Berlin, November 5th

From somewhere comes the sound of small children arguing in German.

Cooper opens her eyes and blinks without knowing where she is. The pain from her facial bruising seems much worse and she realises she's slept on the damaged side. She rolls slowly over and looks around at the unfamiliar cream and white walls and it comes back.

Christina's place. Saturday morning.

She sinks back into the pillows, relieved. It had been a little strange coming into Dreschler's home but the gesture had been welcome and she's grateful for at least the illusion of protection. The smell and weight of the man in the spa keeps flashing into her mind. Here in suburbia she can come to no harm. That's what it feels like anyway and, for now, that will do.

The smell of fresh coffee slides into the room and Cooper swings her legs out from under the covers. She is halfway dressed when her phone rings. Harris. Cooper checks the time. It's seven thirty here, five thirty in Liverpool and when Harris starts talking she sounds tired.

'You have to come back.'

'Right away?'

'That's what Superintendent Searle told me.'

It's an odd way to put it and Cooper picks up an unnatural inflection in her boss's tone. Cooper gets the first hint of the way the conversation might be headed. She says nothing and waits for Harris.

'He wants the Germans to handle their own investigation.'

'Makes sense, ma'am.' Again Cooper waits.

'So you should get a ticket home.'

There is a pause. *Should.* Cooper leaves it hanging. Spit it out, Emily, for Christ's sake.

'You have some leave owing, is that right, Theresa?'

'Uh, yeah, I think so.'

'You do. I checked.'

'OK.'

'And if you use that leave to remain in Berlin then that would be up to you.'

'Yes. I guess. Ma'am.'

'Jesus, Theresa, don't make this harder than it already is.'

'No, sorry, ma'am.' Cooper coughs and when she speaks next her voice is firmer. 'I have some leave owing, ma'am,' she says, 'and, if it's alright with you I'd like to take four days starting today. I might stay in Berlin a little longer. See the sights.'

'At last.' Harris blows out a long sigh and Cooper can almost see her in the Stanley Road office. 'That was like pulling teeth.'

'Sorry, ma'am.'

'Don't take any risks.'

'With the sightseeing?'

'With the sightseeing.'

Cooper starts to ask another question and stops herself. Whatever's happening must be bad for Em Harris to pull a stunt like this. Given what a stickler Harris is normally – and Theresa Cooper has been on the end of more than one undeserved tongue-lashing for not doing things by the book – this is a high risk strategy. Cooper is one of those at MIT who remembers how Harris had done the dirty on Frank Keane. It was less than eighteen months ago and even though the assumption is that Keane and Harris must have kissed and made up since, the question mark remains. Cooper wonders what has pushed Harris down this road. If DCI Keane had still been around then she could have understood. He'd have made sure the enquiry stayed open, no matter what suited Charlie Searle's political game.

She coughs. Keane's gone. There's no point in playing guessing games. Like her mother used to say: if ifs and buts were pounds and pence she'd be a millionaire.

'What?'

'Sorry, ma'am,' says Cooper. 'Got something caught in my throat.'

'Listen, Theresa, if you do see anything interesting . . .'

'While I'm sightseeing?'

'Yeah. If you do, let me know, right? I'm always interested in that kind of thing. Might even get there myself one day. Probably best to use my personal mobile number. Or email. No need for this to register on the MIT records.'

'Of course.'

'And Theresa?'

'Yes, ma'am?'

'Be careful.'

111

Long Carraig, Scotland – Berlin, Germany, November 5th

Wired, alive, the Frankenstein drugs pulsing through his system, Frank reads Harris's file on Felix Hoffen onscreen and destroys her email once the information is committed to memory. He's spent two days conducting his own investigation from Long Carraig.

Harris's intel tells Frank that Hoffen is forty-three and lives in Berlin in what looks like – at least on StreetView – a nice apartment block in Mitte. Hoffen is a native-born East Berliner with a German father and Croatian mother. In 1987 he joined the East German Nationale Volksarmee and was then absorbed into the German Armed Forces after the Wall came down. Hoffen moved to the *Kommando Spezialkräfte* in 1992 and saw action as part of the first Gulf War UN Force as well as other unspecified overseas postings. He left when he was twenty-six, no information trail relating to why. No criminal convictions appeared until 1997 when he did a six-month term for weapons possession in Hamburg. From that point Felix Hoffen dropped from sight. His name cropped up in reports of alleged atrocities in Serbia and Bosnia but nothing stuck. Spurred on by the information from Harris, Frank had done some internet digging of his own and found suggestions of Hoffen as a mercenary. There are links to Mozambique, the Congo, Iraq. Now back in Berlin, Hoffen's name showed up a couple of times in events connected to right wing politics and has occurred on two anti-Nazi web watch lists in relation to something called *Kolumne88*. Frank spends time gathering what he can on *Kolumne88*, much of it from their own websites which have helpfully been translated into English. Images of violence appear. Skinheads, contorted faces, rallies, graffiti, YouTube clips of fights and speeches.

When Frank's certain he has all he can get on Hoffen he takes the laptop to the workshop and smashes the laptop to pieces. He scoops up the broken computer and throws the remnants into the Atlantic. No doubt there'd be ways for a forensic cyber freak to dig it up from somewhere at Harris's end, but it's the best Frank can do. If her email to him about Hoffen is found then Harris's career will be dust. That may be the case anyway – too many risks are already being taken in this business – but at least he's made an effort.

Frank mulls over the details while he's in the air. After negotiating the calmer waters back to Mallaig on the Zodiac left by Paul Finn, he'd driven to Inverness and taken a commercial flight via Dublin, traveling on the Tom Machin documentation without incident. If there is any high level surveillance on him Frank assumes that they are allowing him enough rope. Whatever the truth of it, he lands in Berlin without incident. To his relief, the cancer drugs he's placed in his luggage come through intact.

Frank takes the U-Bahn to the hotel he'd booked online, an anonymous chain hotel on Invalidestraße. In his room he stows his gear and takes his next dose. Ten minutes later he steps out into the Berlin night. Sarah Coughlan may have died without Frank knowing her but that doesn't mean he won't do everything he can to find the people who killed her. What happens after that he doesn't know.

112

Berlin, November 6th

Lydon's gone off the radar. One clear message that he'd acquired the target and then nothing. It's been three full days and the silence tells Hoffen that the courier is dead. Hoffen curses himself for allowing that much time to elapse. he should have known right away. He *did* know right away. He just hadn't done anything about it, hoping he was wrong. It's a mistake.

Leaving his apartment, he closes the door to the street with his mind flashing back to the two calls that followed Lydon's; one to Hoffen and one by him to Lydon's mobile, only one word spoken.

It's the English cop, Keane. Hoffen knew it as soon as he'd hung up. He curses Lydon's secrecy for not letting him know exactly where he'd tracked the guy down to but he doesn't waste too much time worrying; what's done is done and going over old ground is pointless. The good soldier – and Hoffen is nothing if not a good soldier – alters the plan of action in response to events. Keane's disposal of Lydon means that his role as donor for Bruckner's client is over. This Keane *fotze* is trouble. Too much trouble. It's taken four dead to discover that and now, with Gottlenz's cash they have the money anyway. This prick has managed to slip away too many times for it to be dumb luck. Lydon is – *was* – one of the best operators Hoffen had ever come across; devious, single-minded and, above all, effective. Keane had done for him plus two of Gottlenz's crew and managed to vanish into thin air without seemingly breaking sweat. So let Keane stay vanished. Why worry? This thing will be over before the week is out and Keane will be a memory. Forget the Englishman; that's all done with.

Hoffen finds a booth and orders an espresso. He takes out his cigarettes and taps his fingers against the box. Having them to hand makes him feel better.

His coffee arrives and Hoffen stirs a spoon of sugar into it while he weighs up the options.

With funding the remainder of the project no longer an issue, the problems of the next forty-eight hours become much simpler. While Bruckner wasn't difficult to remove, Weiss carries real heft. He will, like Hoffen, have put things in place to prevent his own eradication and is, in all likelihood, considering Hoffen himself as a loose end.

Weiss also brings considerable value to the table as a serving LKA officer. When the dust settles and *Kolumne88* reforms as a far-right political force, they'll need people like Robert. Well-dressed, a slick professional with an impeccable track record, Robert Weiss will become the acceptable face of fascism. The thugs and lunatics are not made for television, for the media. Weiss will stay on. They need him. Hoffen makes a mental note to forge a closer mutually assured destruction treaty. If I go, you go. That sort of thing. It'll work.

Hoffen finishes his coffee and leaves, pulling his collar up against the snow that has just begun to fall. He lights a cigarette and walks north for the last check.

From a recessed doorway across *Christinenstraße*, Frank watches the big German exit the coffee shop and lets Hoffen turn the corner before following. By the time Frank gets to the intersection Hoffen is halfway across the double lane highway next to the *Senefelderplatz* U-Bahn station. Frank pulls down the brim of his cap and speeds up, anxious not to lose his target underground.

At the top of the station steps, he hesitates. If Hoffen is on the platform near the entrance he is sure to see Frank but it's a chance he'll have to take. Frank keeps his head down as he walks onto the platform and is relieved when he sees Hoffen's bulk standing halfway down waiting for a southbound train. Frank buys an all-day pass from the yellow dispenser and waits, his stomach churning. He's had an odd feeling in his guts that's been building for an hour or more. He doesn't know if it's the chase or a side effect of the drugs. Frank wipes his sleeve across his brow.

When the train arrives he stays one carriage down from the target. It's busy enough and he stands with his back to the German watching him via a reflection in a window without too much difficulty. When they pull into *Spittelmarkt* though, Frank loses sight of him and almost leaves the train. At the last moment he spots that Hoffen has found a seat. Two stations later he gets off at *Stadtmitte*.

Above ground Hoffen threads through the streets. The light snow, the first of the winter, is falling more thickly now. On the quieter side streets and on parking lots it settles, sugaring the grey streets with white. Frank errs on the side of caution; better to lose Hoffen than be spotted. But he has little difficulty keeping track. The pavements are sparsely populated and the big German is an easy target.

After some minutes Hoffen emerges onto a large open space criss-crossed with concrete slabs of differing heights, the snow starting to build like icing on the tops. At first, as Hoffen crosses the street towards the slabs, Frank assumes the structure is some sort of public art. It's only when he passes the signs that he realises they are at the Holocaust Memorial.

113

Berlin, November 6th

There he is.

Across the street, Felix Hoffen turns out of his apartment and walks briskly down *Christinenstraße* heading in the direction of the U-Bahn.

Theresa Cooper drains the last of her coffee and puts a few euros down on her table. She shrugs on her coat and is just about to step onto the street when a figure dressed in black emerges from the shadows and heads in the same direction, a tail if ever Cooper had seen one. She steps back into the cafe and averts her head as Hoffen's pursuer walks past the window.

Cooper risks a look at the guy's face and sees something so surreal, so profoundly impossible, that at first she can't make sense of the evidence of her own eyes.

The tail is Frank Keane.

114

Berlin, November 6th

With the weather becoming colder by the second there are few people still at the Holocaust Memorial. It's Friday evening and there are better places to be. Hoffen's been out of sight for a few minutes so Frank tries to do things methodically by taking the ground in sectors, five slabs at a time.

On the second pass he picks him up again. The light's fading now and – *there!* – Frank catches a glimpse of Hoffen turning down one of the avenues between the slabs, heading towards the centre.

Frank scurries after Hoffen, his confidence dropping with each step. It will be next to impossible to track the guy in here. It might be better to wait on a corner for him to leave but the policeman curiosity bites and Frank keeps moving. Keep moving. Keep breathing, keep putting one foot in front of the other until there are no more steps to take. Isn't that all there is?

A stab of pain in his abdomen makes Frank grimace. He experiences a flutter of panic that the pain is from his cancer. Or perhaps the drugs. Even Medavoy didn't know what the side effects might be. He'll give it another hour and then get back to the hotel.

The avenue ahead is deserted. Hoffen gone once more. A couple of tourists wander across the path five or six slabs ahead. Frank meanders through the concrete maze, turning his head at each avenue.

Hoffen is nowhere.

'Shit.'

Frank takes a left turn at random and walks at ninety degrees down another track, this one with the ground rising gently so that after twenty metres his head is above the level of the top of the slabs. He's taking risks now that he wouldn't take normally but he gets lucky and spots Hoffen standing out of the snow in the lee of one of the concrete slabs talking to three young men, all in dark clothes, all with short hair. Frank wonders if it's a sexual pick up; the men have something of the street about them. Maybe meeting rent boys in the Holocaust Memorial would give someone like Hoffen a twisted kick?

The second it takes for Frank to ponder this is enough time for Hoffen to turn his head and look straight at him. As their eyes lock, Frank knows, beyond any shadow of a doubt, that he has been identified.

Hoffen turns his back to Frank and says something to the men. All of them look directly at Frank.

Frank starts moving. Glancing back over his shoulder he sees one of the young guys heading towards the edges of the Memorial, the other in the opposite direction. Hoffen comes straight after him: a pincer movement. Frank is too far from the perimeter to make it before the first guy cuts him off so he dives back into the avenues between the slabs, his feet skidding on the slush, heading deeper and deeper into the maze. As he passes one intersection he almost runs into a young couple, giving them and him a bad scare.

'Sorry,' says Frank and, pushing past the tourists, makes another blind turn then another. Eight or nine slabs away he glimpses one of his pursuers cross the avenue and then, spotting Frank, skid to a halt and come his way, running. Frank turns once more, the slabs now towering above his head, the snow-reflected light becoming more and more sepulchral as they near the centre of the Memorial.

Another of the pursuers appears, this one carrying something in his hand. The object catches in a bar of light filtering through from the street. A knife.

And then Hoffen, about thirty metres further back walking fast. A big man, and getting bigger by the second.

Although it's the briefest of moments, Frank gets the impression that, far from chasing, Hoffen is trying to stop the pursuit. A shadow of concern is on Hoffen's face but Frank has no time to think about that because he turns left and comes face to face with one of the guys. He's young, maybe only twenty, but looks handy. There's no fear showing as he steps towards Frank, a knife in his outstretched hand. Frank runs, turning this way and that and loses the guy. He stops, his back against one of the cold slabs trying to get his breathing under control. A fresh jab of stomach cramp bends him double, almost making him cry out. When he gets back to his feet, tiny white stars dance in front of his eyes. He can hear the muffled slither of footsteps as his attacker tries to figure out which way Frank has gone. There is silence but Frank knows the guy is very close. He breathes out slowly, his breath rising white into the air.

His breath.

Too late, the penny drops that if he can see his own breath in the cold air, so can the attacker. He moves but already the knife is swinging round the corner, the shining blade finding a perfect hit right above Frank's heart.

The impact sends Frank spinning back but the PPSS stab vest he'd bought from Tiny Prior back in Liverpool does its job, the moulded polycarbonate fabric repelling the knife point as effectively as a brick wall.

Frank's apparently supernatural resistance to the knife makes the attacker pause for a fraction of a second. It's enough for Frank to push himself off the slab, swing round and catch the guy with a hard left to the gut. It's been a while since Frank has been in the ring but he always did have a wicked left and this one connects perfectly.

All the breath goes out of the knifeman and he falls forward, putting his arms out to prevent him hitting the slab. As he does, Frank brings his boot up hard into the guy's face and connects again. Blood arcs across the snow as the guy hits the side of a slab and crumples awkwardly, the knife skittering across the thin layer of slush covering the criss-crossed concrete walkway.

Sometimes, and now is one of those times, Frank can feel the cumulative weight of his years of institutional restraint pressing down on him. All these two-bit posturing arseholes, these fucking street-corner, boot-suited scum, these shaven-headed urban guerillas. They all blend, eventually, into one amorphous swamp of obnoxious filth – druggies, crims, dealers, racists, nutters, conmen and creeps. After the cancer diagnosis, after Kath, after killing the men in Helsby, after Menno Koopman and Warren Eckhardt in LA, after a lifetime of doing things by the book, being part of a unit, part of a team, Frank has had it. There is no longer a buffer between himself and reality. No bureaucracy, no correct way of doing things, just life and death and blood.

He picks up the knife and puts it to the throat of the man on the ground, ready to make the score one fewer in their favour. As he steadies himself to make the cut, two more of the goons come into view.

Frank drops the guy and runs, zig-zagging crazily through the labyrinth. Rounding a corner he bangs his thigh hard against the railing of a stairwell cut into the floor.

Narrow concrete steps lead down into darkness. Frank can hear the other two closing in so he takes the chance and clatters down, his feet slipping on the thin layer of snow.

At the foot of the treacherous steps Frank comes face to face with a small security door. There is something written on it in German that Frank can't understand. Above him he can hear boots, voices.

Frank takes a step back and slams the heel of his boot against the door lock. To his surprise it gives easily and he steps through into complete darkness. He closes the door behind him and slumps against it, the sudden pain in his stomach forcing him into a foetal position. The door moves and Frank braces himself to hold it in place. He can

hear angry German *Öffnen sie die verdammte Tür auf!*

Moments crawl. Then, as his strength fades, a series of fluorescent bulbs flicker into life. Instantly the pressure of the door against his back stops and he hears the sound of people running.

'Hey! Was tun Sie?' Another voice. This one inside. Someone in uniform. Frank groans and feels the world closing in, a dark tunnel getting darker. He wants to tell someone he is ill. There is a rising buzz in his ears as the face of Christian Boehne, the Memorial security guard, appears above him, his hand on his pistol.

'Sind sie ok?'

Frank tries to say something but nothing comes out. He closes his eyes and sinks into nothing.

115

Berlin, November 8th

'How long is she staying at your place?'

After being dragged down to an investigation conference most of Saturday that lasted until well after seven, Weiss and Dreschler have pulled an early Sunday morning shift. Both of them look tired.

The LKA office is quieter at weekends and the Ziegler investigation is getting nowhere. This is largely due to Weiss making sure anything useful gets overlooked, a witness report moved here, an informant's notes there. Both he and Dreschler, for different reasons, have managed to avoid being pulled in for the Memorial rally tomorrow.

'What?' Dreschler doesn't look up from her screen.

'Cooper,' says Weiss. 'How long is she staying?'

Dreschler glances across at Weiss. 'I wouldn't have thought she was your type, Robert.'

Weiss raises his eyebrows.

'Anyway,' says Dreschler, 'she's gone.'

'Gone? Like gone back to Liverpool?'

'Not sure. She mentioned something about sightseeing. I got the impression she'd been ordered home.'

'So why hasn't she gone straight back?'

Dreschler pushes her chair away from the desk and makes an impatient gesture with her hands. 'How should I know? Jesus, Robert. I thought you'd be glad she's not clogging up the department.'

Weiss shrugs. 'Just asking.'. He turns back to his screen as Dreschler answers a phone call.

Having Cooper recalled is a bonus. He might not have to kill her after all. After Thursday's escapade had almost gone so badly, Weiss hadn't slept. It had been a close call. Another second or two and he'd have had to kill both Cooper and Dreschler.

Or try. There was no certainty that he'd have succeeded. Both women are experienced police officers. The whole thing could have been a disaster. Now, if Cooper's heading back it would solve everything. But . . .

Sightseeing?

Who goes sightseeing after an experience like Cooper had? Christ, Hoffen is a person who scares *him*. The idea of voluntarily hanging around while he's in the city is not something Weiss would do if he was Cooper. She is either braver than he imagined or dumber. Possibly both. With less than twenty-four hours to go Weiss knows he has a decision to make. Let Cooper go. Or find her and kill her.

'I'm getting some coffee,' says Dreschler. 'Want some?'

Weiss nods, absently. 'You're going tomorrow, aren't you?'

'To the rally? Yes. Eli wants the girls to go.' Dreschler smiles. 'Keep them off school and instill a bit of Jewish militancy in them.'

'I didn't know you were radical.'

'Radical? I'm a German Jew, Robert. We're born radical.'

'OK,' says Weiss. 'You think it's wise? There might be trouble. In fact, it's likely. You know how many nuts that thing attracts.'

Dreschler looks at him curiously. 'I think we'll manage.'

Weiss nods. 'Sure.'

'Was there something else?'

'Yes.' He smiles warmly. 'Don't forget the sugar.'

116

Berlin, November 9th

Frank wakes up in a hospital room. He's surprised. Mainly, and not for the first time recently, that he's woken up at all. A young uniformed cop is sitting on a chair against a white wall. When he sees Frank's eyes open he stands and moves to the door.

'*Krankenschwester, er ist wach.*'

Frank turns his head on the pillow and sees a nurse come in. She leans over him and peers into his eyes.

'*Morgen, Herr Machin.*'

'*Morgen,*' says Frank. 'Where am I?'

The nurse switches to English. 'Hospital. *Sankt Joseph-Krankenhaus.* You collapsed.'

Frank looks at the cop. 'And him?'

The nurse says nothing.

'You were inside the building,' says the cop. 'At the *Holocaust-Mahnmal.*'

'I was . . .' Frank halts. 'I was ill. I fell down the stairs. Next thing I know I was inside somewhere dark.'

'I will get the doctor,' says the nurse.

The cop shrugs and sits down again. He's young. Frank wants to see who his boss might be. He sits up, feeling fine, but he can feel something itching at him. He needs his drugs.

There is silence in the room for a while. Frank swings his legs out of bed and the cop shifts. 'What?' says Frank. 'I'm dangerous?'

'You were in the Holocaust Memorial,' says the cop. 'That's . . . sensitive.' He looks pleased with his choice of word. 'And today there's a big rally. They don't like any surprises, you see?'

Frank does see. He nods. There's something in what the cop says that is of real interest but his brain feels sluggish. He wonders what they put in him. Before he can chase the elusive thoughts further a middle-aged Asian doctor arrives, a nurse in tow. He nods to Frank and looks at the chart offered up by the nurse. After a few moments the doctor scribbles something on the chart and turns to Frank.

'My name is Dr Chatrabaty. I will speak English, Mr Machin. I wonder if you can tell me what happened?' Chatrabaty speaks perfect English.

'I have cancer,' says Frank. At this Chatrabaty's ears prick up. Frank outlines his medical status and sees Chatrabaty's face grow still.

'I see,' he says when Frank has finished. The medic straightens his already immaculate tie. 'That explains some of the blood results. Some interesting things going on in there.' Chatrabaty pauses and smiles bleakly.

'So,' says Frank.

'There is little to be said, Mr Machin. As you know. I am concerned about your fall. That is not something good for someone with your condition. Are you taking any medication? Other than painkillers?'

Frank shakes his head and Chatrabaty purses his lips. 'OK,' he says. 'OK.'

'I can go?'

Dr Chatrabaty shrugs. 'From a medical point of view, yes. But there are two gentlemen outside who would like to speak to you. I will tell them to be kind with you.'

Frank watches Chatrabaty leave. A few minutes later two men walk in the room. They are smartly dressed, forties, unremarkable. One has a black holdall over his shoulder while the other carries a briefcase. Briefcase raises a languid finger towards the uniform and, without speaking, gestures for him to leave. The cop hesitates for a moment before heading for the door. Once he has left, the guy with the holdall closes the door behind him while the other hitches up the crease in his trouser leg and perches elegantly on Frank's bed, his briefcase set on the floor.

'Good morning, Mr Machin.' The voice is British, plummy and precise. The voice of Frank's betters. 'My name is Mr Smith.' He holds out a hand which Frank shakes. Smith waves a hand vaguely over his shoulder at his colleague. 'And that is Mr Jones.'

'Of course you are.'

'That happens a lot,' says Smith. 'We may have to rethink it.' He smiles. 'Now, why don't you tell me and the nice Mr Jones all about what brings you to Berlin,' says Smith. He pauses. 'Frank.'

117

Berlin, November 9th

The temperature drops four degrees on the night of the 8th. By Monday morning the early slush and snow in the city has frozen to iron. Mikkel Steiner, the city coordinator for the remembrance service has been awake since four and is just about the only Berliner glad of the cold. Fewer people means fewer problems. Steiner's job is mostly liaison – a conduit between the city, the police, the media and the rest of the groups intent on making their presence felt during the Holocaust Remembrance ceremony. As far as Steiner is concerned the ideal weather for today would be three feet of snow and a howling gale.

At six, Steiner watches the anti-terror squad make a final sweep through the Memorial. The six-man dog team criss-cross the lines of slabs north to south then east to west. With the museum door having been breached in an incident two days ago, particular attention is paid to that area. Steiner stays in the warmth of his vehicle while they make the sweep.

From an apartment window three hundred metres away, Felix Hoffen watches them approach the slab capped by the device. Next to him in the rented apartment he feels Angelika Lehmann tense.

'Easy,' says Hoffen. Lehmann holds the trigger in her hand and it is one of Hoffen's biggest worries that she will detonate too early, her nerve gone. It is one of the reasons they are side by side.

One of the dogs stops at the slab and begins to sniff. The handler's attention, like that of the animal, is directed at floor level.

'They've spotted it,' says Lehmann. Hoffen puts out a hand and places it on her arm. In the Memorial Square the sniffer dog cocks a leg and pisses on the corner of the slab. After a few seconds both dog and handler move on. The handler does look back once, briefly, at the slab but keeps going. In the apartment, Lehmann moves her arm away from Hoffen's and sits down on the cheap armchair. She lights another cigarette.

Four hours.

118

Berlin, November 9th

Robert might have had a point about the Memorial service.

At nine, when Christina Dreschler and her family are still several hundred metres from the square they can already hear the chanting.

'Achtzig acht! Achtzig acht! Achtzig acht!'

Eighty-eight! Eighty-eight! Eighty-eight!

88. The numerical version of HH. The eighth letter of the alphabet. Heil Hitler.

'Still think this is a good idea, Eli?' Christina asks her husband.

'It was never about being a good idea, Chris. You know that. Hey! Look, they have balloons!'

Rose and Suzanna, six and eight run towards the white tent pitched on the edge of the

Tiergarten. There are row upon row of tents, each of them an organisation there to support the rally: the Jewish Council, Amnesty International, a couple of financial institutions, some German government agencies.

Rose and Suzanna come back holding white helium-filled balloons with an image of a burning candle, the logo of remembrance being used this year.

'See?' says Eli Dreschler. 'Balloons.'

Christina smiles but looks across the corner of the *Tiergarten* to where the police have penned in the lunatics. The white supremacists, the skinheads, and, seemingly everywhere, the black-clad shock troops of the *Autonome Nationalisten* and *Kolumne88.*

There is a bad vibration in the air. Already, younger, less restrained members of the rally supporters are getting angry at the presence of the neo-Nazis. Dreschler notes large numbers of *Die Linke* activists carrying banners with heavier wooden poles than are strictly necessary. There is a very large contingent who seem to be with *Die Linke*, the big radical leftist party, many of them wearing urban combat clothing: hoodies, combat jeans, heavy boots and scarves. Despite the police discouragement, many of them already have the scarves tied across their faces, caps pulled low, hoods up. People are on their toes, adrenalised.

'This is a zoo, Eli,' says Christina.

Eli nods and points across the Memorial to where the media stand is situated. It's on a narrow section of *Hannah-Arendt Straße* at a point furthest from the troublemakers. All streets around the memorial have been coned off. The march will circle the Memorial, running the gauntlet of the Nazis on the other side of *Ebertstraße*.

'We'll stay over there,' says Eli. 'If it gets any worse we'll walk down towards *Wilhelmplatz* and get the train, OK?'

Christina nods. The girls, clutching their balloons look nervous. Both of them keep their eyes fixed on the barriers holding the Nazis. The noise is growing.

'Besides,' says Eli. 'You're a cop. How could anything happen to us?'

119

Berlin, November 9th

'Look at those asswipes,' says someone.

On the top floor of the US Embassy building, a room of people watch the crowds gathered in the square.

Gavin Leland, one of the most senior intelligence officers shakes his head. Like Dreschler, he feels the difference in the air with this one. Unlike Dreschler, he isn't worried about any trouble between the opposing parties. There could be fighting, maybe even a riot. Someone might get killed, but it's all small potatoes. What gets Leland is the idea that they might have missed something, that *he* might have missed something.

'What have we got?' he asks of no-one in particular. 'And don't tell me nothing.'

'Nothing,' says the woman standing next to him. Candice Ortiz is Leland's second-in-command. The two have worked this station for five years, both appointments happening within the same week.

'That's a worry, Candy. How about the guy they found in the museum last night?'

'They did a clean sweep of the area last night. Came up with nothing.'

'I'm hearing that word a lot. Nothing. It's starting to make me nervous. And I don't like being nervous. Reminds me of Mumbai. Got real quiet before that one, remember?'

Ortiz nods. 'Uh-huh.'

'What about the guy in the museum?' Leland is asking out of habit. If Ortiz's people had come up with anything remotely solid they'd

384

have been on to him last night. Ortiz runs a solid crew and Leland has faith in her.

'He's a Brit. Machin. A Tom Machin. Claims he got sick and fell into the museum.'

'Fell? What was he, skydiving?'

'Yeah, I know, but we dug in and we think the most likely thing is that he may have been out trying to score.'

'Drugs?'

'Guys. The Memorial's been getting some popularity on Grindr.'

Leland's face is blank.

'A gay date application.'

'Jesus. At the Holocaust Memorial?' His face wrinkles.

'Well, yeah. Classy. Anyway, we picked up some camera of him with some guys. Wasn't real clear and, like you know, once they're inside that place the lines of sight aren't good.'

'So it was a pickup gone wrong?'

'Maybe. He ran and kicked in the door. The security guard found him slumped just inside. Most of this we only got this morning. He's been unconscious since last night so no-one's been able to interview him. We did check out his ID with the BfV and it comes up clear.'

'Well. That's alright then. I can relax.'

'I'm detecting some cynicism, sir.'

'You noticed? We must be training you better than I thought.' Leland turns his back on the window and leans against the sill. 'You know why I'm not comfortable with BfV. I wouldn't trust those guys if they told me I had two eyes and a nose.'

Ortiz says nothing. Leland's talking about the Fromm scandal a couple of years back. The BfV shredded documents relating to a right-wing terror cell calling themselves the National Socialist Underground. The NSU consisted of three individuals who carried out more than twenty bank robberies, two bombings and nine shootings in a twelve-year period, seemingly without any interference by the BfV. Heinz Fromm, the head of the BfV fell on his sword in 2012 when the story broke. Since then, Leland and his kind have regarded information from that source as tainted at best, willfully misleading at worst.

'So what do we say?'

Ortiz pauses as if remembering. 'Well, he does check out. I got Tanner to run a full check. He's clean. He's sick too. Tanner tells me the guy has cancer. Terminal. The hospital confirmed that.'

'That makes me feel better.' When Ortiz raises an eyebrow, Leland grimaces. 'You know what I mean.' Leland folds his arms. 'So we can leave this Machin out of it? There's nothing?'

Ortiz holds a hand out, palm down and waggles it from side to side. 'Maybe just a sniff of something.'

'I fucking knew it. You had that look. Go ahead.'

'It's not much. His ID checks out like I said. All the databases confirm him as legit.'

'But . . .'

'Well, he was wearing a stab vest.'

Leland raises an eyebrow.

'A stab vest,' says Ortiz. 'It's like a bullet proof vest but f . . .'

'I know what it is.'

'OK. So that was one thing. Which is why we got the Germans to sit on him at the hospital.'

'And the other thing?'

'Well that took longer. I only got it a couple of minutes ago. Machin's rich so I had someone dig into that. It's all legitimate too but . . . at the end of a long string of companies that Machin's money comes from is a name of interest, but not for the reason you might think. Loder Industries.'

Gavin Leland stands. He looks around the office and leans closer to Ortiz. 'You're kidding, right? Tell me you're kidding.'

'It might not mean anything, sir.'

'Christ Almighty, Ortiz!' Leland's raised voice causes every head in the office to turn their way. 'Machin is involved with Loder Industries? When the fuck were you planning to unload that little ball of snakes? I mean, Jesus H Christ riding a fucking Harley, what does it take to raise a red flag around here? Osama Bin Laden applying for security clearance? Hitler's flaming corpse rising from the bunker with a nuke in each paw? Jesus!' Leland, pacing, kicks a wastebasket sending paper skittering across the floor. He puts his hands on his hips and stands shaking his head for a few seconds. When he stops he bends in close to Ortiz, his voice low again, the bile etched into every hissed syllable. 'A guy shows up in our backyard with a mainline connection straight to the motherfucking beating black heart of fucking Loder Industries and that doesn't give you a hot wet fuzzy? *Loder!* Sweet Jesus, we got to let upstairs hear about this one and I can tell you, Ortiz, it's not going to be old Leland standing first in the firing line when Jenks starts shooting.'

Leland, his face set, grabs the tearful Candice Ortiz by the arm and leads her to the corridor. He doesn't know it but it's this action that saves both their lives.

120

Berlin, November 9th

When Theresa Cooper saw Frank Keane in *Christianestraße* she froze, unsure of what she'd seen. In a kind of daze, she left the cafe and fell in behind at a safe distance, tailing a ghost. She thought she'd lost him on the U-Bahn but picked him up again and kept him in sight until they reached the Memorial. There she'd lost him for a while until she saw Hoffen leaving in a hurry. There was no sign of Frank. Torn, Cooper let Hoffen go but Frank Keane didn't emerge. Cooper waited, growing colder by the minute until, unable to stand it any longer and half-convinced that she had imagined the whole thing she had gone back to the hotel, empty-handed and dejected.

Now, in the sharp morning light, the place filled with noise and tension, the Memorial is a different place and the tailing of Frank Keane in the ice fog seemed to belong to another place.

She wanders around the Memorial without quite knowing what she's looking for and trying to tune out the din from the competing factions. Stopping in front of a vast mound of floral tributes laid at one corner, Cooper notices Christina Dreschler walking through the crowds with her family but doesn't stop and speak.

Cooper watches them until they slip from view, feeling uncomfortably like a voyeur.

She is adrift here. Harris's suggestion to stay, so initially thrilling, now seems ridiculous. Without support, without validation, what can she do?

And then it comes to her.

Harris knows that Frank's alive. That explains her lack of emotion at his wake, her strange behaviour on this case. It explains a lot.

Cooper takes out her phone and walks across to a quieter spot behind the media huddle. On the podium erected near the museum entrance block the first of the speeches begins. From the opposite side of the square the speech is greeted with a crescendo of booing. Someone lights a flare and Cooper sees a policeman grappling with a demonstrator. Overhead a police helicopter hovers above the *Tiergarten*.

Unseen by everyone, a green light inside the box containing the bomb on Block 1178 blinks steadily.

Cooper turns her back on the circus, dials Harris's number and, with one finger in her ear, listens to the ringtone.

One.

Two.

Three.

121

Berlin, November 9th

Felix Hoffen lowers the binoculars and steps back from the apartment window. Behind him, Angelika Lehmann holds a mobile phone, her expression flat but her eyes shining. This may have been a commercial transaction but the bomb is two years of her life. This atrocity has beauty when seen from her perspective.

Hoffen nods and retreats into the back kitchen of the apartment followed by Lehmann. They close the door and sit down at the table. Both of them wear gloves and the apartment has been cleaned of all traces they were ever here.

Lehmann closes her eyes and murmurs something Hoffen can't hear. He watches her lips move without comment. When Lehmann has finished she opens her eyes and looks down at the phone in her hand.

'Do it,' says Hoffen.

Lehmann presses a finger to the screen.

122

Berlin, November 9th

'I'm scared, papa,' says Rose. Eli Dreschler picks his daughter up and lifts her onto his shoulders.

'It's OK,' he says, but he knows it isn't. This is no place for children. As soon as the speeches began the mood had started to become even uglier than it had been when they'd arrived and now it threatened to boil over into a full blown riot. As smoke from the flare drifts across the slabs, Eli looks at Christina who has hold of Suzanna's hand.

'Let's go,' says Christina. She leads the way down *Hannah Arendt Straße*, Eli and Rose a few paces behind. As they reach the intersection, Christina spots Theresa Cooper holding a phone to her ear. Cooper looks up and waves a hand in greeting.

Christina pauses to see if Cooper wants to speak but, behind her, Eli tells her to keep moving. Christina waves again to Cooper and that's when she feels the air change.

At the intersection, just as she and Suzanna turn the corner, Lehmann's phone call triggers the aliphatic nitroglycerine in the bomb which detonates at a velocity of 7,700 metres per second sending the ball-bearing payload out in a scything circle of death. Anyone within twenty metres of Block 1178 is decapitated, but the force of the explosion is so intense that the carnage extends for another hundred metres or more. The lucky ones are those protected by the concrete slabs themselves: the main beneficiaries of this being the *Kolumne88* supporters across the square at *Tiergarten*.

Christina Dreschler feels the impact before she hears the explosion.

She registers the steel fence next to her buckling before she and Suzanna are catapulted across the street. A length of shrapnel hits Dreschler high on the shoulder and a ball bearing ploughs a deep furrow across her scalp. Suzanna Dreschler is hit by a fragment of metal which takes off her right foot as cleanly as a surgeon's blade.

Behind them, unprotected by the fence, Eli and Rose Dreschler are killed instantly. Rose, perched high on her father's shoulders, takes the worst of the shock wave.

Theresa Cooper hears Harris answer the phone – *hello* – and then she is flung towards the wall surrounding a tennis court, several ball-bearings taking off part of her skull. She is dead before she connects with the wall.

The media, being closest to the point of detonation are hit hard. Twenty three press are killed and another sixty injured. Forty two police officers, eight Memorial guards, fifteen US Embassy staffers, thirteen tourists, sixty six members of the Council of Jews, nine Berlin council employees and one hundred and thirty one members of the public die in the first millisecond after detonation. Blood and body parts are flung over great distances.

Every window in the US Embassy blows in. On the top floor office, four of Gavin Leland's team are killed. In the corridor, Leland and Ortiz jump violently as several pieces of glass embed themselves in a wall. A severed hand lands in the corridor.

In total, 503 people are killed. Another sixty two will die from their wounds in the following days. The nerve gas kills almost no-one, Roos having made a crucial miscalculation in the mechanism. In the ongoing investigation, this will come to be seen by those who know the details as an almost miraculous escape for Berlin. Even so, it is the biggest single loss of life in Germany since the war.

At the LKA HQ, Robert Weiss, standing and waiting by an open window, hears the explosion and returns to his desk.

It will be a busy day.

123

Berlin, November 9th

When Smith calls him 'Frank', Frank says nothing.

'No reaction?' Smith smiles ruefully.

'I don't know what you expect,' says Frank.

'Hello, maybe?' Smith looks at Frank. 'Or would you prefer if I call you Machin? Or Tom?'

'Mr Machin will be fine,' says Frank. 'Only my friends call me Tom.'

'What friends would those be? The lovely Emily? Or the one-armed Koopman? Charlie Searle probably won't be too friendly if you turn up again. He was most displeased when myself and Mr Jones turned up like the proverbials.'

'Who are you?' Frank is guessing these two are something to do with Lupus but they

don't seem the type. There's something off-kilter about them that makes it difficult for him to see them as cops. They have weight though, that's for sure. The German cop seemed to think they were in charge. Maybe some Euro outfit?

Smith waves his hand dismissively. 'It doesn't matter. Mr 'Machin'. What matters is that we have found you. I must admit that I did have a sneaky feeling it would be Berlin, didn't I, Mr Jones?'

'You did.' Jones remains where he has been since the beginning, leaning against the window.

'You gave the Germans a bit of a scare.' Smith reaches into his briefcase and pulls out the black stab vest Frank had got from Tiny Prior. He holds it by the neck, like a dead bird. 'When they saw this they moved you higher up the list marked "problem".' Smith looks at

Frank. 'Nice bit of kit. Not exactly what your average tourist wears on a jaunt to Berlin.'

'I'm paranoid,' says Frank. 'Goes with the job.'

'What job? You're dead, aren't you?'

'What do you want?' Frank chooses his words with care. Being ID'ed as Frank Keane is a blow but these two don't feel to Frank like they're about to haul him back to Liverpool. This doesn't have the whiff of anything internal.

'Ah,' says Smith beaming. 'That's better . . . Tom. I think I can call you that, right? Now we're getting along.'

Behind Smith, Jones rolls his eyes. 'Can we get on with it?'

Smith raises an eyebrow and looks at Frank, amused. 'He was like this at school, the little saucepot. Never got over me making him warm my toilet seat. Anyway, "Tom", you have arrived at the correct question. We do want something, you're right. We want you.'

Smith hands a business card to Frank. There's a number on it, nothing else.

'Myself and Mr Jones have been following you with some interest since your little episode in America. Came up on our radar so to speak.'

'You're with Loder?' It's the first time Frank has said anything that indicates he is Frank Keane.

'God, no!' Smith grimaces. 'What a grisly thought. Although we do have some common interests. I know Loder were very happy with how things turned out in America. And how discreet you've been since. Despite your troubles.'

'So are you going to tell me what you want?'

Smith nods. 'We'd like to offer you a job.'

Frank laughs and looks at Jones. Jones shrugs. 'It wasn't my idea.'

'Become a spook?' says Frank. 'I can't see myself there. Besides, I don't need a job.'

'Yes, the money. We heard about that. Still, money isn't everything, Tom. I think you still have something to offer our organisation. Particular skills. You don't mind getting your hands dirty.'

'You're Intelligence,' says Frank. 'But there's one thing you have forgotten.'

'The cancer?' Smith smiles. 'No, not at all. If anything it makes it more attractive.' He looks over his shoulder and gestures for Jones to come closer. Jones gets to the bed and takes the bag from his shoulder.

'You see,' says Smith, 'we think you may well survive, Tom.'

Jones unzips the holdall and pulls out Frank's drugs. He hands them to Frank.

'These things work, you know,' says Smith. 'We have it on good authority. Going to make someone a fortune one day. Probably our mutual friend.'

Frank finds it hard to say anything. Whether it's some addictive component of Sheehan's pharmaceuticals, or simply a basic human survival instinct, once Frank sees the drugs it is hard for him to think of anything else.

'Go on,' says Smith as if reading his mind. 'Jab away.'

Frank opens the bag and fills a hypo. He finds a spot on his arm and presses the needle in.

Smith relaxes. 'You'll start feeling much better over the coming weeks, "Tom".' He stands. 'You'll need more drugs of course. More than that lot. And, while I don't want that to influence your decision, we can help with that. I think you know what I'm saying?'

'Let me get this straight,' says Frank. 'Just so I know where we all stand. Unless I take this job you'll stop me getting the drugs that will keep me alive?'

Smith grimaces. 'I wouldn't put it that way, no. Not exactly. But we do offer a safe supply at least until you recover. And then you'll need them in case of a relapse.'

'So that's a "yes"?'

'Well the drugs are untested, Tom. Hard to obtain.' Smith smiles. 'And it's not like there's another supplier on tap. Mr Sheehan's debt only runs so far and I suspect that this bag might be the extent of his generosity. To make it simple: we can get them. If you play nice.'

Frank keeps his poker face. He's about two seconds away from smashing Smith's face in but he doesn't know if he has the strength. And the spook has a point. They are holding all the cards. And the drugs.

'So if I take the job? What, exactly, do you do?'

'Most of the time, most of us do very mundane things indeed, Frank.'

'Tom.'

'My apologies, Tom. You would be our wild card. Someone outside the agency. Someone who knows how to get things done, whatever that might take.'

'You're making it sound like a hit man.'

Smith says nothing and holds Frank's gaze.

'You're fucking kidding.' Frank waits but still Smith says nothing. 'I can't kill anyone.'

'That's not quite true, is it, Tom? There are the two in Helsby. We don't think you killed the woman but we're pretty confident you're the chap who offed the others. Naturally, we could have communicated some of the information to your colleagues but we thought you had . . . potential.' Smith pauses. 'And there's one last consideration.'

Now it's Frank's turn to wait.

'We've been tracking you through your mobile – don't ask me how we found it, we leave that to the spotty herberts at HQ – and monitoring the numbers you call and who call you. As you know, it's possible to build up quite a detailed picture from phone calls. There was a man who came to see you a couple of days ago. He came to the island. A man called Mick Lydon.'

'He's who . . .?'

Smith shakes his head. 'The unlovely Mick spoke with another man when he was at Long Rock. The man we believe you came to Berlin to find. Felix Hoffen. The man responsible for your sister's death.' Smith leans back. 'You already know his address, I believe. Courtesy of Emily Harris. Which is another consideration of course. It would be such a shame if her complicity in all this distasteful business came to light.'

Frank shakes his head, disgust etched on his face.

Smith leans in closer. He's still smiling but now his tone becomes acid and his expression hardens. 'Squeamish? You're probably right to be. We're not very nice people, Tom, because we deal with the very worst people. Hoffen's come up a number of times on our lists here and there, and now it looks like he's involved with some terror outfit. An ambitious rightwing group called *Kolumne88* operating out of Berlin. We got a call yesterday about a technician *Kolumne88* had hired for something. This technician is something of a moron, but needs must, I guess. Anyway, this technician, it appears, has been talking out of school. A friend of his in London, unfortunately for him, got suspicious about the big talk and grassed him up to the counter-terrorist boys who then passed the technician to us for some unknown reason. Maybe because we had a small Berlin interest, who knows how these things work? Long story short is we let him lie and listened in to a couple of calls he made last night. One of the things he mentioned was someone we believe was Hoffen.'

'Believe?'

'This is not a precise art, 'Tom'.'

'Why don't you pick up Hoffen? Get him to tell you what you need to know?'

'That's where you come in. If you decide to take our offer I mean. You're here, you have an additional motivation to discuss matters with Mr Hoffen. Perhaps get some useful information.' Smith smiles. 'We don't mind how you get it. Or what happens to Hoffen afterwards.'

'What about passing him along to the Germans? Can't they get to Hoffen?'

'That's not exactly how things work, Tom. You know what it's like in your line of work. Information is valuable. Hoffen may or may not know anything. The Germans may or may not do something about him. Hoffen belongs to us so we'd like to keep it in house.'

'And if Hoffen has information he doesn't give to me?'

'Then we'll have made a big mistake, won't we? Look, Tom, we handle problems that policemen can't. We clean up and sometimes we stop bad things happening because we're not nice, because we don't worry about the frilly bits around the edges. We just get it done. If we can. Like I told you earlier, this isn't like the movies. We don't have limitless time. You have to force the issue sometimes.'

'Like vigilantes. Judge and jury?'

'And executioner. Don't forget *executioner*.'

'There's a way of doing things.'

'Oh please. Don't give me that sanctimonious brown-rice, one-world drivel, Machin. The cockroaches we deal with make your little Liverpool druggies look like Guardian readers.' Smith breathes deeply and leans back. 'And tell me, did you read those chaps in Helsby their rights before you shot them? With a moody gun you picked up from Tiny Prior. Wasn't exactly by the book, was it?'

'It was self-defence.'

Smith rolls his eyes. 'It's time to grow up, Tom. Do you think your sister was given any chance to defend herself? Do you think . . .'

Smith breaks off as the German uniform steps into the room, his face white. Through the open door, Frank can see people running. Before the cop can say anything Smith's phone rings, closely followed by Jones's. Both men listen to someone talking and then look at Frank.

'What is it?' says Frank.

'A bomb,' says Smith, all trace of his sardonic pose gone. 'A big one.' He looks at Frank. 'At the Holocaust Memorial.'

124

Berlin, November 9th

The windows of the apartment don't break. Although the shockwave rattles the glass in the frames hard, and both of them are rocked on their heels by the pressure wave, Hoffen and Lehmann are too far from the explosion for any damage.

The silence that follows the initial detonation is so complete it feels like all of Berlin has stopped breathing. A second or two later they hear the first screams of the injured. A few seconds after that, the sirens.

Hoffen looks at Lehmann, her head down, tears dropping onto the formica surface of the kitchen table. Her shoulders shake but she makes no sound.

Hoffen walks out of the kitchen to the front of the apartment. His eye is caught by a single drop of blood in the centre of the main window. He gazes at the red spatter for a moment before shifting his focus to the devastation in the square below.

A thick black cloud rises from the bombsite. Radiating out from the point of detonation are what look like the spokes of a broken bicycle wheel, red and black against the snow. The concrete slabs are, mostly, intact. Here and there within the maze, people are moving like zombies, presumably those fortunate enough to have been sheltered from the blast by the slabs. Everywhere are bodies, or parts of bodies. In the avenues down which the explosion funneled, the slabs are smeared with blood and worse. Fires are burning in nearby buildings. The US Embassy has had every window broken.

Hoffen picks up the binoculars and looks across at the *Tiergarten* where people are moving slowly, helping each other. He can see black-clad fascists with their arms around activists, wounded police officers being attended to by skinheads. And everywhere, the screaming of the wounded. He sweeps the binoculars closer to the apartment and something bright catches his eye. He focuses and sees the head of a blonde-haired child wedged in the branches of a tree. There are other parts in different branches that he can't identify.

Hoffen has seen death before. He has caused death before. He has waded through blood and gore. But this is of another order: something beyond comprehension. He had thought he could stand anything but he feels something inside him shift forever. Black guilt settles in his gut and Hoffen knows that it is here to stay. They should not have gone this far. He thought he could do it, and he has, but now, the cold certainty of this atrocity – their atrocity – is all there is. They were wrong. This is wrong.

Lehmann comes and stands next to him. Hoffen hears her saying something under her breath but he doesn't take it in.

'The gas,' she says and then stops speaking.

'It didn't work,' says Hoffen.

He waves a hand to indicate the moving figures. The Zyklon B did not detonate.

'It doesn't matter,' says Lehmann. She has blood on her lips and for a moment Hoffen thinks of the gas, that somehow it has landed here. Then he realises she has bitten her lip. 'What now?'

Hoffen stays silent. In his pocket is the garrotte with which he planned to kill Lehmann. He can feel it coiled there, the steel wire waiting to bite.

'You're going to kill me,' says Lehmann.

Hoffen grimaces. 'I was. I think.' He pauses. 'And I expect you were thinking of killing me.'

'What makes you think I'm not?'

Hoffen gestures out of the window. 'All that.'

'You mean now I'm a good person?'

'I mean that it doesn't matter.' Hoffen sits on the arm of the sofa and puts a hand to his face, kneading the skin at the bridge of his nose. He blows out a long breath and looks at Lehmann.

'What I mean is that, if you are planning on killing me then I won't stop you.'

Lehmann lifts a Glock from her waistband and looks at it blankly.

'I saw bad things before,' she says. She gestures to the square with the gun. 'It happens.'

'It happens because we made it happen.' Hoffen shrugs and stands. 'And I'm not bitching about that. I'm just saying what we did.'

Lehmann reaches behind her and puts the Glock back in the waistband of her jeans.

'So,' says Hoffen.

125

Berlin, November 9th

For several minutes after the hospital room empties Frank does nothing. The two spooks left quickly and the cop had gone with them. Since then there'd been no-one. If what the cop told them was true, that a huge bomb had been detonated in central Berlin, then Frank is the least of their worries.

Until someone remembers that Frank had been found at the Memorial last night. That Frank has connections to Loder Industries. That Frank's already dead. No-one will seriously believe Frank had anything to do with the Berlin bomb but by the time that conversation is over Frank knows he could be dead. These hours after the bomb will be chaotic and loose ends may be tidied up in a hurry. Frank has no intention of being one of those loose ends.

He swings his legs out of bed and almost steps on the holdall left by Smith. Frank lifts it onto the bed and gets dressed quickly.

When he's finished he looks inside the holdall. There are two objects in there besides his drugs. The first is a small leather wallet containing a seemingly blank credit card with a London address on the front. 'Tom Machin. Level 3' is printed in red on the back. Frank pockets the wallet, a small motion signaling a permanent change in his life.

The second object is a gun that Frank can't identify, a vicious looking thing with a fat silencer. He puts the gun back in the holdall and zips it up. Frank shoulders the bag and moves to the door. With every step he moves closer to the shadows, closer to the world inhabited by Smith and Jones. Frank is fading from view as Tom Machin takes shape.

Outside, the corridor is busy but there is no sign of the cop. A small knot of people are gathered round a TV set on the wall which is showing footage from the bomb. No-one is watching anything else.

Frank slips out and keeps his head down. Three minutes later he's outside the hospital and heading for the U-Bahn.

126

Liverpool, November 9th

Harris presses redial but Cooper's not answering. She'd called and then rung off before Harris could answer.

It's almost nine o'clock on Monday morning. Harris is at home after a weekend spent in the office.

She tries Cooper again but gets nothing.

Frustrated, Harris puts down the phone on the kitchen counter and starts making coffee. If it's something important Cooper will call again.

Harris takes a cup in to Linda.

'Thanks.' Linda is leaning forward on the bed to tie her running shoes. 'Can you put it on the table, hon?'

'Where are you running?'

'Down to the docks and along up to Otterspool Prom.'

Linda has been getting into running for a few months – has even joined a regular running club – and Harris is mildly annoyed that she doesn't get asked along. Not that she wants to run. Gym is one thing, running another.

After Linda has left, all lycra and waterproofs, Harris gets another coffee and eats breakfast going over a pile of case notes on the kitchen table. At nine thirty her phone rings again. Harris picks it up and is surprised to see Charlie Searle's ID come up instead of Cooper's.

'I need to talk,' says Searle, his voice sharp.

'Of course, sir. I can be in inside twenty minutes.'

'No need,' says Searle. 'I'm outside. Buzz me in.'

Harris is so surprised that Searle is at her flat that she hangs up without speaking. At the intercom she presses a button and sees her boss waiting impatiently on the street. He's wearing civilian clothes. Harris presses a second button and watches as he steps through the door.

'You heard?' says Searle once he's inside. He looks tired.

'Sorry, sir. Heard what?'

Searle picks up the TV remote and peers at it, puzzled. He hands Harris the device. 'Turn it on. BBC news.'

Harris switches on the TV and the screen is filled with images of devastation. 'Berlin bomb latest,' reads a graphic across the bottom of the screen.

'Happened less than an hour ago,' says Searle, his eyes locked on the TV. 'Six hundred dead.'

Harris feels her knees weaken and she sits down heavily on an armchair.

'Jesus Christ,' says Searle. 'Jesus fucking Christ. What a fucking monumental pile of bollocks.' Harris can't work out if he's talking to her.

For a few minutes they watch in silence. Smoke, blood, hospitals. Mobile phone footage. Film from one of the few surviving TV teams who'd been at the Memorial. Sobbing witnesses and grim-faced anchors. Airports in lockdown, military on alert.

Charlie Searle lets himself slump back against the cushions. 'Have you heard from your chap?'

'Theresa called me at nine,' says Harris.

Searle blows out his cheeks. 'Thank Christ for that! Someone told me she was still there and I was surprised.' He turns to Harris. 'Because I distinctly recall telling you to bring her back.'

'I did,' says Harris. 'But she . . . took some leave and decided to stay.'

Searle's not stupid. 'Ah. I see.' He looks again at the screen. 'But she's alright? I mean when you spoke to her?'

Harris can't face him. 'I didn't speak,' she says, her focus staying on the Berlin carnage. 'She called me but hung up.'

'Hung up?'

Harris gets out of her chair and picks up her phone. She calls Cooper again. Searle can hear the voicemail from across the room.

'And nothing since?' says Searle.

Harris shakes her head.

Searle gets to his feet. 'You need to get into work today,' he says, moving to the door. 'And hope DC Cooper calls.'

At the door he pauses. 'If she doesn't, then we didn't have this conversation, right?'

Harris nods. As the door closes behind Searle she turns back to the TV and dials Cooper again.

127

Berlin, November 9th

Berlin in chaos, the air electrically charged. The transport system shuts down within ten minutes of the bomb. Almost four square kilometres of the area surrounding the square is sealed to traffic. As Frank walks across town to his hotel he sees several troop-laden vehicles driving fast towards the bomb site. There are incongruities: hot-dog sellers still doing a brisk trade at Checkpoint Charlie; Sunday shoppers who either haven't heard, or who don't understand the magnitude of the incident, carrying brightly-colored bags. On one corner a woman walks a pink-painted poodle.

At the hotel there is no-one in reception. In a back room Frank glimpses staff gathered silently around the TV set. He goes to his room, turns on the TV and puts the holdall under the bed. Like everyone else he stays glued to the news. At some point he orders room service and is mildly surprised when food arrives.

In the afternoon he injects himself again and can almost feel the cancer cells dying, the energy returning to his body. On today of all days, Frank, for the first time, allows himself to believe he will survive.

By mid-afternoon no-one has come for him. Although he'd switched hotels he still half expects a knock. But today will be busy for the authorities as will the rest of the weeks and months ahead. Something on this scale takes time to investigate.

The word investigate reminds him of his own reasons to be in Berlin.

Hoffen's proximity to the bombing site now assumes sinister overtones and the TV coverage has shown plenty of footage of the

Kolumne88 goons. There's nothing from Smith about the possibility of Hoffen's involvement. Maybe the bomb has superseded their interest in Hoffen. Maybe they've gone back to London. Maybe they're leaving it up to him. This is a grey world Frank finds himself in. There don't seem to be rules. He thinks about Sarah Coughlan and about the risks Em Harris has taken on his behalf, and about his overwhelming desire to live. He's being played.

At eight, Frank showers, gets dressed, picks up the black holdall and heads into the city.

128

Berlin, November 9th

'Christina.'

Dreschler opens her eyes and sees a figure bending over her, the light from the lamp casting Robert Weiss's face in shadow.

'Christina.' Weiss takes hold of her hand and strokes the skin. There are tears in his eyes. His voice sounds muffled, distant.

Something in her mouth stops Dreschler from speaking. She's in bed, that much she can tell but everything else is surrounded by a dull grey mist. She tries to dislodge whatever's in her mouth but a firm female hand stops her.

'She's too tired,' says a woman's voice. 'You'll have to go.'

'Yes,' says Robert. He shakes his head and places Christina's hand on the bed, careful not to dislodge the drip. Christina wants to ask him questions. Something bad has happened, she knows that much. Why else would Robert be here? Where's Eli?

'We'll get them, Christina.' Weiss's voice falters. 'They'll pay.'

'You have to leave,' says the woman's voice.

Christina closes her eyes and tries to remember but the images are slippery and the effort makes her tired. She gets an image of Rosie on Eli's shoulders but then that's gone.

'Be strong, Christina,' says Robert from a long distance.

Christina Dreschler lapses into unconsciousness.

Weiss closes the door and steps into the corridor. It's a shame about the Dreschlers but what could he have done? He could hardly have told her not to go. He did try. In his way.

As he walks towards his car he takes out his phone and calls LKA.

'I'll be back in ten minutes,' he says. His voice is urgent, business-like and he means it. 'Get everyone assembled. I want to go through tonight's assignment lists.'

It's been a busy day and it'll be an even busier week. Before coming to see Christina, Werner Holz had taken Weiss to one side in the office and told him that he'd be heading up LKA's investigation into the Memorial bombing.

'Obviously most of the high level international stuff will be handled through BfV,' says Holz, 'but I wanted you making sure we do the very best job we can, Robert. I know you'll be motivated on this.'

Weiss had nodded and coughed to cover the emotion in his voice. 'You can depend on me, boss.'

129

Liverpool, November 11th

At her desk before anyone else, and there after most have gone, Harris watches the light creep slowly into the sky above the river. Since the news broke about Berlin she has said little, throwing herself into MIT's workload as if through sheer effort she can lessen the guilt. The day had passed. That was about all you could say.

Take some time, she'd told Theresa.

Have a look around and see what happens.

And what had happened was Theresa being shredded. Everyone's saying it was just chance. Wrong place, wrong time, how could anyone know?

But Harris knows she killed Theresa, no matter what the facts say, no matter what the official line might be. She killed Theresa as surely as if she'd planted the bomb. Get her out Searle had said and she had ignored him because of her own dumb ambition.

Over the past few days the Sarah Coughlan enquiry has been gently wound down. With Cooper gone and nothing coming back from Berlin, all normality suspended in the aftermath of the bomb, Harris knows that they'll let this one go. Cheshire MIT can do what they need to do on their side. If they make headway with either of the two dead men then good luck to them.

Magsi, first of the others into the office, knocks gently and brings in a coffee.

As she drinks it, Harris wonders what Frank's doing.

130

Berlin, November 9th

After the bomb, Hoffen and Lehmann clean the apartment and leave. On a quiet spot between two parked cars the trigger phone is ground underfoot and the pieces dropped in the Spree off the Jannowitz bridge. Lehmann is silent throughout, almost catatonic and Hoffen watches her carefully. He'd seen this reaction before after battle. Lehmann, despite her attempt to place a hard shell around her part in this, is untethered. The idea of violence is always easier to contemplate than the reality. That's why politicians love war so much. It's why boxing is a spectator sport. Lehmann's money won't save her from what's coming and the worst of it is that it's already inside her. Guilt, unless you're psychopathic, is cancerous. You can persuade yourself that you acted in a particular way because of some higher ideal, or because you are more important than others, or because you were temporarily out of control, or following orders, but none of that means anything at 4 a.m. when it's just you and what you have done that haunts you. Hoffen has killed many people and there isn't a day goes past when he doesn't, even if only for a fleeting moment, think of them all. He knows there isn't enough room inside him for the six hundred souls they took this morning. In his head there is one image burned into his retinas so that even when his eyes close he sees the image shadow: the blonde kid's head in the tree. He'll be seeing it forever.

Hoffen knows he should have killed Lehmann in the apartment but doesn't know why he hasn't. In her present state she is a liability. Christ Almighty, *he's* a liability.

His fingers keep obsessively touching the garrotte in his jacket. Maybe that's why he suggests going to his apartment on *Christinenstraße*. Lehmann nods and follows Hoffen upstairs. Hoffen knows it's a dumb idea, that he should keep clear of the apartment for a day or two but his edge has dulled after the explosion.

And he doesn't care. Not really.

They spend some hours watching TV coverage. The numbers are huge. The horror global. Parallels are drawn with 9-11. Lehmann sits motionless.

Later, when it gets dark she takes a long shower. Afterwards she gets into bed. Hoffen showers too and climbs in beside her.

And now this. The bed creaks and the dark room fills with the age-old sound of skin against skin. Lehmann straddles Hoffen and slowly rides. Neither of them make much sound and both of them know this will be the only time this will ever happen. The bedroom is a raft adrift on a black ocean. He has no idea what Lehmann's thought are.

Hoffen puts his hands around Angelika Lehmann's narrow waist and pushes deeper into her. He doesn't know what will happen when they are done so he tries not to think.

This is what it is.

131

Berlin, November 9th

At a corner table of a determinedly beat-down bar called the *Schwarze Pumpe* on *Choriner Straße*, absently turning the card given to him in the hospital by Smith, Frank's putting it together.

Placing Hoffen at the memorial the night before the bombing had set his cop alarm jangling. He'd seen Hoffen at close quarters in Helsby, read his unlovely track record and noted his connections to the neo-Nazis. There was more circumstantial evidence: the expression on Hoffen's face when the goons had been chasing Frank through the slabs. Hoffen wasn't chasing Frank. He was trying to *stop* the goons chasing Frank and attracting attention. Hoffen had been there on a last minute check that the bomb was safely in position. Smith had more or less told Frank that Hoffen was involved with the bomb.

I should call the Germans, thinks Frank. Call the people who deal with this sort of thing.

And then it hits him like a punch to the gut.

I *am* the people who deal with this sort of thing. The words of Dennis Sheehan come back to him. *My people do things you don't want to think about.*

Tom Machin, spook, is exactly who deals with this kind of thing. That's what Smith wants him for. The black holdall containing the gun is right there between his feet under the table.

He drinks his beer and goes over the connection between Felix Hoffen, Lydon, and the Helsby attack. These elements are clearly connected through the clinic, through the abduction of his half-sister, that much is obvious, but for the life of him, Frank can't see how this all links to the bombing. Fundraising? Could that possibly be it?

Frank kicks that one around for a while. It feels like that's not enough but maybe his case, and what happened to Sarah is part of a bigger fundraising scheme. If that's the case, this bombing is huge it means that Hoffen's pursuit of Frank must have been a detail. But Bruckner's connection to Hoffen means that she is part of it all.

Frank orders another beer. When he's finished he knows what's going to happen.

132

Berlin, November 9th

Hoffen puts his back against the bedroom wall, takes a drag on his post-coital cigarette and taps the end into the steel ashtray sitting on his stomach. As if emerging from underwater, the dream-like atmosphere of the evening has faded, leaving him in a state of adrenalised awareness. Clarity is restored. He needs some coke to bring him back to where he needs to be but he's thinking straight again.

With Lehmann in the bathroom, Hoffen looks at his jacket hanging on the back of a chair and thinks about the garrote sitting in the pocket.

He inhales deeply.

There's still time to start putting this right. To start moving in a forward direction. Keep moving. That's all there is. He stubs the cigarette out and, as he swings his legs out of bed, he hears another noise below the sound of running water. It's his phone vibrating against the wooden floor. Hoffen leans down and picks it up.

The number is Mick Lydon's but one glance at the message is enough for Hoffen to know the message isn't from the missing courier.

'I'm the one you've been looking for,' says the message, in English. 'I'm at the *Schwarze Pumpe*. You have ten minutes before I call LKA.'

It's from Frank Keane. The donor. There's no-one else it could be.

And he's at a bar less than five hundred metres from Hoffen's apartment.

Hoffen throws on his clothes, laces his boots and takes his gun from the kitchen. He steps into the bathroom holding the weapon in one hand and his phone in the other. Lehmann looks at him through the glass of the shower door. Hoffen sees her glance at the gun in his hand and then at her pile of clothes on the floor and knows that, like him, she has been thinking that this has been a mistake. Like him, she has been thinking about how to finish this business. He holds up the gun, side on to show it isn't a threat. There are bigger issues than loose ends.

'Your gun's in there?' says Hoffen looking at the clothes.

'Yes,' says Lehmann. She brushes her wet hair behind her ears and stands under the water.

'Never mind that,' says Hoffen. 'We have another problem,' He holds up his phone and Lehmann turns off the shower. She remains where she is and listens as Hoffen explains, still unsure if Hoffen is spinning some story. It's the first time Lehmann has heard Frank Keane's name.

'Wait here,' he says. 'If I'm not back in thirty minutes, then leave.'

'I could leave now,' says Lehmann.

'You could. That's up to you but if there's anyone on your end who has blabbed then you could be taking a risk.'

'The same applies to you.'

'If BfV knew about me they'd be here by now.'

Hoffen turns to the door.

'Thirty minutes.'

He leaves the bathroom door open and turns down the short hallway to the apartment door. Angelika Lehmann stands under the water, watching him through the glass. Hoffen puts his gun in his jacket pocket and steps out of his apartment. As he does so, the fat muzzle of a silencer is pressed hard against Hoffen's temple.

133

Berlin, November 9th

'Stop,' says a voice.

Hoffen's eyes swivel to his right and he sees the Englishman, the cop, bearded now, a black cap pulled low over his face, his gun arm extended.

'What are you going to do, Keane,' says Hoffen, smiling, 'shoot me? You're a cop.'

'Frank Keane's dead, just like his sister.'

Hoffen turns his head fractionally to look at Frank, surprise etched on his face.

'Sister? What the fuck are you talking about, man?'

'My name is Machin.'

Hoffen opens his mouth to speak but this has already gone on too long. Frank squeezes the trigger and shoots the German through the head before he can say another word. Blood and brain spatter up the wall of the hallway with a fat wet sound. The German, his eyes wide, slumps to the floor.

In his peripheral vision Frank sees movement in the apartment and turns to see a naked woman standing in the bathroom. She hesitates for a fraction of a second before dropping to the floor and scrabbling in a pile of clothes. Frank takes three strides down Hoffen's hallway and points the gun at the woman.

'Don't move,' he says but she's coming up fast now, her face set, her hand holding a Glock. Time slows and Frank sees the black eye of the weapon tilting towards him. This woman is part of it, he's sure, but even if she isn't, she is still going to shoot. In these milliseconds abstract concepts of proof and due process become words. Smith had been right.

You know or you don't.

Frank Keane might have hesitated but Tom Machin doesn't. As the Glock turns towards him, time speeding up once more, he jerks sideways and shoots the woman twice, catching her in the chest and sending her skidding backwards on the wet tiled floor before she can get off a shot. She drops the Glock, hitting the edge of the sink with the side of her head and falls heavily half in and half out of the shower enclosure. Water and blood spatter onto the tiles.

Frank's breathing hard, fighting the urge to vomit but also aware of his nerve-endings tingling, of the adrenaline pumping through his body. He's aware of the absolute nowness of the moment he is in, of the lack of distance between his molecules and those of the rest of the universe, of the hyper-real clarity of this environment. Each drop of water appears distinct, every detail of the room, her skin, her blood, the black muzzle of the gun, the smell of hot metal.

This is this. You live, you die. It just *is*.

Frank stares at the dead woman for a few seconds before turning and leaving abruptly, his movements stiff and unnatural. At the door to the apartment he steps over Hoffen's corpse and is halfway down the first flight of stairs before he stops and comes back. Bending, he rummages in the dead man's pockets, finds Hoffen's phone and slips it into the holdall. Frank stands up again and feels light-headed. He braces himself against the wall with his elbow, conscious even in that moment of not leaving prints. He pulls down the brim of his cap and walks downstairs to the street, changed forever.

It had been Frank Keane who entered the apartment block but it's Tom Machin who leaves.

There's no going back.

CAST

Merseyside MIT (Major Incident Team):
Superintendent Charlie Searle. Head of the unit overseeing MIT.
DCI Peter Moreleigh. Head of Merseyside Police Media Unit.
DCI Frank Keane. Current MIT chief.
DI Emily Harris.
DC Saif Magsi.
DC Theresa Cooper.
DC Scott Corner.
DC Peter Wills.
DC Steve Rose.
DC Ronnie Rimmer.
DS Phil Caddick.
DS Blake.
DS Reece.
DCI Paul Perch. Ex-MIT chief.
DCI Menno Koopman. Ex-MIT chief (retired).

Merseyside Police Support Staff and others:
PC John Halloran. Merseyside Traffic Police.
Calum McGettigan. SOC photographer.
Steve Viner. Pathologist.

Operation LUPUS:
Superintendent Mark Milner.
DCI Jane Watson.

UK Intelligence Agency:
Mr Smith.
Mr Jones.

Landeskriminalamt (LKA) State Criminal Police Office, Berlin:
Werner Holz. LKA chief.
Kriminalkommissar Anna Ziegler. LKA investigating officer.
Kriminalkommissar Robert Weiss. LKA investigating officer

Kriminalkommissar Christina Dreschler. LKA investigating officer

B-Kreuz-Scharmer Clinic (Berlin):
Ilsa Bruckner. Surgeon.
Atay. Maintenance crew.
Mesut. Maintenance crew.

Kolumne88 (Berlin):
Felix Hoffen. K88 enforcer.
Sebastian Gottlenz. K88 secretary.
Willy Schneider. K88 enforcer.
Klaus Menckel. K88 enforcer.
Gunther Lamm. K88 member.

Others:
Linda Black. DI Harris's partner, Liverpool.
Christian Boehne. Security/Maintenance crew, Holocaust Memorial, Berlin.
Dr Chatrabaty. Frank Keane's doctor, Berlin.
Sarah Coughlan. Student, Liverpool.
Mary & Dan Coughlan. Sarah's parents. Liverpool.
Eli Dreschler. Christina's husband. Berlin.
Ecklenberger. K88 operative.
Calum Finn. Fisherman, Mallaig, Scotland.
Paul Finn. Fisherman, Mallaig, Scotland.
Angelika Lehmann. Physio (Berlin).
Otto Leutze. Attendant, Berlin Opera House.
Hanna Leunze. Otto's wife.
Gavin Leland. US Intelligence. Berlin.
Mick Lydon. K88 investigator, UK.
Dr Lucas Medavoy. Doctor, Hemswood Clinic, Liverpool.
Candice Ortiz. US Intelligence, Berlin.
Bernie Palmer. Frank Keane's neighbour, Helsby, Cheshire.
Kath Palmer. Frank Keane's neighbour, Helsby, Cheshire.
Dieter Patz. Ilsa Bruckner's boyfriend. Berlin.
Nicky Peters. Victim in prior MIT case. Liverpool.
Bertram 'Tiny' Prior. Fence, MIT informer. Liverpool.
Eric Roos. K88 operative, Berlin.

Dennis Sheehan. Ex-US Sec of State, now CEO of Loder Industries. USA.

Mikkel Steiner. City Co-coordinator, Berlin.

Dr Stevens. Cancer Specialist, London.

Steve White. Victim in prior MIT case. Liverpool.